His new boss is no lady . . .

"So tell me—who are you? There has to be a story here." Sebastian gestured around them. "Because this is not where one would expect to find someone who is obviously a lady."

"Obviously *was*," she retorted. "I am Miss Ivy now, anything I was before is left in the past."

"Were you also a duke who lost his title?" he said, giving her a sly look.

She would not give him what he wanted. Something he was going to have to become accustomed to.

"We do have things to do, Mr. de Silva. Much as I would love to regale you with the story of how I came to be Miss Ivy."

He was keenly aware that he would have to follow her orders—if he wanted to keep this position.

And what other position would you like . . . ? a voice asked in his head.

By Megan Frampton

The Hazards of Dukes
NEVER KISS A DUKE

The Duke's Daughters
NEVER A BRIDE
THE LADY IS DARING
LADY BE RECKLESS
LADY BE BAD
THE EARL'S CHRISTMAS PEARL (novella)

Dukes Behaving Badly
MY FAIR DUCHESS
WHY DO DUKES FALL IN LOVE?
ONE-EYED DUKES ARE WILD
NO GROOM AT THE INN (novella)
PUT UP YOUR DUKE
WHEN GOOD EARLS GO BAD (novella)
THE DUKE'S GUIDE TO CORRECT BEHAVIOR

ATTENTION: ORGANIZATIONS AND CORPORATIONS
HarperCollins books may be purchased for educational, business, or sales promotional use. For information, please e-mail the Special Markets Department at SPsales@harpercollins.com.

NEVER KISS A DUKE

A HAZARDS OF DUKES NOVEL

MEGAN FRAMPTON

AVONBOOKS

An Imprint of HarperCollinsPublishers

This is a work of fiction. Names, characters, places, and incidents are products of the author's imagination or are used fictitiously and are not to be construed as real. Any resemblance to actual events, locales, organizations, or persons, living or dead, is entirely coincidental.

Excerpt from *Tall, Duke, and Dangerous* copyright © 2020 by Megan Frampton.

NEVER KISS A DUKE. Copyright © 2020 by Megan Frampton. All rights reserved. Printed in the United States of America. No part of this book may be used or reproduced in any manner whatsoever without written permission except in the case of brief quotations embodied in critical articles and reviews. For information, address HarperCollins Publishers, 195 Broadway, New York, NY 10007.

First Avon Books mass market printing: February 2020

Print Edition ISBN: 978-0-06-286742-1
Digital Edition ISBN: 978-0-06-286743-8

Cover design by Amy Halperin
Cover illustration by Gregg Gulbronson
Author photograph by Ben Zhuk

Avon, Avon & logo, and Avon Books & logo are registered trademarks of HarperCollins Publishers in the United States of America and other countries.

HarperCollins is a registered trademark of HarperCollins Publishers in the United States of America and other countries.

FIRST EDITION

20 21 22 23 24   QGM   10 9 8 7 6 5 4 3 2 1

If you purchased this book without a cover, you should be aware that this book is stolen property. It was reported as "unsold and destroyed" to the publisher, and neither the author nor the publisher has received any payment for this "stripped book."

To Scott. Thank you for making this all possible.

Chapter One

Everything Sebastian had ever known was a lie.

"You're saying I'm no longer the duke. That I am illegitimate. Do I have that right?" Sebastian Dutton, the Duke of Hasford, spoke in a clipped, sharp tone. A tone he normally reserved for one of his dogs caught gnawing on a shoe.

This was much bigger than footwear.

Sebastian sat across from the solicitor's desk, his cousin Thaddeus Dutton, the Earl of Kempthorne, sitting beside him. Unlike Sebastian, Thaddeus looked as though he'd been up for hours—crisp, alert, and attentive. Likely he had; Thaddeus took his duties in service to Her Majesty very seriously. He had wanted to join the army since he and Sebastian had first played tin soldiers together.

The solicitor visibly swallowed before he replied to Sebastian's terse statement.

"Yes. You do not have claim to being the Duke of Hasford."

He heard Thaddeus emit a gasp, which was the most demonstrative Thaddeus ever got—his gasp was equal to another person's dead faint.

Sebastian had gotten up at a ridiculous time to attend this appointment—normally he would have sent his secretary, but the note from the solicitor's office had strongly emphasized he should attend in person. So he'd roused himself before noon, grouchily drank his coffee, and tried to look somewhat awake as he approached the address indicated on the note.

The cousins were both tall, but there the resemblance ended; where Sebastian was fair-haired and lean, with an easy smile and an even easier charm, Thaddeus was dark, from his hair to his eyes to his sense of right and wrong.

They were opposites, and the best of friends. Dubbed the Angel and the Devil by their friends and family, though there were disputes as to which was which. In appearance, Thaddeus was devilish, but it was Sebastian's attitude toward life that earned him the sobriquet.

You do not have claim to being the Duke of Hasford.

Had the floor dropped out from under him, or was that just how he felt? For the first time, he knew no amount of personal magnetism or supreme confidence would rescue him from the situation.

"So who am I?" Sebastian asked. His words were spoken through a clenched jaw.

"Mr. de Silva," the solicitor replied.

Mr. de Silva, the illegitimate son of a duke. "My mother's name."

"Yes," the solicitor confirmed. "Your mother and your father were not legitimately married, because British law states that a man may not marry the sister of his late wife. And your mother was the late duchess's sister, not her cousin, as she'd told your father." The man cleared his throat. "It's all detailed in the letters she wrote aboard ship."

"Of course she lied," Sebastian said bitterly. He'd always known his mother to be a scheming, heartless creature; her treatment of Ana Maria, his older half sister, proved that. He hadn't known she'd also been a liar.

At least she was consistent in her behavior, he thought humorlessly.

He leaned forward to look at the proof, the seemingly innocuous papers that lay on the solicitor's desk. Yellow, faded, and ragged around the edges, they were proof positive that Sebastian's parents' marriage was illegal. He recognized his mother's handwriting. And her duplicity.

"Where did these come from?" Sebastian demanded. He couldn't succumb to the dark hole that was threatening to engulf him. He had to keep asking questions, to find out what happened so he could understand. If it was possible to make sense of it at all.

The solicitor placed his hands flat on his desk, spreading his fingers wide. "They were found in the duchess's vault box. That is, your late mother." Since she wasn't actually the duchess. "Letters she wrote, but apparently never mailed. We discovered them after the accident."

The carriage accident that took both his parents' lives.

"But that was over six months ago," Thaddeus pointed out. "How is it that these are just coming to light now?"

"It takes time to review all the paperwork after such an event," the solicitor said in a defensive tone. "And we needed to translate the letters," he added.

"Why would your mother lie?" Thaddeus said, turning his intense stare toward Sebastian. "There was no practical reason to hide the relationship."

Thaddeus, ever practical. Always searching for the reason in things. Whereas Sebastian never searched, things just arrived. Like his title, wealth, standing in society, women, and friends.

It was astonishing how quickly one's entire world could be upended. All in the time it took for the solicitor to explain how the letters of Sebastian's mother detailed every last subterfuge.

"My mother was ambitious," Sebastian replied. Unable to keep the animosity from his tone. "She probably persuaded the late duchess that there was some reason to keep their relationship a secret— maybe it would have reflected badly on the family for a sister to act as a companion." He shrugged, as though it didn't matter. Of course it mattered. "The point is that I am not the duke." He raked his hands through his hair, anger coursing through his veins.

The position he'd been trained for since he had been born was not his. The estates, the responsibility, the money, the title, the position—all of it gone.

"Who is?" Thaddeus asked.

Sebastian raised one wry eyebrow as he waited for Thaddeus to figure it out. And supplied the information when it seemed his normally sharp cousin was not processing it. "You're the Duke of Hasford now, Thad."

Sebastian didn't think he had ever seen Thaddeus surprised before. The man was confoundingly strategic, always plotting his next move, anticipating events long before anybody else involved had thought of them. It was what had made him invaluable when they were growing up together—Sebastian usually thought up the mischief, Thaddeus planned out the event, and their friend Nash was there to quash any trouble.

But now Thaddeus looked as though he'd been hit in the head with a heavy object. Or a dukedom.

"That's not—I mean," Thad sputtered.

If Sebastian were feeling more inclined, he'd have to laugh at his cousin's expression and inability to speak in a complete sentence. But he was not inclined. He was furious. With his mother, with his feckless, foolish father, with his own expectations.

"It is." He tapped the papers in front of them. "This proves it." He leaned back, folding his arms over his chest. "And I am plain Mr. de Silva."

His fury changed to fierce protectiveness as he thought of his half sister, at home without any clue of what was happening. "You'll take care of Ana Maria, of course." He knew Thaddeus would have no thought of doing otherwise, but he needed to say it, to retain some measure of agency.

"Of course," Thaddeus said. "But what if I don't want to be the duke?" Thaddeus asked, directing his question to the solicitor. "Can't we just pretend we've never seen these documents? That things are as we always thought?"

Thaddeus was the only person of Sebastian's acquaintance who had never been envious of Sebastian's position, either as a duke's heir or as the duke himself. Which was why he seemed to have forgotten he was Sebastian's heir. Thaddeus had been actively relieved that he was able to serve in the army, serving Her Majesty rather than his own pleasure.

Whereas Sebastian believed that serving his own pleasure meant that those who relied on him would also benefit. That belief applied mostly to the ladies he pleasured, but he took pains to ensure that his staff and tenants were also taken care of properly.

He was privileged, he knew that, but he used his charm and influence so that everyone would like and appreciate him rather than resent him.

Sebastian was shaking his head before his cousin had finished speaking. "You can't refuse it, Thad. That's the whole point of primogeniture and such. And it would be wrong. It would be a lie. You know that."

Thaddeus's eyes widened. "Primogeniture? Since when do you have such an extensive vocabulary?"

Sebastian shrugged. "Since I might have to *do* something rather than just *be* something." It was a return to his normal insouciant self, but it rang hollow.

Thaddeus's expression drew grim.

"You know, it's not the worst thing in the world to be told you're actually a duke," Sebastian pointed out dryly. Thaddeus glared at him, then folded his arms over his chest.

Poor sad duke.

"So what happens now?" Sebastian asked, directing his question to the solicitor.

The man cleared his throat again, looking unhappy. *Have you also been told everything you thought you were is wrong?* Sebastian thought. *I don't think so. So stop making that expression.*

"Well, the Duke of Hasford—that is"—and he gestured toward Thaddeus—"will assume the position immediately. That will include the estates, the ducal holdings, and everything inherited from the late duke."

Everything, in other words. Sebastian didn't have anything of his own, anything that belonged to— what was his name now?—Sebastian de Silva. His mother's last name. The only thing she had been able to leave him, despite her machinations.

The yawning blank of his future widened in front of him. No money beyond what he had on hand. Likely that belonged to Thad, as well. No path forward. No privilege.

"I can't take care of everything right away," Thaddeus said, obviously trying to keep his tone measured. And failing spectacularly. "I command a regiment, it will take time to extricate myself." He sounded desperate. "You can continue for the time being, can't you?" he asked Sebastian.

The solicitor's lips pursed. "That—" he began, before Sebastian interrupted.

"No, Thad." He spoke in a decisive tone. "Much as I would love to help you out by overseeing one of the wealthiest titles in England," he said understatedly, "I cannot." He pointed at the documents. "Those say I cannot. What would it look like if you refused to do your duty? Even for a short time?" He shook his head as he leaned forward. "It would be devastating. The one thing I know in this world is that the Duke of Hasford has responsibilities to the title, to the land, to the tenants and workers, to the country. I've been indoctrinated with that duty since I was born. I cannot betray it." He spoke with the ferocity he normally reserved for flattering a particularly beautiful woman.

Thaddeus clamped his mouth shut, and Sebastian saw a muscle tic in his jaw. That's when he knew Thad wouldn't argue. It was his tell, and Sebastian had taken advantage of it over many card games. But this was one situation where Thad had the winning hand—even though he did not want it.

Sebastian slid the documents back toward the solicitor as he rose out of his chair. Feeling his jaw clench. "I will leave you and the Duke of Hasford to continue your discussion. I presume there is nothing further?" His tone made it clear it would be a presumption if there was.

The solicitor shook his head. "Thank you for coming, Your—that is, Mr. de Silva."

He suppressed a wince at his name. He'd have to grow accustomed to it.

He addressed Thad, noting his cousin's severe expression. Once again, the cousins were in perfect agreement. "I'll vacate the town house as soon as possible, Your Grace. I was planning to launch Ana Maria into Society, so you'll have to take that over. She deserves it."

Whatever happened, at least he knew Ana Maria would be secure. Even if she was also devastated by the turn of events. "I will be available to answer any questions you have regarding the estate management and the tenants and such."

"Seb, you don't have to go right away." Thaddeus looked even grimmer. "This is a lot to absorb, and we'll both need some time to adjust."

Sebastian bit back whatever angry words he wanted to say—it wasn't Thad's fault that Seb's mother had lied. Thad didn't want the title just as much as Seb did. "I'll find somewhere else to go. You'll have to decide if you want to keep the staff. My valet, Hodgkins, will take this hard. If you don't have anyone yet for that position, I'd recommend keeping him on."

The change didn't just mean change for him—it would alter his entire household. His valet, his secretary, the butler, the housekeeper. He had spent six months learning about these people now that he was their master, working with them, assuring them that he was not his careless father. And definitely not his demanding mother. Something he had been thwarted in doing until he had assumed the title. But now the title wasn't his, after all.

He wanted to punch something, someone, but that wouldn't do anything but make his knuckles sore.

"Of course. You can trust me to do what's right."

Sebastian wished he were calm enough to sit back down and review the details of the staff with Thaddeus, try to persuade him to give all of them a chance, even though Thad was rightfully proud of his ability to make a quick, decisive decision. And even though some of the staff were still a work in progress—progress Sebastian had been making, with Ana Maria's guidance.

But he couldn't spend another minute here, not without unleashing his anger, and nobody here deserved that.

"I'll see you later, cousin."

He spun on his heel and walked out of the solicitor's office, ignoring Thaddeus calling his name, nodding at the clerks who were working outside. Maintaining his ducal facade even as his world was crumbling around him.

HOURS LATER, SEBASTIAN was exhausted, hungry, and thirsty. He'd spent the time since leaving the solicitor's office pacing through the streets of London, his mind obsessively churning the information over and over again, as though that would change the outcome. Finally, unable to walk any longer, he returned home. As though home was his home.

He didn't have a home anymore. He didn't own anything anymore.

He wasn't who he'd thought he was anymore.

He'd never truly appreciated the Duke of Hasford's town house until it wasn't his any longer, but as he approached the house he viewed it as others did. The most opulent house on the street, it had over two dozen windows in the front alone, enormous pillars serving no apparent purpose beyond declaring that the owner of the house had so much money he could spend it on useless pieces of marble.

It was elegant and extravagant and shameless.

Rather like him, he thought remorsefully. And like the pillars, he was just as useless. Not even propping up the aristocracy.

"Welcome home, Your Grace." His butler, Fletchfield, hesitated for the slightest fraction before saying his honorific. Meaning the news had already spread here, at least to his butler. No doubt it had already spread through most of Society; that a duke could be de-duked, as it were, would be a scandal for the ages.

"Thank you, Fletchfield." Sebastian gave his hat and coat to the butler. "Whiskey in my office. I'll be down after I change."

"Yes, Your . . ." But the butler's words were lost as Sebastian sprinted up the stairs to his bedroom, turning the knob and flinging the door open.

His valet, Hodgkins, was there, treating him as he usually did. So the news likely hadn't reached beyond Fletchfield. It would, of course, and Sebastian wished he could assure them, all of them, that they would be fine even if he wasn't, but he couldn't make that guarantee, even though he knew Thaddeus would do the right thing. They'd be fearful of losing their positions no matter what—his mother had terrorized them enough during her tenure.

"I'll be changing to go out," he said.

Go out where? a voice asked.

Damned if I know.

He glanced around the room as Hodgkins bustled about, getting his things. He hadn't gotten around to redecorating the master bedroom after his parents died, and everything was done in his mother's style, discreetly tasteful colors indicating just how very expensive it was. The only thing in the room that was truly his was his shaving kit, which his father had gifted to him on his sixteenth birthday. It was engraved with his initials, although they weren't *his* initials any longer, were they?

But it was his, even if nothing else was.

Soon Sebastian was rigged out in his most ostentatious clothing—a gold patterned waistcoat, an elegant black necktie, slim trousers, and a blindingly white shirt—even though he had no place to be. He considered attending a party or five—there were plenty of invitations—but they were all addressed to the Duke of Hasford. Not Mr. Sebastian de Silva.

And he knew that the party guests, those of whom liked to gossip, which meant most of them, would take no time in reminding him he was a mere mister now.

"Damn it," he said to himself as he descended the stairs. He took a quick left into his office, where he spotted the tray with the whiskey right away. "Thank God," he murmured, pouring himself a healthy amount. He'd been spending a lot of time in this room, learning the estate affairs, taking meetings with the staff. Once he'd inherited the title from his father, it had felt crucial that he focus on his responsibilities rather than his pleasure.

He could return to pleasure now. But he didn't want to. Nor would he have the privilege of doing so—he'd have to . . . *work* for his living now?

He'd never considered that possibility when he'd contemplated his future.

The enormity of the change hit him all over again. Nothing was his. Not his clothing, not this house, not anything. Not even the name he'd grown up with. He was Mr. Sebastian de Silva now. Nothing more.

He really needed whiskey, even though that wasn't his either. He knew, however, that Thaddeus wouldn't begrudge him a stiff drink.

He held the glass up to his mouth, then frowned as he spotted the signet ring on his right pinkie.

The signet ring that had belonged to his father, the Duke of Hasford. That was passed on to all the dukes in succession.

He put the glass back down on the table, yanked the ring from his finger, and flung it into the corner of the room.

"Your aim is improving."

Sebastian heard Nash's voice before he saw him. His friend was standing in the shadows, as usual, but emerged into the light, holding the ring, his usual grim smile on his lips.

Nash stood as tall as Sebastian, but where Sebastian was lean and elegant, Nash, the Duke of Malvern, was pure force. He looked more like a stevedore than a duke, and he behaved more like one as well, preferring the company of common men to his literal peers.

He'd grown up with Sebastian and Thaddeus, and the three had maintained their close friendship through inheritance, the army, romantic heartbreak, and feckless parents.

"You've heard." Sebastian picked his glass up and drained it as Nash approached.

He poured a glass and handed it to Nash, who took it and drank it all down, barely wincing at the burn of the whiskey.

"I did." Nash held his glass out for more. "I thought that between you and Thad, you might need me more."

Sebastian snorted as he poured more liquid into Nash's glass. "I'm not certain about that. Thaddeus looked as though someone had deliberately disorganized his papers when we heard the news." He glanced reflexively at the surface of his desk, which was neatly arranged. He hoped his secretary would meet Thad's exacting standards.

Nash chuckled. "What are you going to do?"

That was the question of the day, wasn't it? "I don't know." Sebastian sat down on the sofa, leaning his head back and closing his eyes. "I need to tell Ana Maria. I need to let the staff know, although I suspect the news has already reached them. But first I need to—"

"Get drunk," Nash supplied. "With me at a place where you won't run into as many of those condescending pricks."

"Which condescending pricks?" He waved a hand as Nash opened his mouth. "Never mind, I know you mean all of them. Tell me how you really feel," Sebastian replied dryly. He sat up, slapping his hands on his thighs. "Your idea is a good one, but I can't get too drunk because I need to speak with my sister tomorrow."

Thank goodness Ana Maria was out this evening. He didn't remember where she had gone, but there was no danger Ana Maria would get in any kind of trouble—his half sister was remarkably staid in her behavior, given how wild her younger half brother was. Or had been, until he'd inherited six months ago.

"Drunk enough to take the edge off, then," Nash said. "Miss Ivy's, I think. It's new."

"As long as there is an abundance of whiskey and a paucity of condescending pricks," Seb replied.

Chapter Two

"$\mathcal{M}$y luck has changed," Ivy murmured as she surveyed the room with pride.

Two years ago, she had lost everything: her reputation, her way of life, and a respectable future. Lost on the turn of a card.

But Ivy had fought against what seemed to be inevitable and won. She was now the proud owner—ironically, she had to admit—of a thriving gambling house in London. She would never get back what she had lost, but she could do better—she could control her own future.

The club was still empty, save for the staff, even though it had been open for at least an hour. Late nights were the norm, so Ivy wasn't concerned about the lack of clientele. They would come. They always did.

The club was well-appointed, with comfortable chairs for long evenings of play set near the purposed tables—one for roulette, several for card games, and a few that were intended for customers who wished to drink instead of gamble. Red velvet wallpaper hung on the walls, and Ivy had hunted down a variety of paintings portraying people in various states of gaming, from ladies from the previous century playing faro, to lampoons of gentlemen losing much more than they ought, to even a few whimsical paintings depicting dogs playing cards.

The paintings made her laugh, as did anything she found the slightest bit amusing—it was important, when one's survival depended on serious things like running a business, to keep a humorous perspective.

What was the point in living if you couldn't also enjoy life?

That was Ivy's philosophy, especially now that she was barred from all the traditional things a well-bred young lady should expect.

This was much more fun than being a well-bred young lady.

Miss Ivy's was unusual in that it admitted both men and women of any status. She figured that was more fun for all her customers—who didn't enjoy a spot of flirtation when one was betting on the future?

The only requirement for admittance was that each gambler, male and female, brought enough cash to settle their gambling debts that evening. If they couldn't pay? They were blackballed from the club and were dunned every day until they fulfilled their obligations.

Her policies were at odds with other, older establishments such as White's and Brooks's. The gentlemen who habituated those establishments didn't have to settle up right away, so some of the winners could wait forever. In years past, losing gentlemen would escape to the Continent to avoid payment. Ivy's took the doubt that a winner would receive their money out of the equation.

"Psst! Ivy!" It was her younger sister, Octavia, a girl who could never hide who she was, making Ivy both proud and concerned. Octavia was brash, opinionated, and reckless—taking after her older sister, but Ivy knew how to hide it better.

"I thought we talked about how you are not to be here when the doors are open. What if you're seen?"

Octavia rolled her eyes. "*You* talked about it. I listened. Nobody is here yet, sister. And besides, it is far more fun to be in your den of dubious activities than upstairs working on my embroidery or planning my next good deed."

Ivy laughed at her sister's scornful tone. "You do not embroider, and I believe your last good deed was rescuing those kittens from the cellar. I highly doubt you planned that." She paused. "And you have gotten as much goodness out of the kitten rescue as the animals themselves."

"True," Octavia agreed. "Oh, Carter says she has homes for them, she'll take them there tomorrow."

A relief, since kittens were a cute distraction they did not need.

"I could embroider, at some point in the future," Octavia added.

"Or teach the kittens how to embroider before they leave. They might be in need of some useful skills," Ivy replied with a smirk.

"Or . . ." Octavia said, wrapping her arm around Ivy, "I could come down here and work as a dealer."

"Absolutely not!" Ivy said, shaking Octavia's arm off her shoulder and trying to look like a disapproving older sister. "You are a lady, you have a chance for a respectable future. As long as we keep our relationship a secret. And, though this should go without saying, that you not work in a gambling house. Or, as you put it, my 'den of dubious activities.'"

Octavia was not to be dissuaded from her thoughts, however. "And you? You are a lady also, and you own a gambling house."

"I'm not a lady any longer," Ivy retorted. She'd mourn that loss of status if it didn't also give her the freedom to choose what to do next.

Their father had seen to that—a gamester himself, he had ruined the family by gambling away everything he owned, and several things he did not. Such as his daughter Ivy, who discovered she had been won as a bride by an older man, a gentleman farmer, who wanted a wife to take charge of his adult children and work on his farm from dawn until dusk. Ivy was even more appalled at discovering the man's oldest son was her age.

Ivy had challenged the man to a game herself after discovering her father's loss, and had won, but the damage had been done—her father's wager, her own daring to take back her freedom, had ruined her in the eyes of Society.

But, Ivy had reasoned, she would have been miserable if she had followed what her class dictated, marrying some squire's son and trying to pretend she wasn't as intelligent as she was. The wager and her winning of it merely meant she could chart the course of her own future.

Far better to be a ruined gamester in charge of one's fate than a woeful wife at the mercy of a husband.

Some ladies might have taken that experience to mean that gambling was abhorrent, and something she would never wish to do, or to associate with those who did. But Ivy took it as a sign that risking everything was the only way she would ever be happy.

"Someday, sister," Octavia said in that "far too old for her seventeen years" voice, "you will find your own respectable future." She tugged on Ivy's sleeve. "I could wear a mask, you know. Nobody would know it was me. I know you're short on staff. I could help."

"Absolutely not." Ivy struggled to maintain her stern tone. It would be fun to have Octavia here, she had to admit, but she wanted her sister to wait a bit before shutting the door that led to a respectable future. The gentlemen who gambled here would never choose a gambling house employee or even an owner as a wife.

That was a relief for Ivy, who wanted to be firmly among the regular people. But she wanted Octavia to have a choice, a wider choice than Ivy herself had had. One that didn't depend—literally—on the turn of a card.

Ensuring Octavia's security was the biggest motivation for working so hard to make the club a success—eventually, Ivy thought, she'd make enough money so she could buy a cottage by the sea for her and her sister, hopefully in an area where there were young eligible gentlemen. Gentlemen who wouldn't know of their past life in London.

Not for herself, of course, but for her sister—
Octavia deserved to fall in love and get married.
Ivy just wanted books, tea, and an excellent view.

Ivy heard voices and nudged her sister toward
the door that led upstairs to their lodgings. "People
are coming, you have to go."

Octavia rolled her eyes again, accompanying the
gesture with an exaggerated exhale, but she moved
quickly, and was out of sight before the guests
arrived. There would come a time, Ivy knew, when
her younger sister would no longer follow Ivy's
commands, but at least that day was not today.
Hopefully she could stave off her sister's rebellious-
ness until after they'd moved to that quiet cottage.

Ivy approached the door as the two gentlemen
arrived—and they were most certainly gentlemen.
Men who worked for their livings, even ones who'd
made fortunes, didn't have the air of total entitle-
ment these two had.

She recognized one of the men as having been
in the club before, although she recalled all he had
done the previous time was drink and grunt in
response to any of the other guests' polite over-
tures.

The other one, the stranger, looked like the
manifestation of every man she'd ever dared to
dream about: tall and lean, with a sly grin on a
classically sculpted face. Although, truth be told,
she'd thought the same thing when she had seen
the statues of the Greek and Roman gods in the
British Museum.

This gentleman was not made of stone, however.
That was a good thing. But he wore much more
clothing. Unfortunately.

She bit her tongue before she asked him if his name was Adonis. Although she couldn't suppress her giggle.

He surveyed the room with a discerning look, as though he were appraising everything. He would not find it wanting, she was certain of that.

He caught her eye and his lips curled up into a rakish half smile, as though he was aware of what she had been thinking. Perhaps she would be called upon to explain why she was picturing him on a marble pedestal wearing a fig leaf.

Ivy could keep her expression serene, it was part and parcel of being a good card player, but she was feeling an unduly interested reaction bubbling inside her as he approached. She hoped he had a squeaky voice, or a dislike of ladies with younger sisters, or anything to jar her out of her current fascination.

"Good evening." Damn it. His voice was low and rumbly, making her insides tremble even more. "My hat and coat," he said, removing the items to hand them over to her.

Oh. Well, that was lowering. But it did have the desired effect—he didn't seem nearly as intriguing. Just another example of the aristocratic species, albeit easier on the eyes.

"I'm not—" she began.

"She's the proprietor," the other gentleman said flatly.

The half smile froze on the Assumptive Aristocrat's face. She would have laughed if he wasn't so clearly appalled.

"I of all people should know not to judge anyone by how they look," he said, his tone contrite. "I apologize, I thought—"

"I know what you thought," Ivy replied with a dismissive wave of her hand, wishing his assumption didn't sting. "It's fine. It happens all the time."

Because nobody could imagine a woman who wasn't a maid or a loose woman being at a gambling house. That she was neither, that she didn't fit into expectations, was one of the things that set her, and her establishment, apart.

Now that her insides had been given a good talking-to by his presumption, she could concentrate on what really mattered—making money. The two arrivals were handsome, to be sure, but what mattered more than their looks was the size of their wallets. And how much they were going to lose. They were *marks*, nothing more or less.

Judging by the fine quality of their clothing, they had plenty of money to lose, and she hoped she could lure them into deeper and deeper play—but not enough to ruin them. She monitored all her guests to make sure there wasn't irrevocable damage. Just enough to smart, and to line her pockets with more coin.

"Welcome to Miss Ivy's," she said, gesturing to one of her staff to take the gentlemen's outerwear. "I am Miss Ivy, and I am here to ensure your pleasure."

Adonis gave her a knowing look. Apparently, he recovered quickly from mortification. Or rakishness was so ingrained he could be mortified and flirtatious.

"What game are you interested in playing, my lords?" she continued hurriedly. She would have to watch her words.

The handsome stranger frowned, nearly as deeply as Ivy had just a few moments earlier. "Mr. de Silva," he said shortly. Had she accidentally offended him? By presuming he was an aristocrat rather than a mister?

She didn't think she would point out the irony of his having just presumed information about her that was incorrect.

"Mr. de Silva," Ivy corrected. She hadn't ever heard of him, but then again, she didn't travel in Society circles any longer. She hadn't done so since she'd won the last hand of hazard against her would-be bridegroom.

"And I'm Nash," the other man said.

Mr. de Silva punched his friend on the arm. "The Duke of Malvern. Not everyone has a title they can toss around, you know." He gave his friend a pointed look.

The duke shrugged. Ivy had the feeling he didn't care much one way or the other about his title.

But if he didn't, *she* certainly did—a duke patronizing Miss Ivy's! Even a taciturn stone-like duke was better than no duke at all.

"We might as well play something while we drink," the duke said to Adonis de Silva. He glanced at Ivy. "A game of roulette to start." He looked back at his friend, and his lips nearly curled into a smile. "Who knows, maybe your luck will change?"

As he spoke, Ivy beckoned to Samuel, who stood against the wall wearing the club uniform. Samuel was one of the completely loyal employees who made it possible for a female to own a gambling house. None of her employees argued with her decisions, they didn't think they would be better suited for the position, and they were hard workers who helped make Miss Ivy's the success it had been thus far.

"Samuel is my best roulette spinner." Samuel grinned at her, acknowledging the compliment. She waited for the men to register that a Black man would be manning their table, relieved when they didn't voice any objection, as some of her customers had. Regretfully, those customers were ex-customers, but her staff's loyalty to her was equal to her loyalty to them.

"One more thing, gentlemen."

It was always awkward to remind her customers about the house rule, but if she didn't, there would invariably be someone who claimed ignorance.

"At Miss Ivy's, we pay to play."

Mr. de Silva looked puzzled, as did the duke, but after a moment, the duke's face cleared.

"I'll take care of all of that tonight," he said, shooting a look that Ivy couldn't describe toward his friend.

"Take care of—?" Mr. de Silva asked.

Ivy explained. "Miss Ivy's requires that anyone who gambles must settle their debts at the end of the evening. Pay to play, so to speak."

Mr. de Silva's expression froze. "Because I— Goddamn it."

Ivy started at the intensity of his voice, but reminded herself it wasn't her business. The only thing that was her business was . . . *her business.*

"If you'll step over to my table?" Samuel said, gesturing toward the far corner. The two men nodded, then followed Samuel, sitting down at the roulette table.

Ivy watched them settle themselves, then turned around, relieved she was able to keep herself focused on what was most important. He was just unduly handsome, that was all. She'd had handsome marks in the club before, and she would again—she would just have to figure out how to contain her reaction.

That she hadn't realized responding appropriately to a ridiculously handsome gentleman would be a general side effect of being in this business was her own fault.

And then she chuckled to herself as she thought it out. She'd have to share that with Octavia—her sister did enjoy laughing at her. As she enjoyed laughing at herself.

SEBASTIAN SAT NEXT to Nash, resisting the urge to glance back at the gambling house's proprietor. Miss Ivy. Looking at her, however, was certainly better than being reminded he was now *Mr. de Silva*.

He hadn't expected such a young woman to own a gambling house. Obviously, since he'd mistaken her for a maid. He winced as he recalled his assumption.

Nor had he anticipated she'd be so attractive.

He wondered where she came from, and why such a lovely young woman was the proprietor.

Not that he'd ever pondered what the owner of a gambling house *should* look like. Except that they were usually male, often loud, and frequently obnoxious. She was none of those things. Which was why he'd been so dreadfully wrong.

She was approachably beautiful: short, with wide brown eyes, dark brown hair, a wide mouth, and luscious curves. He wondered what she looked like when she smiled. When those large eyes were suffused with passion. How those curves would feel in his hands.

"Seb?" Nash nudged his arm. "If you're going to sit there and let your mind wander, we can just as well go get drinks and skip the gambling. I'd much prefer that," he added in a grumpy tone.

"No, it's fine, I'm just—" he replied. Nash grunted in response.

Sebastian shook his thoughts free of the exquisite proprietor, glancing instead around the room. Not nearly as compelling. But still interesting.

The room was large, with tables set at specific intervals. The chairs were comfortably upholstered in a dark fabric, while the walls were hung in red, paintings of—was that a dog playing cards?—punctuating the intense color.

Seb squinted at the other paintings. Some of them were what he might expect, but there was a smattering of ones just as whimsical as the one that had first caught his eye.

Someone here had a distinct sense of humor.

Was it her? he wondered.

"What number do you suggest?" Nash asked, interrupting his thoughts.

One dukedom, one illegal marriage, two spouses, two affected children, plus twenty-odd household staff . . . "Twenty-six," he replied.

Nash tossed his chip onto the number, glancing around the room. Likely searching for the server with their drinks.

Sebastian watched as the roulette ball spun around the outside of the wheel.

And leaned back as the ball landed on the red thirteen.

Why hadn't he told Nash to choose *that* number? Perhaps because it would have been too on the nose? *Number thirteen, since all I've had today is bad luck.*

That thought was perilously close to moping. He would not mope. Nobody wanted a mopey duke, much less a mopey *not*-duke. Especially not him.

Thankfully, there was plenty to distract him.

He rose suddenly, turning to look at the other tables in the room. Roulette was entirely a game of chance, but there were other games that required more thinking on the part of the player. Not that Nash would care; as long as the drinks were flowing, his friend was happy. Or at least as happy as Nash ever got. Which was usually slightly to the right of mildly satisfied.

Unless he was embroiled in a fight. Then he seemed intent, focused, and nearly happy.

"Let's try the baccarat table," he said. Nash rose also, following Seb to the table he'd indicated. They had to push through other customers, nearly getting a drink or two spilled on them, while a few of the ladies looked up from their play to appraise them as possible playmates. But Seb kept his gaze firmly locked on the table—he wasn't in the mood this evening, and Nash wasn't one to voluntarily flirt.

They reached the table and sat, Sebastian casting a quick eye at the other players. Nobody he recognized, thank goodness.

Baccarat was nearly as dependent on luck as roulette, but at least there were cards involved. Not just a little ball spinning around a wheel.

If he was going to lose Nash's money—since he didn't have any of his own—he'd rather it be because he'd played the wrong card than because a ball took the wrong bounce.

Funny how gambling wasn't nearly as enjoyable when you had literally nothing to lose.

His life had changed irrevocably that afternoon in ways he couldn't imagine. The thought of not being able to afford anything—he had never had that. He didn't know what things cost, much less how much money one needed to afford them.

A woman stood at the table, obviously the dealer. Yet another unusual aspect of this club—Sebastian didn't think he'd ever seen a female dealer. She was an older woman with sharp features and black hair scraped back into a severe bun. She wore equally severe clothing and no gloves. She nodded at them, then resumed efficiently shuffling a deck of cards.

Sebastian heard voices and turned around to see people coming steadily into the room. Some of the people he recognized, so he snapped back around. He didn't want to have the "oh yes, I am an illegitimate nobody" conversation with anybody right now. Or, worse yet, have them be unaware of his changed status and treat him as an important personage, not some poor bastard who'd discovered his true heritage.

He could still hear a few bits of conversation around him and picked up on some accents that did not belong to the cream of Society. It appeared Miss

Ivy's was egalitarian in its clientele in both gender and class. *Bring your money, come in.* It was an easy equation, almost impossibly simple to parse.

He wondered how many members of the House of Lords sniffed at Miss Ivy's, either because of the unsuitable clientele or because they lacked the cash necessary to play. No wonder Nash liked it; it was as devoid of false pretense as he was.

"How long has Miss Ivy's been open?" he asked the dealer. She shot him a look that indicated she did not want to waste time answering questions. He responded by giving her one of his easy smiles.

It did not work. She only looked more forbidding.

When he'd lost his title, had he lost his charm?

"I'll take over, Caroline." Miss Ivy nodded at her employee, who almost seemed to soften, and then stepped away.

"Not just the proprietor, but also a dealer?" Seb asked.

She shrugged, a touch of pink on her cheeks. Why had she stepped in, anyway?

He wouldn't be Sebastian, now not the Duke of Hasford, if he didn't believe it had something to do with him.

She tapped the deck of cards on the surface of the table. "Place your bets."

Nash nodded at Seb, who shrugged and placed one of Nash's chips on the player side.

Miss Ivy shuffled the cards, then dealt two for the player, two for the dealer.

Seb added the numbers up quickly in his head, but not as fast as Miss Ivy did. Impressive.

"Player wins," she said, sliding a chip to join the bet.

"I can ask you, since your dealer wasn't inclined to answer." Seb tried his smile again, this time with much better results. He saw her eyes widen, and her throat move as she swallowed. If he were not a good card player, he would have grinned at her reaction. "How long have you been open?"

She tilted her head as she calculated. "Approximately six months."

Ah. No wonder he hadn't come here before. Six months ago was when his parents had died. And he hadn't had time for pleasure in the time since. "And your clientele is . . . ?"

Her eyebrows drew together. "Why are you so interested, Mr. de Silva?" She frowned. "You're not from Crockford's, are you?"

Sebastian held his hands up in surrender. "No, I promise. I'm just interested." He put his hands back down on the table and leaned forward, his voice taking a conspiratorial tone. "Besides which, I'd be a horrible spy if I were just asking the questions directly, wouldn't I?" It felt so much more normal, and like himself, to be teasing a lady. And thank goodness he hadn't lost his charm, after all.

Her expression eased, and she nodded. "Excellent point. Although perhaps you *are* a horrible spy."

Seb chuckled. "What would a horrible spy be like, anyway?"

She laughed, her entire face expressing delight. He had to concentrate on keeping his expression neutral; her smile was nearly blinding. It wasn't the sensual smile that ladies intent on seduction wore. It was wide, and sincere, and made him want to live up to its promise. To conjure the joy of the smile, to be worthy of all that brilliance.

And where did that idea come from?

The loss of a dukedom must have done something to his brain.

"Please share all your secrets so I might report them back to your rival," she said, lowering her voice to sound more masculine.

"Tell me who your most profligate customers are so I can lure them away to my establishment," he rejoined.

"And while you are at it, please indicate which of your employees are the best at their jobs. Purely for interest's sake."

They shared a smile for a brief moment.

"Well," she said, smoothing her expression, though her eyes still danced in laughter, "since we have established you are not a spy, perhaps we should continue the play."

"Yes, I would prefer to lose money rather than listen to you flirt," Nash said in a dry tone.

She opened her mouth as though to respond, then snapped it shut again. Her cheeks got pink.

"Stop complaining and place your chips on the dealer," Seb said to Nash, who complied, giving Sebastian a knowing look.

Fine, Seb wanted to say. *I was flirting. Can you blame me? I am me, and she is lovely.*

"Dealer wins," Miss Ivy said after a few minutes, jolting Seb from his thoughts. She nodded toward one of the workers, who stepped forward at her gesture.

He looked smugly at Nash, who was already rolling his eyes. "My entire life might be in shambles, and tomorrow is in doubt, but at least I am still able to predict a turn of the card." Poking Nash was nearly as much fun as teasing ladies.

Nash drew his chips toward him, flipping one at Seb. "Here, let me be the first to stake your future." The worker had stepped away, and he felt her focus back on the two of them.

Sebastian caught the chip, placing it on the table, shifting it between player and dealer. At last he decided where to place it, then glanced up to meet her eyes. "I'm betting on the dealer," he said, watching as her eyes widened and she took a few short breaths.

Perhaps his luck hadn't entirely changed.

Chapter Three

I'm betting on the dealer.

Ivy didn't think she'd ever been so flustered before. More accurately, she didn't think she'd *ever* been flustered before. But he'd smiled, and she'd felt wobbly around the knees and somewhat light-headed, as well.

Either she was reacting to him, or she was coming down with something.

She did not think she was getting ill.

Ivy had long wondered why other women got so silly around gentlemen. She was able to keep her composure, why couldn't they? There was simply no reason, in her opinion, to see a handsome gentleman and suddenly start to blush and flutter one's lashes and start speaking as though one were unsure of everything that came out of one's mouth.

Only here she was. Blushing and fluttering.

Annoying herself.

"You're betting on the dealer," she said, only her words had that lift up at the end that made them sound like a question. Damn it. "You're betting on the dealer," she repeated, as though it were a statement of fact. There. Much better.

"I see no reason not to," he replied in a low voice. A voice that made Ivy think of all sorts of things she had never thought about before.

"I'm taking the player," the duke added, sliding his chip onto that square. Ivy nearly jumped; she'd forgotten he was there at all.

She was not thinking straight at the moment. She should be focused on her customers, all of them, not this particular one. He was a mark. They all were.

It was just that this mark was so pleasant to look at. That was all.

She took a deep breath and vowed not to look at him for at least a minute. She could go for a minute, couldn't she? She was stalwart, resolute, unflappable Ivy. Ivy of the Worried Concerns. Ivy of the Steadfast Plan. Not Ivy of the Fluttering Lashes or Simpering Voice.

Instead, she stared down at the cards, dealing them out and holding her breath as each card was revealed. "Dealer wins," she said after a moment. After a minute of not looking at him.

And then allowed herself another glance. His eyes gazed resolutely at her, his lips tugging upward in a half smile.

"I knew it," he said in a soft tone of voice.

His eyes were the most unusual color she'd ever seen—almost amber, although she supposed others might say they were hazel. Of course he would even have beautiful eyes. Hers, she knew full well, were brown. Boring, ordinary, dull brown.

She exhaled, her deplorably brown eyes darting around the room as she tried to calm herself. And then felt her chest tighten as she glanced over at the opposite table. A young, auburn-haired woman clad in a mask was acting as the dealer, her slim fingers deftly dealing the cards.

Damn it.

"If you will excuse me, gentlemen," Ivy said, nodding toward Caroline, who was at another table. Caroline returned to the table where the duke and Mr. de Silva sat, and Ivy sped across the floor, anger warring with relief. Anger at Octavia for doing something Ivy had expressly forbidden, and relief that she was distracted for a few moments.

She went behind the table and grabbed Octavia's arm, whispering sharply into her ear. "What in God's name are you doing here?"

Octavia's eyes danced behind the mask. Perhaps today was the day that her sister would no longer obey Ivy's commands. "I'm helping out, Miss Ivy," she replied in a demure tone. "I understand that you are in need of some assistance."

"Miss Ivy, your new dealer is extraordinary."

Ivy turned to see who the speaker was. And nearly groaned aloud when she saw it was Lady Massingley, who would have been the person Ivy cited as her most profligate customer, if a poor-at-his-pursuit spy had asked.

"Thank you," Octavia replied, accompanying her words with a curtsy.

Lady Massingley flicked a coin across the table, which Octavia snagged handily.

"You are bringing me luck," Lady Massingley said. "Double or nothing," she said, sliding her whole stack of chips into the middle of the table.

"You see?" Octavia said in a smug tone.

"Fine," Ivy said in a low voice. "Just for tonight. And do not, under any circumstances, remove that mask."

"Yes, Miss Ivy." Octavia's tone was cheeky, and Ivy had to remind herself not to drag Octavia away. First, because it wouldn't be appropriate for the proprietor of Miss Ivy's to be seen in a scuffle with one of her supposed employees. Second, and more practically, Octavia was taller than Ivy, and she didn't think she would be able to do it anyway.

"It's a clever move, having your dealers behind masks."

Ivy jumped as she heard Mr. de Silva's voice behind her. She spun around, nearly falling into him. She hadn't realized quite how tall he was; of course she was rather short, but her head only came up to his chest. She kept her eyes on his waistcoat. It was gold, with an intricate pattern on the fabric. Gold buttons were an impudent addition that should have made the waistcoat look gaudy. But instead the overall effect was that of a confident man wearing clothing that would look good on only one person—and that person was him.

He was lucky in his clothing choices, too, apparently.

"We all want to pursue our pleasure anonymously," he continued. Thankfully oblivious to her assessment of his raiment. "And what better way to make everyone equal than to have them behind masks? You should supply them to the guests, as well." His gaze took in the room, which by now was about three-quarters full. "You allow anyone entry, do you not? Provided they have money?"

"I do," Ivy replied, curious to hear his thoughts. So few people actually considered why she'd set the club up as she did.

"That kind of—dare I say—revolutionary aesthetic lends itself well to anonymity. If everyone is masked, then we are all the same, are we not?" He chuckled. "I've never thought so much about equality before," he said in a speculative tone.

Ivy turned the idea over in her mind, suddenly intrigued. Perhaps Octavia's attempt at disguise would turn out to be an asset for the club.

"That is exactly what Ivy's is to be," she said in an enthusiastic tone. "A place where anyone is the same as anyone else. Its only requirement is the universal measure of egalitarianism—money."

"Although it is most likely that those with privilege are most likely to have it," he remarked dryly.

She thought of her father, a baron whose family went back to William the Conqueror. And yet who didn't have enough money to fund his weakness. And of the other members of the aristocracy she'd heard of who were thousands of pounds in debt, and yet other members of the aristocracy continued to gamble with them because they had noble blood. "And most likely to moan about it when they lose it. When they lose their privilege."

"Mope," he said.

"What?"

"*Mope* about it when they lose their privilege." It sounded as though he was issuing a reminder.

"Moan, mope, whatever," she said, gesturing dismissively. "The point is, yes. Miss Ivy's is for everyone." Ivy gestured to one of the passing servers, snagging two glasses from the tray. "Here."

"Thank you." He took a sip, then looked at her with a surprised expression. "It's excellent."

She nodded, pleased at the compliment. "If everyone is equal at Miss Ivy's, then everyone should have equally excellent beverages."

"I like the way you think, Miss Ivy," he said, tipping his glass to her. He took another swallow, nodding in satisfaction. "So I am presuming you are responsible for choosing the paintings? The ones with the duplicitous dogs are particularly charming."

She smothered a giggle. "Yes, I find it's so much more fun to work in pleasant surroundings. And knowing that those dogs are up on the walls trying to hide their scandalous deeds makes me smile every time I think about them." She leaned toward him to speak in a lower tone. "You're the first customer to notice them. Bravo, Mr. de Silva."

He shrugged in mock humility. "It's only a matter of paying attention. Especially to something so intriguing."

And then he looked at her, and she felt the force of his gaze. He certainly was a rakish sort. She'd seen the smile he'd aimed toward Caroline, who'd been immune. It seemed as though his charm was as natural to him as breathing; she wondered what it would be like to have that kind of innate charisma?

It would definitely serve her well in her role as gambling club proprietor. If she could lure customers in merely by charming them, she would make a lot of money far more swiftly than she currently was.

"Mr. de Silva, I believe you are flirting with me," she replied, relieved to hear her voice sound strong and playful. She wouldn't want him to know how he'd affected her breathing, for goodness' sake.

"I *did* say I would bet on the dealer."

She exhaled as she took another sip of her champagne. He was a charmer, this Mr. de Silva. It was a good thing she was a sensible woman and not a flighty girl, or she'd have her head turned.

A very good thing, a stern voice inside her brain reminded her.

Oh, do shut up, she replied. Hadn't she just said she liked working in pleasant surroundings? And Mr. de Silva was very pleasant indeed.

"As I was saying," she said, determined to prove to herself and her quarrelsome brain that she could continue a conversation with an attractive gentleman, "Miss Ivy's is for everyone." *Everyone with money, that is.*

"For everyone," he echoed. He downed the glass as his sharp gaze glanced around the room. He gestured with the hand holding the glass so it looked as though he were about to offer a toast. "That table over there, they're playing hearts?" He shook his head. "Terrible for the players, it's just a way for the house to make money."

Of course it's just a way for the house to make money. This is my house, and I wish to make money. "Just don't tell them that," she replied.

"Hearts is a losing game," he declared. She wished he would keep his tone down. "Everything is luck. You could have a king in your hand or a joker. Or you could think your joker was a king, and only find out you're wrong when it's too late." Now he sounded contemplative. She began to relax; if he just declaimed about luck, he wouldn't sound any different from any other of her customers, who were quick to blame anything when they lost.

Unfortunately, he quickly returned to the topic of games. "The players here would do better playing écarté or loo."

"Could you lower your voice please?" she hissed.

"Or whist!" he exclaimed, sounding enthusiastic. "Even though whist is what your grandmother plays. Or is that faro?" he mused, tilting his head in question.

She appreciated that he seemed to be interested in the games she offered, but she did not want any of her customers to get scared off because he'd laid out the odds of their winning. And he would not lower his voice.

"If you would just step over he—" Ivy said, speaking in the low tone she wished he would mimic. She regretted that this wasn't near one of the regular times the local police stopped in for a quick check of the premises. Not to arrest him, certainly not for talking, but it might shut him up better than she could.

"It's faro," he said in a decided, and decidedly not quiet, tone. "Hearts doesn't require any skill." Ah, insulting the customers' ability as well as pointing out how difficult it would be to win. A winning hand for losing business.

Damn him for being as observant and analytical as it seemed he was.

"Mr. de Silva, if you would—?" Ivy tugged on his sleeve, but he shifted away from her grasp.

"I should go advise those people what to play," he said in a determined tone. And then began to walk away.

She took a deep breath, then prepared to follow. To wrestle him to the ground, if necessary.

He hadn't gone more than a few steps when the duke walked up, thank God, clapping a hand on his friend's shoulder. "I think it's time we go home, Seb."

Mr. de Silva shrugged his friend's hand off. "I haven't finished, Nash."

The duke crossed his arms over his broad chest. "I think you have. Remember you're not—" And he frowned. *What had he been about to say?*

The duke glanced at Ivy, giving her a look that seemed to say, *Don't worry, I'll take care of this.*

Do not dare chase my patrons away, Smarty de Silva, she thought.

"I just wanted to tell them, Nash, about luck. It's entirely unpredictable."

"The very definition of luck," she muttered.

"I wanted to tell them that if you are going to play hearts," he continued, still speaking to his friend, "just make sure you keep track of the cards. That means don't drink too much. Don't let yourself get distracted," and at that he turned to grin wickedly at her.

His charming flirtation would not make her forget he had nearly cost her business.

"You want I should toss him out?" Henry asked, low at her side. Henry was a boxer, but was also uncannily savvy with money, and acted as Ivy's security and accountant. She'd met him when she'd attended an illegal fight, wanting to see how those cash transactions were handled prior to opening Miss Ivy's. Henry had gotten the worst of it when his opponent used an illegal weapon to stab Henry in the side. Ivy had taken him to a doctor, and he had refused to leave her side since.

She'd found it was awfully handy to employ a large financially literate man who could also toss disruptive patrons into the street.

"If he says another word," Ivy replied. "Then yes."

"Seb, time to go home," the duke said, flinging one long arm over Mr. Business Ruiner de Silva. "Come on."

Henry grunted in approval beside her.

"Not ready yet," Mr. de Silva expostulated. "I haven't said anything to them. Just to you, who isn't interested in playing. And her, who knows already," he added, glancing at Ivy.

I think you've said plenty, Ivy thought in exasperation.

"We're done, Seb," the duke declared. "You can come share your theories another time."

"If he's welcome," Henry muttered.

"Ssh," Ivy hissed back. Her desire to see him gone was equal to her wish to keep the duke as a returning patron.

Mr. de Silva twisted to look at Ivy. "You've got a good business here, I like the masks." Speaking as though completely unaware he'd come close to wrecking things—if not forever, at least for this evening. As though he merely had to speak, no matter what he said, and he'd be applauded. The arrogance of it made her shake.

"Thank you, Mr. de Silva," she managed to bite out. "Your Grace."

She and Henry watched as the duke led Mr. de Silva from the premises as that gentleman kept trying to engage her customers. Thankfully, his large friend eventually resorted to yanking him by the coat collar, eventually bundling him into a carriage outside.

"DAMN IT, I was out of line, wasn't I?"

An hour or so later, Sebastian cradled his snifter of brandy as he sat on Nash's excellently designed couch. The couch—designed to fit Nash's body if he chose to nap on it—was in Nash's library, which was less a library and more of a place for Nash to pace and drink.

Actually, any place would become that eventually. Sebastian knew it was because Nash would otherwise find himself in far more fistfights than he was normally in. Which were a lot. Nash had a temper.

Although Seb had opinions, so perhaps he shouldn't judge.

Nash took a swig of his drink. "It depends on what you mean by out of line." He was sprawled on a chair to the right of the sofa, one leg swung over the arm. "If you think wanting to tell people that a business is out to take their money is the definition of out of line." Nash spoke in a dry tone and Sebastian winced as he thought about what he'd said.

That everything—one's life, one's self—is dependent on luck. *That* had been the real truth of it, not that she would know that. She would only see that he had been about to scare off her customers. Not that his recent loss of luck was an excuse, but it was an explanation. He wasn't usually—which was to say never—so tactless.

Or had he been, and nobody had ever told him, because he was a duke? Privilege existed in places he'd never even contemplated before.

Nash continued. "You only spoke the truth. Businesses do want to take people's money. Otherwise, why else would it be a business?"

"Yes, but it wasn't my place to share that information."

"So you were an ass," Nash said with a shrug. "It's not like you haven't been one before." A pause. "For that matter, it isn't as though *I* haven't been an ass before." As though that was news to anyone.

"It's unusual for *me* to be an ass," Sebastian said in a pointed tone. He got up and drank the rest of the brandy, beginning to pace.

He snorted as he realized what he was doing: drinking and pacing. Just like Nash.

"It's probably the shock of hearing the news," Nash commented. "What with being disinherited and all. And because of your position, it's unlikely anyone ever allowed themselves to visibly express if you were an ass. Take comfort in that." He spoke ruefully; it was likely Nash wished more people would tell him the truth. Nash hated lying nearly as much as he hated the trappings of his title.

Nash got up as he spoke, walking to the table where he'd placed the brandy, pouring himself another draught, then raising it in question to Sebastian.

"No, thank you. Not after nearly ruining that poor woman's livelihood just because mine is gone. I feel like a churl."

"Better a churl than a useless bastard." Nash spoke in a flat tone. "Though you're that now, too," he said, sounding as though he were remarking on the weather and not on Sebastian's complete change of status. Sometimes Sebastian wished Nash were a little less truthful.

Sebastian raised his brow. "A useless bastard? Too on the nose, unless I can find something to do with myself. Then that would make me a useful bastard. I don't suppose you have an opening for a former duke, do you?"

Nash snorted. "I barely want to have a current duke." Nash's antipathy toward his title was a well-trod subject. Literally as well as figuratively, since he tended to pace as he voiced his aggravation.

"Look," Nash said, his tone softening, "you're arrogant, it's in your nature as well as your nurture. That's one of the reasons I tolerate you." He returned to his seat on the chair, leaning his elbows on his knees.

Sebastian laughed in reply as Nash continued. "But you're not unkind." Nash spoke gruffly, unaccustomed as he was to sharing his thoughts. "You didn't want to damage Miss Ivy's business by scaring off her customers." He shrugged, returning to his natural mien. "If anything, you believed that a well-informed customer would be likely to take more risks, since they'd have more confidence."

Sebastian acknowledged Nash's rare words with a nod of agreement. Even though the result had not been what he'd intended. And definitely not what *she* wanted. "If I were still a duke," he began ruefully, sitting down on the sofa, "I could just glide with my entourage, drop a tremendous amount of money at the club, and discuss the high quality of play. That would secure Miss Ivy's position in Society."

But I'm not.

He rose, unable to keep himself still. "I'll need to go apologize. I'll also need to learn how to keep my mouth shut."

"Along with how to not be a duke."

Ouch.

Nash leaned against the back of the chair, looking like a king on a throne. "You can't go tonight, it's too late. You'd better go see Miss Ivy tomorrow, before the club opens. You can stay here if you want."

"Since I have no better place to go," Sebastian replied. And then he winced. "That sounds as though your house is a last resort, that's not what I meant at all."

"Shut up, I know what you meant." Nash rose, striding over to the door and opening it wide. "Finan! Get your Irish arse in here!"

Nash's butler, formerly his batman, walked into the room, a tolerant expression on his face. "Your Grace has requested my Irish arse?" he said. He nodded toward Sebastian. "Your Grace."

"Not anymore," Sebastian murmured.

"Seb is staying here tonight, make up his usual room."

Finan nodded. "Do you need more brandy?" he asked, glancing over at the near-empty bottle.

"Not any for me tonight," Sebastian replied. He already knew waking up tomorrow was going to be painful, given everything that had happened today. He didn't want to add a hangover on top of it.

"Nor for me," Nash added.

"Well, that's a first," Finan said.

Nash growled.

"Come up in a few minutes, Your Grace, the room should be ready for you." Finan directed his words to Sebastian.

"Thank you, Finan."

Finan raised his eyebrows in mock surprise. "At least one of these dukes has a polite bone in his body. Unlike some I could mention."

Sebastian snorted in laughter, making Nash glare at him.

"Just go take care of it," Nash replied.

"Right away, Your Grace. Absolutely, Your Grace." Finan walked briskly out of the room as Nash shook his head.

"Insolent bastard," Nash muttered.

As though it bothered Nash at all—if anything, he'd probably see Finan's impudence as a tribute.

"You know," Nash said, "you can stay here for as long as you want."

Sebastian took a deep breath at the reminder. "I could go home, Thad would be fine with it—"

"But you wouldn't." Nash knew him well.

"No. No, I wouldn't. What my mother did, she did for her own security. Just so she wouldn't have to survive on her own. I can't do the same thing."

Nash nodded. "I understand why, but don't be an idiot. Stay here if you have nowhere else to go." It was the closest Nash had ever come to admitting he cared.

"I won't be an idiot, I promise." At least not more than he already was. "Thank you. At least I have a few things to do tomorrow," he continued, a hint of humor in his tone. "I'll apologize to the lady, give Ana Maria the news, and then figure out what to do with the rest of my life. As well as where to live."

"It's a plan. I wish I could have that schedule," Nash said, glancing around his comfortable room as though it were a prison.

Odd that Sebastian was the only one of the three of them who actually wanted a title—and was the only one who had no right to one.

"It's too early for His Grace," Finan said as Sebastian emerged from the guest bedroom. "Do you want I should wake him?" he added in a hopeful voice.

"No, don't bother him."

Sebastian had woken with his agenda fully on his mind, but with the added realization that he needed to get some things from his house before continuing.

And he did not want to see anyone, so he'd have to be swift and stealthy about it.

Which meant getting up earlier than he had ever gotten up before. Even earlier than the day before, when he'd had to go to the solicitor's office.

"I will bother him for his carriage, though," Sebastian continued. "It can take me home, and then can wait for my bag. I believe I'll be staying here for a few more nights."

Finan didn't say anything, just lifted his brows in surprise. Seb knew he'd get the truth of it all from Nash later anyway.

"Of course, Your Grace."

"Not that," Sebastian replied, but Finan was already halfway down the stairs. "Not Your Grace anymore," he murmured as he walked out the door into Nash's carriage. Heading back to the home that was no longer his to retrieve the few items he would feel comfortable taking so he wouldn't be venturing into his new life with only what he'd worn the night before.

"FLETCHFIELD, I'VE JUST come to collect a few things." Sebastian nodded to the butler, whose expression was a mix of sympathy and surprise. An expression he'd likely be seeing a lot in the future. If his former peers didn't ignore him entirely.

He strode up the stairs to the landing, turning right to head to his room. To the duke's room, that is.

"Your Grace!" Sebastian's valet, Hodgkins, scurried into the room behind him. Sebastian took a deep breath to compose himself, then turned around. His valet's expression was the same as usual, so the news still hadn't broken. Sebastian would have to tell him himself.

Hodgkins had been one of the footmen prior to Sebastian's father's death, and Sebastian had always noted Hodgkins's impeccable grooming and elegant style, even in the wardrobe his mother had deemed appropriate for a duke's footman.

The late duke's valet had wished to retire, and Sebastian hadn't hesitated a moment before promoting Hodgkins to work as his own valet after his mother had died—the one his mother had insisted on was condescending and had only been given the position so he could report Sebastian's goings-on to his mother.

Sebastian had kept the man quite busy, indulging in many goings-on prior to his parents' deaths.

"Hodgkins, can you find my thickest boots?" They were likely downstairs, leaving Sebastian time to assess what he would need and start to pack.

Not that he had ever packed before. But apparently the rest of his life would be marked by things he had never done previously but would have to do now.

Like apologize. Or make a living.

"Of course." Hodgkins nodded, then left the room.

Sebastian withdrew a satchel from the bottom of the wardrobe. He would not need what he had worn, and was still wearing, the night before. He doubted if elegant evening wear would be an essential element of his future life.

But he did like the gold waistcoat quite a lot.

He removed his jacket and then the waistcoat, folding the latter into some semblance of neatness. Or not, actually. He hadn't folded anything before.

He had a lot to learn.

He found a clean white shirt, shucking his current one onto the bed. Then he changed his trousers and rummaged in the wardrobe and chest of drawers to find clean linen, more shirts, and a few more pairs of trousers. He took his shaving kit as well, placing it on top of the pile.

Glancing skeptically between the pile of clothing now on his bed and his satchel, he shrugged and began to stuff it all in. If it all came out wrinkled? He'd ask Finan to help him sort it out. Even though that meant not learning.

He'd ask Finan to demonstrate what to do. There. That was better.

"Your Grace, your boots." Hodgkins froze as he took in what Sebastian was doing. And then drew himself up stiffly, his entire person radiating offense. "Has my work not been satisfactory? If there is something you wish I had done, perhaps you can—"

"No, it's not that," Sebastian replied, cutting him off. "You'll hear eventually, but I want to inform you myself. I would just ask"—and here it got tricky, since he didn't want Hodgkins to have to lie—"that Lady Ana Maria not be told until I can tell her."

"Of course, Your Grace." Hodgkins's expression eased.

"I—Well, the thing is," Seb began. This was even more difficult than he'd imagined, and it was to Hodgkins, not to his beloved sister. Perhaps he should view this as a practice run so he didn't entirely muck it up. "It turns out that my cousin, the Earl of Kempthorne, is actually the duke. I—I am not."

He exhaled as he spoke, glad to have the truth out there, somewhere, even if it wasn't all of the truth to all of the people.

Hodgkins's mouth had dropped open.

"And while I am welcome to stay here, the new duke has assured me of that, I would prefer to stay . . . elsewhere." He gestured toward the satchel. "So I am packing a few of the things I will need."

"Yes, Your—" And Hodgkins's expression froze so comically, Sebastian was sorely tempted to laugh.

But he didn't. The last thing his earnest valet needed was for his not-duke employer to laugh at him.

See, I can be cognizant of other people's sensitivities. He had just never done it before.

"I'll send for more things once I know where I am to live." Sebastian spoke in a tone that indicated he knew that there would be a place for him to live when he knew nothing of the sort.

Perhaps he could get a position upon the stage. Acting as though he knew things when he did not.

He leaned down to pick up the boots from where Hodgkins had put them, then picked up the satchel and swung it onto his arm.

Sebastian paused to clap a hand on Hodgkins's shoulder. "Thank you, Hodgkins."

"Of course, Your—" Hodgkins replied.

"Goodbye," Sebastian said, cutting him off so Hodgkins wouldn't be entirely appalled. "Remember about Lady Ana Maria. I'll speak with her as soon as I can."

And with that, he was down the stairs and out the door, heading to his new life. Though he didn't know where, for how long, or with whom.

Just that it wasn't this.

Chapter Four

Ivy emerged from the club, blinking at the sunlight. It was nearly noon, and she'd been unable to sleep past eight o'clock, which meant that she'd gotten approximately five hours of sleep—the club remained open as long as the players were wanting to play, and Lady Massingley had been surprisingly sprightly until close to three. But she'd been losing, so Ivy was more than happy to be exhausted the next day. Not that she was *happy*, per se; she was still irritated about the incident the previous night, especially since she'd allowed herself to be lured in by his charm and good looks.

But she had to stop thinking about it, and him. "Apples, bread, cheese," she chanted to herself, clutching the empty basket resting on her hip. She didn't normally take care of the shopping, their maid Carter did, but today was the day Carter was taking the rescued kittens to their new homes. Ivy didn't think it was fair to ask Carter to do the shopping on top of that, so she'd volunteered.

And it was a welcome distraction from her thoughts.

"Miss Ivy!" a voice called. A male voice, a voice belonging to the gentleman who'd chased off several of her patrons the night before.

So much for being sufficiently distracted.

"Mr. de Silva," she replied in a short tone, continuing to walk. He fell into step beside her, shortening his long stride.

He'd removed his waistcoat, but his hair was ruffled, and his cheeks were dark with stubble. Had he not gone home?

Perhaps he had gone to a pub and told everyone there about the hazards of drinking.

And then gone to a stable and discussed the various injuries one could incur while horseback riding.

Mr. Unwelcome Words de Silva.

"Miss Ivy, I completely understand if you don't wish to speak to me, but you must allow me to—"

"If you understand I don't wish to speak to you, then why are you speaking to me?"

Had anyone ever told him to stop talking before?

And why was she allowing herself to be so irritated?

"Fair point. But let me just apologize for my behavior last night."

She stopped walking, turning to regard him. "It wasn't your behavior that I object to, it was that you were about to discuss the inner workings of the play to the players. You do realize you were on the verge of driving away my customers?"

He winced. "I do. At least I did once I'd thought about it. And I want to make it up to you."

She met his gaze. He really was handsome. It irked her. "So come lose money in my establishment."

His expression tightened. "That is not possible."

She raised her eyebrows in disbelief. "Because you're such a good player? *Do* try to lose, Mr. de Silva, it will be a novel experience."

"It's not that." He looked away from her, off into the distance as though he was thinking. "I haven't had to measure my words before, and I regret that I said the things I did. I really do admire the unique aspects of your establishment. I was out of line."

"You were." Her words were direct, but her tone was softer. It did sound as though he was truly regretful.

"Where are you going? May I accompany you?" He spoke as if unaccustomed to asking. Likely he didn't ask, he just *did*. Like the previous evening.

"Uh . . ." she began. Did he not know how that might look? Not that she had a reputation to lose or anything. But he didn't know that.

He shook his head as he spoke. "That was not well done of me, I apologize. Again. I do not seem to know how to behave in certain company."

Drat. She could never resist helping a person in need. And this gentleman seemed needy.

"I am going to buy," she began, then tilted her head up to recall, "apples, bread, cheese." She shrugged. "You are welcome to keep me company on such an important errand, if you want," she said with a self-deprecating tone.

They were walking toward the market, people streaming hurriedly past them, forcing them to walk closer together. Her shoulder brushed his arm, making both of them shift unsteadily for a moment, and then he took her arm and looped it through his. She opened her mouth to object—he hadn't asked, after all—but it felt lovely, so she thought she'd rather not.

She reminded herself sternly to reprimand him if he took further liberties.

But right now, she didn't mind. Apparently her indignation could be mollified if the result felt pleasant. She wanted to smack herself for her pliable standards.

"The thing is," he began, "I didn't intend to chase your customers away."

"It doesn't matter what your intent was, the result was that you were on the verge of it."

"Intentions don't matter," he said, sounding as though he weren't replying to her, but commenting on something else. "The results are everything." Once again, his thoughtful tone made it sound as though he were having a separate conversation somewhere.

"Yes, well," she replied. She wondered who he was arguing with inside his head. "It's not that you were wrong. I mean, we both know that hearts is a game anyone can play, and anyone can win at. There is very little skill involved."

"Loo and écarté take more skill."

"As you said last night."

"I was an ass, wasn't I?"

"Indeed." But her tone was amused, and she looked up at him, a smile on her face.

"But what I said before is true. Your club is distinct, far more interesting to me than Crockford's."

"Because Miss Ivy's allows ladies to play?"

"That is an attraction, I admit." He paused. "But that's not all of it. Requiring the players to settle up before they leave, letting anyone in as long as they have money—it's a radical concept. Quite innovative."

"Thank you," Ivy replied. "Here we are," she continued. They were stopped in front of a cart overflowing with apples.

"Miss, sir, how can I assist?"

The merchant's head popped up from behind the cart, his cheeks as red as his apples. Ivy suppressed a giggle.

"I need apples," she said.

"It appears you have come to the right place," Mr. de Silva murmured beside her. She bit her lip to keep from laughing.

"What kind?" the merchant asked.

"Uh—" she began.

"I've got the Harvey, the Laxton's Superb, the Maiden's Blush, and the Cox."

"Maiden's Blush, I think," she decided. Apropos for the day. "Enough to make a pie and have a few left over."

He placed the apples in a bag, handing them over the cart. Mr. de Silva took them in one hand, sliding the basket off her arm with the other, then placed the bag inside the basket.

"That'll be two and eight," the merchant said.

Ivy withdrew her wallet from her skirt pocket, handing him the coins.

"Apples cost two and eight," she heard Mr. de Silva say in a musing voice.

"Bread and cheese next?" he said, taking her arm again.

"Bread and cheese," she confirmed.

AN HOUR LATER, he was walking her toward the club, having shared some of the food she'd bought. He had waited patiently as she made her purchases, even though she had told him he needn't bother—he'd apologized, she'd accepted the apology, and that should have been that.

But.

But he was still here, and he still held her arm, and her basket, and he was such a pleasure to look at, even if she couldn't do more than steal a few glances at him.

Pliable standards. She had them.

"Well, thank you for escorting me to the market. It was nice not having to carry all of these things myself." She took the basket from his grasp.

"And thank you for accepting my apology," he replied.

"Would you want to come inside to continue the discussion?" She smiled. "Now that there are no customers about, I would like to hear your opinions on how we could improve Miss Ivy's. I am certain with so many opinions you are bound to have some on that matter."

And then she wanted to wince at the invitation. Of course he didn't want to come in, he merely felt bad about chasing her patrons away.

"I'd love to."

Oh.

"It's not as though I have anything else to do."

Oh. That put an entirely different spin on his reply. And who was he, anyway, not to have anything to do in the middle of the day?

It didn't matter. What mattered, what always mattered, was finding and implementing good ideas.

She slid the key into the lock, then pushed the door open. The club stood empty, the chairs all pushed against the wall in preparation for the floor getting mopped. "Through here," she said, stopping to place her basket on one of the chairs before walking across the floor. She flung the next door open, stepping into the hallway. Straight ahead was the door that led upstairs to the private rooms, which is where she and Octavia lived, while to the right was her office, which was basically a glorified term for the room where all the necessities for the club were stored: extra dice, alcohol, cleaning supplies, and whatever else was needed.

"Come into my office." She led the way, going to sit behind the desk where she did her paperwork.

If she were the lady she'd once been, she would have blanched at inviting a gentleman to spend time with her alone. As she would have at his asking to accompany her on her errands. But she was a businesswoman, and he had advice to share.

"Please sit." She gestured to the well-worn wooden chair opposite the desk as she sat in her own chair, the mate to his.

"Is it too early for a drink?" she asked.

"Never," he replied, a grin on his face.

She bent down to retrieve the bottle of whiskey she kept in her bottom drawer along with two glasses. He nodded affirmatively as she held them up.

"Here," she said, sliding one glass across her desk to him. He sat as though on a throne, not in her spindly office chair, his legs planted on either side next to the chair legs, his hands resting on his thighs. A king amongst the clutter.

"To Miss Ivy's," he said, lifting the glass.

She smiled, raising her own glass as she took a deep swallow. The whiskey burned as it went down her throat, and her chest immediately felt warmer. At least she could blame that on the alcohol, and not on him.

"Excellent," he commented. "Like your champagne."

"Yes, and our food is even better." She couldn't disguise the pride in her voice.

Another one of Ivy's rescues, her chef, Mac, was an Irishman who'd trained in the celebrated chef Alexis Soyer's kitchens. He had remarkable talent, but of course no aristocrat would hire an Irish chef. And Mac was far too talented, and aware of his talent, to settle for less than what he was worth. That made him tricky to manage, but the food was delicious. Word was already spreading that there was fine food as well as fine gaming to be found at Miss Ivy's.

"Well," she said, finishing her whiskey and setting the glass down on the surface of her desk, "what ideas do you have for me?"

So. This is how it felt to be asked one's opinions and advice because of one's actual opinions and advice, not because it would flatter the opinion giver, or bestow some sort of reflected splendor onto the asker.

Perhaps not being a duke wouldn't be the barren nightmare he imagined.

No moping, he reminded himself.

Just reality, he retorted.

Seb finished his whiskey, nodding affirmatively when she gestured toward the bottle again. Now it didn't seem quite as important that he dull his mind, but her whiskey was truly excellent, and he didn't know when he could afford its quality himself. He was glad, however, he'd accepted her offer of bread and cheese—he needed to keep a clear head for—well, for the rest of his life, since he couldn't afford any kind of misstep.

Which reminded him he still had to figure out what to do with the rest of his life. And that the rest of his life was a vast unknown chasm. What did people who were not dukes do, anyway?

But now, he still had whiskey and conversation with an intriguing woman. He could table the whole "rest of his life" question until later.

"Masks, as I said last night." He tilted his head to stare at the ceiling. "I suppose you could also have special evenings." The ideas were whirling through his head. As though his change of circumstances had freed something inside him.

It was refreshing for him to actually be *thinking*. Not just pushing things along, or attending something because of who he was, standing silent as he acknowledged his importance.

He wasn't important anymore. He was the illegitimate offspring of a duplicitous woman. But he could be the *useful* illegitimate offspring of a duplicitous woman. So that was an improvement.

"Special evenings such as costume night, where your guests arrive in costumes from another era. Or one evening where the wagers aren't based around actual money, but around transactions." He thought of the possibilities. "That could be quite intriguing," he added.

Her cheeks flushed, and he surmised she had come to the same conclusions he had. Conclusions that seemed far more intriguing if *she* were involved.

Well, at least he knew that if he was no longer a duke, he would still be a rake.

"Your ideas are certainly creative," she said. She took a deep breath. "So tell me, Mr. de Silva, why aren't you running your own gambling hell?"

His immediate reaction was to be affronted—how dare this woman suggest that he actually work at something?

But then he realized his response would be insulting even if he was still a duke. This woman was working at something, something that clearly mattered to her. She was obviously proud of her accomplishments and wanted to improve her business. She served the best food and drink, even though similar establishments made do with mediocre fare because their clientele would accept it.

And if he were still a duke, he wouldn't have even gone to the club in the first place to see what she'd done. He'd have gone to a party, getting fawned over by people whose names he could scarcely remember. Being eyeballed as a prospective husband by any number of conniving mothers.

But that was far too harsh. He needed to remind himself that he was still Sebastian, even if he didn't have a title.

The reality was that he did have some friends whose presence at that party would have made it tolerable. Who would have shared a commiserative glance at an obsequious comment? He had been depending on those friends to help Ana Maria navigate Society; he doubted practical Thaddeus would be able to charm people as well as he could. In fact, he knew *that* was a sure bet.

And Nash—Nash much preferred the society of ex-soldiers, sailors, merchants, and anybody who wasn't an aristocrat to anybody in Society. When he wasn't roaming the streets of London in search of a fight.

Oh. She was still waiting for his reply, not pondering his change of circumstances. Or his friend's lowly predilections.

Given that she didn't know about either of them. "I suppose because I'd never thought of it, not until now." *Because I was too occupied with being ducal and whatnot.*

"Not that I want you to open your own establishment," she said quickly. "Would you mind if I used some of your ideas?" She wrinkled her brow. "What is it you do, anyway? I hadn't asked yet, that was very rude of me."

He waved his hand. "This and that."

"Oh," she replied, a slight frown on her face. "I would be happy to offer you payment for what we've discussed."

Well. Payment. He'd never had to think along those lines before. "Thank you. For now, if you wouldn't mind pouring me some more whiskey, that would do." He pushed his glass across the desk. She poured a generous amount and pushed it back, then poured more in her own glass. Less than his, but still enough.

"To new ideas," she said, raising her glass.

"To new ideas," he echoed.

His new idea? That he wished he could find a way to drink whiskey during the day while still making a living.

But that wasn't possible. Or if it was, it meant being a duke, and he'd already tried that and been rejected. Unfortunately, he had no excuse anymore. He needed to return to Nash's and ponder his future. He finished his drink, then rose and bowed.

"Thank you for an engaging afternoon." And he meant it—he hadn't been so mentally engaged in years, if ever. Mostly he said things and people agreed: "Should we take to your bed for a night of pleasure?" "Could I have that waistcoat in four different shades of red?" "I would like to purchase that horse." Things like that.

"Thank you, Mr. de Silva," she replied, rising from her chair.

He nodded again, then turned and walked out of the room, conscious that he'd just spent time with an adult woman to whom he wasn't related that hadn't involved parts of their anatomy.

He'd have to get used to new things every day from now on.

IT WAS FAR later than she'd thought when she finally glanced at the clock. She'd had to rush to get dressed for the evening after his departure, and she'd barely had time to down a cup of tea with Octavia, their daily ritual, before starting work.

The club had been exceedingly busy all evening, which was gratifying, but exhausting.

But it was now just after two o'clock in the morning, several hours since she'd returned home, and the last player had gone, and she could finally relax.

"That will be all, Henry." Ivy turned to address the rest of the staff. "Everyone, we're finished for the night. Good work."

The staff nodded, filing out as they placed the various tools of their profession on the shelves close to the door. Henry was the last to go, giving Ivy one last searching look. She gave him a reassuring smile. He was always concerned when there was a lot of cash on the premises, and there was a lot of cash this evening.

Octavia had snuck down again wearing her mask, taking a place behind the same table as the evening before. But Lady Massingley had returned as well, and had continued to lose, so Ivy had suppressed her wish to march her sister back upstairs.

It had been an excellent night overall for Miss Ivy's following the excellent afternoon for personal Ivy; Mr. de Silva had spent a long time in her office, both of them discussing various ideas for the club. Some of them were ridiculous, of course, but there were many that would distinguish Miss Ivy's from the other gambling houses, especially Crockford's, which was by far the biggest establishment in London.

Ivy could only hope for a fraction of Crockford's success, but that fraction might be larger if she implemented these innovations. Perhaps more importantly, Mr. de Silva had talked to her as an equal—not as a foolish woman who was trying to make a go of a business.

"Why are you all flushed?" Octavia narrowed her eyes as she stood in front of her sister. "What have you been doing?"

Ivy planted her hands on her hips, relieved to have a distraction from her . . . distracting thoughts.

"What have *I* been doing?" she retorted in a self-righteous tone. "I have not been acting as a dealer against my older sister and guardian's express wishes."

Octavia rolled her eyes. So much for an older sister's authority.

"I was *helping*. Lady Massingley lost everything she brought with her, which means the club gained. That would not have been possible without my assistance."

"Oh, believe me, Lady Massingley would have found a way to lose without you," Ivy said in a dry tone of voice.

"It was so much fun, Ivy," Octavia said, sounding far too enthusiastic. "You have to let me work down here. You don't know how boring it is up above stairs in the evening, knowing there is all this happening while I am stuck up there. And with the kittens gone, there isn't even any company."

"Poor you. Having to relax in the evening, perhaps reading a salacious novel, while your sister works to keep a roof over your head."

"That's just it," Octavia said triumphantly. "If we both work here, we are both keeping a roof over our heads. Why should you bear all of this alone?"

"Because," Ivy replied, taking her sister's arm and walking with her toward the door leading to upstairs, "you deserve to have whatever future you want. And that would not be possible if you work here." *You are my responsibility. I won't have you getting entangled in this, not when it means no respectable gentleman will have you.*

She had given up her own hopes and dreams the evening her father had wagered her. But she wouldn't give up on Octavia's.

Although her sister was proving to be an asset.

Stop thinking that, she reminded herself sternly.

Octavia dragged her feet, wriggling her arm to try to get Ivy to let go. She might be close to an adult, but she still behaved like a child sometimes.

"When are you going to let me choose the future I want, Ivy?"

She didn't sound childish, however. She sounded determined.

"You don't want this." Even to her own ears, Ivy's words sounded hesitant.

"Isn't that up to—?"

But the rest of Octavia's words were lost as both women heard a crash from the front door and turned toward the noise. A figure burst in, falling onto the nearest table. Another figure followed, brandishing what appeared to be—a cribbage board?—over his head.

Ivy wished Henry hadn't left, after all.

Her eyes darted around for any kind of weapon. A deck of cards wasn't going to do anything. Nor were the various pairs of dice left on the table. And the roulette wheel was fastened securely.

Finally, she saw a broom in the corner, left after the staff had swept up, and seized it, hoisting it over her head with the brush part at the very top. No doubt she looked ridiculous, but she didn't think the intruders would offer a critique of her defensive stance.

And if they did, she would brain them with her broom.

Which, to be honest, she was planning on doing anyway. She raised the broom, whirling it in the air as she tried to figure out which miscreant she should hit first.

"Ivy!"

Octavia's shout made her pause, the broom frozen in the air.

"Look!"

Ivy followed where Octavia was pointing, recognizing Mr. de Silva as the second of the intruders. He met her gaze, nodding briefly before launching himself onto the other man's back. "Caught him trying to break in," Mr. de Silva called. The man twisted, but was unable to dislodge Mr. de Silva, whose delighted expression would have made Ivy laugh, if the situation wasn't so dire.

He lifted the cribbage board into the air and struck it down with a satisfying thwack onto the other man's head, making the man stumble onto the table, sending Mr. de Silva flying over the man's head and the table, landing on the floor on the other side.

The man he'd struck slumped onto the table, suddenly still. Ivy held her broom up high as she cautiously approached him.

"Octavia, see to Mr. de Silva, please," she ordered.

Ivy peered at the would-be burglar, whose face was on the green felt of the table. Blood leaked from his nose, a dark stain spreading rapidly on the table. Damn it. She had just gotten this table recovered. She could see the man's body rising with his breath, so she knew he hadn't been irreparably damaged by the cribbage board.

Death by cribbage board would be very difficult to explain to the authorities.

Now she had to figure out what to do with him. What to do with both of them.

"He's unconscious, but otherwise fine," Octavia said, returning to stand beside Ivy. "Is that one dead?" Her tone wasn't appalled, and Ivy wondered if she had done irreparable damage to her sister's character by exposing her to this world.

Then again, this was the first such incident they'd ever had. So perhaps it had been part of Octavia's makeup all along.

So maybe she did belong on the gambling floor?

That was a question for another time, however. Now she had a fallen criminal and a fallen hero to worry about.

"Can you go out and find a policeman? Just wait at the entrance if there isn't one right away." The last thing she needed was for her daring sister to go venturing into London in the middle of the night.

When she'd first opened, Ivy had spoken with the chief constable in the area, discovering he had a penchant for excellent food, and therefore making sure she always brought out a plate of Mac's best dishes when he was around. In exchange, Chief Constable Tildon had promised regular police visits.

"Can't we just punish him ourselves?" Octavia leaned in to peer at the thief's face. "Although his nose appears to be broken, so perhaps that is punishment enough. You just had that table re-covered, didn't you?" She made a tsking noise. "Remarkable they both managed to knock themselves out."

"Go fetch the policeman," Ivy ordered, nudging her sister near the door.

"I'll deal with you in a moment," she said to the still-unconscious thief, stepping to the other side of the table and bending down to look at Mr. de Silva.

Thankfully, his nose wasn't broken. Given that it was such a nice nose. He stirred as she looked at him, and she exhaled in relief. She wouldn't want him to have to go to hospital because he was defending her club.

With a cribbage board.

Which was odd, to say the least.

She shrugged, then placed her palm on his forehead, smoothing a few strands of hair away from his face. He moaned, and she murmured some soothing noises in his general direction.

"Constable Duxworth is here, Ivy," Octavia said. Ivy rose and turned, recognizing the policeman as a regular patroller.

"This is the man who tried to rob us," Octavia continued, pointing at the man on the table. Constable Duxworth, a middle-aged man with an impressive mustache, leaned around the table to take a look at Mr. de Silva.

"And this one, too?"

"No, no, not at all," Ivy replied hurriedly. "He saved us. We'll be responsible for him, if you can just take this one away."

Constable Duxworth gave her a skeptical look, but because she'd been on the receiving end of several such looks since she'd opened, she didn't let it bother her.

"I'll take him down to the station. He won't be bothering you young ladies any longer." He spoke in a patronizing tone.

Ivy placed her hand on Octavia's arm as she felt her sister start to bristle.

"Thank you, Constable."

He grabbed the man by the back of his collar, lifting his head off the table, then turned to place the man's weight on his back, beginning to drag him out of the club. Ivy and Octavia followed, Ivy wincing at how roughly Constable Duxworth was treating his prisoner.

Not that she felt sorry for the man, but all the jouncing he was undergoing was going to hurt when he eventually woke up.

"Thank you, Constable," Ivy said again before shutting the door. She leaned against it, taking a few deep breaths. She hadn't allowed it to register during the fracas, but her heart was racing, and she was in a heightened state of panic. And that was even before she dealt with Mr. de Silva, who had already made her heart race.

"What do we do about him?" Octavia said, nodding toward the man in question.

Both sisters looked at him, still slumped on the floor. Ivy supposed she could have tried to make him more comfortable, but he was mostly unconscious.

"Uh—do you think we can bring him to our apartments? He can sleep in the spare room."

Octavia gave Ivy a skeptical glance. "You mean where we put our things when we don't know where to put them?" She looked back at Mr. de Silva. "I don't know this gentleman, but he is clearly a *gentleman*. He's not going to want to be stuffed among our old dolls, your abandoned knitting projects, and all our books."

"He doesn't have a choice, does he?" Ivy retorted. "Either he stays on our floor here, or he goes to sleep with Mrs. Buttercup."

Octavia snorted. "Mrs. Buttercup is not that kind of doll!" She regarded Mr. de Silva as though calculating. "We can probably bring him through to our apartments between the two of us. You're short, but you're strong."

"Thank you for the praise," Ivy said dryly. "You take his legs, I'll take his shoulders."

By the time they'd gotten Mr. de Silva to the spare room, Ivy had soaked through her clothing and Octavia had cursed her no fewer than five times.

Mr. de Silva mumbled occasionally, but offered no assistance otherwise.

"He's very handsome," Octavia remarked as Ivy drew up the covers under his chin.

"Oh, is he? I hadn't noticed," Ivy replied. There was never an inopportune time to practice her bluffing.

"He is! Just look at him."

Ivy smothered a grin, delighted at her success. *I have looked at him, sister. I have.*

Chapter Five

Sebastian cautiously opened one eye, then the other, uttering an audible groan at the light flooding the room. Why did his head hurt so much? Was it possible he had drunk that much?

And why hadn't Hodgkins closed the drapes? He knew Sebastian didn't like to wake until well past noon. Keeping the room dark was essential for an uninterrupted sleep.

Not to mention, why was his ceiling so close to his face? Had it been moved in the night?

Although that was ridiculous. Clearly he was not in his own bedroom. But where the hell was he?

"You're awake," a voice said. A female voice. One he thought he recognized, but everything felt and sounded fuzzy. Seb turned his head to where the voice came from, wincing at the pain.

"Don't move too quickly, you'll just get a headache."

"I already have one," Seb growled in reply.

A cool hand was placed on his forehead, and Seb closed his eyes, nearly drifting off to sleep again. This bed was more comfortable than his own. He congratulated himself on his choice of bed partners last night—a comfortable bed was a welcome bonus to whatever sport he'd engaged in.

"Who are you?" he muttered. Rude not to remember who he'd spent the night with, but it was ruder to pretend to remember and then get caught out in a lie.

"Miss Ivy," the voice said in an amused tone.

"Ah, Miss Ivy," Seb repeated, his brain sifting through his memory. And then his eyes shot open, and he stared at her standing above him. She wore a plain blue gown, her hair scraped back from her face. Her expression was concerned, and he wondered just what he'd done to elicit that reaction.

He hadn't been disappointing, had he? He'd never disappointed a woman in his life. At least not in that way.

"Did we . . . ?" he began.

Because if they had, and he couldn't remember, he was going to be furious with himself.

"Certainly not!" Miss Ivy snatched her hand away, folding her arms over her chest. She had a lovely bosom. "You don't remember?"

"Enlighten me," he said, stretching his fingers out to touch her gown. It was worn, and soft to the touch.

She snatched it away, looking ruffled. "I don't know why you had returned, but you did a great deed last night."

He smirked.

"Not *that* kind of deed," she continued, rolling her eyes. "Goodness, you'd think after being knocked unconscious you wouldn't be quite so determined in your rakish pursuits."

"Knocked unconscious?" No wonder he felt as though he'd been . . . knocked unconscious. "Rakish pursuits?" he added, his tone humorous.

"Yes, as I said, you returned as there was a man trying to rob the club. My sister and I were alone. I don't know what would have happened if you—"

"So I was a hero," he pronounced with satisfaction.

He didn't have to look at her to know she had an aggravated expression on her face.

He shouldn't tease her, but it was just so much fun.

"Of sorts. You hit the man on the head with a cribbage board."

That sounded odd. And not at all like him. If he were going to hit someone, he'd use his fists.

"And then you tripped on one of the tables and fell on your head." Her tone, and her description of the event, did not seem heroic. In the least.

He frowned. "Ah. So I am in your home?"

"Yes. We do have to thank you, Mr. de Silva. I don't know what would have happened if you hadn't returned—"

"Mr. de Silva?" he repeated, entirely confused.

And then it all came rushing back, his memory of what had happened in the solicitor's office, the evening with Nash, the apology he'd offered, the time spent pondering his future, all accompanied with a sharp sense of panic.

As though he were falling off a cliff with no idea of what awaited him. Which would be merely a moment of panic if it wasn't also entirely true.

"Damn it, I have to get going." He sat up suddenly in bed, groaning at how his head reacted to his movement, but keenly aware of time ticking by.

As a duke, he hadn't been answerable to anybody. Plus, he'd always been accompanied by various servants. But he was on his own now, and he had no idea if Nash was concerned about his not appearing home that evening. What had he done? Right, he'd returned to Nash's house for dinner, and then was too restless to settle down. His roaming had brought him to the club, hoping for a chance to speak with her again. Even though it had been ridiculously late, what had he been thinking?

Which meant he hadn't made it to Nash's house. Would his friend be concerned?

Likely not, knowing Nash. But Finan might be.

"You'd better not. Let me get you some tea."

"Tea will not solve anything," he said firmly, swinging his legs over the side of the bed. His boots were on the floor, and he was still clad in his shirt and trousers. So he really had just been knocked unconscious. Drat. Although that meant he hadn't disappointed her in that way, so at least there was an upside.

A moment of bleak humor in the midst of all this uncertainty.

He got to his feet, sitting abruptly back down as his head started to spin.

"Tea," she said firmly, walking out of the room and closing the door behind her.

He lay back on the bed, his legs dangling off the edge, staring up at the ceiling.

He needed to start his new life. Whatever that would be. After he told Ana Maria. Not that he knew what he would tell her. What would he tell her?

The truth.

Well, yes. The truth. It wouldn't affect Ana Maria directly, except it would confirm what both of them already knew—that Sebastian's mother was ruthless and wouldn't let anything stand in her way. Not her husband's daughter or British law.

And even though he knew it had nothing to do with him, he didn't want to be the reason she was disappointed again.

Damn it.

But thinking about her meant he wasn't contemplating what the hell *he* was going to do.

He sat up again just as Miss Ivy returned holding a tray of tea things. She placed it on the bureau to the right of the bed, nudging what appeared to be an ancient doll with one eye missing to make room for the tray. He glanced around, taking in the details of the room.

An enormous bookshelf was at one end, stacked with books put in any which way. Dolls ranged along the surface of the other bureau he could see, all in various stages of disrepair. Taxidermic animals sat between a few of the dolls, while an enormous bust of some glowering man stared straight at him. Pieces of bric-a-brac were scattered around, seemingly without a thought toward decoration.

"This isn't your room, is it?" he said, unable to disguise his tone of voice.

Because if it were, and he had been here for a romantic interlude, he'd have to ask himself just how much he wanted to have relations in this setting. The room was . . . *unsettling*, to say the least.

"Are you back to thinking anything happened last night, Mr. de Silva?" She shook her head, beginning to pour the tea. "This is not my room. I slept in my own room, thank you very much. How do you take your tea?"

"Not at all, if I can help it," Seb replied.

She gave him an exasperated look.

"Fine," he said, waving his hand. Not as impressive a gesture when he was effectively in bed. "A bit of milk, no sugar."

She nodded, then handed him a cup and saucer. She made her own cup and sat back in her chair.

"I did a lot of thinking prior to the incident last evening," she said. She took a sip of tea while Seb studied her.

Her expressions shifted as she thought, and he wondered just what was going through her mind. He could see she was debating something and saw when she'd made her decision.

"You'd make a terrible card player," he remarked.

Her eyes widened, and for a moment it actually seemed as though she was about to growl. "I would not! I do not! I am an excellent card player as it happens, Mr. de Silva. How do you think Miss Ivy's is so successful? It is not because I am a terrible card player." He wanted to laugh at her outraged tone.

He shrugged deliberately, accidentally spilling some tea onto his leg, which made him jump. "Blast," he exclaimed, putting the cursed tea on the side table next to the bed.

She was laughing, damn her, one hand held up to her mouth, her eyes dancing with humor. He couldn't help but join her. It was funny, and he definitely deserved her laughter. Plus he *had* been rather obnoxious when he'd believed he was a duke who had spent the night with a lady.

"Although I do not play cards with my clientele, at least not often. Sometimes I sit in when there is a large pot and the player likes to feel as though anyone could win or lose." She shook her head as though impatient. "But that's not important. I am wondering, Mr. de Silva—if your position is one you would consider leaving," she began, lacing her fingers together. "I would like to offer you a job at Miss Ivy's."

MR. DE SILVA was staring at her as though she'd sprouted an additional head. Was it such an odd question? And if it was, all he had to say was no. He didn't have to look at her as though she'd just arrived on this planet.

Although she could understand that presumption if he thought this was her bedroom. It was filled with detritus from her childhood, plus several of Octavia's odder interests, including the time she thought she might want to be a taxidermist. She'd even thought of a name for her shop—Dead on Arrival.

"Uh—" he began.

"If you have a position you don't wish to leave, I would understand," she interrupted. "Or if you believe it would be beneath you—" This same scenario had not been nearly as difficult when she'd hired Samuel and Henry. But neither of them was *this* gentleman.

"No," he said.

She blinked. "No, what? No, you are absolutely not interested in working here, or no, you don't have a position, or no, it isn't beneath you?"

"No, I don't have a position." He looked thoughtful, and Ivy nearly held her breath to hear how he'd answer. She'd never thought of hiring a second-in-command before, but the club was doing well, and Mr. de Silva had so many interesting ideas. Ideas she knew her clientele would love.

Plus he was obviously a gentleman, and she'd realized there was a certain group of patrons she would never lure into the club if they thought a fallen lady was entirely in charge. Hiring him would pay for itself in no time. If she could increase the club's revenue, she would be set that much sooner. Perhaps there'd even be enough money to give Octavia a reasonable dowry so she could get married.

She winced as she imagined Octavia's inevitable response to that idea.

She'd cross that marital bridge when she came to it.

"So do you want to work for me?"

Mr. de Silva took a deep breath, his hands curled into fists on either side of him. "I have to do *something* with myself," he said in a bitter tone. What was that about? "I would," he said in a louder voice, meeting her gaze. "Thank you."

He looked and sounded humble now, the first such time she'd thought that about him. Perhaps there was more to him than a man of clever ideas and rakish pursuits. Or maybe there was less to him, since she had no idea who he was. Making her impulsive decision even more impulsive. But that was how she worked, and thus far, her instincts had been proved right.

"I am grateful for the opportunity." A pause as his brows drew together. "But what do you want me to do?"

Ivy couldn't help the immediate and completely inappropriate thought that first came to her: *a fig leaf, a pedestal, and perhaps a gaming table.*

Even though she should absolutely not be thinking any such thing, since the thought was so inappropriate.

For one thing, he was to be her employee, and there were *rules* about such behavior, even though it was normally a male employer and his female employee. For another, she didn't know if he was already involved or perhaps even married.

And then there was the fact that he appeared to try to flirt with every female, so she'd never know if he truly liked her, or she was just convenient for the time. He hadn't been successful with Caroline, but he had tried.

That was a lowering thought. But it had the benefit of making her realize just what a horrible idea it was in the first place.

Even though she still found him ridiculously handsome.

"I want you to help me implement some of your ideas from last night, help me manage the club. Perhaps work as a dealer occasionally." She shrugged. "We'll have to see. There is a lot to do, and not a lot of people to do it."

"I'll need a day or two to—to settle my affairs," he said. He looked pained again, and she opened her mouth to inquire about it. But that wasn't her business—his working for her was, but nothing else, she reminded herself firmly.

No matter how handsome or charming or rakish he was.

"And," he said, taking a deep breath as he spoke, "I suppose I should tell you who I am."

"So who are you?" she asked. Unless he was a spy, or a serial cribbage board attacker, it didn't really matter.

He gave a chuckle devoid of humor. "Until two days ago, I was the Duke of Hasford. But because of some recent information, it turns out that I am not."

"The Duke of Hasford?" No wonder she'd pegged him as a gentleman. He was one of the highest such gentlemen in the land. Or *had* been. So what was a gentleman who used to inhabit such a prestigious title doing defending her club with a cribbage board? Now tucked up in her spare room as though he were just another one of Octavia's collected items?

She had so many questions. But again, it wasn't her business.

Besides which, she knew as soon as Octavia found out, her sister would waste no time getting all the details, so her curiosity would be satisfied without having to ask him for clarification.

Which made her principled decision not to ask him a lot less principled.

"Yes."

"Well, Your Grace," she said, a wry grin on her face, "when would you be able to start working?"

Chapter Six

Sebastian felt stunned by the past forty-eight hours.

Literally stunned, since it seemed he'd been knocked unconscious the previous evening. But also figuratively stunned; he'd gone from being a duke with all the privilege and prestige in the world to being an illegitimate nobody.

But he'd also, somehow, miraculously, found something to do that did not involve moping or bemoaning his lot.

Which were somewhat the same thing, he had to admit. Perhaps he could get a position supplying synonyms to perplexed conversationalists.

He had left Miss Ivy's an hour or so ago, and was wending his way back to the town house, which he could no longer call home. He didn't have a home any longer.

He had to shove those thoughts aside. Better would be to think out the details of some of the ideas he'd mentioned to Miss Ivy—his new employer. His thoughts were scattered, veering from shock at his change in circumstances to excitement about what might lie ahead.

But first he had to go to his not home.

He needed to see Ana Maria and explain everything. Hopefully she hadn't heard yet.

His chest tightened as he anticipated her likely reaction.

It wasn't until after his mother died that she had been treated as an equal and valued member of the household—before that, she'd been treated as an unpaid servant, doing whatever tasks his mother had assigned her. Their father was too scattered to notice his wife's treatment of his daughter, and Sebastian hadn't been able to dissuade his mother either—the most he'd ever been able to do was behave so recklessly himself that he'd taken the duchess's attention away from Ana Maria.

It was one of the many reasons he'd been relieved when he'd been informed of his parents' deaths. Ana Maria didn't deserve to be treated so poorly, and his only comfort was that eventually he would become the duke and he could change all that.

Ana Maria was always cheerful, even when scrubbing floors and peeling potatoes, but it was only in the past six months that she had seemed to relax, though she still had a habit of cleaning things, despite Sebastian's reminders that they had servants for that. She had finally agreed to enter Society, though she had balked at having a traditional come-out.

Her life was about to be altered again, after having just seeming to settle.

As was his, of course.

No moping, a voice inside his head admonished.

I'm not moping, *I'm* pondering, he rejoined.

Humph, the voice responded. *A synonym provider might suggest those were the same thing in this context.*

Thank goodness he arrived at the door before a fully blown fight could break out between the voices in his head.

It swung open before he could knock, Fletchfield regarding him with a concerned expression.

"Your—yes, uh, you are home. Your sister has been worried about you. She is in your library."

Sebastian handed his hat and coat to Fletchfield, then stood and regarded the library's closed door. This would be the worst of it—telling Ana Maria.

He loved his sister. She was the one who'd taken care of him when he was little, when his mother was off tending to her duchess duties. Ana Maria had read to him at night and stayed with him when he'd had nightmares. They had been each other's sole comfort in the house; their father wasn't usually present, either in person or in mind, and his mother was not a kind woman.

And when he had inherited the title, he had reassured Ana Maria that she had a proper home with a loving family of two. Now he was going to have to tell her that she was being abandoned, albeit unwillingly. Just as her mother had unwillingly abandoned her at birth.

Damn it.

At least she would be living with Thaddeus, who cared for Ana Maria even if he didn't understand her nearly as well as Sebastian did.

"Sebby!" Ana Maria emerged from the library, wearing one of her old work gowns that Sebastian had tried to toss in the rubbish. Her dark hair was pulled into a bun, as usual, but also as usual her curls had made a run for it, spiraling around her face, giving the impression that even her hair was delightfully fun.

She grabbed him in a tight hold, and he allowed himself to feel the warmth of her embrace for a moment of respite.

"You've returned, I was worried, you usually send a note if you'll be—uh, out all night." Her delicate way of referring to his spending the night with one of his many ladies. She continued speaking, her words tumbling out faster and faster. "And when I asked the staff if anyone had heard from you, they all gave me the strangest looks. Though they did say you were at Nash's house, but I couldn't figure that out, since why would you spend the night there when you could be here?"

So it seemed the staff knew, even if his sister didn't. They must be frantic with worry about their futures—he hoped Thaddeus would take possession soon and sort it all out.

He withdrew from her embrace, then held her at arm's length. "We need to talk."

"What is it?" Her expression was concerned, but not yet worried.

"Let's go into the library. We'll need some privacy."

"BUT—BUT THERE must be some mistake! Why did those letters just turn up? And why would your mother do something like that?"

Ana Maria's expression was incredulous, and Sebastian had to admire how she continued to believe in the good of people, even when they showed her who they were, time after household-drudgery time. His mother had never hidden her dislike of her husband's first child, quashing any attempt to allow Ana Maria to take her rightful place as a duke's daughter.

But Ana Maria refused to be quashed, just making her own joy in whatever task she tackled. Sebastian had often shaken his head at how she'd always contrived to make a game of whatever terrible task the duchess had assigned her. As though she'd been rebelling against the chores in her own optimistic way.

She paced back and forth in front of his desk while he leaned on the mantel of the fireplace watching her frenetic energy. He suddenly felt exhausted, whether from being knocked unconscious or his entire world changing, he couldn't say.

At least he wasn't moping. Thank goodness for small favors.

He tried to keep his tone measured so as not to exacerbate Ana Maria's agitation. "It doesn't matter why. It just matters that it's the truth."

She turned to face him, planting her fists on her hips. "Well, if you're not the duke, and you have to leave here, I'm coming with you. If you're not here, it's not home." Her expression was determined, and his chest hurt at the palpable sign of her love and caring for him.

He was shaking his head before she'd finished speaking. "You can't, Ana Banana." The childhood nickname emerged without his thinking about it. "Be reasonable. Thaddeus will take possession of the house, and has promised to give you everything you rightfully deserve—your place in Society, the chance to find a husband who is worthy of you. Following me won't do any of that." One of the best parts of inheriting the title was that he would finally be able to help Ana Maria—he couldn't bear it if she turned her back on all of it just because of his situation.

"What if I don't want it?"

Sebastian snorted. "Funny, that's exactly what Thad said. That he didn't want to be duke. He asked if we could just pretend that we hadn't seen the documents and letters."

Ana Maria flung her hands into the air. She was always dramatic with her gesticulations, something her stepmother had deplored as part of her Spanish heritage. As though Sebastian's mother hadn't also been Spanish. But Sebastian's mother was the epitome of a reserved English lady in her demeanor, and the duchess was constantly reminding Ana Maria to be less exuberant. Reprimands that Ana Maria refused to heed. "And why didn't you? That would be far better than this situation."

Sebastian kept his gaze on her until her eyes dropped to the floor.

"It wouldn't be right," he said softly. "It wouldn't be the truth. You know we all promised to be truthful with one another, no matter what anyone else might say. You, me, Thad, and Nash. Who would we be if we just ignored what my mother did?"

Ana Maria's expression softened, and she walked up to Sebastian, tears in her eyes. "I am so sorry, Sebby. It must hurt to know the duchess was so . . ." She paused, as though unable or unwilling to speak the word.

"Conniving?" Sebastian supplied. "Duplicitous?" he added. "It's a relief, honestly. My whole life I wondered what it was about her, about me, that made it impossible for us to care for one another."

He shrugged. "Now I know it wasn't me. That I wasn't undeserving of love."

"You deserve love," Ana Maria replied, her tone fierce. "And you know that no matter what, I love you."

Sebastian reached forward to draw his sister into an embrace. "I love you, too." He buried his nose in her hair. "You'll tell the staff officially?" Even though he knew they knew. But it was the way of things, to pretend not to know things until one was directly informed.

"Of course," she replied.

He held her for a few moments, wishing he could take her with him. But she didn't deserve his future, and besides, he wanted to enter his future without feeling encumbered or responsible for anyone else.

If he were to fail, he wanted it to be his failure alone, not drag anyone else along with him. If he succeeded? Well, then perhaps he would return and invite Ana Maria to join him. Wherever he ended up. But hopefully by then she'd have found her own happiness.

"You'll let me know where you're living?" Ana Maria held his hat, running her fingers over the brim. "Oh! And your dogs—what about them?"

Damn. Another ducal responsibility that wouldn't belong in his current situation.

"Can you take care of them? Just until I figure out where I am going to live?" As though it were a simple matter of just deciding. Even though it wasn't.

"Yes, of course," Ana Maria said in a bright tone. She frowned as she thought, then reached into the pocket that hung at the waist of her gown, drawing out some coins. "Here. You'll have more immediate use for these than I. Now that Thaddeus is going to manage me. 'Ana Maria, you are going to dance, and you are going to enjoy it.'" She lowered her voice to imitate Thad's imperative tone, and Sebastian couldn't help but laugh at her mimicry.

"Thank you." It was awkward, taking the coins. He'd never had to carry cash around; dukes just asked for things and they got them. Mere illegitimate misters likely had to pay right away. But Ana Maria would be hurt if he declined, and he did need some money, after all.

"What are you going to do?"

He didn't reply, at least not right away. But seeing Miss Ivy's had given him a spark of an idea that hadn't burst into any kind of flame until just this moment. If a lady could open a gambling house, then why couldn't he do something equally risky? Why wouldn't he?

"I might go into investing."

She looked puzzled. "Investing?"

"Yes," he replied, feeling more enthusiastic as he began to think on it. "I know shipping companies are always looking for investors. If I can make enough money to put a stake into some sort of venture—"

"Do you need more? I am certain Thaddeus would give you the—"

"I don't want charity." His tone was sharp, and he immediately felt terrible for using it toward his beloved sister. "That is, if I have a goal beyond no longer being a duke, that will give me purpose. I need something to point toward. Getting enough money to make my own way in life would do that."

Because it was no longer enough just to be—he had to *do*.

"You can achieve anything, Sebby, once you put your mind to it." He was shaken by her absolute faith in him. "You'll be just as good at investing or whatever it is you end up doing as you are a duke." He gave her a wry look, at which she rolled her eyes. "Fine. A brother, you are still an excellent brother."

"Thank you, Ana Banana," he replied. The clock struck quarter past, and he realized it was getting late. Besides, if he stayed here any longer, he might give in to Ana Maria's pleading looks and stay here, which would ensure he was a useless bastard, after all. "I need to get going."

"You'll let me know where you are? Will you be at Nash's?"

"I'm not certain." His hoped-for future did not entail living with his friend the Fighting Duke. "But when I am, of course I'll let you know." He gestured toward his hat, which she held out for him to take. He glanced beyond her to where Fletchfield stood, having given him his coat. "Thank you for informing the staff," he said in a low tone meant just for her ears. "I told Thaddeus he needed to make certain they were taken care of."

"They will be," Ana Maria replied. "But who will take care of *you*?"

His heart squeezed at his sister's forlorn tone, and he leaned forward to kiss her on the cheek. "I'll be fine."

He'd have to be. Ana Maria should be free of worry, should finally be able to live her own life, not spend time fussing about him.

He'd succeed, if not for himself, then for his sister.

"Make sure Byron gets good long walks in the afternoon. Otherwise she'll try to bite Keats."

"I will," she promised. "Do you want to say goodbye to them?"

"I think this goodbye is all I can handle," he said, trying to keep his tone light and failing. Because it was true—he and his sister had never lived apart, and while of course they would see one another, everything was different now.

God. Everything was different now.

"Goodbye, Ana Maria," he said softly. He turned and walked out the door as quickly as he could, feeling both anxious and excited about what his new future would bring.

IVY SETTLED A dispute between her chef and her servers, managed to persuade Octavia not to buy a particularly hideous hat, and took the deposit—saved by the cribbage-board-holding Mr. de Silva—to the bank.

And it was barely teatime.

"You offered him a job?" Octavia said in disbelief. "But I'm right here, you could have hired me!"

They were sitting in the small parlor between their two bedrooms. Regardless of their schedules, Ivy and Octavia met up every day at this time to review the day and have a small moment of sisterly affection. Even though Octavia's affection was frequently tinged by complaints. Such as this one.

The parlor was thankfully clear of the items found in the spare room—Ivy winced as she realized what Mr. de Silva had seen when he had woken up.

Ivy took a sip of her tea. "He has skills you do not. He is a gentleman, for one thing." She cleared her throat. "He used to be the Duke of Something, actually." Octavia's eyes grew round, and she opened her mouth, but Ivy kept speaking. "And what's more, he is not my sister who should be working on being respectable." It was a losing battle, she knew that. Eventually Octavia would refuse to listen to her older sister, and Ivy would have to accept that she'd be involved in the club. But Ivy wouldn't be doing her job as her sister's guardian if she didn't at least try to persuade her otherwise.

"Humph." Her eyes sparkled. "Was he really a duke? How do you not be a duke after being one?"

"I have no idea. I did not intrude," she said in a prim tone, trying to remind her sister it was rude to pry.

Octavia's expression brightened. So she hadn't taken the hint. "At least he is very good-looking. He'll make the time pass more quickly on slow evenings."

Ivy squelched the inappropriate thoughts of just what Mr. de Silva could do to make the time pass more quickly. She was really going to have to give herself a stern talking-to regarding her newest employee.

"The mysterious former duke," Octavia sighed, her expression growing dreamy. "He must have a dark past. Perhaps he lost his first love in a tragic storm, and he finds solace only in games of chance." She bolted upright. "Do you think he lost the dukedom in a wager?" She shook her head. "No, it doesn't work that way." She scrunched up her face in thought. "There has to be a reason he's here. Maybe he wants to make amends for his past mistakes."

"By rescuing damsels in distress. Armed with a cribbage board," Ivy finished dryly. "Honestly, Octavia, you should try your hand at writing gothic novels. Your imagination is well suited for it."

Octavia folded her arms over her chest. "Perhaps I will. And I will use my real name to publish under—Miss Octavia Holton—so that everyone knows it is me."

Ivy shook her head. She wished, not for the first time, that Octavia had just a fraction of the practicality it seemed Ivy had in spades—so to speak.

"Miss?" Their maid stood at the door. Carter was the daughter of one of Ivy and Octavia's father's workers who'd lost his job when their father had lost everything. Ivy had packed Carter up, along with Octavia and a ridiculous number of dolls, and had come to London.

"Yes?"

"There's a gentleman here. Says his name's Silver."

"Mr. de Silva, yes. Please show him in."

Carter nodded, then turned back to walk down the hall.

"Oooh, the mystery man in the flesh!" Octavia exclaimed.

"You'll excuse yourself. We have business to discuss," Ivy said in a brisk tone. It wouldn't do to let Octavia and Ivy's employee spend too much time together—Octavia was nothing if not completely and totally irresistible, and Ivy could say the same about Mr. de Silva. She did not want her sister getting romantically entangled with anyone, at least not until she'd secured her future.

Plus it was obvious Mr. de Silva was a shameless flirt, and Ivy didn't want her younger sister to mistake flirting for anything else.

"You don't let me have any fun," Octavia groused, putting the remaining biscuits on the tea tray into a napkin. "I'm taking these as punishment."

"Fine," Ivy said. It was a small price to pay.

"Mr. Silver," Carter announced.

He stood at the door, glancing between the two sisters, an appreciative grin on his face.

No, no, no, no, a voice clamored inside Ivy's head. *Don't be all charming to my sister.*

"Mr. de Silva, you've arrived. I thought you needed a day or two to settle your affairs?"

She heard Octavia suppress a snort.

"That is not what I meant," Ivy said reprovingly. "Mr. de Silva, may I introduce my sister? This is—" Well, drat. She hadn't had to formally introduce her sister since they'd arrived. She couldn't call her by her real name in case he knew their family, but she didn't know what she could call her.

"I'm Miss Octavia," Octavia said, holding her hand out. Mr. de Silva took it, his lips curling into a devastating smile.

Double drat.

Well, if she had to flirt as shamelessly as Mr. de Silva to thwart any flirtation between the charming man and her sister, she would.

What a noble sacrifice.

Hush, you, Ivy rejoined.

The only issue now was finding the right words to flirt with—she didn't have much, that is to say *any*, experience flirting. Just like being flustered. She had experience gambling with blackguards, negotiating with vendors, hiring workers, and bargaining with landlords, and she'd even found herself on the receiving end of masculine interest, but she had no experience with flirting.

Triple drat.

Octavia rose, brushing crumbs from her lap. She held the napkin full of biscuits in her left hand, a mischievous smile on her lips. "Ivy tells me I have to excuse myself, so I am going to do that."

"Because you always do as I say," Ivy commented in a dry tone.

Octavia beamed. "Exactly." She held her hand out to Mr. de Silva. "It was a pleasure to meet you, I look forward to working with you."

"And I with you," he replied before Ivy could contradict Octavia's assertion that the two would be working together. Her sister shot her a smug look, then walked out, shutting the door behind her.

Ivy plopped back down on her chair, exhaling sharply.

Mr. de Silva gestured toward Octavia's seat. "May I?"

"Please do," she said.

But before he could sit, the door shot open again, revealing a large gentleman clad in a military uniform. His expression was fierce and determined, and she wondered if her new employee was wanted by the authorities in addition to being a former duke.

That would be ludicrous, even for one of Octavia's gothic novels.

"Thaddeus." Mr. de Silva didn't seem surprised, but Ivy certainly was.

"We have to talk." The gentleman replied before glancing at Ivy. "Ma'am."

Mr. de Silva addressed Ivy. "This won't take long." It sounded like a threat—not directed toward her, but to the stranger. "I assume we'll find some privacy in the game room?"

"Yes, of course," Ivy replied. Should she grab the cribbage board and follow?

Mr. de Silva strode past the military man, grabbing him by the arm to pull him toward the door as he walked. She couldn't hear the specific words, but there was no mistaking Mr. de Silva's stern tone.

SEBASTIAN WALKED QUICKLY down the hall to the game room, Thaddeus close on his heels. He shouldn't be surprised Thaddeus had found him so quickly, but he was surprised at how much he didn't want to see his cousin. Not now, not when everything was still fresh and raw.

But that wasn't Thad's fault.

He took a deep breath as they entered the room. Empty as promised. The tables were neatly arranged in rows, the room looking a lot larger with nobody in it.

The table he'd apparently stumbled over was at the far end, a dark stain on its surface testament to the earlier fracas.

He shut the door behind them, then turned to face his cousin. "Why are you here?"

Thaddeus gazed steadily at him. But Sebastian wasn't one of his troops, and he wouldn't be cowed by Thad's implacable stare.

Eventually, Thad sighed, raising his eyes to the ceiling. "I should have been here before. I shouldn't have let you leave that office the other day. Why am I here? Because we're family. Because this is a terrible situation, and I want to make certain you're all right."

"Because you feel guilty."

Thaddeus shook his head, then paused and nodded. "Yes. I suppose I do. This is too sudden. We need time to arrange things. To adjust."

He'd said something similar in the solicitor's office. "Are you saying that to me or to you?"

"I am here because I'm concerned about you." Thaddeus spoke through gritted teeth. "I had to take care of some things before coming to speak to you. I also knew you would be completely annoying." At least one thing hadn't changed—Sebastian still knew how to most efficiently aggravate his cousin.

Another skill he could add to his list of post-duke qualifications.

Sebastian spread his arms out wide. "I'm fine." He paused. "Not to mention annoying."

Thaddeus did not laugh. "I've spoken to Ana Maria. She's worried, as well."

"Of course she is." Sebastian's tone tightened. "As are you. Thank you for coming. But I promise, I am fine."

"I was hoping you'd come back to your—that is, the town house."

"*Your* town house."

"This doesn't have to be an argument, Seb. We're family. We can work together to get through this."

"Get through what?" Sebastian shook his head as he started to pace. "It won't do either of us any good to pretend things are as they were." As of just—how long? Had it only been two days? "You need to learn your new responsibilities, and I need to learn how to survive."

"What if we could do both? But together?"

"I won't live at the town house, Thad." The thought of his being there but not belonging would make his skin crawl. He'd grow to resent his cousin as much as he resented his circumstances.

"You could go to the country. I'm certain one or another of the houses could use a Dutton in residence." Thad's tone was as close to pleading as Sebastian had ever heard it.

His cousin truly cared for him, was worried about him, he knew that, but his proposed solution was not what Sebastian wanted—charity in the guise of familial obligation. Hadn't he vowed not to be dependent on the new duke's largesse? Even if it were Thad dispensing the charity, it would still be charity.

The idea he'd had when he'd spoken to Ana Maria, the one about investing. He snatched that glimmer of hope and held on to it—he had to make *something* of himself somehow. He *would* make something of himself. He just needed time and money. The former he had, the latter would come . . . in time.

Sebastian had skills, skills beyond his renown in the bedroom. And he could turn to those as a last resort if necessary.

Though advertising his services might be awkward. *Available for a Fee: A Gentleman for Profound Pleasure. 100% Satisfaction Guaranteed.*

"I'd want to pay you, of course," Thad continued, unaware of Seb's wayward thoughts. "You'd be doing me—that is, the dukedom—a great service."

Thaddeus's tone sounded convincing. No wonder his men followed him wherever he ordered. If Sebastian hadn't already been decided on his course of action, he might have almost been persuaded. After all, it wouldn't be the worst thing to go work on one of the duke's estates. He knew most of the properties, he'd have authority by proxy as well as by knowledge. He could likely find some measure of happiness there.

But it wouldn't be his choice. It wouldn't be something he had found on his own, something that relied on who he was and what he could do, but rather who he was related to. Or who cared for him.

There was time to retreat to the country, if necessary. He could fail at any time, and he knew Thad would be there to help him out. But he wouldn't accept that, not now, not when he had his sights set on his own opportunity. And the means to get there—he and Miss Ivy hadn't negotiated what he'd be paid yet. Perhaps he could leverage that to his advantage.

"Thanks, but no," Sebastian said. "I know you mean well, but this isn't what I want to do. Not now."

Thaddeus's lips pursed. "I should have expected this answer. You always were stubborn."

Sebastian grinned. "And handsome and charming and—"

"And far too full of yourself," Thaddeus interrupted, back to sounding like the stuffy cousin Sebastian had met fifteen years previous. Which he promptly dispelled by grabbing Sebastian in an enormous bear hug. Sebastian was the taller of the two cousins, but Thaddeus was broader. His embrace was more like a smother.

Sebastian clapped his cousin on the back, then withdrew, holding on to Thad's arms. "I promise I'll reach out if I need help. But until then, you're going to have to let me do this on my own." He paused. "And I promise not to come lecture you about the right way to be a duke."

Thaddeus snorted. "You probably should. And don't lecture me for giving you this." Thaddeus took his wallet from his breast pocket, withdrawing some bills and stuffing it into Sebastian's hand, curling Seb's fingers around it.

Sebastian glanced down at his hand, then back up at Thad. His cousin's expression was forbidding, almost grim. Thad only looked that way when he was in the throes of some deep emotion, and Sebastian felt a pang at how this situation had upended Thad's life, as well—his cousin had only ever wanted to serve in Her Majesty's army, and now he wouldn't be allowed to.

"Thank you, Thad."

His cousin nodded, then spun on his heel and walked out without looking back.

Sebastian stood in place for a few moments. He had always taken his chosen family—Ana Maria, Thaddeus, and Nash—for granted. They were there for him, and he was there for them. He'd never imagined he'd have to call on them for anything; he was the heir to a dukedom, after all. And he hadn't even called this time either—they'd just come to offer their help and support.

If he hadn't just lost his entire identity and had no idea where his life was going, he would have thought this not-being-a-duke thing wasn't that bad.

But he had, and it was. Although thanks to Miss Ivy, he wouldn't have to sell his sexual skills, at least not right now.

Chapter Seven

"Everything settled?" Ivy asked as Mr. de Silva returned to the parlor. She peered past him, looking for the large military man. And then heard distant footsteps, and then the door shutting.

"Yes. My apologies." Mr. de Silva sat down, crossing one lean leg over the other. "My affairs were not as settled as I'd thought. It won't happen again."

Ivy waved her hand. "It is of no concern." She gestured toward the tea tray. "I know your opinion of the beverage, but would you care for tea?" She accompanied her question with a questioning look. "Or are you in need of something stronger?"

"Something stronger would be much appreciated. Family has a way of driving one to drink."

"Ah, so that gentleman is a relative?"

Mr. de Silva's expression tightened. "Yes, he is the actual duke, as it turns out. And my cousin."

Ivy rose, walking to the cabinet where she kept the alcohol. She opened the door and bent down, shifting the half-empty bottles of sherry to find the whiskey tucked in the back, pulling it out with a triumphant exclamation. "I knew we had some. Here," she said, opening the bottle and pouring whiskey into the delicate teacup.

"Are you going to have any?" he asked as she handed him the cup.

She tilted her head in thought. "I believe I will." She picked up her own tea, drank it down, then splashed whiskey into her cup. She raised it up in his direction. "Cheers!"

"May we never want a friend, nor a bottle to share with him. Or her," he said, nodding in her direction.

They both drank, Ivy relishing the burn of the alcohol down her throat.

"How do you lose a dukedom, anyway?"

He raised his brow—at her cavalier tone? Of course, he didn't know she had lost her respectability, too. Not that she'd be sharing all that information with him, not right now at least. "My mother. She withheld some crucial information, information that invalidates my claim to the title."

She waited, nodding at him to continue.

His jaw clenched. "She pretended she was the first duchess's cousin, not her sister. And then she married her sister's widower, which is against the law."

"That's a very odd law," she remarked.

He nodded in acquiescence. "Odd, yes, but also a law, which is the more important aspect of it."

She took a sip from her cup. "Do you get along with him? Your cousin?"

He nodded. "I do. I suppose that makes it harder in some way."

"How?"

He twisted his mouth in thought. "Thaddeus and I, we are as close as brothers, and yet we are totally different. He is, as you can see, a military man. And I?"

She leaned forward. "Yes. And what are you, Mr. de Silva?"

He met her gaze, and Ivy could see the frank honesty in his eyes. "I don't know," he said softly. "I hope to find out."

"Maybe working at Miss Ivy's will help," she replied. At least she hoped so.

He nodded as he took another sip. "I believe it will." He crossed his arms over his chest. "I've never had to think about who I am before. It's just been a fact. Like the blue sky, or that coffee is infinitely preferable to tea, and whiskey is even more preferable."

"Spoken like someone who has never had his opinion questioned," she replied. *A duke, second only to the royal family. And who would dare to argue with the royal family?* "I might have to argue with you about the sky—you do know we live in London, don't you?" She wrinkled her nose. "More often than not, the sky is gray."

"Ah, but if you drink enough whiskey, it is blue, my lady."

She felt herself stiffen. "I am Miss Ivy. Not 'my lady.'"

His eyebrows rose. "Duly noted." He frowned. "I suppose I never have been questioned. Something I'll have to learn."

"What else do you want to learn?" she asked.

He downed his drink, then regarded her with a grin. Not the rakish smile she'd been expecting, but something less practiced. More enthusiastic. As though he couldn't wait to share his thoughts with her.

Only Octavia normally looked at her that way,

and Octavia's thoughts usually ran to how Octavia should be allowed to do whatever she wanted, no matter what Ivy said.

She wondered what Mr. de Silva would do if he were allowed to do whatever he wanted.

"So where do we start?" he asked, setting his cup on the table beside him. "With my employment?" he added in response to Ivy's blank stare.

Well, at least he wasn't able to read her thoughts. She wished she could point out that she was a good card player after all, since he'd had no idea what she was thinking, but then that would require that she disclose what she was thinking, and she could barely allow herself to think it, much less say it.

"Do you have a place to stay?" she blurted. Better than the alternative conversation. The one that involved them and his handsomeness and her enthusiasm for the same.

"Pardon?"

"A place to stay. You mentioned you'd be needing a place."

His eyebrows drew together. "I do. I was staying with a friend, but—" He clamped his lips together.

Ivy took a deep breath. "You can stay here."

His eyebrows shot up. He took another swig from his cup. "Here? With you and your sister? That would be . . ." He paused, then downed the rest of the liquid, stretching forward to pluck the bottle from the table and pour more into his cup.

Inappropriate, scandalous, indecent, wicked, and outrageous. "It would be, yes," Ivy said. "But it is also practical. You are just setting out on your own, and it is clear it would be good to have someone on the premises besides me and Octavia. In case another situation like last night occurs. Although I would expect you to be armed with something else," she added hastily.

His lips curled into a wry smile. "A cribbage board is not what I would normally choose to hit someone on the head with, I promise. Are you certain? About me staying here? Because it would be an easy solution, but it would also be—"

He excelled in leaving out the words that would tarnish her reputation.

"Yes. It would. But since I have no expectations, it is not relevant." She wanted to be as clear as possible about that; she was not in the market for a husband. She did not want him thinking anything of the kind.

What she wanted was someone far more difficult to find, a person who could help her with the club's success.

He looked as though he wanted to ask about that, but shook his head instead. "Then I accept." He winced. "Does that mean my room will be the one I woke up in?"

She gave him a commiserating look. "Yes, unfortunately. You and Mrs. Buttercup."

"Mrs. Buttercup?"

"Yes, the doll on the shelf. Missing an eye?"

"Ah, yes." He finished his whiskey, then rose. "Please inform Mrs. Buttercup I will take possession of the room in a few hours." He held his arm out to her. "Meanwhile, should we go elaborate on our discussion from last night?"

She stood also, taking his arm. Of course her insides did a traitorous flip. But his arm felt so solid, who could blame her traitorous insides?

"Tell me more about your relative. The imposing one who seemed as though he wanted to issue you some orders. Which," she added, looking up at him with a wry grin, "it appeared you would not take."

"I only take orders from my boss," he replied, accompanying his words with a rakish wink.

Oh. So much for not thinking things she shouldn't. And he hadn't answered her question. But he had made her feel entirely too aware of their unusual situation.

As soon as the words were out of his mouth, he regretted them. Not to mention that wink.

Not because he didn't want to take orders from his boss; he did. But that also summoned tantalizing images of taking orders from a woman—specifically, *her.*

What would she ask him to do, if she took that power?

Stop it, Sebastian, he chided himself. She might find him charming, because everyone did, but that didn't mean anything more. Nor should it; it would be entirely inappropriate for him to dally with his boss.

Although the word *dally* was intriguing.

"Where are you taking me?" he asked, then winced as he realized those words made him think of even more inappropriate things.

When he'd been a duke, such thoughts had been natural. Appropriate. Practically ducal. But now that he was supposed to be a simple man earning his living, defining himself by what he could do, not who he was, those salacious thoughts and images were not suitable.

"We're going to the main room," she replied, nothing in her voice indicating her thoughts had gone where his had.

Thank goodness, he assured himself.

"I need to move the damaged table out of the way, and I thought you could help me," she continued. "And I could list all the games we offer at Miss Ivy's."

Games. He'd like to play some games. With her.

Damn it.

"You already know about roulette and baccarat," she began, speaking in that businesslike tone that nonetheless entirely piqued his nonbusinesslike interest. "We also offer craps, faro, blackjack. On Monday nights we offer whist only—we found whist players don't like the noise associated with the other games, and they do end up spending a lot of money, so it is worth it to restrict the game to only that."

"Have you had other nights where the play is limited to a certain game?"

She shook her head. "No, I've considered it, but I wouldn't know what game to offer."

He shrugged. "What game makes the house the most money?"

She rolled her eyes. "Oh, I should have thought of that." She tilted her head in thought. "Oh, but I did! Mr. de Silva, I am not new to this business."

He deserved that rebuke. He needed to go beyond the rudimentary to impress this woman, he knew that already. Was his brain up to the task?

Well, if not, at least it felt like a challenge. *A goal.* Something he relished in his current frame of mind.

"Of course. My apologies."

She shook her head. "I shouldn't be so sharp. It's just that other people, other *men*, have come to Miss Ivy's to tell me everything I am doing wrong, and suggested that if I only had a man assisting me, the club would be much more successful."

Sebastian felt himself start to bristle. But then he was overtaken by curiosity. "So what made you offer me the position? When you had so many others clamoring for it?"

"Your ideas are different. And you didn't posit them in a way that condescended to me or implied that only you could implement them." She grinned. "Plus you did foil that miscreant quite handily."

"Ah. So because I treated you as an equal in thought and whacked someone with a cribbage board I deserve a position?"

She gave a wry smile. "Odd that it would be a former duke, of all things, who should impress me with his equality. And skill with an unusual weapon." She dipped into a curtsy, a mocking expression on her face. "Thank you, Your Grace."

"I'm not that any longer." He couldn't help his sharp tone. *I'm not anything any longer.*

She rose, regarding him with a skeptical look. "It is bound to be noticed, you know. If you work here. People from your world do patronize Miss Ivy's. Which you know yourself because you yourself came here."

She had a point, he had to admit.

"You're going to have to get accustomed to it. To this," she said, spreading her hands out to indicate the club. "If you own the situation, nobody can get the best of you about it." She paused, then grinned again. "Your Grace."

Sebastian raised one of his haughtiest eyebrows in response. To which she just laughed. He held his hands up in defeat. "Fine. I'll work on tempering my response."

"Excellent, Your Grace," she teased. Her eyes gleamed with laughter, her mouth was smiling, and all he wanted to do was kiss her.

HER NEW EMPLOYEE was nearly—*nearly*—as prickly as Ivy herself. It was a relief, honestly, to have to deal with someone who wasn't entirely pleasant.

Her staff, with the exception of her hotheaded Irish chef, were all accommodating, sharing their thoughts but never speaking up to Ivy. Octavia was her own situation, of course, but she wasn't—yet—working at the club.

Which left Mr. de Silva. Her very own duke.

She couldn't resist teasing him. Not only because it was delightful fun, but also because she'd been speaking the truth—he would have to negotiate people who knew who he was, or had been, in the club. And he couldn't very well speak to them in that frosty, dismissive tone of voice. Not if he wanted to keep his position.

Plus it was a good early test of how they would work together—he needed to be able to listen to her, and follow her orders, if they were going to make this work.

Whatever *this* was. She still had no clue why she had so impetuously asked him to work for her, except that it felt right. A business person had no business, so to speak, being impetuous. Especially not a *female* business person, whose strength of character was even more scrutinized than any random man who might have opened a gambling club.

But she couldn't and wouldn't spend any more time thinking about her latest employee. They were here to work. To roll up their sleeves and figure out how to make Miss Ivy's even more successful.

She wondered what his forearms looked like. What with the rolled-up sleeves and all.

Stop that, Ivy.

"Right. Well, so those are the games we offer," she continued, making certain she was speaking in her usual measured tone.

He was regarding her with an odd expression—had she upset him with her teasing?

No, it didn't seem like that. His gaze was focused on her mouth, and she felt self-conscious, licking her suddenly dry lips. His gaze sharpened at that, and her insides knew with certainty—even if she herself refused to admit it—just what he had been thinking about.

"And I think the first and easiest of your ideas to implement is to have an anonymous evening," she continued, hoping she didn't sound flustered.

"Masks so that nobody knows who the others are?" He spoke in a low tone, one that resonated throughout her body. "So that anybody is as equal as the other?" He stepped toward her, his gaze still on her mouth. She trembled, but not from fear—fear she understood, and knew how to combat. Henry had shown her a few moves to disable a man if he posed a threat. She would have unleashed them the evening before, aided by her weaponized broom, if Mr. de Silva hadn't deployed his cribbage board.

It was a very different emotion from fear. Something that she had only just started to feel, and it had—not coincidentally—made its appearance when he had.

"A duke could play a game with a lady not from his world and nobody would be the wiser?" he added. She was not imagining the silky tone of his voice, how it had lowered so that only she could hear it.

Not that there was anybody else in the room, anyway. They were entirely and thoroughly alone.

They were entirely and thoroughly alone.

Because she was his employer, and he was her employee, and she had just met him.

Oh my Lord. What was she even thinking?

Entirely inappropriate, Ivy, she reproved herself. Not to mention it seemed as though flirting was in his blood—he didn't mean anything by it. So if, theoretically, she were to launch herself in his general mouth area, he would likely be completely astonished and tell her he did not want to kiss her, despite his flirtatious tone.

"Well," she said, relieved that she sounded like her usual self, "yes, we will definitely schedule in a masked evening. Your first task will be to write up a plan for how to let the patrons know as well as people who might not have thought of Miss Ivy's as a place for their gambling custom."

"Certainly." He sounded as though he were offended—had she done or said something?

Although that should not matter, not when he was working for her.

"And there's the table."

"Don't you have anybody else here who could help me move it?" he asked.

"Because I am female?" she said, feeling her temper start to rise. There were far too many instances of people doubting her because she was a woman. She did not want him to start off his tenure as her employee doing the same.

"No," he replied in a mild tone. "Because you are the boss. You shouldn't have to be doing manual labor. That is one thing I know for certain, having been a boss of sorts myself."

Oh. Of course.

"No, it's just me," she said as she walked to one end of the table. "Besides which," she added in a wry tone, "the owner of a gambling house has a much less lofty status than a duke." She frowned as she looked down at the surface of the table. The stain had darkened, and the table would need to be entirely re-covered, damn it. "I'd just had this done," she said in a mournful tone as she placed her hands under the edge.

He went to the other end and looked at her. "Perhaps we can take this as an opportunity. Maybe choose a different color for the table? Make it a special privilege to be sat here?"

"The whole point of Miss Ivy's is that everyone is equal," she said, unable to keep herself from sounding aggravated. It didn't seem to bother him, however; he just grinned in reply.

"Lift," she ordered, and then they started to carry the table toward the door that led to her office, both of them shuffling under the weight.

"But some are more equal than others," he replied with a twist of his lips.

"That makes no sense, and you know it," she retorted.

"But what if their bonus equality comes through merit? Perhaps they've won a tremendous amount at the club?"

"So why would we reward them? We want them to *lose*, after all."

They were now through the door, and Ivy felt the strain in her arms. She regretted not waiting until there was another worker there, but her stubbornness was stronger than her muscles.

"The point is, you could make something distinctive. We can figure out what it will all mean later, but I think you should consider doing some things differently."

"I—" she began.

"You already do things differently," he interrupted. "Here, let's slide the table against that wall."

They were just outside her office, thankfully, since her arms were starting to tremble.

"Fine," she said, letting him guide the table inside.

He maneuvered it so it took as little room as possible, and she let go with an exhale of relief.

"As I was saying," he continued, gesturing for her to sit, "you already do things differently. I apologize, I wasn't saying things clearly. I think that what you have here is an opportunity to continue your work by questioning everything."

She sat down, her posture completely inappropriate for a lady of her previous position, but completely appropriate for how exhausted she was. "Question everything?"

"Yes, like that!" he replied.

She laughed in response. "I didn't mean that to be as clever as it sounded. I was actually asking."

He sat down also, crossing one long, lean leg

over the other. "But that's exactly what I mean. To ask instead of accept. To push forward instead of settle."

She considered his words. "I suppose that is what I have always done," she said slowly. "I never thought about it before."

"Nor did I," he said in a rueful tone.

QUESTION EVERYTHING. HE'D never done that before—he'd known, and accepted, that he was the heir to a dukedom. Then he'd known and accepted that he was able to charm anybody into giving him what he wanted: sweets and toys when he was younger, kisses and more as he got older. Then he was the duke, and everything was even easier, even though he'd been determined to be the best kind of duke.

Now everything was harder. And it was important for him to do as he'd advised her to—question, push forward, and try to improve.

Dukes weren't expected to improve. They were just expected to *duke*.

But illegitimate men who had no idea how they were going to survive—well, they either had to figure it out or slink back to become an encumbrance on their relatives.

Not that he had an opinion about his options or anything.

"What are you questioning now?" she asked.

He wasn't surprised she was asking; in the short time he'd known her, he'd seen she was remarkably observant.

So he had observed her strong observational skills.

Which was not only redundant, but another thing he'd never done before.

"I was thinking about the turn of events that led me here," he replied.

"Do you miss it?"

He snorted. "It's only been a few days, of course I miss it. It's the most privileged position one can have. I'd be an idiot not to miss it."

"Oh," she said in a soft voice. "Of course."

"I'm sorry," he said, shaking his head. "I didn't mean to imply it was a stupid question."

"You didn't have to imply it, your tone indicated it." At least she was back to using a teasing tone.

"I suppose it did." He paused. "It will be difficult to lose the habits of being a duke, even though I've lost the dukedom."

"You mean the arrogant tone and the assumption that a duke is always correct?"

"Ouch," he replied with a mock grimace. "Tell me what you really think of me." His tone grew serious. "But yes. It's not as simple as losing everything," he continued, shaking his head at his own insouciance, "it's a matter of finding who you are."

Finding who you are.

The words resonated in the air around them, and he found himself staring at her, drinking in her wide-open eyes and sincere expression. She obviously knew who she was, and that was obviously different from who she was before.

That was his goal now. He had a purpose, a mission, that was more than just mere survival.

He just hoped he'd like himself as much as he had before.

"So tell me—unless there is something else we need to be doing," he added hastily, "who are you? There has to be a story here." He gestured around them. "Because this is not where one would expect to find someone who is obviously a lady."

"Obviously *was*," she retorted, stressing the second word. "I am Miss Ivy now, anything I was before is left in the past."

"Were you also a duke who lost his title?" he said, giving her a sly look.

His teasing had the effect of lightening her affect. She acknowledged the question with an incline of her head, then seemed to consider her answer. And then not give him what he wanted, after all.

Something he was going to have to become accustomed to. Something he had never been accustomed to before.

"We do have things to do, Mr. de Silva. Much as I would love to regale you with the story of how I came to be Miss Ivy, and the history of the gambling house in general." Her neutral tone belied her words.

She stood suddenly, and he bolted upright as well, keenly aware that he would have to follow her lead—follow her orders—if he wanted to keep this position.

And what other position would you like? a voice asked in his head.

That is not appropriate. She is my boss, my employer, and I cannot jeopardize my position by embarking on a relationship with inevitable heartbreak.

Because his affairs usually ended when he got bored, or found somebody else more intriguing, leaving the lady wishing he could offer more. He was never rude to the ladies, but he was definite in stating that the ending was just that—an ending.

Although he wasn't certain that would be the case here—she was far more intelligent than his previous amours, and she was also clearly independent, and would be more likely to break things off if there was the slightest hitch. She had to be even more aware of their unusual circumstances than he.

"I want to introduce you to the staff," she said, picking up what appeared to be a ledger from her desk and sliding a pencil behind her ear.

He had to admit he found that delightfully endearing.

"Of course." He swept his hand toward the door. "Lead the way, boss."

"Follow me, Your Grace," she replied.

Chapter Eight

$\mathcal{I}$vy walked swiftly down the hallway and back into the main gaming room. A few of her staff were already there, even though Miss Ivy's would be closed for a few more hours. They'd been doing that almost since the club opened.

When she'd asked why, Samuel and the others had replied that they wanted to ensure the experience at Miss Ivy's was the most satisfying of any gambling house in London, so that meant making certain the temperature was perfect, the chairs and tables were clean and comfortable, and the play ran smoothly.

Preparing all of that took time.

On the other side of the room was the entrance to the kitchen, where Mac was already terrorizing his own band of incredibly loyal servants. Ivy left the menus up to him, as much because he was so stubborn he would just make what he wanted to no matter what she said, as because what he chose to create was inevitably delicious.

"Good day, Miss Ivy," Samuel said, pausing in his work. His eyes narrowed at seeing Mr. de Silva.

"Good day, Samuel," she replied. She glanced to Henry, who had just walked in. His eyes also narrowed at seeing her newest employee.

Of course they'd be suspicious of him—he was clearly from the Society they catered to, not from their world. Her employees considered anyone like Mr. de Silva just a mark, not a person who could possibly offer any value beyond how much they could lose in an evening.

"Samuel, Henry, I'll make the official introduction at the meeting before the club opens tonight, but for now, I want to introduce Mr. de Silva. He'll be assisting me with some new ideas for the club."

"What's wrong with the old ideas?" Samuel asked, not taking Mr. de Silva's outstretched hand.

"Nothing is wrong with them, that is why we're going to add more." Mr. de Silva spoke before Ivy could, his tone mild in contrast to Samuel's belligerent one. "Miss Ivy's has already embarked on a bold idea—that of having anyone welcome in the door, regardless of who they are. As long as they have enough money, they can game. But Miss Ivy and I were talking and thinking about ways we could emphasize that equality to make it seem more exclusive to game here."

"So a gambling house that is exclusive while still allowing anyone in?"

Ivy nearly laughed at Henry's skeptical expression. Although she appreciated his ability to identify an oxymoron.

"Precisely," Mr. de Silva replied, an easy smile on his face. "Miss Ivy will explain it more when we've figured out the details."

"Humph," Samuel said, looking Mr. de Silva up and down. He glanced to Ivy. "I trust you know what you're doing, Miss Ivy," he said. He jerked his chin at Mr. de Silva. "Just so anyone else knows that if there's something off about someone, we'll take pains to remove that person."

The threat and the promise were crystal clear. Ivy would be annoyed if she also wasn't incredibly honored that her staff was so protective.

"I can see why Miss Ivy values you so much." Mr. de Silva didn't raise his voice or become defensive, both of which must have been difficult for a recent duke.

"We'll see you at the meeting," Henry said, taking Samuel's arm and leading him toward the kitchen.

Ivy watched them walk away, Henry speaking into Samuel's ear as Samuel glanced back at them.

"It's a lucky thing I am confident of my ideas," Mr. de Silva said after a moment. She felt him come to stand beside her, and she looked up into his face as he spoke.

His gaze was focused on the two men, so she had a chance to look at him a little more closely. There was stubble on his face, and she wondered if he even knew how to shave himself, given that he must have left a valet behind.

And then followed that up with the idea that perhaps she should ask him if he wanted her to help him.

The thought made her breath hitch.

And then she practically seized when she realized that his lack of a valet might also mean he wouldn't know how to dress himself. And perhaps he might need assistance with that also.

She was such a terrible boss to him already—thinking inappropriate things whenever she was in his general vicinity.

But at least she could console herself with the fact that, thanks to her poker face, he would never know what she was thinking.

Unless she did something that would tip him off.

She would never do that. Never. And meanwhile, he had just said something, and instead of replying, she'd begun thinking about razors and the planes of his face, and how he might need help getting into—or out of—his shirt.

"They are very protective," she said. He looked at her quizzically, then nodded in understanding. Of course she'd taken so very long to answer he probably forgot what he'd said. "Just remember that when you decide to become a gambling-house spy," she said, shaking her finger at him.

He chuckled in response.

Sebastian shifted on his feet, then straightened his shoulders. What stance should one take when one was trying to look entirely competent but non-threatening?

He had no idea. He'd never had to look nonthreatening before. Or, to be honest, entirely competent. He just *was*.

"You're looking very fierce." Miss Octavia had popped up on his left side, leaning in to whisper in his ear. She was taller than her sister and was more beautiful than pretty. If he were a complete cad, he would have tried to flirt with her. But he was not, and besides, she was his boss's younger sister. He'd gotten enough warning from his friends about their sisters to know that a sister was completely out-of-bounds, romantically. Not to mention she was entirely too young.

"I was *trying* to look nonthreatening," he said in a low tone.

The staff of the gambling club were filing into the main room, most of them giving him curious glances. Miss Ivy was engrossed in a conversation with a large red-faced man, who Sebastian assumed was the chef; he wore an apron, and carried a large wooden spoon, which he kept gesticulating with.

"You are failing miserably," Miss Octavia replied. She turned to face him, then put her hands on his shoulders. "Here, put those down a little." He jumped at her touch, at which she rolled her eyes and pushed harder. "And maybe smile a little bit?"

He complied.

"No, not like that!" she exclaimed. "You look positively menacing." She stepped back, tilting her head to look at him. "That must be the aftereffect of being a duke. A former duke," she amended hastily. She waved her hands vaguely toward him. "Just think of something mildly pleasant. Like a lukewarm pudding, or perhaps a tree with its leaves just starting to fall."

"A tree? A lukewarm pudding?" he said, raising his eyebrows. "Those are certainly evocative images."

She beamed. "You think so? I am considering being a novelist. Ivy says she wants me to have a respectable future"—and her frown indicated what she thought about that—"but I want some adventure." She glanced over at her sister, who had finished with the chef and was walking toward them. "I think Ivy should have some adventure, too." She looked up at him, mischief in her gaze. "Don't you?" Her intent was perfectly clear.

Sebastian had never wanted to be a diplomat, navigating difficult conversational territory, but he desperately wished he had diplomatic skills now. At least he was a good card player, so he wouldn't reveal what he was thinking in response to Miss Octavia's question.

Miss Octavia would either be shocked or delighted at where his thoughts had gone. He wasn't certain which he'd prefer.

"Everyone, I have an announcement."

Thankfully, Ivy spoke before he had to come up with something. Though he couldn't stop his brain from thinking about the kinds of adventure he'd like to lead Miss Ivy into—things involving gambling tables, and cards, and very specific and unusual wagers.

He forced himself to think of lukewarm pudding as Miss Ivy continued speaking.

It wasn't helping.

"I have asked Mr. de Silva to join us to help grow our business."

He didn't have to look around to see the many skeptical expressions on the staff's faces.

"And he and I will be working together to implement some exciting new features for Miss Ivy's." She stopped speaking, then looked at each of her staff members in turn, as though she was reminding them who was in charge.

He respected that. If he had still been a duke, he would have stolen the gesture to enforce his authority.

"Does anyone have any ques—?" Only her words were lost as the door to the outside was flung open, revealing Ana Maria and his dogs, Byron and Keats.

The latter two hurled themselves across the floor to jump on him, barking enthusiastically.

"I'm sorry," he heard Ana Maria yell from across the room. She wore a colorful ensemble that made her look as delightfully frothy as any other young lady in Society. *Bravo*, he thought. "Come back, Byron! Keats!" She ran across the room, then pulled up short as she spotted Sebastian.

"Down," Sebastian ordered, and the two obeyed, both of them gazing up at him adoringly.

"No wonder they tore in here like that," Ana Maria said. She glanced from Sebastian to the ladies, her eyes wide in interest. "They must have smelled you. I was just on my way to the dressmaker's, and I thought they needed a walk. And here you are."

Sebastian suppressed a groan at his dogs' keen sense of smell. And his sister's blatant curiosity.

"These are yours?" Miss Octavia asked, bending down to scratch behind Byron's ear.

"Good evening, I am the du—that is, Mr. de Silva's sister." Ana Maria stumbled over his name as she held her hand out to Miss Ivy.

"It is a pleasure to meet you," Ivy replied. She glanced at Sebastian, an amused expression on her face. "Your dogs are very excited to see you."

He looked back down at them. Byron's tongue was lolling out of her mouth, while Keats was turning in a circle preparing, Sebastian knew, to sit on his feet.

"But now they're here, and so are you." Ana Maria tilted her head in thought. "I wonder, could you take them? You must be living somewhere, I know you're not with Nash. Just look at them, they're so much happier now."

The sisters both looked down at the dogs, who were staring adoringly up at Sebastian.

"Take care of them?" Sebastian repeated. "I don't think that's—" he began.

"Of course he can," Octavia interrupted. "Dogs should be taken care of by the person they love most in this world, shouldn't they?"

"Octavia," Ivy said in a warning tone.

"I agree," Ana Maria said, beaming at Miss Octavia. Two meddling peas in a mischievous pod. She turned to Sebastian. "Can you give me your address? I can bring them over after my appointment."

"He's living here," Octavia answered before Sebastian could, and he suppressed a wince as he realized that everyone in the room had heard that, and all of them likely had a strong opinion about his proximity to Miss Ivy.

Ana Maria blinked a few times, startled, then took a deep breath. "Well, then. No need for me to wait after all, you can just take them." She stepped forward, giving Sebastian a quick kiss on his cheek. "And I will leave, I can tell I've interrupted something important." Her eyes twinkled as she spoke, and Sebastian wanted to curse his sister for her keen skills of observation.

"No, wait." Ivy and Sebastian spoke at the same time, then met one another's gaze.

"Goodbye. I am late for my appointment. The dressmaker is working on a gown for my party." She wrinkled her nose at that. "It was a pleasure to meet you all," she added hurriedly, edging toward the door.

And then she was gone. Leaving Sebastian with

his two dogs, an interfering younger sister, an outraged staff, and a discombobulated boss.

Dogs. Not only had she rescued an ex-duke,
it appeared she was also going to rescue the ex-
duke's two dogs, neither of whom seemed to be
sufficiently meek about their imminent rescue. And
they'd just managed to get rid of the cats. Drat.

One of the dogs was walking around the perimeter
of the room, sniffing everything and everybody,
glancing back at Mr. de Silva every few feet. The other
dog was curled up on Mr. de Silva's feet, occasionally raising its head to sniff its owner's knees.

"I apologize for this," Mr. de Silva said, making
a vague gesture. "My sister is so softhearted, she
probably has been hearing them whimper and is
worried about them." He gingerly removed his feet
from underneath the now-sleeping dog. "I'll find
other arrangements."

Ivy shook her head. "No, you don't have to do that."
She gave a weary sigh. "Octavia wants you to have
them here, and I won't get any peace if I reverse her
position. So I should just cede the battle and let them
stay." It was the same way with the kittens. Thank
goodness Carter had come to the rescue.

Mr. de Silva's mouth tightened. "I don't want
to impose on you. You've already done so much
for me, giving me employment and a room. You
shouldn't have to do anything you don't wish to."

Ivy's mouth curled in a wry smile. "All of us
have to do things we don't wish to." She held her
hand up to stop him when she saw he was about to
speak. "And honestly, this is one of the least oner-

ous things I've had to do." She looked over at the dog who was currently staring at Mac as though he had something tasty hidden in his pocket. "Besides, they'll offer a warning if anyone tries to break in, won't they?" She looked back at him, raising one eyebrow. "Far better than a cribbage board, don't you agree?"

He gave a reluctant smile. "I suppose. Although I don't like the idea of anyone taking advantage of you, even if that person is me."

"It was your sister," she pointed out. "And I know how sisters can be."

Both of them looked over at Octavia, who had gone to stand behind one of the tables and was obviously practicing her dealing skills, while Caroline watched over her.

"She wants to work in the club," he remarked.

Ivy sighed. "Yes, she actually donned a mask the other night and snuck in. The night you first came here, as a matter of fact. I have been trying to keep her away from it—"

"Why?" he asked.

"Because she deserves a reasonable future, away from all this."

He gave her an incredulous look. "But all this is good enough for you? You undervalue yourself, Miss Ivy. And," he continued, lifting his chin toward Octavia, "you have to give your sister the same choice you took yourself."

Ivy felt her chest tighten. "I didn't take my choice. It was made for me." The resentment was always there, even though the club was doing well. Resentment that she had to be intelligent enough not to end up with a future she didn't want—what if she had been less fortunate? An irony, given her profession. But still.

There were other women out there who were never given a choice. Ivy couldn't rescue them, but she could hold out the possibility for her sister. But not if her sister foreclosed on a respectable future, and that future would only be gained if Ivy could get Octavia safely away from London and the club before she turned eighteen.

"You have to trust her. You have to trust yourself," he replied softly.

She turned on him, the words spilling out before she could pull them back in. "I *only* trust myself, Your Grace. I can't depend on anyone but myself. Not anymore."

She swallowed, hard, then stood there, trying to regain her usual measure of aplomb. The cool demeanor that was required for a woman who owned her type of establishment.

"Who hurt you, Ivy?" His tone was low, but fierce. As though he wanted to go assault that person with far more than a cribbage board.

She shook her head. "No. No, you don't get to hear my secrets, not when you're a person I only met a few days ago. Not when you're my employee." *Not when you might leave with my secrets at any moment.*

And then she froze, knowing those words would cut anybody, never mind it was an ex-duke she was saying them to.

His expression stilled, and he dipped his head in a brief nod. "I see. If you will pardon me, I will go work on some plans."

He turned and walked away, his entire bearing rigid, Ivy watching his back recede and his dogs follow him, resisting the urge to run after him and apologize.

They'd just met. He was working for her. She didn't need to apologize for anything. She was in charge. He didn't get to ask those types of questions. Not yet. Maybe not ever.

So why did it feel as though she'd done irreparable damage?

Chapter Nine

*I*f he were still a duke, Sebastian wouldn't have left. He would have squared off against her, continuing to press his point until the inevitable happened—they fell into bed. And then they would have taken their anger out on each other with vigorous fucking on satin sheets.

But he couldn't. And what's more, even only a few days later, he could see that he didn't want that any more either. Granted, he knew he was charming and handsome. *That* wasn't going away with the dukedom.

Now, if he wanted to coax a woman into bed following a heated argument, he was going to have to rely entirely on himself.

Game on, he vowed as he strode back to his room, Byron and Keats at his heels.

"Your Grace." He stopped in his tracks and began to turn around.

This time, the honorific wasn't said in her teasing voice. This time, it came from the largest of the disgruntled men Ivy had introduced him to. The other one, the Black man who had spun the roulette wheel that first night, stood beside the large man. Both of them were wearing matching expressions that were . . . not friendly.

"I am sorry," Sebastian said, glancing between them. "I don't recall your names."

"Of course you don't," the first one said. He gestured toward his companion. "He's Samuel, I'm Henry. We've both been with Miss Ivy from the start. We know she's determined to have you work here, but we wanted to warn you."

Samuel nodded as he spoke. "You might have been a fancy gentleman out there, but here? You're just another employee. And all employees, even former dukes, have to work hard. Especially former dukes," he added, folding his arms over his chest.

"I intend to," Sebastian replied through his clenched jaw.

"You might intend to," Henry said. "But things for the rest of us are different than they are for you lot."

"You do know I'm not part of that lot any longer."

Henry snorted. "Right, or why else would you be here? Slumming in a gambling club, and not even the biggest one?"

"But just because you aren't still one of them doesn't mean you know all about what it's like here. For one thing," Samuel said, staring Sebastian straight in the eyes, "we all do the work. We don't just call for someone else to take care of unpleasant tasks. And we don't favor certain people over others." He lifted his chin. "What'll happen when one of your lord types comes in and breaks club rules?"

Sebastian's chest tightened. He'd barely spent a thought on what would happen when one of his former peers saw him working. That was a failing on his part. The ignominy of the scene washed over him, immediately followed by shame that he wouldn't be proud of who he was now. But he wasn't. Not yet.

"I'll do my job," he replied stiffly.

"Of course you will." Samuel's tone belied his words.

"Miss Ivy doesn't deserve to be betrayed by her own employee," Henry said. "You'd best remember that." Now he folded his arms over his chest, as well. He certainly was a large man. "There's no changing her mind, and for some reason you want to be here, but let me tell you, you won't be staying."

"Is that a threat?"

Henry slowly shook his head. "No. Not a threat. A *prediction*. You won't be able to stomach it here, working as you'll have to. Just make sure you give her enough time before you leave. And you will leave, we know that. But while you're here, you'd best behave."

Exact words he had spoken to his dogs.

Did she think that also? That he wouldn't be able to stomach it here?

"I will take your advice into account," Sebastian said, unable to keep the cold, duke-like tone from his words.

"You do that."

And then the two men turned and walked away, leaving Sebastian even more keenly aware of the discrepancy between who he had been, who he was now, and who he hoped to be.

BYRON WAS SETTLED against his hip as he worked. There was no desk in his temporary room, so he was sitting on the bed—still unmade because of course there were no servants to take care of it, and he hadn't figured out how to do it himself yet—and he was propped against the headboard, already feeling the strain in his neck.

Not to mention the strain of being viewed with suspicion by at least two of his fellow employees.

And yet, somehow, he'd never felt better. More useful.

He'd heard noises in the hallway, and knew she must be out there, bustling back and forth from her office to the club, then upstairs for something, giving orders to the maid, and back down again. He'd resisted the urge to go out and speak to her. Mostly because he didn't know how he felt, even the next day. Was he upset that she had refused to confide in him? Was he regretting his strong reaction? Did he want to establish that they were employer and employee, nothing more?

And was this the first time he hadn't been entirely certain?

He could answer that definitively. Ironically, since the answer was yes.

"Mr. de Silva?"

The words were accompanied by a quick knock, then the door opened before he could respond. Miss Octavia stepped inside, her gaze immediately going to Keats, who was lying on the floor next to the bed. She rushed forward to kneel down and place her hand on his head. "He's friendly, isn't he?"

"Well," Sebastian replied dryly, "if he weren't, you would know by now."

She glanced up at him, smiling. "How old is he?"

"I'm not entirely sure." He cleared his throat. "I am not his original owner." He had gotten the dogs from a local farmer, who'd had them as a deterrent against rodents intent on eating his crops. The farmer had sold his farm to Sebastian's father, who was going to install a new tenant on the land. A tenant who had a fear of dogs.

The duchess hadn't cared about what would happen to the dogs, but Sebastian had, so he'd managed to persuade his mother that owning dogs was a mark of a proper English aristocrat.

That was seven years ago, and Byron and Keats had been with him ever since.

"What are their names?" Miss Octavia asked, scratching behind Keats's ears.

Sebastian paused before replying. "Uh—that is Keats, and this is Byron. Byron is a girl."

Her eyes brightened, and she smiled. "How did you name them?" She drew her brows together. "You did name them, didn't you?"

He shrugged. "Yes, I went through a period where all I did was read poetry and dress like the Romantics."

She laughed, shaking her head. "I would not have thought you to be the romantic type." She thought for a moment, then spoke again. "In the pining-over-a-distant-love kind of way. I have seen you flirt, so I know you are romantic that way."

The retort was on his lips, but he didn't speak. Was he romantic now? He had been, back in those days. He'd thought at the time that his cold mother was merely the product of her upbringing, that there was warmth lurking within. That his careless father was just distracted, not unloving. That his sister actually enjoyed the drudgery she was forced into.

He'd been so naive. No, he wasn't romantic now. He was realistic.

"But I am not here to discuss your dogs, lovable though they are." She gave Keats one last pat, then rose. "You have done something to Ivy, I don't know what." She gesticulated toward the door. "She's been stomping around ever since, and—"

"I can apologize," he said.

"Oh no, don't!" she replied, shaking her head vehemently. "It is good for her to be ruffled, she is entirely too settled. Do you know," she continued, planting her fists on her hips, "that she thinks she will never get married?"

I have no expectations.

"Not that I want you to marry her, far from it." She spoke in a dismissive tone, and he felt immediately argumentative—*Why not?* he wanted to say.

But of course he didn't want to marry her either.

"I want someone to argue with her, as it appears you've done. Someone besides me, of course."

"Why?"

Miss Ivy's younger sister was wasted in the gambling club; she should have been ensconced in Society, dazzling young gentlemen with her mischievous charm and convoluted schemes.

Although he didn't think she would agree.

"Because everyone here thinks she is absolutely marvelous!" Miss Octavia's exasperated tone told him what she thought of *that*. "And she is content to just work on the club. Her goal is to make enough money so she can go live quietly in a cottage somewhere." A dismissive snort accompanied her words.

"I take it you don't think that will suit her?" Sebastian replied amusedly.

"Of course not! Ivy should give herself as much opportunity as she wants me to have. To have fun, to fall in love, to have a marvelous future."

"And how do I fit into that?"

"You have already challenged her. I haven't seen her that worked up since the night she won the wager."

The wager. He would need to discover what that was all about. But he wanted to hear it from her directly, not from her sister.

"So you want me to work her up?" Sebastian replied.

She beamed at him. "Exactly! And it could be fun for you, too. I doubt that you have ever met anyone like Ivy before. She is very smart, you know."

No, he hadn't. He'd met smart women, of course, but none he'd deem capable of running a business. None that would ever deign to run a business, in fact. Nor did he think those women—those *ladies*— would inspire the same sort of devotion it appeared she inspired in her staff.

"I will do what I can," he replied.

"Excellent." She gave Keats one last scratch, then turned and whirled out of the room, leaving Sebastian to consider just what he'd agreed to.

A game. A wager. A *challenge.*

This not-being-a-duke thing was proving to be far more interesting than he'd ever imagined.

Not that he'd ever imagined it.

"I UNDERSTAND YOUR concern," Ivy said, "but there is no reason to be alarmed, I promise."

Ivy was sitting in her office, behind the desk, as Henry and Samuel stood facing her. Their expressions had not changed.

So much for her reassuring words.

"The thing is," she continued, leaning forward to make her point, "Mr. de Silva is here with some interesting ideas. If they don't work—if he doesn't work—then I will get rid of him."

Samuel looked skeptical.

"How long will you let him stay?" Henry asked. She could see his fists balled up, as though he wanted to go punch Mr. de Silva at this very moment.

It was a good thing Henry didn't have access to a cribbage board.

"Because we don't want you to get hurt."

Ivy's eyes widened as she absorbed what Samuel had just said. "Hurt?" She narrowed her eyes. "How do you mean *hurt*?"

Samuel glanced at Henry, who shrugged in reply.

"I won't get hurt." She lowered her gaze to her desk. Thankfully, there were some papers that required her attention. "I'll be up later."

It was a clear dismissal. She waited as they still stood there, then exhaled as they exited the office, closing the door behind them.

Hurt. Did they think she was going to do the unthinkable and fall in love with him? He was her *employee*. It wouldn't be appropriate for her to be in a position to get hurt by her employee.

What's more, he might be plain Mr. de Silva right now, but he wasn't of her world. Her new world, the one she had made for herself.

She had no doubt that he would return to his previous life once he realized what it meant to inhabit this new world. It was hard, far harder than he likely knew. Not only would he have to shave himself, he would have to adjust to being entirely without servants, without power, without privilege.

It was clear the new duke wanted him back, as did his sister. Once he was done sulking about the change in his life, he would go back.

And she would have gotten the benefit of his ideas, so perhaps she could quit this life, too.

The club was fun; the work was hard, but it was satisfying.

That was a conversation she would have to have with herself at another time.

For right now, she knew she would not allow him to be in the position to hurt her, no matter how charming or handsome he was. No matter that he was going to be living in her home. No matter that she had already thought about his forearms, his stubble, and what it might be like to undress him.

Oh dear. She was already in so much trouble.

"Miss Ivy?"

Ivy raised her head sharply at the interruption. She'd been engrossed in balancing the accounts— who knew a gambling club could spend that much money on glassware and replacement dice, for goodness' sake—and for a moment, was startled at seeing such a tall, handsome gentleman standing at her doorway.

"Mr. de Silva," she said, reminding herself to breathe. "Come in."

He walked in, his eyes focused on hers, his expression neutral.

Right, he had been irked with her last time they'd spoken.

"What is it?" she asked. She curled her mouth into a slight smile. Not so much as to be encouraging, but not so little as to be censorious.

She'd never had to think so much about managing an employee before.

Then again, she'd never had a remarkably handsome ex-duke as an employee before either.

"May I?" He gestured toward the chair.

"Please."

He sat, crossing one long leg over the other. He leaned forward to put a few pieces of paper on her desk, sliding them toward her. "My ideas for the club."

She drew them near her, then looked up at him. "Before I take a look, we should discuss what happened yesterday."

Because if they couldn't get past it, they wouldn't be able to have a working relationship. And she'd rather cut her losses now than tread carefully around him, or vice versa.

His mouth thinned, and he took a deep breath. "I apologize. I should not have presumed." She saw his throat move as he swallowed. "It is not an excuse, but I haven't had to do . . . any of this before," he said, gesticulating widely.

She held his gaze a moment before nodding in reply. "That is completely understandable. It is a difficult position to be in, I presume." She wanted to add, *I know myself*, but that would be leading him back into a situation where he'd want to ask questions, and she wouldn't want to answer.

And yet—and yet she wanted to tell him that he wasn't alone. That even though of course she hadn't been a duke, she had been a lady, with every expectation of following the usual course that ladies did: come out in Society, meet a gentleman, get married, live comfortably for the rest of her life, having children and taking tea.

Perhaps it would give him some measure of comfort to know it was possible to survive, even though she was absolutely certain he would eventually grow tired of this working-for-a-living life and return to his relatives.

But meanwhile—"It can't happen again."

"It won't. Not unless you give permission. Thank you," he said, his tone sincere.

"Let me take a look at what you've done," she replied, lowering her gaze to the papers.

She read for the next ten minutes, acutely conscious of him sitting there. Not that he was doing anything but sitting, but still. It wasn't usual for her to have an insanely attractive gentleman watch her do anything, so it felt odd.

"These are good." She tapped the papers. "It's good you laid out the strategy for implementation. It's easy to come up with ideas, but it's not always as easy to follow through on the plans for them." She glanced back down again. "These ideas are fun."

He raised his eyebrows at that, then shifted in his chair. What could she have possibly said to make him react like that?

"Speaking of fun," he began, his expression returning to its natural rakishness, "your sister doesn't think you have any."

Ivy froze. Of course she should have anticipated Octavia would have An Opinion about what Ivy was doing. She had said as much to Ivy in the past few months. But she hadn't thought that her sister would share her thoughts with the club's newest employee.

Although she suspected why her sister had done just that.

She felt her cheeks heat, and knew she was close to matching the red pockets on the roulette wheel.

"Octavia is far too interfering," she replied, meeting his gaze. "And I do have fun."

His expression practically challenged her to prove it.

So she rose, slowly, crooking her finger at him in an indication to come closer.

He stood, uncoiling his lean frame, and walked to stand in front of her. Just standing. And looking. Not reaching for her, or otherwise indicating what he expected. What he wanted.

Well, he might not be speaking the words aloud, but she knew what *she* wanted.

And she was going to act on it. That was what independent businesswomen did—they saw something and they went for it. A piece of property, a viable business proposition, a spectacular opportunity.

A handsome gentleman with charm and wit and intelligence.

A spectacular opportunity, indeed, she thought as she grasped the back of his head and drew him down to her mouth, pausing to let him decline if he wished.

The alacrity with which he fastened his mouth on hers told her that he did not wish.

And now they were kissing.

SHE TASTED EVEN better than he had been imagining. Sweet and luscious and open. He placed his fingers at her waist, holding her lightly, bending down to meet her mouth. She was so much shorter than he that it was awkward, but it was oh so worth it. Even if he had neck strain afterward.

He'd never not been the pursuer. He'd always been the one in control, in charge, of any situation, not just one involving amatory pursuits.

But today was an anomaly, an anomaly that would likely last the rest of his life—he was following someone else's lead. Letting her direct what was happening, whether it was discussing their future work at the club or following her desires.

Thank God she had. He didn't know if he could have resisted for much longer—not when she licked her lips with that pink tongue, her raised color indicating just what she was thinking about.

But it was even more delicious for having waited.

She held his face down to hers, her fingers digging into his scalp as they threaded through his hair. He wanted to preen like a cat under her touch, but that would require lifting his mouth from hers, and there was no possibility he was going to do that.

She made a small noise in the back of her throat, and he gripped her tighter, raising her slightly, spreading his fingers across her torso.

Her tongue was sliding tentatively into his mouth, and he sucked it inside, feeling her shock at the action. Nearly releasing her then since he didn't want to startle her or seem to force her into something she didn't want, but then she made another noise, and her tongue tangled with his as she slid her hands down his back to link together at his waist, pulling his body closer into hers.

Which brought his cock in contact with her body, and it reacted predictably, hardening as she continued to kiss him, an enthusiastic fervor tempering the kiss, making him lose his mind and forget everything but the taste of her, how close his fingers were to her breasts.

And then she brought her hands back up over his shoulders, sliding down his chest, pushing the lapels of his jacket aside, touching his chest under his shirt, making him wish he wasn't wearing anything at all, so she could touch him better.

He groaned, bringing his right hand up to close over her breast, squeezing its lush fullness, pushing his cock closer against her.

It felt good. So good. And they were both still fully clothed, his cock straining in his trousers, their mouths fused together as they licked and sucked with an equal amount of passion.

He took his hand away, bringing both his hands around her, under her bottom, lifting her up, and setting her on top of her desk.

Now *this* was a game he wanted to play.

Her legs widened, and he stepped between them, wrapping his arms around her body, holding her up as he ravaged her mouth. And she ravaged his.

It would be just a matter of time before he ran

his hands up her legs, pushing her skirts up so his throbbing cock could find its purchase.

Slow down, Sebastian. This isn't one of your experienced ladies.

So he tried to stop thinking about her willing warmth, the satisfaction he'd feel at thrusting into her. How he wanted to cover her nipple with his mouth, suck the tight bud as she arched under him.

Admittedly, he was not doing a good job not thinking about all of that.

But then they heard a door, and sprang apart, her still sitting on the desk, her face flushed, her mouth bruised and swollen.

She looked gorgeous.

Her eyes widened in shock, and she held her hand up to her mouth, which had opened to an *O* of surprise.

"Oh my God, I am so sorry. I didn't mean—" she said, shaking her head as she leaped off the table. Her hair fell forward into her face, so he couldn't see her expression.

They heard footsteps, and her gaze darted toward the door. "It won't happen again, I promise. I am not in the habit of taking advantage of my employees, you have to forgive me." She spoke in a rapid whisper, her tone agitated.

"Yes, of course." It was an automatic reaction, one bred into him as a gentleman. Not that he was that any longer, but his training still remained.

Had a lady ever apologized for kissing him before?

Of course not. Nor should they.

He frowned as he realized precisely what she'd said. That she was sorry she had kissed him. That it wouldn't happen again.

Not only did he not want her to be sorry—
sorry!—she'd kissed him, he definitely wanted it to
happen again.

He wanted to show her all the fun they could
manage.

Chapter Ten

Oh my God. What had she done? Who had she done? Why had she done it?

She could answer all of those questions just by looking at him. By speaking with him, having him apologize to her for his presumption. By feeling appreciated for her intelligence and business savvy.

Lord.

"Ivy?"

Octavia spoke just at the door, and then the door opened, and her sister stepped inside. Mr. de Silva's two dogs trailed at her heels. Octavia's glance darted between the two of them, and it appeared that she suppressed a smirk.

Humph.

"Oh good, I was actually looking for you, Mr. de Silva. And here you are. With Ivy." Octavia's voice dripped with smug satisfaction.

Ivy resisted the urge to roll her eyes at how obvious her sister was being.

"Here I am." His voice was a bit ragged, and Ivy felt a surge of triumph at having affected him so.

"I was hoping you would allow me to take Byron and Keats out for a walk," Octavia continued, gesturing toward the dogs. "They started following me to the gambling room, and it seems as though they are restless, as am I, and I thought we could all use a walk. Unless you two wish to take them out?" she said with what Ivy knew to be a deliberately disingenuous smile.

"No," they both replied in unison.

"I have too much work, Octavia," Ivy said. "I cannot speak for Mr. de Silva."

"I wish to hear your sister's thoughts on my work."

And what work is that? The thought came unbidden to her mind.

Because she was wondering if she was a good kisser at all. She'd been kissed only a few times before, and none of those kisses was as satisfactory as this one had been. But she knew he had likely kissed many more people than she, and she wondered how she ranked among those.

It seemed as if he'd liked it, judging by the hardness she'd felt against herself, but that could be just because he hadn't been with a lady for a day or two. Since she had no idea how often he was with ladies in the first place.

That would be an awkward question to ask. Not to mention entirely and thoroughly inappropriate. *What is your regular rotation of females? One a week? Two a week? More?*

If it were more, she'd be surprised he wasn't constantly yawning. Servicing ladies had to be a fatiguing exercise. At least, she would imagine it would be if it were him.

She felt herself growing warm and wanted to squirm at the image it conjured in her mind—him unclothed, panting from his exertions, a completely satisfied young woman underneath him. With the young woman looking suspiciously like her.

Octavia shrugged. "Then I can take them out, if that is fine with you, Mr. de Silva."

"Call me Sebastian," he said in a curt tone. Ivy and Octavia both looked at him in surprise.

"I don't mean to be rude. It's just that Sebastian feels far more comfortable than Mr. de Silva."

"Ah," Octavia replied. "Sebastian, might I take your dogs out for a walk?"

"Yes, thank you, Miss Octavia."

Octavia grinned. "Just Octavia, since you're just Sebastian."

"Just Sebastian," he murmured. As though he was reminding himself.

"Come on, then," Octavia said, tugging on the dogs' leashes. She shot one last knowing look at Ivy, and then shut the door.

"Byron and Keats?" Ivy asked, wanting to steer the conversation away from what just happened, the grading of kisses, and her overly enthusiastic imagination.

That shiver was just because it was cold.

Even though it was not at all.

"I went through a Romantic period," he replied. His gaze moved from her eyes to her mouth. "And now I'm not certain I ever left."

"No!" she snapped, startling them both. "We can't do any of this," she said in a softer tone, gesturing to the space between them. "Even though I'm the one who started it," she added.

He looked as though he was about to speak, but then he pressed his lips together and nodded.

"You understand?" she pressed.

Another nod. He looked almost angry.

"Let's return to the work at hand," she said, waving

her hand toward the papers on her desk. The papers that had gotten crushed when he'd hoisted her atop them.

"Of course, Miss Ivy."

She was about to tell him he could call her just Ivy, as Octavia had, but that would further blur the lines between them—he was living with her, he was working for her, and now he had kissed her. Or she had kissed him. They shouldn't be on such familiar terms with one another. It would just encourage . . . familiarity.

"Excellent." She took her seat again, gesturing to the chair opposite. "If you please?" she said. She nearly added his given name, but that seemed thoughtless considering what she had just said.

She started to read his work again, only to find her mind was entirely clouded. That kiss. That moment. That feeling.

Yes, she'd been kissed before. Yes, even by the occasional handsome man; she'd met a few in her tenure as Miss Ivy, proprietor of the newly fashionable Miss Ivy's.

But he was so much more than any of them, and she needed to push that all away so she could focus on what was important: the club, and making money, enough money to leave the club behind and go live somewhere else.

Although that was sounding less and less appealing by the day. By the ex-duke, if she were being honest.

Damn it.

DAMN IT. Was he less charming now that he was no longer a duke?

No, because she hadn't known him until he wasn't a duke.

But he'd never had a woman so thoroughly deny him before. Of course he had to respect that. It was the right thing to do, regardless of their respective positions. But that he was her employee made it even more important.

Not that he needed this job, precisely. Not for survival, that is.

"What are you paying me, anyway?" he blurted.

Better to ask questions she could answer than ones she could not: *Why don't you want to kiss me again? Have I lost my charm?* and most important, *Why don't we work on having fun together?*

She looked up with a surprised expression.

"Pardon?"

"My salary. I don't believe we discussed it." He spoke in an authoritative tone of voice, even though he honestly had no idea how negotiations between employer and employee were supposed to be handled.

Her cheeks began to color, and she looked embarrassed. "Of course, Mr. de Silva—"

"Sebastian."

"I apologize for not discussing this when I hired you. How much do you require?"

Ah, here is where it got tricky. Because until a few days ago, he hadn't had to think about money in terms of how much he needed to live on. He just gestured, and things would get paid, and he would always have enough for his needs.

He had no idea how much rent cost, how much food cost, how much even a new razor cost. Which reminded him that his razor was getting worn, and he must be looking ragged.

Thank goodness he did know how to shave, or else he'd have had to ask her to assist him.

"I don't know," he replied. "It depends on my duties, I suppose." As though he had a clue what he was talking about.

She frowned at him. Had she figured out he had no clue?

"Shall we say thirty pounds a year?"

He'd spent four pounds on a hat for Ana Maria two weeks ago. She'd protested, but he'd insisted, telling her the cost was less than he spent on a good bottle of whiskey.

The disparity between the two was striking.

And at this rate, his future goal of investing was so far off in the future he might have expired by then.

"Seems fair." Even though it didn't. Because if a hat or alcohol could cost a month's wages, what would a suit of clothes cost? Or a horse? How would he be able to live on that?

Just like everybody else who isn't a duke does.

"I would pay you more," she continued, "but I accounted for the rent you won't be paying us. Should you find you wish to move elsewhere, I will adjust accordingly. And I presume you'll be taking your meals with us, as well? We provide meals for the staff on the nights we know will be especially busy."

Living with her. Taking meals with her. It was essential, at least according to her, that he maintain a distance. And yet they would be together now nearly all the time.

He'd have to develop a hobby to keep him out of the house when he wasn't working.

Byron and Keats were going to get plenty of walking until he figured that hobby out.

"Well," she said, "now that that is settled, I want to implement the Masked Evening as soon as possible—say next week? Does that give you enough time to prepare?"

Preparing meant buying masks and letting the customers know. That didn't seem too difficult, although he knew there were likely to be unanticipated problems.

"Yes." He spoke with a confidence he didn't necessarily feel. But he was going to have to grow accustomed to pretending to know what he was doing until he actually did.

Speaking of which— "Can we agree to a bonus incentive?"

She regarded him quizzically.

"If," he said, his thoughts running furiously fast, "if I am able to draw in the type of customers you wouldn't have thought attainable, could you perhaps consider additional monies?"

She twisted her mouth in thought. "That might work. Let me speak with Henry about it and see what kind of parameters we can set up." She arched her brow. "And may I say I admire your boldness to ask for more when you've barely begun working."

"Uh—" he began, only to stop speaking as he saw her laughing face.

"It's fine, you wouldn't know unless you asked. And you're correct, there are likely to be people I couldn't have lured into the club alone."

He felt a deep sense of satisfaction—he had a goal, one he was working toward. If his goal took ten years, or twenty? At least he would be looking forward.

"But meanwhile," she said, "you should meet with Mac."

He shook his head in confusion.

"The chef."

Oh. The large red-faced man. Sebastian hoped he wasn't as anti-Sebastian as Samuel and Henry were.

"To discuss the menu for that evening. We should have food that looks like other food—sort of a delicious nod to the evening's theme."

"That is an excellent idea," he said in surprise.

"I have them, occasionally," she replied dryly. "Such as when I opened this club, or when I hired you. Although that remains to be seen," she added with a smirk.

"It will be." He rose, leaning over to take his work back. "I will be on the floor at night to observe and help out when required, and I'll be working on the Masked Evening during the days. I might not see you at meals."

"Oh, of course." Her face was expressionless. Did that mean it bothered her? Or did it not bother her?

He might've misspoken when he'd told her she must be a terrible card player. He couldn't read her at all.

But damned if he didn't want to kiss her again. His hand still prickled from where he'd touched her. His scalp tingled from her fingers. He could find somebody else to kiss, he knew he only needed his charm and looks to acquire that, but he strongly suspected it wouldn't be the same.

He wanted to kiss *her*.

OCTAVIA BURST INTO Ivy's office, slamming the door behind her. Ivy had spent as little time in the house as possible since that day she kissed Mr. de Silva, so she hadn't seen her sister very much. She'd even missed their regular afternoon tea appointment a few times, and the other times, she'd gulped her share down and rushed off claiming work.

"Good afternoon to you, too, sister," Ivy said in a mild tone.

Octavia stomped toward Ivy's desk, then plopped down into the chair in front of it. "Do you mind telling me what is going on with you?"

Ivy tensed. "What do you mean?"

Her sister rolled her eyes. "As though you don't know. You've been cranky for several days now, this is not like you."

Nor is kissing my employees, and yet here I am, she thought.

"Business is engrossing," Ivy replied, shuffling some of the papers on her desk.

Octavia slapped her hand on top of them. "Stop that. I know you're not that busy, not so busy you have to be actively unpleasant."

Ivy drew her brows together in a frown. "Actively unpleasant?" She hadn't realized. "If so, I apologize."

"Not *if* so. It is so." Octavia settled her hands in her lap. "I accept your apology."

Ivy exhaled, then picked up her pencil and held it in a manner that clearly indicated she was ready to get back to work. "So if you don't mind . . . ?"

"I *do* mind. You have to tell me why." Octavia leaned forward, narrowing her gaze. "I don't think it is such a stretch to think it has something to do with Sebastian."

Sebastian. Her sister had grown accustomed to calling him by his first name immediately, and used it constantly. *Sebastian, would you want to take Byron and Keats for a walk? Sebastian, pass me the butter. Sebastian, did you see the patron last night? She was irked you weren't her dealer.*

But Ivy hadn't. She *couldn't.* Because to admit that kind of familiarity would lead to other familiar things. Things that kept her lying awake in her bed at night. Things that her imagination ran wild with, meaning Ivy found it impossible to sleep. Impossible to sleep—that was it. An all-purpose excuse.

"I've had some trouble sleeping as of late. I am sorry." She tried to imbue her tone with the right combination of sorrow and fatigue.

"It's not that." Octavia's firm words meant that her attempt had failed. "I wish you could allow yourself to enjoy something, Ivy."

"Is that why you urged Mr. de Silva to bring some fun into my life?"

"He told you that? I would not have thought he'd be so bold." Octavia sounded admiring. "But yes." She held her hands out as she explained. "We have a rare opportunity here, Ivy. We have a gentleman, a very handsome, charming gentleman, in residence in our house. It would be a disservice not to utilize him to his utmost ability."

Ivy gawked at her sister. "Utilize him to his—? Octavia, he's not a tool."

"No, he's a man." Octavia accompanied her words with a smirk. As though she knew that Ivy was already keenly aware of that. "And you are a woman."

"So are you!" Ivy wished she had thought before she'd spoken. She didn't want her sister ensnared by all of Mr. de Silva's flirtatious charm.

Octavia rolled her eyes. Again. "I see him as a friend. Perhaps a friendly cousin. He is too old for me," she said scornfully.

Thank goodness. Although that just meant that Octavia believed he wasn't too old for Ivy.

"Just try to get yourself out of this grouchy mood," Octavia said, rising. She glanced at the watch pinned to her bodice. "I promised Sebastian we would go out with the dogs now. We've been exploring London together. Until now, he's only seen the areas a duke would see."

"What areas are you showing him?" Ivy asked in alarm.

Octavia made a tsking noise. "It's not as though I am taking him anywhere more disreputable than a gambling house. But he wanted to get some new linen and get some whiskey." She shrugged. "He didn't know where people, regular people, went to purchase those items. So I showed him."

Linens and whiskey. The necessities for a former duke, now gambling-house employee.

"Well. Thank you for that."

"So you'll consider what I said? About being less unpleasant?"

Leave it to her sister not to sugarcoat her words.

"I will."

Octavia grinned. "Maybe have some fun, even?"

"Get out of my office," Ivy replied, gesturing to the door. Her tone was stern, but she couldn't help but smile.

A WEEK LATER, and his desire for her hadn't abated. And her expression and treatment of him remained coolly distant, as was appropriate for an employer and her employee.

It was frustrating as hell.

"Taste."

Mac didn't wait for Sebastian to respond before shoving something into his mouth. Thankfully, Sebastian knew that all of Mac's food was delicious, so he didn't hesitate to start chewing.

"Mm," he said, nodding at the chef. He and Mac had found common ground on dogs and the running of the British government, so the two had become friends within a short period of time.

Thank God, because Samuel and Henry were only now just beginning to thaw. He'd nearly thanked them for their not-so-friendly advice, since their words rang in his brain anytime he was working—reminding him that he was on unfamiliar ground, and that he had to prove himself.

Mac didn't seem to judge anyone as long as they liked his food, and Sebastian liked his food quite a lot.

"What is it?" he asked when he could speak again.

Mac grinned in delight. "It's duck and quince pie. It's like a meat pie, only it's actually stuffed with duck and quince."

"Hence the name," Sebastian said dryly.

"You may not have noticed, Your Grace," Mac said, fully aware it would annoy Sebastian, "but the people on the streets often buy meat pies from vendors. They are generally foul tasting, using meat I wouldn't give to your dogs."

"Well, since I caught you feeding sirloin to Byron the other day, that is not much of a condemnation."

Mac waved his large hand in dismissal. "The point is, it looks like one thing and tastes like another."

"Perfect for the evening. Miss Ivy will be pleased her idea was so successful."

Mac had already perfected the recipe for lobster cakes disguised as biscuits, and pastries masquerading as cheddar cheese, so the duck and quince pie would just about finish the special selections for the Masked Evening.

"Miss Ivy!" Mac called, leaning to one side to peer over Sebastian's shoulder. Sebastian forced himself not to turn to look at her; it was difficult enough to share a living and working space with her, as he often discovered himself staring at her when he hadn't realized it. If he could just not stare at her when he did realize it, perhaps she wouldn't notice he was obsessed.

He wasn't obsessed. No, not that. He just wished to speak with her, perhaps discover if his memory was playing tricks on him—was her mouth that delectable? Her curves that luscious?

But instead he was relegated to staring at her like he was an urchin peeking into a kitchen window.

"Good evening, Mac. Good evening," she said to him. She hadn't said his name since he'd asked her and Octavia to call him Sebastian. She found myriad solutions to avoid addressing him at all.

Was it possible she was just as obsessed with him? His past duke self would have assumed she was.

But now, now that he wasn't who he thought he was, and things were entirely different, he wasn't certain. Now that he was working for a young lady instead of working to get a young lady into bed, well, that was an entirely different situation.

"Are we ready for this evening?"

The question was rhetorical, since she knew full well they were—she'd ensured it, with her lists and her reminders and her ability to focus on any potential weaknesses.

He admired it. She would make an excellent duke, what with all the managing and negotiating one had to do in that position.

He'd ventured out to meet with some of the people from his old life, and after the initial awkwardness about the scandal of his title, he had gotten their commitment to stop by, fulfilling his promise of bringing more well-heeled and important people into the club. He and Ivy had agreed to terms on a bonus, and both had been working furiously hard in preparation.

"We are absolutely ready, Miss Ivy." In contrast to her, he always said her name. Whether it was a rebuke of her not giving him permission to call her by her Christian name, as her sister had, or a reminder to himself of their professional relationship, he didn't know. He did know that every time he said her name, her expression changed, such a fleeting frown on her face he'd thought he was imagining it the first few times.

But no. For some reason, his calling her Miss Ivy irked her. So of course he did it as often as possible.

"Taste this." Mac held the other half of the pie out to her, and she took it, popping the whole bit into her mouth. She chewed, nodding in approval. "It's very good," she said, licking her lips to retrieve an errant crumb.

Damn it. He wished seeing that didn't make his cock twitch. Thinking about other places she could lick, were she so inclined.

Though she wasn't. She'd made that clear with her words directly following the kiss, and by her behavior in the week since.

Her sister, however, was as friendly as Miss Ivy was distant. Sebastian had found himself asking questions about their life before coming to London, before opening the club. Octavia was an open book except for when it came to how her older sister settled on opening a gambling club in the first place. But he heard all about Ivy's teaching lessons to Octavia, since their father couldn't seem to hire a proper governess; the various scrapes from which Ivy rescued her sister; and how much Octavia did not wish to go live in a country cottage.

Sebastian found himself sympathizing with Miss Ivy, who was clearly trying to keep her younger sister contained, even though that sister was equally determined not to be so.

He wished they were friendly enough for him to tell her so. But anytime their conversation threatened to move beyond a professional relationship, she suddenly announced she had somewhere else to be.

He strongly suspected she did not always have somewhere else to be.

Chapter Eleven

Ivy suppressed a sigh as she glanced over at him. It appeared he did indeed know how to shave himself, his smooth skin revealing the sharp angles of his face.

She hadn't been able to stop thinking about that kiss. And she knew, she just knew, he hadn't been able to stop either. She could tell, from the way he would look at her—hungrily, as though he wanted one thing, and that thing was her.

It excited her, to be honest. As well as terrified her; she was enough of a savvy London inhabitant to know some of what happened between a man and a woman. She'd had to learn caution walking around the streets by herself, since a gambling club owner did not have the same responsibility to keep a maid with her at all times. And she'd seen some of that activity in certain areas—a woman on her knees in front of a gentleman, his head thrown back, his expression one of deep ecstasy.

She was curious. And she wanted to stop being so skittish about it all. She was a young London woman, not a noble lady who had to watch every aspect of her behavior. He would leave as soon as he'd had enough of this life anyway; she didn't want to regret not taking advantage of his presence while he was here.

Plus Octavia had urged her to have fun. She couldn't disappoint her sister, could she?

"Could you come with me to my office?" she asked him. He looked as though he was startled by her request. Likely because she'd managed not to spend more than a few minutes alone with him since their kiss.

But damn it, she needed to clear the air. She wasn't an innocent girl who had time to spend conjuring up dreams of a perfect romance. She was a businesswoman who had to get on with things.

"Certainly, Miss Ivy."

She felt her mouth twist at hearing him say her name so formally. She knew he did it to bother her, she could tell by the smirk on his face. But in some contrary way—and she hadn't realized until now that she was contrary—that pleased her, because it meant that he cared about her reaction. She wasn't just a kiss that had happened a week ago and was now receding into the distance.

Plus—and she should be ashamed, but she absolutely wasn't—she knew that regardless of what his female habits were before, he hadn't been with anyone else since. She knew because he was working all the time, and if he wasn't working, he was sleeping or out walking his dogs with Octavia.

Ivy was relieved that Octavia had adopted him as a sort of big brother rather than treating him as someone to be flirted with. They went walking for an hour every day, and each time Octavia returned with a fresh bit of information about her new employee—he was very fond of his sister, he liked the work he was doing, he was frustrated with not knowing how to do his own laundry.

"Is there something wrong?" he asked as they walked down the hallway to her office.

She didn't reply, just gestured for him to enter and then shut the door behind him. "Sit down, if you would."

He did, regarding her warily.

"Your work is excellent, I am not here to relieve you of your duties or anything," she said.

His expression eased. "So what do you want to talk to me about?"

She made a noise of frustration, gesturing between them. "This. This awkwardness that we can't seem to get over. It was just a kiss!" she exclaimed, as much to herself as to him.

He rose at her words, walking slowly and assuredly toward her. Giving her time to stop him, only she couldn't. She could just watch, feeling her breathing speed as he approached.

"It wasn't just a kiss," he replied, sounding regretful. "I wish it were, or I'd have been able to forget it." Now he was standing directly in front of her. She could see where he'd cut himself shaving. Perhaps he did need assistance, after all. "I've tried, but I can't." His gaze settled on her mouth, and it felt as though he was already kissing her. "I keep recalling your taste. How you dug your fingers into my hair. How you responded when I caressed you. What your breasts felt like under my palm." His voice was growing more ragged, and she found herself leaning in to him, her own breath growing shorter, her whole body feeling prickly, but in an exciting, sensual way.

"Oh," she sighed. "I can't forget either." She tilted her face toward him in an unmistakable invitation, and he reached to slide his fingers to her jaw, stroking the skin there. She couldn't help herself, she bit her lip at his touch, and he growled as he lowered his mouth to hers.

He paused, just for a moment, long enough for her to refuse him if she wanted to.

But she did not want to.

Instead, she arched up to meet him, grabbing his hand at her face and drawing it down to her waist, putting her other hand on his back to pull him into her.

He wrapped his other hand around her, tugging her up so their mouths were firmly pressed together, the only sound in the room their breaths. And then he opened his mouth, and she slid her tongue inside, unable to suppress the moan she made deep in her throat.

She felt his hardness against her, and she shifted so she could press that part of her that was aching against his leg. He deepened the kiss, and she surrendered to the sensation of his tongue tangling with hers, his hand now at her waist, sliding up so his fingers were just under her breast.

She felt as though she was about to burst, she craved his touch, craved him everywhere, if she was being honest. He placed his palm on her breast and squeezed, making her feel a vast want all over.

He drew his mouth away to press his lips at her neck, drawing the tender skin into his mouth and biting gently. She made a soft noise, and he chuckled. She could feel him tugging on her gown to draw it up, and she felt the air on her ankle, her calf, until the fabric was up over her knee.

"Oh," she moaned, and rubbed herself against his leg, shameless in her desire. He responded by sliding his fingers up and then down into the neckline of her gown, warm against her skin, searching for something.

"Ahh," she said as his fingers stroked over her nipple. She had had no idea that would feel so good. And then he pinched it between his fingers, and the slight sting sent skittering sparks through her, and she twisted in his embrace, pulling him against her as she leaned back on the desk.

He moved his mouth from her neck to her upper chest, and she felt his fingers working on the fabric until her breast was exposed. He made a savagely primal sound before covering her nipple with his mouth.

She gasped as he licked her there, his fingers pressing into her skin, his other hand on her thigh under the skirts of her gown.

Her hand went to his waist, and then she curled her fingers into the waistband of his trousers, biting her lip as he continued to pleasure her.

She uncurled her fingers, flattening her palm to skim down, over his hardness, brushing it up and down until she grasped him through the fabric. He shifted, giving her better access to him, and she gripped him, caressing his length as much as she was able.

She had never done any of this, but she'd been a ruined lady running a gambling establishment for six months now; there were things she had heard about, and she was grateful she had paid attention through her embarrassed haze.

She had never felt more gloriously in control, nor had she ever felt so remarkably passionate.

She wanted to devour him, to have him do the same to her, to discover what it felt like when the passion crested.

"Miss Ivy," he said, his voice a rough whisper.

"Just Ivy," she replied, a smile curling her mouth at his adhering to politeness despite what they were currently engaged in.

"Ivy, I want to bury myself in your softness. I want to strip you of this gown and take you on top of this table."

Each word made her feel as though she was on fire. She squirmed on the table, wanting more, wanting all of it.

"But we have to stop."

And he gave her nipple one last, regretful look as he removed his hand from her thigh, stepping back from between her legs.

"Why?" she asked. Her voice was husky.

"For many reasons, not least of which is that I wouldn't want your first time to be on top of a wooden desk," he replied in an amused tone.

She sat up, pushing her disheveled hair back over her shoulders. "How do you know this is my first time?"

His eyebrow arched, and he gave her a wry grin. "It's either your first time, or I am extraordinarily good." His smile deepened. "And while I have been known to be rightly proud of my skills, it is more likely to be the former."

She laughed as she shook her head. "You truly are proud." *Well deserved*, she wanted to add. Her whole body tingled from his touch. "But yes, my first time on a desk doesn't sound appealing, once you put it that way."

He held his hand out, and she took it, sliding off the desk to stand on the floor, shaking her skirts back down. She kept eye contact with him as she put her bodice to rights, tucking her breast back into her shift and gown.

"So what now?" she asked, raising her chin.

His gaze raked her up and down, and she trembled in response. "I like this game, Ivy. This might be the most pleasurable pursuit under your roof. Although I wouldn't want just anyone to play."

She stepped forward, grasping him by the neck. "No. It should be just us." *For as long as you're here.*

"So shall we continue to play?" he murmured. He was still under her hold, as though ceding control.

She liked how that felt.

"Yes," she replied, lifting up to press her mouth against his. "But now we have to prepare for tonight."

"As you wish, Miss Ivy."

She rolled her eyes. "Whatever you say, Your Grace."

THE CLUB LOOKED spectacular. The windows, which were normally discreetly shaded in dark curtains, had been redone in gold and red fabric, black masks on the finials. The chairs were covered in gold fabric also, black masks tying the fabric together at the back.

The staff had outdone itself with cleaning, as well. The wooden floors gleamed, every surface was dusted and polished, and the staff themselves looked impeccably groomed.

The food—all disguised as other foods, as Ivy had suggested—was served on trays that had been covered in green felt, matching the gambling tables. The staff were all wearing masks, although theirs were black, while the guests wore gold.

She'd also taken extra care with her own outfit—usually she chose gowns that were subdued. She didn't want to attract any more attention than she already would, given that she was the lady proprietor of a gambling house. But tonight she'd deliberately picked one of her more daring gowns, cut low in a dark red color, with darker ruffles at the bottom of the skirt. Would he admire it? she wondered. Would he even notice?

Even with a mask on, Ivy could pick out Sebastian. First there was his height, which made him stand out from the rest of the gentlemen in the room. And his clothing was impeccably fit, molding to his long, lean lines. Clearly costing far more than nearly everyone else's, a vestige of his former duke days. And then there was his hair, which glinted gold in the candlelight, literally drawing her eye.

But since she was apparently generally obsessed with him, she'd still be looking at him if he were standing in the corner with a bucket on his head.

So there was that.

He didn't belong here. He wouldn't be here for long, but in the meantime, she could stare to her heart's content.

As she watched, she saw another tall gentleman

draw near, and recognized him as the gentleman she'd first met him with—the Duke of Something, she couldn't remember what. But a duke was once again in her establishment, and that was reason enough to call the evening a success.

The customers all seemed to be enjoying the Masked Evening, and unlike most evenings, when the clientele segregated themselves by class, as indicated by their speech and clothing, tonight they were deliberately choosing to sit with people not of their world. Nobles sat next to merchants, solicitors sat alongside actresses, and ladies were beside ladies' companions. It was as though they were playing the game of anonymity as well as games of chance.

Henry had asked for additional security for the house bank this evening, which Sebastian had taken care of before Ivy had even heard of it. Henry had been thawing toward Ivy's newest employee of late, although Samuel still remained skeptical.

The club was making money, and people were having a good time, two things that were often mutually exclusive. The drama of the evening, the audacity of deciding to play cards or dice with someone you would not normally acknowledge— that added an extra luster to the night.

Her body tightened as he walked toward her.

"Are you pleased?" Sebastian asked, his voice low. He stood at her elbow, just behind, as though aware of his position in relation to hers.

That shouldn't mean as much as it did to her, but it absolutely did.

She turned to him. He wore a black mask, as she did, making him look even more rakish, if such a thing were possible. "I am. This is good work." She hesitated, then added, "Sebastian."

"Thank you." A pause, then a chuckle. "Ivy."

"Is it your thought that we will institute these evenings regularly?"

He shook his head. "I think it will have more impact if it is a surprise—if, when the patrons arrive, they are given masks, and won't know what evening it will happen."

"Unexpected anonymity. I like it."

"You do?" he replied in a husky tone.

Suddenly, the room felt as though it contained just the two of them. Him, standing close so they could hear one another. His gaze through the mask fixed on her. She felt all his primal energy, as if she could feel his desires. Likely because she felt those desires herself.

But— "Now is not the time for flirting," she said in a low voice. "We are supposed to be working. Ensuring everything goes well this evening."

"I can both flirt and ensure everything goes well." He accompanied his words with waggling eyebrows, making her laugh.

"Can you—?" she began, only to stop when they heard a loud noise a few tables away.

He was already rushing over when Ivy identified what it was—an unsteady patron, likely the imbiber of too much of her excellent wine, had tipped a chair over and was staring belligerently at Samuel, who was staring just as intensely back.

Oh no, oh no, oh no. And the night was going so well. These things happened on occasion, of course. Usually Ivy and her staff were able to identify a potential problem. But tonight's increased activity and unusual atmosphere meant they were more likely to miss something. Which, apparently, they had.

"Gentlemen," she heard Sebastian say, his hands out in a placating manner, "let us discuss."

"Your dealer is cheating!" the gentleman replied, pointing a finger at Samuel.

Many of the patrons gasped—cheating was a serious accusation, and if it were thought to be true, the club would lose business. And it did not escape Ivy's notice that the gentleman had chosen to accuse a man of color.

Samuel folded his arms over his broad chest. "He put his bet on red. The wheel came up black."

"Ten times?" the gentleman retorted.

Samuel shrugged. "Not my fault if the wheel is not in favor with you this evening."

"My good sir, perhaps I can interest you in playing at another table?" Sebastian placed his hand on the gentleman's shoulder, effectively steadying him. He began to walk away from Samuel's table, steering the gentleman.

Ivy was about to exhale in relief when the gentleman shrugged Sebastian's hold off him, then took his own mask off, discarding it on the floor.

Ivy recognized him—a young lord who was arrogant even without the benefit of alcohol. Then she watched as he reached forward to Sebastian's face, yanking his mask off.

"I knew I recognized you!" the gentleman said accusingly.

Sebastian nodded, taking the mask from the gentleman's hands. "Yes, my lord. We have met." He spoke in a terse tone, but his expression remained calm.

"You're the one whose mother lied. A once mighty duke, now a bastard working here."

His jaw clenched, and she saw his friend the duke start to move toward them, only to stop when Sebastian flung his hand up. "Nash," he said in a warning tone, his gaze never wavering from the tottering lord.

As far as she knew, he hadn't seen many people from his former world. At least not in the club; she presumed he'd been speaking with some of them, since he was working toward the bonus they'd negotiated. Had he even dealt with his feelings and reaction to his change of circumstances? If she thought about it, it seemed as though he'd buried himself in work and walking. Certainly Octavia would have told her if he had spoken about it at all. He hadn't been to visit his sister, nor had she or the intense military man made a reappearance.

She'd wondered about that, but it wasn't her business. Especially since she'd been struggling to keep their lives from intersecting through personal connection.

Which, as her bruised mouth and awakened desire could attest, had not gone all that well.

She held her breath as he opened his mouth to speak.

Chapter Twelve

Sebastian squelched his urge to punch young Lord Linehan in the jaw.

Not that it wouldn't feel good; it would.

Not that he didn't deserve it; he did.

But he could see what would happen if he did, and none of the results would make it worth the satisfaction. Sebastian would get a reputation as a bitter hothead, Miss Ivy's would be known as a refuge for said hotheads, and the aristocracy would chatter amongst themselves that Miss Ivy's was not a safe place for people like them.

So no, he couldn't punch him.

"My lord," he began, taking deep breaths in an attempt to calm himself, "it is true that I have recently suffered a change of circumstance."

The club had quieted, and it seemed as though most everyone there—patrons and staff—were waiting to hear what he was going to say.

For that matter, *he* was waiting to hear what he was going to say. He didn't have the slightest idea, since telling Lord Linehan he had decided not to punch him in the jaw was probably not a winning diplomatic strategy.

Lord Linehan wobbled before replying, "A change of circumstance?" Only, because he was slurring, it sounded like, "A shange of shircumstance?" Sebastian looked at him, shaking his head.

There would be no point in punching him. He was young, and drunk, and likely feeling overwhelmed by the many varieties of people in the club. So he was putting on a bravado he likely didn't feel, aided by wine, and it would be beneath Sebastian to do anything but try to resolve the situation.

Besides which, he thought Miss Ivy might like it if he did.

So he wasn't entirely altruistic.

"Do you need me to hit him, Seb?" Nash asked in a low growl.

"No, I've got this," he replied, nodding at his friend.

Nash nodded, then his lip curled as he cast one last look toward Lord Linehan, who was starting to look truly frightened—no doubt because the Dangerous Duke had him in his sights.

"Go somewhere and try to look less intimidating," he added. Nash chuckled in surprise, then returned to his table, gesturing for more wine as he did so.

"My lord," he began, pulling a chair from a nearby table and dragging it toward Lord Linehan, "you are so fortunate." He nudged the swaying gentleman into the chair. "You can go anywhere and be admitted because of who you are." He gestured to one of the members of the staff, who walked over to him. "Coffee, please," he said. The staff member nodded, then walked toward the kitchen.

Sebastian dragged another chair next to where Lord Linehan sat, straddling it backward to face him. Lord Linehan was blinking heavily, and Sebastian thought it was just a matter of time before he fell asleep. "I know you didn't mean to be rude in Miss Ivy's establishment. An establishment that welcomes all, regardless of who they are." The patrons who were listening nodded, and Sebastian knew that at least some of them felt as he did. "I would urge you not to take anything for granted— not your position, not your wealth, not anything. You never know when it will be taken away."

Lord Linehan regarded him through bleary eyes. Had he understood anything? Likely not, but the more important point was that the room's other inhabitants had.

"Don't want it to be taken away," Lord Linehan mumbled, his head swaying forward.

Sebastian gestured to Henry, who strode toward him. "Can we get Lord Linehan a hansom home? And pay the driver in advance so he won't have to?"

"Excellent idea," Henry said, not sounding as begrudging in his praise as Sebastian might have expected.

"Didn't mean anything," Lord Linehan continued. "Sorry to be—" And then he stopped speaking, his head bobbing onto his chest.

"He's out, I think," Sebastian said to Henry. Henry didn't reply, just stepped forward and picked him up with no appearance of effort. He tossed the young lord over his shoulders and walked out, a cluster of guests murmuring as he did so.

"Well, I believe we can all now testify to the strength and quality of the wine." Ivy spoke in a carrying voice, clapping her hands together as she did so. She addressed the staff arranged along the walls. "Can we ensure all our guests have plenty to eat and drink? Miss Ivy's is for pleasure, after all."

The staff dispersed toward where the wine was kept, and soon every patron's glass was filled to the brim, most of them chuckling about the inebriated lord and his attempts to start an argument. A few spoke to one another in low voices, and Sebastian kept his eye on them. He knew full well how quickly public opinion could leap over to another side. He'd seen it often enough, even if he hadn't been the recipient of it.

But thus far it was just a few murmurs. Something they'd have to be aware of.

Situation defused, Sebastian thought with satisfaction. And he didn't need to punch anyone. Or have Nash punch anyone. Even though Nash likely regretted that.

"Thank you, Sebastian." Ivy spoke in a low tone, her eyes constantly assessing the room and the crowd. Did she never stop working?

Oh yes, she did. When she was kissing him. So if he were to kiss her again, he would be doing a service, ensuring she wasn't always thinking about the club. About her duties, what she perceived as her responsibilities toward her sister.

And he wouldn't be thinking about anything either.

"I used to take things for granted. As he did," Sebastian replied. "Until one day the things weren't there." He had avoided thinking about his situation by throwing himself completely into his new job.

.

But it crept up, and he couldn't keep himself from feeling the anger stirring. So much anger, anger he would have to deal with at some point.

"And now you have to—?"

"Take things as I find them. Find things I want to take."

He wanted to take *her*. Not only because he seemed to be ludicrously intrigued with her, this intelligent business owner and lively companion, but because taking her would push the anger away in favor of more passionate feelings.

Using sex as avoidance.

WHEN IVY HAD ever thought about what a gentleman would have to do to entice her into a romantic situation, she had never thought of "speak in a reasonable and logical manner." And yet here she was. She'd been unable to look away from him while he was dealing with the truculent lord. His measured tone, his levelheaded demeanor, his consideration—all of that made her insides melt.

She had been concerned he would start a fight, because that is what proud gentlemen did.

But he hadn't. Instead, he'd spoken to Lord Linehan as though the other gentleman was someone who could be reasoned with, who was intelligent enough to perceive what he was saying.

To put it more bluntly, she wanted to kiss him at this very moment. Even though they were in the main room of the club, with all of her staff around, and her sister—who would likely cheer if she acted on her desires.

Find things I want to take.

She knew what he was referring to, of course. She wasn't that unaware of her effect on him. She'd felt it, literally.

"What are you thinking about?" His low voice interrupted her thoughts. Although no, they hadn't—because he'd asked what she was thinking about, and he knew damn well what she was thinking about.

"What do you think?" she replied, slowly lifting her gaze to meet his. He drew in a deep breath, his eyes going to her mouth.

They were standing near one another, not even touching, and it felt as though he had his hands all over her.

He leaned to whisper in her ear. Still not touching her, though his breath tickled her skin. "I think I want this evening to end. I think I want to take what I can find. Perhaps in your bedroom."

"Oh," she gasped, the words sliding down her spine like a caress.

Was she thinking about doing that?

Absolutely she was. After all, she had no expectations. This wasn't going to be a permanent thing anyway. They both knew that.

She was already ruined, at least in the eyes of Society. And she didn't give a tinker's damn about anybody's opinion of her, not anymore.

"Sebastian." Octavia spoke sharply, making both of them jump. She had something in her hand, which she held out to him. "This came for you just now."

He glanced briefly at Ivy, then took the item, which appeared to be an envelope. Ivy stepped away to give him privacy, although part of her wanted to stay and read over his shoulder. But what if it was a love letter? What if one of his past ladies wanted to be current? Would she tolerate that? How could she say no if that was the case? They had no hold on one another. For that matter, she could go out and find an additional lover.

Only the thought of that made her chuckle, since the idea of even the one was daunting enough. How would she possibly juggle two?

She'd have to ask his advice: *How can I maintain a business while also maintaining romantic interludes with two gentlemen?*

"I have to go," he said, stuffing the letter back in the envelope. Ivy's heart sank. Another lady, then. "It's my sister, she needs me."

Ivy's relief warred with her concern that something serious had happened to his sister.

"Nothing terrible, I hope," Octavia said, asking Ivy's question.

He shook his head. "No, it's just—it's just something to do with the family." His expression was set, determined, and Ivy could see the vestiges of his former ducal self. Not that he hadn't looked like that in the club, but it was clear now that he had been consciously trying to tamp down his arrogance.

Albeit not always very well.

She had to admit that his arrogant aristocrat look was quite appealing, in a "tell me what scandalous things to do to you" kind of way.

Unfortunately he had to go take that demeanor elsewhere.

"I'll be back when I can," he said. He didn't wait to say anything to her, to acknowledge that there was something more here than employer and employee.

Nor should he, a voice reminded Ivy. *Remember? This is a game you two have decided to play. And like a game, it isn't serious. He doesn't need to treat you as anything more than what you are—his employer whom he also kisses on occasion.*

Men did it all the time, so could she.

"Please send our best to your sister," Ivy said.

"I'll take care of Byron and Keats," Octavia added.

"Thank you," he replied, speaking to Octavia. Barely looking at Ivy.

Stop noticing that. This is just showing you what you already know to be true.

She and Octavia watched him leave the club, stopping to say something to Samuel, and then to Henry, and then out the door.

"I wonder what that is about," Octavia mused. "Maybe they've discovered it's all a mistake, and he's still a duke."

Ivy held her breath for a moment as Octavia's words resonated through her. That would be a wonderful thing for him. Although it would foreclose on her short career as a sexual adventuress. Still, a small price to pay for his returning to the life she knew he must love. Who wouldn't?

Power, prestige, money, lands, parties.

All of it, to a lesser degree, had been within her grasp. Before her father gambled with fate. Hers, specifically.

Did she miss it?

She hadn't thought too much about that before. She'd assumed she had missed it, but when she considered it, she realized she didn't. Not in the way that would impel her to try to return.

Which meant that if Octavia was correct, he and Ivy would not meet again, beyond a perfunctory goodbye. There was no place in a duke's life for the scandalous owner of a gambling club.

And she would be fine with that. She *would*.

"No," SEBASTIAN SAID, waving away the hansom that had slowed near him. He'd get there faster in a cab, but he didn't want to be cooped up inside. It was odd. Now that he'd been on his own—for what, a week? two?—he treasured his freedom of movement. A duke was free to do whatever he liked, of course, but there were always people around, trying to help, or asking questions, or requiring assistance of some sort.

Being a regular person, a mere illegitimate son, meant that he was answerable to no one except his employer.

Ana Maria's note hadn't said much, just that he should come straight away and that nobody was in danger. So why was she sending him a note this late in the evening?

He had deliberately avoided thinking about her and Thaddeus since he'd come to Miss Ivy's. Not difficult, since the work was so engrossing. But now that he was allowing himself to, the emotions were roiling within him, making him aware he hadn't truly dealt with anything yet. Just smothered it under a pile of work and desire.

The duke's town house wasn't very far from Miss Ivy's, and he was there before he truly wanted to be—then again, the trip could have taken years, and he would have thought the same.

The door opened as he walked up the steps, making it obvious they'd been anticipating his arrival.

Fletchfield greeted him at the entrance. "Lady Ana Maria is waiting for you in the library," he said. He gestured toward it as though Sebastian would have forgotten, and Seb had to suppress his annoyance. He hadn't been gone *that* long.

He strode toward the library, flinging the door open and stopping when he saw both Ana Maria and Thaddeus. Both of whom looked guilty.

"What's going on?" he asked, glancing between the two of them.

Ana Maria rushed forward, her dark eyes glistening. She was always prone to tearing up, but that didn't explain why Sebastian felt a reciprocal prickle in his eyes.

"It's so good to see you," she said, clasping him in a tight hug as she buried her head on his chest. He looked over her head at Thaddeus, who appeared to be his usual impenetrable self, albeit not in uniform, as he usually was.

Of course. He'd had to resign his captaincy to take over as the duke.

He wore clothing that Sebastian might have chosen himself for an evening at home—an elegantly tailored suit, crisp linen, and polished boots.

Sebastian saw the glint of his father's signet ring on Thaddeus's finger.

"What's going on?" he repeated, directing his question at Thad.

Ana Maria released him, dabbing at her eyes and going to sit on the sofa. Thaddeus went and sat behind the desk—previously Sebastian's desk—and gestured for Sebastian to sit also.

It made sense that it would ache, to be here and not belong, but that didn't lessen the sting. He didn't want to sit, he didn't want to be here at all.

This was why he had stayed away. It was painful to be in a place where he wasn't who he'd thought he was. That was why reinventing himself at Miss Ivy's suited him.

Not to mention the lady herself.

"I asked your sister to send the note. So if you want to blame anyone, you can blame me."

"But I agreed," Ana Maria rushed to add. "And Thad wanted to wait until tomorrow, but once I heard he wanted to speak to you, I knew I couldn't wait."

"You haven't said what it is." Sebastian spoke in a curt voice.

"I need your help," Thaddeus said, in a tone that didn't sound at all like Thad. Mostly because him asking for help was like Sebastian wanting advice on how to seduce women—it didn't happen, and what's more, it wasn't necessary.

"He does," Ana Maria echoed. "And I do, too."

Like Thad, Ana Maria was garbed for an evening at home, albeit in far more lively colors than the monochrome Thaddeus. Her gown was made of blue patterned silk, the fabric shot through with gold thread that created a shimmering effect. He didn't think she was sweeping floors in that outfit, thank goodness.

"What kind of help?" Sebastian couldn't contain his skeptical tone. Because it was late at night, and he didn't think Thaddeus needed the kind of help Sebastian was likely to offer at such an hour.

"It's your valet and your secretary. They're arguing over who will prepare me for whatever party they've said I have to go to." Sebastian wanted to laugh at Thaddeus's clear tone of disgust. And at what an obvious ploy it was. "Both of them believe they are the proper person. But that's not even the half of it." Thaddeus ran a hand through his hair in clear frustration. "I don't know how you do it—did it." He gesticulated at the desk, which was strewn with papers. "There's always something to be done."

"And?"

"And I don't want to do it." Thaddeus looked at Sebastian, who was still standing. "For God's sake, sit down." He sounded more like his usual self when he was ordering Sebastian to do something.

Sebastian sat, relieved Thaddeus hadn't changed that much.

He regarded the two of them for a moment as he crossed his legs. "Tell Hodgkins and Melmsford that Ana Maria will be taking care of it from now on. That way, neither man loses face." He exhaled. "As for the rest of it? You don't want to do it. How is that my problem?" He paused. "I don't wish to be cruel, but this isn't my life anymore."

He hadn't needed to hurry over here just to resolve a pride squabble between servants. But he supposed he wouldn't point that out to either one of them.

"Yes, it is." Ana Maria spoke in a passionate tone, leaning forward in her seat. "You belong here, Seb. Fixing the issue between the valet and the secretary so quickly proves it. You belong here as much as Thad and I do."

Sebastian was opening his mouth to reply when Thaddeus spoke.

"It doesn't matter who has the title. We're family."

Sebastian's words froze in his throat. *We're family.* They were, and yet he didn't know if he could be here. Not just because he was too proud to return to a place where he wasn't the same person anymore—he wished that weren't true at all, but he had to admit it was, partially—but because he didn't want to be here. He wanted to be somewhere where he had a purpose, one that was his alone.

He didn't want to end up like his mother, desperately clinging to a situation because it was more comfortable than the alternative.

"I'm not as good at this as you are, Sebastian." Thaddeus shook his head in disgust as he regarded his desk.

"He has been wonderful," Ana Maria retorted.

Sebastian allowed a half smile to curl onto his lips. "I thought I could never live up to the responsibilities either, at first. Give yourself time, Thad. It took me at least a month before I was comfortable. It's only been two weeks."

"Two weeks without you in the house." Ana Maria kept her gaze locked on him. "We want you back here. We miss you. And you could—"

She hadn't even finished speaking before Sebastian was shaking his head. "No, you don't want me back. I know you miss me, but if I return things will be as they were, only not—I'm not the duke. I'm Mr. de Silva, the illegitimate son of the late Duke of Hasford, God rest his malleable soul." Images of her, of Octavia, of Mac, even of Samuel and Henry, filled his brain. They needed him. Or, more accurately, he needed *them*.

"I don't want to be here, Sebastian. I don't want to take care of all of this."

"And you said you'd help with my debut," Ana Maria added.

Sebastian frowned. "All I'd do if I return is drag you down. You deserve to enter Society with as little scandal as possible. It's already going to be awkward, what with the change in circumstances. But if I'm there, everyone will be talking about me."

"I'd be fine with that, honestly," Ana Maria replied. She grinned. "I *like* talking about you." She tilted her head back as she continued. "How much trouble you like to get into, that you used to drool in your sleep, your hatred of tea."

It would be amusing if he weren't so uncomfortable being here.

"You can't hide from who you are, Ana Maria." She straightened in surprise. At his sharp tone? "I am not the duke. Thad is. You are the daughter of the Duke and Duchess of Hasford, and you deserve the chance to be seen for who you are. And you are wonderful," he added more softly. "I can't hide from who I am either. And who I am, at the moment, is the employee of a gambling house." *And I'm pretty good at it, too.*

He hadn't realized just how proud he was of his work until now. He'd been so intent on forgetting everything that came before, concentrating only on the work at hand, that he hadn't reflected on what he was learning. Who he was becoming.

And that he had goals that extended beyond his time at the club.

"There's no way I can persuade you to come back?" Thad rose from his chair, clasping his hands behind his back as if he were at military attention. "If there's anything I can do to make you reconsider, I'll do it."

Sebastian took a deep breath. "Look, I don't know for how long I'll need to be away." He shrugged. "Come to me in a few months, perhaps? Maybe with another idea for how this could work?"

Thaddeus leaned back in his chair. "I will do that." It was a promise. "But you have to give us your word you will give me a fair hearing. When I come to you."

"And you have to visit at least once a week. I miss you so much, Sebby."

Ana Maria's voice trembled, and Sebastian felt his chest tighten in response. He wasn't certain he deserved Ana Maria's love—he wasn't certain anyone did, honestly—but he wouldn't deny her request.

"I will. Two days from now." Tomorrow there would be things to discuss about the Masked Evening and planning to be done for the next event.

"I'll expect you," she said with a smile.

Sebastian rose, not wanting to be in the house for a moment longer than he had to. Eventually he could do it, but not now—not until he knew who he was, not just who he was not. "Thank you." He cleared his throat. "For your care. I wish we could be as we were, but that's just not possible. But we might end up being better."

Ana Maria and Thaddeus both looked startled, and he wondered if he had ever said anything this profound before. Not that it was that profound, not compared with people who regularly declaimed very important things, but his previous interactions with them had never touched on anything close to that—it was unspoken, who they were. It was known. And now it wasn't any longer.

"Two days," Ana Maria said.

Sebastian nodded, then glanced at Thaddeus, who returned his nod.

He walked out the door, his chest tight, his heart hurting. But knowing that for him, at least, there was no other way.

SHE HADN'T INTENDED to wait up for his return. It just happened.

Octavia had gone to bed about an hour ago, rolling her eyes in disbelief when Ivy said she still had some things to go over. Carter had followed a few minutes later, stifling her yawns with her apron.

Ivy did have things to do, she always did, but she couldn't concentrate, not with knowing he was out there and not here. The only beings who were inside were her, her sister, and his dogs.

The dogs would likely be able to help in a dangerous situation, but she would much prefer to have him here. For obvious reasons.

She smoothed her expression as she heard footsteps coming down the hall, and then his head appeared in the doorway to her office.

"You're back!" she said, as though startled out of her work. She'd carefully put a stack of papers on her desk and had even managed to glance at some for a few seconds.

"What are you still doing up?"

His hair was disheveled, as if he'd been running his fingers through it, and he'd undone his neckcloth, revealing his bare throat.

She gestured to the stack of papers. "I was too

excited about this evening to sleep, so I thought I'd work through some of this."

He walked into the room, his expression unlike one she'd seen on his face before.

"Are you all right? Is your sister all right?"

He sat down in the chair, the one she'd begun to think of as his, swinging one leg over the other. "I am, and she is fine."

"That's a relief. But if you will forgive the intrusion, you don't seem fine."

He dropped his head to gaze at the floor. "I don't know what I am." A pause, and then his head shot up and he met her gaze. "And that's the problem. I don't know what I am."

"Is this about being a duke or not?"

He nodded. "Yes. I've tried to just put it behind me, as though it was something that was in the past, and I wouldn't have to deal with it, but it doesn't work that way. There are always entanglements."

"What kind of entanglements?" It hurt to see him so unlike his usual self.

"My sister, my cousin, my staff. My dogs," he added after a moment. "I promised my sister I'd visit."

"I was wondering why you hadn't. But it wasn't my place to ask." And she wasn't sure she wanted the answer anyway. What if one of his visits persuaded him just to return permanently?

He snorted, giving her an amused look. "So it's perfectly fine that we've kissed, that I've put you on that very desk and had my hands on you, but you can't ask me if I'm going to see my sister?" He shook his head in mock dismay. "Miss Ivy, you are as hypocritical as some gentlemen of my acquaintance."

Her cheeks turned red, both from embarrassment at the truth of his words and at the words he was saying, evoking the images and feelings she'd had when they'd been doing those things.

"You know," she began, "I had a similar experience to yours. Not as extreme—I certainly didn't lose a dukedom—but I did lose what I had known about myself."

He leaned back in his chair, his expression thoughtful. "Is this when you are going to reveal something about yourself, something personal that blurs the line between employer and employee?"

She made a noise indicating her rueful recognition of his pointed comment. "As you observed, we are far beyond that now." She raised one of her eyebrows. "Far, far beyond that," she said in a wry tone. "But if you don't wish to talk about it, if you want to go to bed or something—"

"Go to bed with you?" he asked.

Her eyes widened. "No! I did not mean that at all." She'd forgotten they'd discussed that much earlier in the evening.

He chuckled. "I knew you didn't, more's the pity."

Although a part of her wondered if she *did* mean it, at least partially.

He tilted his head, regarding her. The slight lift to his lips indicating he might have figured out what she was thinking. "I want to hear it. I want to hear *you.*"

Chapter Thirteen

"You probably know I wasn't raised to be the owner of a gambling den," Ivy began.

"Who among us is?" he shot back, making her laugh.

"And it's unlikely that someone as lofty as you were would ever have heard of my family, but we came from good stock. My father was a baron, and my mother was the daughter of an earl." Her face grew sober. "She died soon after Octavia was born, and our father raised us." She met his gaze, a wry smirk on her lips. "Not very well, as you likely can see."

"Go on," he urged.

"And my father was . . . *careless* with our upbringing. He didn't seem to notice if things were wrong."

"Sounds familiar," he replied. If his father had been more observant, if he had realized what kind of woman he'd taken as a second wife—it all would have been different. If his father had just asked more questions so as to discover the truth, they would not have even gotten married in the first place.

Sebastian wouldn't have been born, for one thing. He wasn't going to be so mopey as to say that would have been a better thing—he liked being alive far more than he would like not being alive. But how he came into being complicated things, clearly.

"And he also was reckless in a few important ways." She took a deep breath. "He gambled recklessly, for example."

"And yet you have opened a gambling house?"

She nodded ruefully. "I know. It seems ridiculous, but it is something I am good at."

"So what happened?" Because something had to have happened. It always did. And if it hadn't, it always would.

She shrugged. "My father lost a wager, one where he'd staked me. I was supposed to be married to a Mr. Fallon. He'd won honestly, and he had every right to take me."

He had every right to take me. Sebastian felt his throat tighten at hearing how close she'd come to having her life irrevocably changed because of a feckless parent—not that he had anything in common with that, did he?

"But then you did something," he said. Even without her telling the story, he knew she had done something to change her fate. It was impossible to know her for more than a few minutes and not realize she would not settle. Not for an unpleasant future, not for a less than completely loyal employee, not for a mediocre gambling house.

"I did." Her expression altered, to one that was both mischievous and chagrined. "I challenged Mr. Fallon to a new wager."

"What were the stakes?"

She hesitated. Were her stakes as scandalous as the ones he'd imagined? And if they were, would she permit him to go punch this Mr. Fallon in the jaw for having dared at all?

Thank God she had won.

"The stakes were that if he lost, I would not have to marry him." Another pause. "And if he won, I would marry him." He heard her take a deep breath. "I tried to leave that as the wager, but he pointed out—rightly—that he had already won that particular bet. It would be ungentlemanly for me to try to win the same bet over again." She bit her lip as she regarded him. "So I promised that if I lost, Octavia would marry his oldest son."

He absorbed what she'd said, reviewed it in his mind against what he knew of the sisters. "She doesn't know, does she?"

She shook her head emphatically. "No. And I haven't had the courage to tell her. She would be furious. But I knew"—and she leaned forward, her expression fierce and determined—"I knew I would win."

"Gamblers are always that confident, but you know as well as I do that their confidence doesn't always guarantee the results they want."

She lifted her chin. There was the ferocious lady he'd come to know—and desire.

"I had a plan if I lost. I had enough money to send her to our mother's sister. Our aunt. She doesn't like us, she never liked our father. Octavia wouldn't have forgiven me either way, but at least she wouldn't have had to marry my stepson." A wry expression crossed her face. "And I knew Octavia would find a way to escape sooner rather than later. While still despising me." She paused. "But I won. And then our father died, and I took my money, plus what he'd left us, and came here."

"I think you should tell Octavia about the wager," he said, her shaking her head in refusal even before he'd finished speaking. "She trusts you to take care of her. She deserves to know."

"I can't. Not yet."

"Just think about it. You'd have had to tell her if you lost, after all."

"I'll consider it," she replied tersely. "So when I won," she continued, "I took it as a sign that I should do something with my gambling knowledge."

"No wonder you were so irate when I said your face was expressive."

She raised her eyebrows. "I believe you said, *You'd make a terrible card player*, when, in fact, I am an excellent card player."

Except he could read her, at least in certain things.

"I stand corrected," he replied mildly.

Her eyes narrowed, as though she knew what he'd said didn't match up with what he felt. Perhaps she *was* an excellent card player.

In which case he should try to shield his thoughts from her, given how often they ran to them being naked and supine together.

Or not.

She did want to play, after all, didn't she?

"THANK YOU," she said.

He frowned in question. "For what?"

She shrugged, feeling more vulnerable than she had in months. She had just shared something with him she hadn't even told her sister, for obvious reasons. It had barely been two weeks, and yet she felt as though she could trust him.

That was even more rare than kissing. Although the kissing was nice, too.

"For listening."

Her heart did a funny little flip at seeing his lopsided smile. It wasn't a smile meant to charm or seduce; it was a genuine smile borne of genuine emotion.

At least she thought so. If it wasn't, he was a far better card player than anyone she'd ever met, and she would have to ensure she never wagered with him.

Unless she was willing to lose. Which would depend entirely on what they were wagering.

God, she hoped he wouldn't leave to go back to his old life before she'd gotten all of her questions answered.

"I am honored that you confided in me, Miss Ivy." Her breath caught at how sincere he sounded. First her heart, now her lungs.

He was affecting her entire body. And this time, it wasn't with his touch, but his words.

"I didn't know what I was going to do with myself when I lost my title. I thought I'd lost who I was. And I could have, if I'd let it. But then I met you. Call it luck," he said with a grin.

"I told you I was lucky," she said smugly.

"You did. Remind me not to play games with you. Unless I am willing to lose." His gaze slid silkily over her as he spoke, and she shivered in response.

"So who are you?" she asked after a moment.

He looked away from her as if pondering the question. She saw his thoughts flit across his face, and felt her breath catch—again—at the raw emotions she saw there. So many, and so varied. From regret, to anger, to hope, to satisfaction.

"I don't know yet. Not entirely. But this work, and this," he said, gesturing to the space between them, "this is allowing me to find out."

This.

This relationship. This situation. This game.

It would only last awhile, she knew that. He would eventually return to being who he was before—not a duke, but a gentleman. She knew his family would present a solution to the problem that would allow him to maintain his pride while still maintaining his previous circumstances.

But in the meantime, while he was here, he was hers. Hers to talk to, to spar with, to confide in. To kiss. To do more than that.

She wanted more than that. And his body's response told her the same, although she wouldn't just assume his brain would follow his body's inclination.

Although then she'd have to say it all aloud, which made her internally cringe with anticipatory embarrassment. But how could she do it if she couldn't even say it?

"This is more than I'd expected," she said at last.

He met her gaze. "So much more."

She rose and began to walk toward him. He stood also, but didn't move, just waited for her to approach. She liked that. That he wasn't rushing her. That he was confident enough that she would come to him to just wait.

"Thank you, Sebastian," she said, raising herself up on her tiptoes so she could kiss his cheek.

He turned his head, and she wondered if he was going to kiss her again. But he didn't; he lowered his mouth to just below her ear and pressed his lips to her skin so softly it almost made her cry.

"Thank you, Ivy."

He lifted his head and gazed at her with a single-minded intensity that she felt through her entire body.

"I'll be heading to bed," she said in a quiet voice.

"Good night, Ivy," he said, just as softly.

"Good night."

Knowing, as she walked out of the room, that this—whatever *this* was—meant far more to her than it should. She would get hurt, she knew that. But she also knew that she would emerge from *this* a more knowledgeable and confident person.

"WHERE ARE YOU going?"

Octavia seemed to appear out of nowhere, her expression avidly curious. As it usually was, Sebastian had observed.

"I'm off to tea with my sister." Ana Maria's politely worded summons had reminded him that he had promised, that she was only free this afternoon, and that she would chase him down if he didn't appear by four o'clock.

"Oh! Your sister, the lady who brought Byron and Keats? Can I come?"

Sebastian opened his mouth, not sure of what to say when she answered for him.

"Oh, of course I can't. You haven't seen her much since you left, and it would be awkward if I were there." She looked mournful, and Sebastian almost found himself urging her to come with him. Even though she was correct in that it would be entirely awkward.

"But you'll have to bring her to have tea with me and Ivy soon," she added, her face brightening.

Octavia was possibly the most mercurial person he'd ever met. He felt as though he could get whiplash from her constant shifting of emotions.

"Ivy and me," he heard her sister say.

He turned to see her, dressed in a plain gown that indicated she was about to retreat to her office for paperwork. Because she did that most days, and then worked in the evenings. How much did she sleep? She must be exhausted.

But she didn't look it. She appeared fresh and cheerful, giving him a conspiratorial glance as she approached.

"Me and Ivy just sounds better," Octavia protested.

"Our governess would be ashamed of you," Ivy replied, but her tone was amused.

"'Our governess' meaning you? Yes, you should be ashamed of yourself," Octavia said.

Of course. She'd mentioned her father being feckless, leaving the raising of Octavia to her older sister. Ivy had been responsible for Octavia's education as well as her survival? Small wonder she was so protective of her younger sister.

It was how he felt about Ana Maria, even though she was older than he, in years, at least, and had proved herself to be perfectly capable of her own survival. Perhaps it was a better descriptor to say he was concerned with her happiness. That was why he'd been so insistent she finally have a coming-out party, that she indulge herself with beautiful gowns and all the books she'd been denied the reading of while toiling under his mother's stern gaze.

"You are seeing your sister?" Ivy asked.

He nodded. "I'll be back an hour before the club opens."

"Unless she persuades you not to come back."

Sebastian's denial froze on his lips. What would he do if Thaddeus and Ana Maria had concocted some plan that would allow him to keep his pride as well as his position?

Two weeks ago, he might have leaped at the chance.

But two weeks ago he hadn't had the bone-deep satisfaction of a job well done. Two weeks ago he hadn't met her, hadn't kissed her. Hadn't touched her. Hadn't tromped for miles with her sister and his dogs through parts of London he would have never seen if he hadn't lost his status.

"I'll be back," he repeated, striding toward the door, an uneasy feeling creeping through him.

He was never uneasy. If anything, he had always been entirely easy—satisfied in his life, confident in who he was, assured in his interactions with others.

Until now.

"Sebby!" Ana Maria launched herself at him, making him stumble backward almost back out the front door.

He wrapped his arms around her and hugged her tightly. He'd forgotten—or he'd tried to forget—how much he cared for his sister.

"How are you?" he said, stepping back and holding her at arm's length.

She looked wonderful, but that didn't mean she necessarily *felt* wonderful. She wore a fashionable day dress that would be impossible to clean in, not only because of the pale pink color, but also because of the vast amount of fabric and ruffles and what he could only term as thingamabobs, since he had no idea what they were. Some sort of strewn-about decoration that caught the light as she moved.

"I am good." She spoke in a firm voice. He knew her tells well, which meant he knew she was not entirely good. She'd employed that tone frequently when speaking with his mother. "Come into the sitting room, I've asked for tea."

He followed her down the hall to the sitting room, a room he'd seldom used. It had been the late duchess's, the one she called him in to discuss his most recent outrageous behavior—beginning from when he would dodge his lessons by taking a horse from the stables to when he would dodge his responsibilities by bedding a widow instead of courting a debutante.

He wasn't dodging anything now.

Ana Maria held the door open, and his eyes widened as he walked in. She'd changed the room completely. Gone were the staid colors his mother had favored. Now the room was a riot of color, various shades of red mixing with gold and purple. It was lush and opulent, and it had a startling effect. It was also far more in line with his sister's natural energetic exuberance. It suited her, and he hoped it would continue to emerge. She had squelched it in response to his mother, but there was no need for that now.

"Do you like it?" she asked. She didn't wait for his reply before continuing. "I wanted something that would make me comfortable to be in. Thaddeus refused to let me see any of the bills, and then he kept asking about each item in the room. 'What about the credenza? You're going to change the color of the settee.'" She lowered her voice in a reasonable Thaddeus imitation. "So finally I just gave up and made the room precisely as I wished it. And," she said in a pleased tone, "it seems I have a talent for matching colors. A few of the other customers asked for my advice."

The room was remarkable, and the colors went surprisingly well with one another. Perhaps his sister had as many hidden talents as it seemed he did.

He walked around the perimeter of the room, taking note of the stuffed bookshelves, the two excessively upholstered chairs, the low table cluttered with scribbled-on bits of paper and invitations, two broken fans, and a wilted bouquet tied with a green velvet ribbon. All signs that Ana Maria was finally able to express herself.

"I love it," he said, lowering himself into one of the plush chairs.

She sat next to him, a wide smile on her face. "I am so glad. Thaddeus makes this odd face when he comes in, so I don't think he's all that fond of it. Even though he paid for it," she added with a chuckle. She glanced around, sighing deeply. "I feel comfortable here, Sebby. I don't feel comfortable many places, but I do here."

Sebastian leaned forward to take her hand. "Tell me about that. What is making you uncomfortable?" He narrowed his eyes. "Who is making you uncomfortable?"

She shook her head, taking her hand back at the same time. "It's not anyone but myself. I know you and Thad want me to find a gentleman and get married, but there isn't anyone who likes me in that way that I like."

He rolled her words around in his brain. "So—there is someone you like in that way who doesn't see you that way?" He wasn't accustomed to obfuscatory language, so it was difficult to parse her meaning.

Her cheeks blazed pink, and he knew he had somehow managed to figure it out.

"Never mind that," she said hurriedly. "How are you? We miss you. And I have to admit I don't entirely understand why you can't come back."

Sebastian took a deep breath before he spoke. "I'm not certain I can explain it to you." He gave her a smile. "Mostly because I am not entirely certain myself. Just that it wouldn't be right for me to be here, having been who I was, and have Thad here, as well." He leaned against the back of the chair. "It's like you doing what you used to do before—cleaning, and managing the staff, and everything else my mother demanded. It's not that you can't do it anymore. It's not even that you despised doing it, since I know you actually enjoyed certain parts of it, you perversely cheery person. But it wouldn't be right."

She tilted her head in thought. "I suppose that makes sense."

"Tea, my lady." Fletchfield walked into the room holding a tea tray, setting it down on the low table in front of them. "And may I say it is a pleasure to see you, Your—Mr. de Silva."

"Thank you, Fletchfield. It is a pleasure to be seen."

The butler smiled at Sebastian's wordplay, then nodded toward Ana Maria. "Is there anything else?"

She shook her head. "No, thank you. I just want to visit with my brother awhile."

"I will remind you that the Duke of Malvern is coming to take you riding in an hour."

"Thank you, I will be sure to change before then."

"Very good, my lady." Fletchfield bowed again, apparently for good measure, then walked out of the room.

Sebastian's eyebrows rose. "Riding with Nash?"

Ana Maria immediately began fussing with the tea things. "It's nothing. He's merely doing a kindness, taking me out riding."

Sebastian refrained from pointing out Nash seldom, if ever, did kindnesses for anyone. Beyond suggesting he take his newly unduked friend drinking, that is. And even that impetus was fueled by alcohol.

"So tell me about the gambling house. Miss Ivy's. Was Miss Ivy the one who said Byron and Keats should stay?"

"No, that was Miss Ivy's sister, Miss Octavia." He couldn't help but grin at thinking about her. Octavia's personality was as wildly exuberant as Ana Maria's newly redecorated room. And already as exuberant as he hoped Ana Maria would be, eventually. "Actually, I think you would like Miss Octavia. She is a bit younger than you, but you are similar to her."

He paused as he thought more; Ivy wanted her sister to enter Society, even though she would not.

Perhaps he could do her a good turn by encouraging his sister and hers to make their debuts together?

Although Octavia might not like that.

"I would like to get to know her. Both of them, since you're living with them now."

He laughed at her expression, a mix of disapproval and avid interest.

"It just happened, you know. Miss Ivy knew I didn't have a place to live at the moment, and since we both anticipated I'd be working a lot, and need to be at the club often, it made sense for me to stay there." *Plus I want to be certain she's safe.*

"Hm." Ana Maria took a sip of tea. She frowned, then shook her head as though to clear it. "Never mind that. I don't want to hear about anybody other than you. You promise me you are fine?"

He considered the word—*fine*. Fine, when said casually, could mean just fine. Not wonderful, but nothing was currently horrible at the moment. Was he that type of fine? Or was he the type of fine that meant that things were actually good?

He wished he knew himself.

But he could answer the question. "Yes, yes, I am fine. Perfectly fine."

"Good." She finished her tea, then glanced at his cup, a wry smile on her lips. "You haven't changed that much—you still don't care for tea."

"Perhaps that is why I was stripped of the dukedom," he said in a humorous tone.

She laughed in response, then her expression got serious. He braced himself for whatever she would say—prior to the unduking, he'd been incapable of refusing any of her requests. She made so few of them, and they were usually something small. Except when it came to living here. That he would not do, not until he had utterly failed in the outside world.

"I want you to promise me something, Sebby."

He took a deep breath. "You know I will try. What is it?"

She blinked rapidly, and her color heightened. "Well, a few somethings, to be honest." She took a breath, speaking rapidly. "I want you to come to at least one party with me, and you'll need to dance with me also."

"For you, Ana Banana, I will."

Her smile warmed her whole face. "And I want you to try to forgive your mother." She held her hand out to silence him. "What she did seems unforgivable—"

"It is," he interrupted.

"But she must have had her reasons. They may not ever make sense to you, but you do know she had your welfare at heart."

After she'd married her dead sister's husband. He inhaled sharply. "I will try." He regarded her steadily. "Have you forgiven her?"

She returned his gaze, unwavering honesty in her eyes. "I have." His sister. Kind in the face of cruelty, determined to survive, even if it meant peeling every potato ever dug.

Forgiving of someone who had done her a grievous wrong.

"Then I suppose if you can, I should."

"Thank you," she said softly. She nodded in thought. "And I will send invitations for my party to Miss Ivy and her sister, as well."

"I don't think—" he began, thinking of Ivy's likely response.

"I don't care." Her cheeks were bright red, matching her new curtains. "They are a part of your life, and I am a part of your life, and I want to know them."

"Couldn't you just invite them to tea?" Sebastian asked in a mild tone.

She made a face at him, and he laughed. "I could and I will, but that's not enough. It's obvious that they were gently raised, and I know what it's like to press your face against the glass, wanting to be invited in."

He didn't think Ivy had ever pressed her face against the glass. And if Octavia had, he would have wagered her subsequent action would be to smash the glass, but he didn't tell Ana Maria that.

"If that is all, I believe you have a riding habit to change into. For your ride with Nash?" he said, watching her closely.

Her reaction did not disappoint. He saw her catch her breath and her fingers tighten around her teacup, and then she swallowed.

Hm. He would never have thought his older sister and his close friend would be suitable for one another. They seemed more like brother and sister, at least in his view. He'd have to observe to make sure Ana Maria didn't get her heart broken. Because if she did, Nash was going to have his nose broken. Possibly also a few ribs.

"Yes, well, thank you for coming."

She rose, holding her arms out for a hug. He wrapped her in his embrace, wishing he could just settle and return here, the not-duke living in the glory of his former title. It would make both his sister and Thaddeus happy.

But it wouldn't serve him. He wondered if this is how his mother had felt when confronted with her possible futures. If it was, he might understand a little better why she had made the choice she did.

"I love you, Sebby," Ana Maria said, her words muffled in his chest.

"I love you, too," he replied.

Chapter Fourteen

"If you're going to work on the floor—"

"*Since* I'll be working on the floor," Octavia said, interrupting.

Ivy gave an exasperated sigh. "Fine. *Since.* Always with a mask on. Can I keep speaking?"

Octavia waved a lofty hand. "Go on."

The two sisters were in the sitting room, it being teatime. Ivy had been too busy with work to speak with Sebastian, and then they'd both been too busy at the club to do more than interact about club logistics.

Still, she'd noticed he seemed quieter than usual. She hoped nothing was wrong. She also hoped, perversely, that nothing was right—that his sister hadn't come up with a plan to have him return to the family fold. She'd miss him, not just because of *that*, but also because he was so good at engaging the customers, and they were already working on his next idea—Special Wager Night.

She shivered in anticipation as she thought about it.

"You were saying?" Octavia prompted impatiently.

"Yes. Of course." Ivy took a sip of tea, trying to settle her thoughts. "Since you'll be working on the floor, I have a few rules to insist upon."

Octavia rolled her eyes. "Of course you do."

"First, always wear a mask. The second rule is that you are not to flirt with any of our customers."

Octavia smiled. Flirtatiously.

Ivy pointed an accusing finger at her sister. "That is just what I am talking about. You will be working, Octavia. You cannot spend time flirting."

Octavia blinked her eyes in an innocent manner. "But you and Mr. de Silva, what do you call that?"

Ivy froze, wishing she didn't feel her face flush. Knowing, by Octavia's shrewd expression, that her sister had observed her reaction.

"Ha!" her sister crowed. "You are so easy to read." *You'd make a terrible card player.* Her tone grew teasing. "Did he do something to divert your attention?"

Besides manhandling me on my desk? Manhandling I very much enjoyed?

"Uh—"

Octavia clapped her hands and bounced in her seat. "I knew it!"

"Octav—" Ivy began in a warning tone, when there was a knock on the door.

Thank goodness.

"Come in," she called.

Carter opened the door, Henry lurking behind her. If such a large man could be said to lurk.

"I know this is teatime, Miss Ivy, but Mr. Henry has something urgent."

"Come in, Henry. Thank you, Carter."

Carter's gaze darted between Ivy and Henry in avid curiosity.

"You may shut the door behind you," Octavia said in a firm tone.

Ivy was impressed—Octavia was usually the sister who indulged the staff in whatever it was they wanted. Apparently she was changing with the news she would now be an employee herself.

Henry waited until they heard the door click closed, and then he addressed Ivy.

"You know it's Whist Night."

Yes, the one night during the week that Ivy let her staff manage the club. The clientele was generally older, the patrons appreciating the club's quiet so they could play their games.

"And that Lady Massingley is here—"

"On Whist Night?" both sisters said in surprise. Lady Massingley liked to gamble, a lot, and she seemed to like losing a lot of money. At least, that is what she did when at Miss Ivy's, and she kept returning, so that was the only supposition they could make.

"And she brought her nephew with her, too."

"So what is the problem? Besides the fact that the play is likely too staid for Lady Massingley."

"She and her nephew are talking about what happened the other night with Mr. de Silva and that drunk lord."

"What happened? Nothing happened. Mr. de Silva took care of it." Far better than she would have expected, honestly.

"He did, but that's not the story Lady Massingley and her nephew are sharing. From what they're saying, Mr. de Silva took offense at that lord's recognizing him, and banned him from the club. They're saying that they're wondering who'll get banned next, since the bast—that is, Mr. de Silva seems to be in charge now."

There were so many things Ivy could get furious about that she couldn't figure out which one to focus on first.

Fortunately, Octavia was willing to take up the challenge.

"But that is ridiculous! Sebastian didn't take offense at all, and he merely sent him home in a carriage. And Ivy is entirely in charge, she has hired Sebastian, not knuckled under to him." Octavia looked at Ivy, squinting her eyes. "Unless you have?"

Ivy's eyes widened in shock. "Of course not! Lady Massingley and her nephew are repeating gossip that isn't even true." She rose so quickly she slammed into the tea table, making the dishes clank together. "I'll just go see what this is all about." She couldn't keep her voice from trembling with self-righteous anger.

"Just a moment, Ivy," Octavia said, holding her hand up. "I know it is rich for me to say this, but perhaps you want to wait a moment to let yourself settle down?" Her sister gave Ivy an appraising look. "You seem rather—perturbed."

"I *am* perturbed," Ivy retorted. It was one thing for people to assume things about her because she was the club's owner, and formerly of the aristocracy, but Sebastian had done everything right and he was still getting maligned? That was intolerable.

"Then go on." Octavia made a shooing gesture. "I'll be right behind you."

Ivy walked swiftly out of the room, nearly running over Carter, who had been just outside the room.

She'd probably heard everything, but that couldn't concern Ivy now. What *did* concern her was Sebastian—she knew it had to have been difficult for him to keep himself from reacting as his former self would have—arrogantly, rashly, dangerously. That he hadn't, but was being castigated? Her club possibly held in ill repute?

No. That would not stand.

As she strode into the gambling room, she realized she felt as outraged and determined as she had those few years ago when her father had staked his daughter as a wager.

Then, she'd known if that outcome had occurred that there was no trusting her father not to do the same thing with Octavia when his luck had soured. It had been the thought of that, and not her own future, that had propelled her to act as she had.

And now she felt that same furious rage.

"Miss Ivy, the lady and her nephew are just over there." Henry had followed right behind her, and now was pointing to a table near the front, where anyone going in or out would observe its occupants.

Wonderful. Perhaps she should have sold tickets.

"Lady Massingley?" Ivy said as she approached the table. The lady in question turned, revealing red cheeks and bleary eyes, indicating she'd been imbibing more than she usually did.

Seated next to her was a gentleman, presumably her nephew. His gaze fastened on Ivy, and his lips curled back into a feral smile.

She did not like this nephew straightaway.

"This is the proprietor, Aunt?" he said, flicking his finger toward Ivy.

"Yes, Miss Ivy." Lady Massingley's expression faltered, as though she was realizing just what she was doing.

The lady was a good soul, Ivy had found; she loved to gamble, she didn't mind losing vast sums of money, and she always had a kind word for her dealer.

But, it seemed, she was also vulnerable to gossip, especially if it was dealt by a relative.

"I wish you would explain why Lord Linehan was treated so badly," Lady Massingley began, shaking her head. "Tossed out on his ear, banned from the establishment—"

"If he was banned, my lady, it was not by me. Perhaps his family asked him to stay away?" Ivy tried to keep her tone mild, but it was difficult, what with Lady Massingley's nephew's clear interest in stirring things up.

"I have not met your young relative," Ivy said, nodding toward the nephew.

"Yes, this is my nephew, Mr. Charles Jennings. Charles is staying with me for a few days." She smiled at him. "He is almost like a son to me."

Ah, no wonder. Ivy knew Lady Massingley had no children, and if this Charles was expecting an inheritance, it would be in his best interest to separate his aunt from the place where she lost excessive amounts of money. She couldn't blame him for the attempt, but she also wouldn't allow him to besmirch the club's reputation.

"And there is the bast—apologies, ladies," Mr. Jennings said, even though Ivy knew he wasn't sorry at all.

She felt Sebastian come up behind her, and she took a deep breath.

"Mr. de Silva," she said, turning to him. She nearly took a step back—he appeared to be as angry as she felt. *No, no, no, don't say anything*, she chanted in her head.

"Yes, Miss Ivy. Henry says there is some discussion as to what happened the other night?" As he spoke, his gaze shifted beyond her face, his eyes narrowing as he glared at Mr. Jennings. "Jennings." He spoke as though he did not like the other man.

"Hasford. Or no, you're not Hasford, are you?" Mr. Jennings's tone dripped with disdain. "Mr. de Silva. A bastard, as it turns out. A bastard who is responsible for turning a gently bred lord away from this establishment. Everyone is talking about it."

"Are we to be treated as poorly?" a man at a nearby table shouted. Ivy heard the increasing murmurs and hushed conversation with dread, knowing the entire incident could blow up in a matter of moments, ruining everything she'd worked so hard for.

Sebastian ignored the question, instead walking past Ivy to face Mr. Jennings. Mr. Jennings raised his chin, his expression belligerent. The two men glared at one another as Ivy watched, holding her breath. It would be perfectly within her rights to intercede, but if she did before Sebastian had a chance to resolve the situation, neither of them would know what he would have done.

Although if she did wait, and Sebastian escalated the situation, Miss Ivy's would suffer.

Business that depended on managing men's pride was very difficult.

"We moved in the same circles, once. I might not have liked you, but I did not think you would come into my place of employment and make a scene. I suggest you leave." Sebastian spoke quietly, but firmly.

Not perfect, but not inflammatory.

"Who are you to tell me to go? Are you the owner of this place?" Mr. Jennings sneered. "You've said it yourself, it is now your place of employment. You presumably draw a salary to obey a woman's orders. You do not dare to speak to me so."

"I dare, Jennings." Sebastian's voice held a menace that brought Ivy's anxiety back.

"You dare because you have nothing left to lose. Because you *have* nothing."

The club had stilled, most of the patrons not even trying to hide their eavesdropping. Ivy held her breath.

Sebastian straightened to his full height, his hands curling into fists at his side.

She'd not actually seen Sebastian as he must have been before—absolutely certain that whatever he did was right. And if it wasn't, that nobody would call him out on it. She suspected this was what he used to be like, before he was humbled—relatively—by his loss of status.

"If you believe I have nothing, then you won't mind stepping outside with me. You have nothing to lose." That was definitely a threat.

"You want me to leave the club because of what I have said about the poor treatment here? Because of what I said about you?" Mr. Jennings raised his voice as he spoke, meaning that everyone in the club, even the few who were trying to pretend they weren't curious, could hear.

Damn it.

Sebastian moved in close, leaning down to speak inches away from Mr. Jennings's face.

"When I'm through with you, you'll wish you had noth—"

"Mr. de Silva," Ivy interrupted.

He turned his head to look at her, and for a moment, it seemed he didn't even recognize her.

"Yes?"

She made a gesture for him to face her. He did, albeit slowly and somewhat menacingly. Once he had his back turned to Lady Massingley's table, she spoke.

"Mr. de Silva, please let me speak with Lady Massingley and Mr. Jennings. I am certain we can resolve all of this."

His expression was determined. Grim. He didn't move, just stared at her as though an internal conflict was raging within him—listen to his employer or sock Mr. Jennings in the jaw? She could see it as clearly as if he had spoken the words.

"This is what happens when you allow a bastard to mix with polite company. Small wonder his sister is making her appearance in Society without him. Or perhaps she is just as much of a nothing as her brother?" Mr. Jennings asked.

Ivy winced, her whole body stiffening in anticipation of his likely reaction.

He turned back, raising his fists as the people in the club uttered a collective gasp.

"Mr. de Silva." She spoke in a firm tone, one that would hopefully remind him he worked here. For her.

He didn't move.

She spoke again. "Mr. de Silva," she repeated, louder and more urgently.

He turned back. Thank God. She raised her chin, keeping her gaze locked with his. "Wait for me in the office," she ordered.

Would he obey? For a moment, she wasn't certain. But then, finally, he gave a brief nod, walking swiftly past her toward the door that led to the office.

She heaved a sigh of relief.

"Well! I wonder at you having such people working for you, Miss Ivy," Lady Massingley said. Her voice shook.

Ivy couldn't blame her; he was entirely and thoroughly menacing, and she saw now just how intimidating a gentleman could be when his anger was aroused.

She was shaking, too. These kinds of things happened every so often, but since Ivy was female, she was usually able to subdue the complaint. There had been a few times she had had to enlist Samuel and Henry, but if it came to that, the person with whom they were dealing was actually banned from the club. She couldn't recall more than a few times it had occurred.

But this—this had escalated far more quickly than ever before, simply because of who he was.

She'd have to have a serious conversation with him, and soon.

She'd have to ask him what world he belonged to, and demand that he live up to her expectations for as long as he chose to remain here. And if he chose his previous world?

She'd have to reconcile herself to whatever decision he made.

But in the meantime, she had to assuage Lady Massingley and her obnoxious nephew sufficiently so that the club wouldn't suffer.

It would be galling, given how provoking Mr. Jennings was, but a business owner didn't have the luxury of being offended by a well-paying customer.

Chapter Fifteen

Sebastian stalked past the maid, who took one look at him and darted away down the hallway.

That brought him up short. He was angry, but the only person he wished to terrify was Jennings.

That miserable backbiting worm.

He'd known Jennings when he'd been a duke—at that time, the other man had been as kowtowing and obsequious as could be imagined. Which meant that Sebastian neither liked nor trusted him. But he was pleasant enough when he tried, and Sebastian hadn't ever bothered with putting him in his place.

He should have. He should have found a place from which Jennings couldn't emerge, preferably at the bottom of a muddy trench.

Sebastian strode into Ivy's office, around her desk, reaching into the drawer where she kept her whiskey. He planted it on the desk, then looked back down for a glass.

None there.

Never mind, he didn't need a glass.

He unstoppered the bottle, raising it to his mouth as he took a swig. It burned, nearly as much as Jennings's words.

You have nothing left to lose. Because you have nothing.

"Mr. de Silva."

She stood at the doorway to the office, her lips pressed tight.

He put the bottle down slowly, gently, on her desk.

Her eyes tracked his movements, then returned to his face, meeting his gaze.

"Do you mind shutting the door?"

She frowned. "Pardon?"

"So you can rebuke me in private. I've had enough public humiliation."

Her eyebrows rose. "That was not public humiliation."

But she did as he'd asked, shutting the door and then walking toward him, keeping her eyes locked on his as she did.

"What would you call it?"

She uttered a derisive snort. "Two men taunting one another." She came to stand beside him. "Sit."

He opened his mouth to retort, then shrugged, sliding past her to sit in the chair facing the desk. The chair he'd sat in the first time he'd been here, when she'd treated him as a valuable resource, not just someone to flatter and cajole. Because she didn't know who he was. Who he had been.

Damn it.

"As I said," she continued, seating herself behind the desk, "two men taunting one another. Although I will say he started the trouble."

"The bast—" he began, then stopped speaking. Because *he* was the bastard, wasn't he? That was what Jennings had so nastily pointed out. But more importantly, she was his employer, she should be able to speak without interruption.

"The point is, Mr. de Silva," she said as his eyes narrowed. *Mr. de Silva?*

He supposed he deserved that.

"I understand you were provoked, but it is crucial—*crucial*—to maintain calm at all times, no matter how unpleasant a customer might be. My business depends on it, and so, by extension, does your livelihood."

That was a far more dangerous threat—that she'd fire him. That not only would he lose his position, the place where he felt valued for who he was, not undervalued because of who he used to be, but that he would lose her.

"I understand," he replied.

"I'm not finished," she said, holding her hand up. Her expression was stern. "This is not a game." She uttered a snort. "Despite what we provide to our customers." She lifted her chin. "I expect you will return to your family at some point."

She did? Just as Samuel and Henry had also predicted. That stung, too.

Didn't she want him to stay? Just a little bit?

"But I do not have that luxury. This, Mr. de Silva, is my life. If I am to support myself and my sister, to make certain we need not make any choices that will ruin our lives, I need to ensure my clientele is satisfied. Which means not getting a reputation as an establishment where it is likely its patrons will end up in an altercation with its staff."

His throat choked with all the words he wanted to say. That he knew he could not and would not say. Not if he wanted to remain where he was.

"I understand," he repeated. Forcing himself to breathe.

He'd been reprimanded before, of course; his mother was continually carping at him to change his behavior. But he'd never before agreed with the reprimander.

"I hope you do." She rose, and he did as well, his anger making his posture rigid. "If you will excuse me."

He clenched his jaw as she swept out of the room, not looking at him once.

Had he ruined whatever they had together? Was the game over?

And why did it feel like so much more than a game?

Goddamn it.

IVY WAS SHAKING by the time she reached her bedroom. She twisted the knob, exhaling in relief as she stepped inside.

"Are you all right?"

Octavia was seated at Ivy's dressing table, a concerned expression on her face.

Ivy took a deep breath. "I am fine."

Octavia's brow rose. "You don't look fine."

Ivy snapped. "How do I look, then? As though I've had a belligerent customer accuse the club of having an out-of-control employee? As though I saw the possibility of all this going away in an instant because some preening gentleman wanted to score points on someone he clearly resented? Because it was more important for two gentlemen to maintain their pride than for me to maintain my business?" She shook her head as she sat on her bed. "I'm so tired, Octavia. I just wanted to hire him to help out. I should have thought all this through as soon as I found out who he used to be." She gave a disdainful chuckle. "I should have known not to trust anybody from that world."

"That's not fair," Octavia replied, her tone irate. "Sebastian was provoked by that worm."

"Do you know how many times I've had someone test me at the club?" Ivy shot back. "You don't because I didn't let it become anything. I am not a former duke with an abundance of male pride."

It hurt, that he hadn't given a thought to anything beyond himself. That first time he'd kept a clear head and defused the situation. But the moment it became personal, from someone it was clear was antagonistic toward him? He reacted as any proud aristocrat would.

"You're correct, I don't know." Olivia rose to face Ivy, a pugnacious expression on her face. "And that's because you've been so determined to keep me out of everything. You know that I do not want the life you want for me. I want to do what you did, risk everything to make certain our future was secure."

"No, you don't." Ivy spoke in a voice thick with emotion. "Do you know—do you know what I risked?"

"Marriage to that old man, I know."

Ivy shook her head. If Octavia was determined to emulate her sister, she needed to know what her sister had done.

"Not just that. Father had already wagered that." She licked her suddenly dry lips. "Octavia, I need you to understand what I did. You might not forgive me—"

Octavia's expression froze. "Forgive you?"

Ivy swallowed. "Yes. I've wanted to tell you since it happened, but I needed you to come with me. I wasn't certain you—"

"Tell me what?"

This was the right thing to do. She'd known that even before Sebastian had said she should. She couldn't keep secrets from her sister. Nor could she continue to work toward what she thought her sister deserved—perhaps her sister would end up marrying someone from her own class, but that was up to her. Not Ivy.

It was hard to admit, especially for someone who had grown so accustomed to being in charge, but she couldn't manage Octavia's life anymore.

"I wagered you."

Octavia's eyes widened and her mouth dropped open. "Me? To marry Mr. Fallon instead of you? How could you?"

"Not that. Mr. Fallon had already won my hand from Father, so I said you would marry his oldest son if I lost."

Octavia wavered where she stood, her eyes blinking as she absorbed Ivy's words.

"You. Bet. Me." Her words emerged as though they were being forced through her mouth. Ivy kept her gaze on her sister, willing herself not to turn away. She'd held Mr. de Silva's feet to the fire for what he'd done, and Octavia deserved no less.

"I did. I had money for you to escape if I lost—I would be shamed for reneging on my gamble, but it wouldn't matter because I would have married Mr. Fallon anyway. But he wouldn't take the wager any other way."

"If you had the money to escape, why didn't you take it?"

It was a reasonable question, one Ivy had asked herself many times since that night. The short answer was she hadn't been thinking about herself, only about her sister. Though that made her sound like a martyr, and she certainly was not that.

"I don't know. I think—I think I felt as though you deserved the chance to leave more than I did."

Octavia shook her head. "You're an idiot."

Ivy took hope in Octavia's tone—it didn't sound as though her sister was absolutely furious with her.

"But you did win, so you didn't have to tell me what you'd done. Why are you telling me now?"

Another good question.

Ivy exhaled. "I suppose it's because I agree with you. You shouldn't have to do what I want you to do. If you want to work at Miss Ivy's, even without a mask, that's up to you. But you should understand the risks to doing anything—you might end up losing a wager, one that would have profound consequences for you and your family. Because you're my family, Octavia."

Octavia's expression softened. "I haven't absorbed exactly what you did, and I certainly don't understand why you didn't just leave, but I do know why you thought you had to do what you did."

Ivy chuckled. "That means you are far more understanding than I am. Since I still don't understand. But it meant we ended up here and are happy."

Octavia peered at her, and Ivy's breath hitched. Octavia's inquisitive look usually meant that Ivy was about to have to answer a very difficult question.

"Are you happy?"

Ivy exhaled. She had just promised to tell Octavia the truth, hadn't she?

She took a long pause as Octavia gave her an impatient look. "I suppose I am." That was a surprise. She had assumed, all along, that being in London was just a stop to another place. That when she had enough money, she would turn her back on the club and the city. But that would mean turning her back on her staff—Samuel, Henry, Mac, Caroline, and the rest of them—and not being in charge of something. Yes, she liked being in charge. She should admit that to Octavia, as well.

Although she'd revealed a lot for today, and she doubted that it would come as a surprise to her sister, anyway.

"I am glad to hear it," Octavia replied. "I am as well, although—" There was that mischievous smile that Ivy dreaded nearly as much as the inquisitive look. It meant that Octavia was hatching plans inside her beautiful brain.

"I promise," Ivy said, before Octavia could speak, "that I will never keep you in the dark again about anything. As long as you promise that you will never do anything to put yourself in danger."

"I promise," Octavia said.

"Are you happy here?"

Sebastian started at hearing Octavia's voice. He'd slept surprisingly well and had gotten up earlier than the rest of the household, taking Byron and Keats for an early morning walk.

Carter greeted him with a freshly made cup of coffee, and he was making notes on the Masked

Evening. There were things that had worked well, and he was generally pleased with the results, but he knew there were tweaks that could be made to improve the experience.

It kept his mind from wandering to what she had said, and how she must have felt. He had, as she'd said, jeopardized her livelihood, and that was unacceptable. For him as well as her. When he'd been a duke, none of that would have mattered; he could have tossed enough money to salvage the situation, or he wouldn't have noticed it was a problem in the first place.

But he had to be a lot more considerate now that he was not a duke. Something he would have argued with before—he'd never considered himself a selfish person, necessarily, but he'd never done anything for anybody else if it didn't also benefit himself. Even championing Ana Maria had reaped rewards, because she was his emotional resource in the household, and he hadn't wanted to lose that.

"Sebastian?" Octavia sounded impatient. Of course, he hadn't answered her question.

"Give me a moment. It's not as though you asked me if I wanted tea."

She snorted. "I know what the answer to that would be. A very condescending no." She peered at his cup. "Besides which, you already have coffee."

"Am I happy?" Sebastian repeated. He turned to look at Octavia, suddenly suspicious. "Why are you asking me that? Does your sister think I am not? I do not want to leave here." Especially not now, not when he had so much to prove. To her and to himself.

"No, should Ivy be involved in the discussion? You sound worried." Octavia's tone was mischievous. He'd never dealt with such a challenging lady before—that is, not one he wasn't sexually involved with. Ana Maria was far more staid than Sebastian was, whereas Octavia . . . well, it was clear how headstrong and determined she was. No wonder Ivy was so concerned about her younger sister.

"No, she should not be involved in the discussion," he rebuked. "Am I happy?"

"You know, if you say it a few more times, I am certain the answer will come to you. Tell me, were you this befuddled by questions when you were a duke?" She shrugged. "Never mind, likely you were, it's just that nobody told you."

"I was not!" Sebastian retorted, knowing she was teasing him, but still unable to resist the bait.

"Answer the question."

"Yes, I will. And—yes." And it was true, wasn't it? He hadn't thought much about it. Or he had, but he had thought about it in terms of what he had lost, not what he had gained. But he had gained—a purpose, a home of sorts, friends. Family, since he thought of Octavia as his irksome little sister.

"Excellent." She sounded smug.

"Why are you asking all of a sudden?"

Another shrug. "I asked Ivy last night, and it took her a bit to reply—you two have that in common— but she said she was, as well. And sounded nearly as surprised as you did. Another thing you have in common."

That smug tone again. He knew Octavia harbored not-so-secret wishes for him and her sister, her knowing looks and occasional smirks had told him that. But he didn't want her to get her hopes up for their future, especially after last night.

"Your sister and I—it's complicated." Octavia rolled her eyes, as though that was obvious. "I like her, and I like working with her. But we're too different, we're—"

"You're so similar!" Octavia expostulated. "You're both clever, you undervalue yourselves, and you are surprisingly fun to be around."

"Thank you, I think?" Sebastian shook his head. "I have never been accused of undervaluing myself, by the way. If anything, most would say I think too highly of myself."

"When you were a duke, doing your duke things, I suppose that was probably true. But ever since you started working here, you've been surprisingly thoughtful. As though you were aware that this was all new to you, and you didn't want to pre- sume. Undervaluing, as I said."

"None of that means anything in terms of me and Miss Ivy." He spoke in his most forbidding tone, the one that he used to use as duke when he'd been forced to bring someone to heel.

She waved her hand in dismissal. Apparently she did not speak Forbidding Duke. "I was just think- ing, though, that if you and she were to marry then she'd give up her ludicrous idea of buying a cottage at the seaside." Her disgusted tone made him laugh. "We could all stay here, and you two could run the club."

If you and she were to marry. He hadn't consid- ered that possibility, not since she'd said she never wanted to be married. But that was before. Before they'd kissed, before they'd started playing their game, before any of it.

Damn it. He couldn't think about that now. Even though that was all he wanted to think about now. He tried to keep his tone light when he spoke again. "What would you be doing in this remarkable fantasy of yours?"

"I'd be the hostess. Ivy is good at it, but she does not enjoy speaking with people as much as I do. I would be able to convince all of them to spend more money while you two were off somewhere counting it."

"Have you talked to your sister? Not about the two of us," he added hastily, "but about your own aspirations?"

"I have." Her expression grew more somber. "She said I should be free to make my own choices, but she reminded me that there are risks to everything."

He could hear her saying it, too. Tilting her head up proudly as she spoke, the physical embodiment of a woman who had taken a risk—taken several risks—and had emerged triumphant.

He admired her. Her future wasn't stripped away from her as his was; she had a course she could have taken, a course that most people would have accepted. Instead, she had forged her own path, not letting bad luck—literally—decide anything for her.

Whereas he? He had been sailing along happily enough until his future was yanked away with a few letters by a duplicitous mother.

What would he do if presented with a real choice? What would he do if he could *create* his own choice?

With a future that would be acceptable versus one that was fraught with peril?

That was an interesting question. One he hoped Octavia wouldn't ask him, since he wasn't sure how he would answer. He knew how he hoped he would answer, but it was impossible to know a thing, he'd realized, until you were in the thick of it.

If he were to prove himself to be the person he hoped he was, he would have to find a real choice so he would know for certain. A real choice that would tell him—and the people who cared for him—what he valued most.

Chapter Sixteen

"Can I come in?"

Ivy raised her head, her traitorous heart catching as she saw him. It had been over a week since the incident, and while they hadn't avoided each other as they had before, they hadn't spoken alone since then. She'd noticed he had kept himself perfectly in line, even though there had been some customers who had attempted to lure him into an argument.

What was it about people that made them want to cause that kind of trouble? She suspected that it was natural human behavior coupled with who he had been—his arrogance was tempered now, but it was still there. Imagine how insufferable some people found him when he was the duke, wielding his authority as lightly as if he was turning over a card.

He was dressed in an immaculate suit, and she wondered if he had pressed it himself, or—more likely—if he had cajoled Carter or Octavia or one of the club staff to take care of it for him.

"Please."

She gestured to the chair in front of her, folding her hands on the desk surface as he took his seat.

For a moment—a long moment—he regarded her intently. As though he was trying to read her mind.

I don't know my own mind, so you'll have no luck, she thought ruefully.

"Can I take you out today?"

She blinked, startled. "Take me out? Where?" She gestured to her desk, to the room in general. "I have a lot of work to do."

"You always have work to do. What about fun? Didn't your sister mention how you didn't have enough fun?"

Ivy felt her cheeks heat as she recalled what "fun" they had engaged in. No more of that; she was his employer, and she needed to prove she could maintain a calm mien. As opposed to, say, stroking his penis through his trousers. Among other things.

"I think I've had enough fun," she replied, trying to make herself sound stern and in command. Instead, however, she sounded wistful. Recalling how it all felt?

"We can do or not do whatever you like," he said, his gaze still intent on her face, his tone low and earnest. Not as though he was trying to charm her into something, but as though he actually wanted this. Whatever this was. "I thought we might visit some bookshops. Perhaps have a cup of tea at a café."

Books and tea?

"Are you running a fever? You are offering to drink tea?"

He grinned, crossing one long leg over the other. "I know that might seem odd, given my forthright opinion on the beverage." His expression grew serious. "But I miss you, Ivy. Not just—" And he gesticulated between them, his meaning clear. She felt herself flush even more. "I miss talking to you. I know you said eventually you wanted to take a cottage somewhere and read books and drink tea. And while it doesn't sound ideal to me, if it sounds ideal to you, I want you to get the chance to prepare. You'll need plenty of books if you're going to live there for the rest of your life."

Ivy's breath hitched at his words. *The rest of your life.* Before, when she'd wanted to escape and keep Octavia safe, it had sounded wonderful.

Now, however?

She had to admit it sounded boring. Admit it to herself only, though, since Octavia would get that smug look on her face and he—well, he might draw the wrong conclusion about what she wanted. She'd told him she would never get married when they'd first met, that she had no expectations. No matter how delightful their interludes were, they both knew they were temporary. She couldn't do anything to make him question that.

"Books and tea," she repeated, rising from her chair. "I'll get my wrap, and we can go out. Samuel will welcome the chance to open the club without me. He has been pressing me to relinquish some of the day-to-day duties."

"As I have," he murmured, getting up from his own chair as she walked by him. So close she could smell his scent, the faint warm odor of freshly pressed wool.

She missed him, too. Not just *that*, although now that she had experienced that, she missed it very much. But she missed him, the camaraderie they shared, the ability to analyze any situation quickly and come up with a clever summation.

Octavia was interested in the club, but she was interested in the day-to-day workings of it, not what would make it a success or a failure over the long term. He was the only person thus far who she'd sensed had as much global understanding of what it meant. Samuel came close, but Samuel hadn't much experience with the aristocracy, and didn't understand what it would take to make them loyal customers.

Sebastian did. Far more than she, and she was of the world also.

If she had to work with him, just *work* with him, doing none of the other things, she would be satisfied. She would have to be, especially since she would have to keep herself in check. He could likely find someone else to sate his appetite—had he already?—but she already knew she would not enter into such a relationship lightly, and she was too busy to entertain the prospect, anyway.

If only—

But the scenarios she was dreaming of would require that they meet outside of the club, beyond the employer/employee relationship, and it was inconceivable to think that a powerful duke would have ever treated her as an equal.

He treated her as an employer now, not as an equal. It didn't seem as if they would ever be able to bridge the great divide between them.

"WHERE TO?" SHE asked, taking his arm. He glanced down, only to frown when her hat obscured his view of her face.

"I've only been to the bookshop a few streets away," she continued, her words floating up from underneath that stupid hat. "It has a limited selection." She tilted her head to look at him. Much better. "It would increase sales if the proprietor rotated his stock more frequently, or at least cleaned more often. There are books there that clearly haven't been touched in years, judging from the dust. It does not offer a pleasant experience."

He smiled down at her. "You can't stop yourself from thinking about business, can you? Perhaps you should consider opening a bookshop near your little cottage when this is all a memory."

"Humph," she replied, glancing away as though uncomfortable. Interesting.

"I thought I'd take us to Hatchards. You haven't been there, have you?"

She shook her head. "No, though I've heard of it."

"And then tea. All the tea we can buy, and I will drink it."

She laughed. "It's not as though it is my most fervent hope that you drink tea, by the way. I find it rather endearing, honestly, that you loathe it so much."

"What *is* your most fervent hope?" He regretted the words as soon as they emerged from his mouth. He knew what his most fervent hope was, and it involved neither books nor tea. Damn it. He was trying to treat her as a friend, not as a lover. And yet here he was, asking her questions that might lead to a disconcerting place.

She exhaled, squeezing his arm as they walked. "I can't answer that," she said in a quiet voice.

Can't or won't?

Does it matter?

"The shop is just over there on the next street," he said, congratulating himself for not speaking the words aloud.

"Ah," she replied in a stiff tone of voice.

Hatchards was busy, and Sebastian and Ivy were separated nearly right away. She wanted to purchase some novels for Octavia, while he was hoping to find something to give Ana Maria. She'd received so few presents in her life that it was a joy to give her something as simple as a new handkerchief. Thankfully, since that was likely now all that he could afford.

He scanned the volumes on the shelves, shaking his head in dissatisfaction as he read the titles. Ana Maria had no need of books that purported to teach her how to live a righteous life; if anything, he wished there was a book that would give her instruction on how to misbehave.

Likely Hatchards was not the right establishment to find that kind of book. And it would be odd for her brother to give it to her, anyway.

Scratch that idea.

He browsed through a few more aisles, grimacing when he saw the collected works of Plato, Aristotle, and the other boring philosophers who thought they were better than everyone else.

He had thought he was better than everyone, too, and yet it turned out that he was entirely wrong.

"Ah!" he exclaimed, drawing a book from the shelf. Its illustrated cover featured a young woman wearing plain clothing, carrying a broom and a mop, a cap on top of her head. But the artist had given her a delighted expression, and there were curls escaping from the cap while an older woman with a witch's hat atop her head looked on, a fond expression on her face. *"Cinderella!"*

It was almost too perfect. He grinned as he tucked it under his arm, anticipating the look on Ana Maria's face when he gave it to her.

Perhaps he'd save it for the night of her party, since it seemed she was determined to have him there. At least he'd have a purpose, and he could borrow it to read if the ballroom and the guests became unbearable.

"OH, SHE'LL LOVE this one," Ivy murmured to herself as she plucked a book from the shelf. The title, *Count Peccadillo and the Lost Hours*, was written in garish red letters, a few trickles appearing to indicate blood dripping from some of the letters.

"There you are." Sebastian walked to her side, peering over her shoulder at the book. "That looks about right for Octavia I'd say." He sounded amused.

"Sebby!"

Ivy and Sebastian turned at the sound of the lady's voice. Mr. de Silva's sister stood in the aisle, a wide smile on her face.

She wore a purple cloak that ended halfway down, the skirts of her dark pink gown showing underneath. The cloak had black military-style frogs closing it, and the gown was ornamented by wide black bands of shiny fabric running vertically along the bottom. The entire effect was certainly remarkable, but it suited the lady's overall joyous demeanor. Ivy couldn't help but return the smile.

"Ana Maria," Sebastian replied, sounding stiff. "Miss Ivy, may I present my sister, Lady Ana Maria? Ana Maria, this is Miss Ivy."

Lady Ana Maria extended her hand for Ivy to shake.

"It is a pleasure to see you again, Miss Ivy. Perhaps we might actually have a conversation, now that I am not occupied with Sebastian's dogs."

"A pleasure."

Lady Ana Maria clapped her hands together and glanced between the two. "And you are both here, this is perfect!"

"Ana . . ." Sebastian began in a tone of warning.

"Hush." Lady Ana Maria spoke in an older sister tone of voice, one Ivy knew well herself. She shot a pointed look toward her brother, who immediately closed his mouth. "This is between me and the lady. Miss Ivy, I would like to personally invite you to my coming-out party. That is, I am well overage for a debutante, but I never got to . . ." she said, her expression regretful. "Anyway, I am finally having one, and Sebastian promised he would be in attendance. I would love it if you and your sister could come, as well."

"I don't think—" Sebastian tried again.

"Sebastian." There was that tone again. Lady Ana Maria had intriguing hidden strength of character, it seemed.

Ivy's chest grew tight at what he was likely thinking, if not about to say: *I don't think the owner of a gambling house is an appropriate guest at a young lady's coming-out ball. Even if we have touched one another with mouths and hands and such.*

"Thank you for the invitation, my lady, but—"

"No." Lady Ana Maria used her older sister tone again. "Please don't decline, I don't know many people, and I like even fewer of them."

"We have just met," Ivy pointed out dryly. "You could end up disliking me."

She heard Sebastian smother a snort of laughter. At least he wasn't trying to find a way to prevent her from attending.

"But you seem nice, and parties are fun—aren't they?" It sounded as though she might not actually know. "And Sebastian will be there because he promised he would, so you'd know someone. I mean, besides me."

Ivy knew it was the worst idea to accept, but sometimes one had to agree to the worst ideas because the person proposing them was so earnest and kind. Not to mention someone who employed the older sister tone as effectively as oneself.

"Yes, thank you. In that case, my sister and I will be there."

Lady Ana Maria's smile grew even wider, though Ivy would not have thought that possible. "I will send the invitations." She leaned over to kiss Sebastian on the cheek. "Goodbye."

She stepped away in a whirl of vibrant color, leaving Ivy feeling as though she'd been flattened by a strong wind.

"Your sister is very insistent," she said.

"Yes, she certainly is." He sounded rueful as he took her arm. "Let's pay for our books and then go find something to drink."

"Tea?" she asked in a mischievous tone.

"If I must," he groaned in mock agony.

She chuckled as they walked to the front of the shop.

AS IT TURNED out, there was a small café a few blocks from Hatchards. Sebastian glanced around to make certain he didn't know anybody there, since he didn't want to get into a fracas. Again.

Thankfully, the customers were primarily nursemaids with their charges. Unless he had mortally offended some child in some way, and he was fairly certain he hadn't, they could have their drinks in peace.

He glanced at the menu, shrugged, then handed it to Ivy. "At least they offer a variety of the loathsome beverages."

She took the menu, looking briefly at it before setting it down on the table. They sat across from one another, very close because the table was quite small, the chairs little spindly things that Sebastian thought were designed with women and children in mind, not with grown men who liked to sit comfortably.

"What will you have?" the server asked.

"Tea for two, please," Ivy answered.

The server nodded, taking the menu as she walked away.

"You didn't purchase any books for yourself. Only for your sister. Why was that?"

She looked self-conscious. "I suppose it is because I tend to think of Octavia first, and me second."

"You know that's not the way to live, don't you?"

She sighed. "I do, especially since my thinking about Octavia generally isn't in line with what she is thinking about herself. So perhaps I am not as altruistic as I think I am."

He leaned forward. They were only about six inches apart from one another. Her tobacco-colored eyes were focused on him, and he felt a sudden but not unexpected desire for her. To see those eyes sultry in passion, to have her gaze at him with sated approval.

Goddamn it.

"You are that, it is also that you believe yourself to be correct at all times, as well." He drew back as the server walked over to lay their tea things out.

"So I am nobly suffering for no good?" Her laugh was rueful. "That is remarkably idiotic. I should think about what I would like to do."

"And what is that, Ivy?" He held his breath waiting for her reply.

"You asked me before what my most fervent hope was. I couldn't answer. I wouldn't answer. But the answer is that you know, Sebastian," she said in a low voice, looking up at him with a purposeful look on her face.

"I believe I do," he replied, trying to keep his tone even and measured. "I didn't know if things had changed between us, and I didn't want to presume—"

"Things *have* changed between us. But not everything. I still want the same things I did before."

He took a sip of his tea. He still hated the taste, but it gave him a chance to think. He'd never had to think of what to say or how to say it to any woman he'd been involved with before—if things weren't mutual, then it ended. Simple as that.

But she was anything but simple. And he was anything but cavalier in his dealings with her. That had changed.

"I am glad," he said at last.

"You promised we would play," she said in a whisper. "And now that I know you aren't on the brink of ruining my livelihood with your arrogance and temper—"

He snorted in response.

"I want us to continue the game. It can only be for a short while, anyway."

It was on the tip of his tongue to ask why, but there was no guarantee that she would answer as he wished. Not that he knew what he wished in the first place.

Things were certainly a lot simpler when he was a duke. For the obvious power and money reasons, yes, but also because he hadn't had to care about anyone beyond his family. Or he hadn't bothered to care.

Now he cared. He thought he might care very much.

That unnerved him.

Chapter Seventeen

Ivy's body prickled with anticipation as they made their way back to the club.

Not that she thought they would walk in and he would immediately ravish her, but because she knew what she wanted. And now so did he.

Although if immediate ravishing was in the offing, she would acquiesce enthusiastically.

He had insisted on carrying her purchase, so both books were tucked under one arm, while he held her elbow with the other. The sun still shone, but the shadows were growing longer, and she knew there wasn't much time before she had to return to work.

But it had been a lovely respite. And things with him felt . . . better. If not settled. Because she was definitely unsettled when she was around him.

"I'm thinking about your fervent hope," he said in a low voice, the tone of which sent a shiver down her spine. It promised all sorts of things, things that could only be spoken of in quiet tones between the two of them. "And, knowing your inability to stop working for more than a few hours, I wonder if we can combine the two."

"It will take more than a few hours?" she blurted in surprise.

He laughed, a knowing chuckle that made everything warm all over.

"If I have my way, yes." A pause. "And I will have my way."

"Ah." Trying to keep herself from gasping or moaning or just wrapping herself around his entire body.

"The day after we first met, we spoke about a special wager night. Where the customers could stake whatever they desired. Or that their opponents desired."

She licked her lips, since her mouth suddenly felt dry.

"And what is your idea?" She sounded breathy. Something it appeared he heard, as well, since his grip tightened on her arm and he seemed to emit some sort of growl.

"I propose that we practice. Play the game ourselves to see how it goes. If you want to."

If she wanted to? He knew the way to her heart—no, not that, not her heart—the way to her interest was to combine her personal and professional passion.

"I do want to." So very much.

"I'll need time to prepare. I want to have everything as we think it might be when we do the real thing. So—three days? That would make it the day before Ana Maria's ball."

"That sounds excellent." As though she were truly an employer approving an employee's plans, and not an eagerly lustful female anticipating a partner's sexual play. "Will you require anything?" she asked.

"That is an intriguing question," he replied. His voice was full of wicked promise. "I require only your complete and utter participation. That if it doesn't feel right, that you will let me know. I may not win our specific wager, but I will walk away with your pleasure at the end of the night."

Her body reacted immediately to his words, her breasts feeling as though they ached within her gown. The image of him sucking her nipples made her breath catch, and she faltered so that he had to steady her.

"I plan to have you off your feet for the entire evening, Ivy, so this is a good start," he said, lowering his head to whisper in her ear. "Even as I am on my knees."

If she didn't have his arm for support, she would have definitely fallen over then. Because the image of him kneeling before her, his hands roaming on her skin, his mouth—well, his mouth just there, even though she wasn't certain that happened. But if women did that to men, then it stood to reason—and passion—that men did that to women, as well.

She wanted him to do that to her.

She wanted to do that to him.

She wanted it all. It was, as he'd said, her most fervent hope.

And it was only three days away.

SEBASTIAN STRODE DOWN the hall after escorting Ivy to her office. Not that she needed escorting, but he needed to be with her as long as possible.

He was sorely tempted to kiss her, but he wanted to ensure that she was as desperately hungry as he was, that she was anticipating their evening together with as much eagerness as a desert traveler coming across a cool spring.

Plus Samuel was waiting for her, so it wasn't practical.

He walked into his room, nodding at Mrs. Buttercup as he shut and locked the door behind him. "Afternoon, ma'am," he said with a grin. Byron and Keats weren't there, likely out walking with Octavia.

Good. He needed the time to be alone, so he could plot out just what he was going to do in three days. They would fuck, he knew that, but he also knew it wouldn't be a fast coupling. He wanted to savor it. He wanted to make it as pleasurable as possible for her, which meant taking his time.

Running his hands over her luscious curves, cupping her breasts in his hands as he lowered his mouth to lick and suck her nipples. Sliding down to kiss her belly, to grab hold of her thighs as his mouth plunged into her warmth.

And now he was hard, with only his hand as a recourse.

He stroked his erection with his right hand while he undid the placket of his trousers with the other, his cock springing free after he'd opened them. It took just a moment to put his hand inside his smallclothes to grasp himself.

It wasn't her soft, small hand, but it would do. Especially if he imagined it was hers, her bright, curious eyes watching him as she ran her hand up and down his shaft.

Perhaps she'd be sitting on the tabletop, her legs spread so he could see her soft folds as she stroked him. Watching his face to see what he liked, adjusting her grip and tempo in response. Putting her other hand to use on herself so he could see what she liked.

He gripped himself harder, stroking faster as he envisioned the scene. Thinking about her fingers rubbing herself, her eyes growing hazy as she brought herself closer to climax.

You first, he might whisper.

She'd shake her head, unable to resist a dare. A gamble. *No, you.* And she'd increase her rhythm on him, perhaps drawing her other hand away from herself to play and tug at her nipple as she kept her eyes on his cock.

He felt the orgasm growing, his movements more rapid, until he spasmed, feeling the climax through his entire body. Gasping at how intense it was, far more than what was usual when he was on his own.

Three days was a lifetime away.

"It's just us here, Ivy." Octavia waved at the closed door as she spoke. "Come on, tell me."

Ivy didn't bother to feign innocence. "He and I, we're—"

"Oh, Ivy!" Octavia launched herself toward her sister, wrapping her in an enormous hug. "I told him you should get married."

Ivy froze in Octavia's embrace. "Uh—we're not getting married."

Octavia drew back, a puzzled frown on her face. "You're not? But then what are you—ohh!" she said, her eyes wide. "You're—*Ivy!*" she said in a shocked tone of voice. "What happened? How on earth do you discuss such a thing? I am impressed by you, sister."

"Reach in that cabinet behind those bottles and hand me the whiskey. I'll need it before I tell you. But I will tell you—no more secrets, remember?"

A knock on the door made both of them turn. "Yes?" Ivy called.

"The post, miss," Carter replied. "And a footman brought something also."

The invitation to Lady Ana Maria's party. Something to distract Octavia with. "Come in."

Carter opened the door, handing the small stack of letters to Ivy. The invitation was on top, and Ivy picked it up and waved it toward her sister. "I forgot to mention this"—*because I was too preoccupied thinking about getting my hands on Sebastian*—"but Sebastian and I ran into his sister, and she said she would be sending an invitation to a party. I presume this is it."

Carter was still in the room, clear interest in her expression.

Ivy sighed. "We might as well all look at it." She undid the seal, then withdrew the letter and read it quickly, handing it to Carter. "It's in four days, we were invited to the Duke of Hasford's town house for a party to introduce Lady Ana Maria to Society. It's not precisely her coming-out ball, since she is a bit older than the usual debutante, but it seems as though she hasn't been properly introduced."

Carter handed the letter to Octavia, who barely glanced at it before addressing Ivy. "What will we possibly wear? It's far too late to get anything made up, and I don't know if we have anything suitable."

Ivy nodded. "I've thought of that. We'll go pay a visit to Madame Delyth's, she makes clothing for theater people, I am certain she will have something she can rig out that will work."

Octavia grinned in response. "Perfect! The two most unsuitable ladies in London wearing clothing that might have appeared on the stage. I do like your thinking, Ivy."

Ivy returned her sister's grin with a self-deprecating smile. "I know how to operate in a crisis," she said in an overly modest tone.

"I can't wait until the party," Octavia exclaimed.

And I cannot wait until the evening before, Ivy thought.

"Carter, can you go into our wardrobes and check if we have the appropriate accessories to attend an evening function?" Octavia asked.

Carter curtsied her acquiescence, a pleased smile on her face. Ivy knew the maid's status would be improved in her circle of friends if it was known her employers had attended a party at the Duke of Hasford's town house.

"Shut the door, if you please," Octavia called as Carter walked out.

The door shut behind her, and Octavia turned to Ivy, her expression of delight replaced with an interrogative look.

"You have to tell me everything."

Ivy felt a blush creeping onto her cheeks. "Nothing's happened yet!" she said. "I mean—"

Octavia's eyes widened. "So things have happened, but not all the things? My goodness, Ivy, you are far more adventurous than I would have imagined!"

It likely wasn't a good thing for Ivy's reputation that Octavia was so admiring.

"I don't know what has come over me, I have to admit," Ivy said slowly. "He's—well, he's good to converse with, and he is very sharp in terms of business. And then—"

"And then—?" Octavia prompted as Ivy fell silent.

"I do like him. Very much." Had she admitted as much to herself yet?

Likely not, since she was terrified of getting hurt. *Too late*, a voice chided in her head. *He's going to leave, and you'll suffer.*

"So why aren't you thinking of marriage?" Octavia asked, sounding both puzzled and judgmental. That was a talent.

"He hasn't asked." Of course it was far more complicated than that. But hopefully it would satisfy her sister.

"That wasn't my question." So much for satisfying Octavia's constant curiosity. "You came to London thinking we would only be here for a short time, just long enough to make us able to have a modest life on the beach or whatever." She sounded thoroughly scornful, and Ivy wondered at her own cluelessness not to realize that life would not suit Octavia, no matter how much it might suit Ivy.

Even though she wasn't certain it would suit her now. It was a terrifying thought, the idea that she might deviate from her course of action. Usually, always before this, she saw what she had to do and she did it. She didn't question herself or the steps she'd take to achieve her goals; she'd just do.

But now, the plan she'd laid out for herself wasn't as appealing. It wasn't just due to his appearance in her life. Although the sensual pleasure she'd felt with him definitely added to her wanting to stay here. How could she be a loose, scandalous woman in a small town?

Well, she could, but she would quickly run out of gentlemen to be loosely scandalous with. Never mind that the only person she wanted to do any of that with was him.

Drat.

"But it seems," Octavia continued, and Ivy had to remind herself what her sister was discussing, "that you might be rethinking all of that. Especially since I will not be accompanying you, no matter how enjoyable it might be to live in a place where every single person knows your business." She paused. "So my question stands—why haven't you considered marriage? If not to Sebastian, then to some other gentleman who strikes your fancy?"

All the answers that rushed through Ivy's head— that she needed to keep Octavia as her first priority, that no gentleman would want her given her scandalous past, or even that she wasn't certain she could stand to be with another person who wasn't a relation for the rest of her life—rang hollow, and she knew Octavia would see right through her.

She was scared.

Scared of committing to someone or something forever. Scared that things would have to change as her life changed.

She was scared. And that was not whom she believed herself to be, strong and determined. So she'd need to consider everything she knew about herself as well as what actions she wanted to take in the future.

The first step, thank goodness since it was the step she definitely wanted to take, was to be bold and adventurous with him, even though such behavior would ruin her in Society's eyes. But she wasn't in Society, her wager and taking her inheritance to purchase a gambling house instead of a husband had already taken care of that.

So she should do as she wished.

"Perhaps I will consider a different future," Ivy said slowly. "You've made it abundantly clear that you do not want what I had envisioned, so I should start to think what I want." She paused. "But he and I—that's not a permanent possibility. I just don't believe he'll stay out here when he could return to his aristocratic family none the worse for wear. He's slumming it with us, and eventually he'll leave." *Eventually he'll leave.*

If she kept repeating it to herself, would it hurt less when it inevitably occurred?

Octavia opened her mouth as though to argue, but apparently decided against it.

Ivy continued. "But that doesn't mean it's him or nobody. You're correct, I need to be open to the possibilities."

"Huzzah!" Octavia cheered.

"Huzzah," Ivy echoed.

The bigger question was what possibility would be the best one for her? And how would she possibly achieve it?

"YOU'RE CERTAIN YOU want five yards of ribbon, sir?"

The clerk accompanied her question with a curious look. Not surprising since Sebastian doubted he looked much like a person who would be dabbling in ribbon.

"Yes. Five different shades, a yard each." He kept his tone firm, hoping the clerk wouldn't ask him how he was planning to utilize the ribbon. *I'll be*

wrapping it around the lovely naked form of my lover,
and hoping she'll be doing the same to me.

My lover.

It was odd to think of Ivy, gorgeous, delightful, intelligent Ivy, as his lover. Not just because they weren't technically lovers yet, but also because it seemed such a narrow word for who she was to him. She was his employer, his friend, his fellow disgrace from Society.

He should thank Nash for bringing him to Miss Ivy's on that fateful evening, the same day he'd found that everything he'd ever known was a lie.

Only to discover, eventually, the truth about himself—that he would be able to survive and thrive, even without the trappings he'd taken for granted. That he could find connections that weren't dependent on who he was.

That he wouldn't return to that time, even if it were offered with all the trappings he'd taken for granted before.

"Sir?"

The clerk's tone was impatient, as though she had been speaking for some time.

"Yes, pardon?"

"Do you want the red or the blue?" The clerk held up two spools of ribbon, one in each hand. "I've already cut the purple, green, white, and pink."

"The red."

The clerk nodded, putting the other spool down and reaching for the scissors.

"No, all of it," Sebastian said. It was far too tempting an image to resist—Ivy swathed in ruby-red ribbon, lying atop the gaming table. Perhaps still wearing her stockings, but nothing else.

"All of it?" the clerk said in surprise.

"Yes." Sebastian dug in his pocket for his money, tossing coins and bills on the table. "Take what is owed." Since he had no idea how much any of this would cost, nor how much of his current money it would take. Just that he needed to buy it.

So much for leaving his aristocratic habits behind.

But it would be worth it. Well worth it.

"WELCOME, LADIES!"

The dressmaker greeted Ivy and Octavia at the door to the shop, waving them inside.

The first impression of the room was one of exuberance: bright patterned bolts of fabric on large shelves, boxes and bags stuffed with accessories of all kinds, spilling out their contents on the massive table in the center of the room. The proprietor was equally exuberant—the fabric of her gown was a dizzying array of colors, ornamented with randomly scattered flowers and bows. The effect was whimsically charming, and Ivy couldn't help but smile.

Even though the thought of her wearing something similar to Madame Delyth's gown was slightly terrifying.

"Come in, have a look around. Your note said you have an evening affair to attend?"

Ivy's eyes widened in shock until she realized Madame Delyth could not possibly have been referring to *that*.

Octavia spoke as Ivy was trying to keep herself from blushing. "Yes, we've been invited to the Duke of Hasford's home to honor his cousin Lady Ana Maria."

Madame Delyth clapped her hands together. "Wonderful! I believe I have a few gowns left from the production of *Twelfth Night.*"

"It's not a costume party," Ivy said.

"No, of course not. But the gowns were quite modern in construction, and they should be grand enough for a duke's home. Let me go find them."

She bustled out in a whirl of color as Octavia turned to Ivy, a delighted expression on her face. Ivy gazed at her sister, recalling how she had felt when she'd been fitted for her first evening gown. She'd been so naive then, even though she'd felt wise beyond her years. But at that time she'd envisioned a future with a kind, loving husband, a home filled with children, perhaps a dog or two.

Not being the owner of a gaming establishment catering to anybody with a penny in their pocket.

"What are you thinking about?" Octavia said, peering at Ivy. "You look so wistful."

Darn her sister for being so observant.

"Here we are!" Madame Delyth announced, her arms overflowing with fabric.

She dumped the gowns on the table and began separating them. "I thought perhaps the green one for you," she said, nodding toward Octavia, "and then this one for you."

Ivy gasped as Madame Delyth plucked the gown from the table. It was beautiful, far simpler in design than Ivy would have anticipated, made of a sumptuous gold fabric that practically glittered.

"Ivy, that's lovely," Octavia said.

"It is."

Madame Delyth raised the gown up, walking toward Ivy. "Let's see if it suits your coloring before you try it on. I do have others, but—"

"This one," Ivy interrupted. Now that she'd seen it, she couldn't imagine wearing anything else. "This is the one."

"It complements you," the dressmaker said in an admiring tone. "It makes your hair look richer, and your eyes sparkle. Don't you think so, Miss Octavia?"

"I do. Ivy, it's perfect."

"Let's hope it fits."

"It will fit, and if it doesn't, I will alter it. No need to worry about that, I promise you," Madame Delyth said reassuringly. "You can go over there and try it on. And then we'll see what else it might need."

Ivy took the gown, her breath catching as she thought about his reaction to seeing her dressed like this. Properly, as though she were still in that world. As though she were someone he might have met while still a duke. Neither of them who they used to be, but returning to that world nonetheless.

"Ohh, Ivy," Octavia sighed as Ivy returned wearing the gown. "It truly is perfect."

"Just a bit of hemming, and I'll have to adjust the neckline," Madame Delyth said, examining Ivy. "You have a lovely bosom, you should show it more." She motioned for Ivy to turn around. "It won't take but a few days."

"Good, because the party is in three days," Octavia replied.

"I will have it to you by the day before," the dressmaker promised. "I am so glad it will be getting more use, it is truly one of my favorite creations.

You look better in it than the actress who wore it on stage," she added in an admiring tone.

"Thank you." Ivy looked down at herself, the fabric swamping her feet. "I wish I weren't quite so short," she commented ruefully.

"I can use the fabric from the hem to run up a little purse that will match. Perhaps ornament it with some ribbons."

"What an excellent idea," Ivy replied.

"You'll need gloves, too," Octavia said, examining Ivy with a critical expression. "And a necklace of some sort for your lovely bosom."

Ivy made a face at her sister, who just laughed.

"I cannot help you with the jewelry, but I do have some gloves you could try." Madame Delyth walked to the other side of her table and drew a box down from one of the shelves. "I believe they are—yes, here they are." She handed them to Ivy, who placed them against the fabric of the gown.

The gloves were made of gold satin, just a little worn at the thumb, but nobody would notice that. They were a slightly darker color than the gown, and one might have supposed the combination would be overly opulent, but instead the effect was of a lustrous regality, the warmth of the two shades of gold making for a literally rich feel.

"This is all too much," Ivy said, shaking her head.

"I'll bill you," Madame Delyth promised, a wicked glint in her eye. "And besides, when those ladies see you looking so fine, they'll demand to know where you purchased your gown." She shrugged in false modesty. "And you will tell them from the most exclusive couturier in London. So it will be well worth it."

"Thank you," Ivy replied. She glanced down at the gown again, taking a deep breath. For one night, she was going to return to her previous life as a respectable Society lady. To feel what it might have been like if her father hadn't gambled away her future and she hadn't taken it back.

If she had the chance, would she want to return permanently? What did she want, anyway? She'd promised Octavia she would consider her own wants and needs—and part of that was continuing her activities with Sebastian—but she still didn't know what she wanted for her future. Or perhaps she did. She just had to be brave enough to get it.

But wearing this gown, and the accompanying confidence it roused, she was fairly certain she could do anything.

Chapter Eighteen

"Are you ready?"

Sebastian stood at the doorway to Ivy's office, dressed in his most elegant attire. It was just past one o'clock in the morning, which would usually still be very busy in the club, but it was Whist Night, so the clientele had begun to leave around midnight, all of them gone by half past the hour.

Ivy rose from her chair, the butterflies that had been fluttering all day and all evening as she worked in the club manifesting to a veritable tornado inside her belly. "Are we going out? I am not dressed for it," she said, gesturing to her clothing. She wore what she usually wore on the floor—a simple dark gown that didn't call attention to itself but was appropriate for a businesswoman. She had resisted the urge to do anything differently today than she usually did—she didn't want to imbue the evening's plans with any more importance than he would likely give them.

Although of course she knew she was lying to herself. What they would do that evening would be tremendously important, at least for her. And, she knew with a small amount of pride, it would mean something to him. So her attempts to minimize it all were merely attempts to keep from breaking her own heart when he inevitably left.

"We're not going out," Sebastian replied, a knowing smile on his face. He held his hand out to her. "Would you care to accompany me onto the gaming floor? I believe we have some games to play."

His words sent a wicked shiver through Ivy's body. This was it. She—and he—were going to do this. All of it. And there would be no obligation afterward, no promises made, so no promises would be broken.

She took his hand and he drew her forward, pulling her close to him. He looked down at her, his expression earnest. "If you wish not to play, for any reason, you know you just have to tell me." He paused, taking a deep breath. "I want you to be absolutely certain about all of this."

She smiled in response. "I am, Sebastian. I want this. I want *you*."

He let out a long breath. "I was hoping you would say that. Follow me."

He turned, still holding her hand, leading her out of the office and down the hall to the gaming room.

She couldn't help but gasp as she entered—he'd worked a miracle in the half hour or so after the last customers had gone. The refinished table, the one the would-be assailant had bled onto, was in the middle of the room, the other tables having been pushed to the side. The table itself held a few packs of cards, a bottle of champagne, two glasses, candles, and dice. Ribbons had been tacked onto the side, cascading down toward the floor. He'd covered two of the chairs the same way he'd done them the night of the Masked Evening, and a blanket was folded on one of them.

Only a few candles still burned at the edges of the room, lending the space an even more clandestine feel. Light pooled onto the table, making it the focus of attention. She glanced at him, meeting his gaze and nodding in assent. "It looks very mysterious and alluring."

His smile deepened. "Like you."

She snorted in reply. "Hardly. I have shared all of my secrets with you, haven't I? And I'm hardly allur—"

"Stop," he said, his mouth curling down in disapproval. "You've captured my interest since the first time I walked in here with Nash. The way you spoke to me with your own opinions, interested to hear mine. I had never met anyone who actually wanted to hear me. That is more than alluring. It's seductive." His voice was low, sending sparks skittering along her spine. His gaze traveled down her body, making her feel as though he were touching her. "And the way you look and feel and respond is irresistible."

"So I'm alluring because I listen?" she replied in a saucy tone of voice, tilting her face toward his.

"Minx," he said, the word punctuated with a soft chuckle. He put his hand on her shoulder, drawing her into his body. His fingers went to the back of her gown, and started to work on the buttons. She made a movement as though to turn around, but he shook his head. "Not yet."

He lowered his mouth, hesitating for a fraction of a second before pressing his lips to hers. His fingers worked rapidly at the back of her gown.

She already felt heated, as though every fiber of her body was responding to him, was calling out for his hands, for his mouth, for his—yes. That. If she was going to have congress with it, she should be able to mention it, if only in her mind, shouldn't she? His penis. His man part. His cock. She'd felt it when they had been intimate before, but she hadn't named it, not even in her own thoughts.

Cock.

That part.

His lips were nibbling on hers, and she opened her mouth, his tongue sliding in to tangle with hers. She felt his hand at the center of her back, spreading the fabric of her gown apart. She felt his fingers pluck at the laces of her corset, and she put her own hand back there to speed up the process. He chuckled softly against her lips, swatting her hand away. "I want to do this," he murmured. "All by myself."

She drew back, meeting his gaze. "Shouldn't we be wagering or something? I had imagined that clothing removal would be an aspect of losing a wager."

"Or winning," he retorted.

She inclined her head in agreement.

"As always, Miss Ivy, you make an excellent point." He plucked his hand away and rested it at her waist, drawing her close so their lower bodies touched. She felt that part of him, the cock part, hard against her belly. "Let's review the possible guidelines for the evening. You'll want the customers to feel safe, so we won't allow wagers that will put anyone in danger."

He bent his head to place his mouth on her neck.

His lips were warm, and her eyes closed slowly in response as he dragged a kiss from her ear down to her collarbone. His fingers tightened on her waist. "We'll want to have monitors on all the wagers for the evening." He was whispering against her skin. She had never found club business to be erotic before. "Traditional wagers with money will not be allowed, but the same rule applies—all bets have to be paid in full at the end of the evening."

"Mm," she murmured as his hand reached up to squeeze her breast. She wanted to writhe against him, push that aching part of hers against him.

He chuckled, low and knowing. "Patience, Miss Ivy. By the end of the evening, not immediately."

"I don't want to hear all the rules, Sebastian. I want to play," she replied, running her hand from his neck down his chest to there, resting her fingers lightly on top of his trousers. His expression tightened, and she smiled.

"Let's play, then," he said in a growl, reaching down to swing her up into his arms, shoving aside the cards and dice to place her on the table.

She reached down to grab the fabric of her gown in her fists, sliding it slowly up her legs.

"Nobody said I couldn't cheat," she said as he gazed at her hungrily.

"CHEAT, HM?" SEBASTIAN said, placing his hands on the table, watching her expression change to one of anticipation.

"What—what are you going to do?" she asked, her voice soft and breathy.

He leaned forward. "What do you want me to do?"

She swallowed. "Everything. I don't have the words—"

"Do you want me to teach you some words?" The thought of his Ivy demanding he lick her sweet cunt made his knees buckle.

A wicked smile spread across her face. "Yes. I do know a few already."

He arched a brow, reaching one hand to put it on her revealed leg. Her skin was soft, and he suppressed the urge to just take her, quick and hard and fast. That would be immediately satisfying, of course, but he wanted to draw her pleasure out for her. Make certain she was satisfied before he was.

"Tell me." He moved his palm so it was on the inside of her leg, then began to draw it slowly up. Past her knee and onto her thigh, where it rested for a moment as he met her gaze.

She took a deep breath, licking her lips. "I know that your part there is your cock." She nodded toward his trousers, emphasizing the *k* part, and accompanying her word with another lick of her lips. "And that your cock goes inside me."

"Or in your mouth," he suggested.

Her expression grew sensual. "Yes, I've seen that, it looks quite intriguing."

The thought of her watching and getting excited by viewing the act made him even harder. Would she want to be watched by others as she sucked him? As he was fucking her?

Another appealing image. He reached down to adjust his erection, and she shook her head.

"No. That is mine right now, not yours." She lifted her chin. "Undo your trousers."

"Are we wagering anything?"

He didn't know if he could speak more than a few words, much less come up with a suitable wager, but he had promised they would be testing the idea out tonight. Even though doing anything but indulging in slow carnality was not at all appealing.

She shrugged. "Maybe later. Right now, I bet that you can teach me some things that will be . . . intriguing for both of us." She winked at her play on words. "Undo your trousers," she said again.

His hand went to the placket of his trousers, and he began to undo them, watching her as he did so. Her gaze was fastened on what his fingers were doing, and her eyes widened as he drew his cock out from his smallclothes.

"Oh," she gasped, biting her lip.

"Is that a good 'oh'?" If it wasn't, he didn't want to know, but he needed to ask, to make certain she was still on board with all of this.

She nodded. "Mm-hm."

"Do you want to see me touch myself? So you can touch me?" His voice was ragged.

"Mm-hm."

"Take the top part of your gown off."

She glanced up at him, the corner of her mouth lifting in a half smile. As though she knew just what torment she was about to put him through.

"Do you want to see my breasts?" she asked, sliding the gown off one of her shoulders.

"I want to see them and then I want to kiss them, Ivy. Suck on them until you beg for mercy."

He saw her shiver as she undid the other shoulder. Then, still meeting his gaze, she got onto her knees and moved forward so she was at the edge of the table facing him. His gaze lowered to her breasts, which were at eye level. He waited as she slid her arms out through the armholes, shimmying so the whole front fell forward.

Her corset didn't cover the tops of her breasts, but her shift did. And he desperately wanted to see her nipples. Wanting to know how they tasted, too.

"Your corset."

"Yes, sir," she said impudently, reaching one hand around to loosen the strings. She undid them, tossing the corset to one side.

Now she was just in her shift, her gown bunched around her waist. She gestured to the shift. "This, too, I suppose?"

"Now, Ivy."

She chuckled, positioning herself so she could pull the garment up and over her head. That, too, got tossed to the side.

"Lord, Ivy." Her breasts were gorgeous—full, and round, and topped with cherry-colored nipples. Darker than he had imagined.

His hands covered them, and then he leaned forward to draw his mouth from the top of her chest to one plump breast. Sucking the soft skin into his mouth, dragging his teeth gently on the delicious bite, then wrapping his lips around her nipple.

"Ahhh," she moaned, and she shifted forward so her body was on the edge of the table. He wrapped his arms around her, moving so his cock was pressed up against her mound.

Knowing she could feel how hard he was.

He sucked and licked her nipple, playing with it as it grew taut, hearing her soft sighs and moans above his head.

"More, Sebastian," she said, putting her fingers in his hair to press him closer. His face was buried in her soft curves, and his hips had unconsciously started a rhythmic press against her.

He hadn't come like this since he was young, but he knew he could with her and be just as satiated as if he were cock-deep inside.

He drew back, releasing her nipple from his mouth with a satisfying pop. He glanced up at her face, flushed with desire. "Take your gown entirely off," he commanded, leaning down to toe his shoes off as he spoke. Quickly followed by his trousers, and then his shirt, which he drew over his head.

She hadn't moved. Instead, she was staring at him, an avidly curious look on her face. He had always known he was handsome, and that his body was pleasing for ladies to regard, but he'd never felt so intensely regarded before. Just like everything she put her attention to, her focus was intense and direct.

"Your gown?" he prompted, gesturing to her.

She took one last look at him, then hopped off the table, bending forward to pick the bottom of her gown up and over her head.

And just as he'd imagined it, she was entirely naked except for her shoes and stockings. Her waist was small, curving into wide hips, surrounding the patch of dark hair at her entrance.

He reluctantly raised his eyes to her face. She looked apprehensive.

"What is it?" he asked. "We can stop, if you want."

She was already shaking her head before he finished speaking. "No, I just"—she gestured to herself, then at him—"I'm—and you're—and I don't know."

He stepped forward, placing his hands at her waist and bringing her close against him. His cock arched into her soft belly, and he couldn't suppress a groan. "You're gorgeous, Ivy. All of this soft roundness, your curves. I can't wait to touch you everywhere and bury myself in your warmth."

She looked up at him, her hands at the small of his back. He watched her expression shift into a mischievous one as she put one palm on the cheek of his arse, squeezing. Then she leaned her head over to one side, peering around to look at his back. "My goodness, Sebastian. Your"—and she squeezed again to indicate what she was talking about—"is remarkable."

He uttered an unexpected laugh. "Remarkable? I have never heard my arse described that way. Or any way at all, honestly." He slid his hands around her back and clasped her arse in them, squeezing as she had. "Soft and round, like a peach."

She looked at him as she took a deep breath. His arse still in her grip.

"It's time for you to teach me, Sebastian."

Chapter Nineteen

$\mathcal{L}$ie back on the table."

She glanced behind her, skeptical that she could hop back up without looking ridiculous, given that she was both naked and short.

"I'll help." He didn't wait for her to reply, but put his hands at her waist and lifted her effortlessly.

The green felt of the table tickled her skin. She glanced around, spotting the blanket he'd left folded on the chair. "I think we should put that down. I don't want to have to cover this again."

"Always practical," he replied, a wry grin on his face. He unfolded the blanket, laying it on the table, then tucking it under her as she raised herself up on her arms.

"And now you," she said, indicating he should join her.

He vaulted onto the table with ease, lying down as he rolled her on top of him. Every part of them was pressed together, skin to skin, his erection pressing into her body, his arms wrapped around her, holding her tight.

"I'm not hurting you?" she asked.

"Only in the best way, Ivy."

"So—what now?"

"What do you want to do?"

She liked that he asked her, even though obviously he was the more experienced with all of this. "I want to see what you taste like. I want to put your cock in my mouth."

She felt him shudder as his eyes closed. "God, yes, Ivy."

She raised herself up off his body, shifting down so she was right there. It was large, and long, and appeared to defy gravity by waving in the air. It did look rather funny, come to think of it.

Not that she'd tell him that.

She took it in her hand, wrapping her grip around him. He uttered a groan.

"Too tight?" she asked, relaxing her grip.

"No, tighter."

Hm. Interesting. She tightened her grip, and then leaned forward to lick the top part with her tongue. Swirling it around the head of his cock as though it was an ice.

From the sounds he was making, he liked that a lot.

"Can you—can you take me inside your mouth?"

"I'll try. You're awfully big," she replied.

He chuckled, which sounded more like another groan.

"Or my mouth is small."

"I like the first option better," he said, sounding strained.

She opened her mouth and guided his cock into it. It tasted musky, and she inhaled his scent as she continued to lick him.

"Yes. Like that. God, Ivy," he said, his hand coming to rest on her head. She slid her mouth down as far as she could. "Slide your hand up and down, like this," he said, putting his hand on hers. She followed his rhythm, moving her mouth in concert with her hand. She could feel him tremble and shudder, and she relished how powerful she felt.

She kept it up for a few minutes, until he squeezed her shoulder. "You should stop, it's—I don't want to spend before I get the chance to make you come."

She didn't understand entirely what he had said, but she understood the gist of it, so she drew her mouth off him. His cock was wet from her mouth.

He opened his eyes and looked at her as though he was dazed. She had done that. Ivy, Risk Taker and Business Owner, had brought Sebastian to this mindless state with her mouth and hand.

Excellent work, Ivy, she thought, leaning back on her heels.

He propped himself up on his elbows, his gaze slowly returning to one of sensual appraisal. "That was incredible," he said, shaking his head. "And now let me show you what I can do."

Within seconds, she was on her back and he was lying next to her, one leg slung over her body. He kissed her deeply, his hand sliding across her body, lingering on her hip, moving closer to *there* with each caress.

And then he *was* there, and she gasped against his mouth, her body arching up off the table.

His fingers stroked her, just where her body was clamoring for him. He broke the kiss, now moving so he could kiss her breast. Take the other nipple into his mouth.

It was nearly overwhelming, but she didn't want it to stop. Ever.

"Do you like this, Ivy?" he murmured against her skin.

She made some inarticulate noise of approval, and he chuckled.

His fingers began a slow, rhythmic caress there. "Is that—what are you touching?"

He lifted his head to meet her gaze. "It's your cunt, Ivy. Did you not know what to call it before?" The grin on his face was wicked. "Say it," he urged.

"You've got your fingers in my cunt," she replied, sounding breathless.

"I've got my fingers in your sweet cunt, Ivy," he corrected. "And I know it's sweet even though I haven't tasted it yet."

Her eyes widened; so it was something people did. Something *he* did.

"Does that idea intrigue you?" he asked softly. He kissed her breast again, then began to make his way down her body. "The thought of me kissing you there?"

"Mmph," she replied, hardly able to think, much less speak.

He pressed a kiss against her belly, and then shifted so he was right there, his face right there, looking at her most intimate place.

Her cunt.

And then he licked her, and she yelped, banging her hands down on the table.

"Is this all right?" he asked. "Remember we can stop if this is too much."

"It is," she began, only to shake her head as he began to draw away. "It is too much, but I don't want you to stop. Don't stop, Sebastian," she said in a pleading voice.

"Tell me what you don't want me to stop," he said. He kept his intense gaze locked with hers. "Tell me," he said again, caressing her there.

"I don't want you to stop kissing my—my cunt," she answered, adding a moan as he immediately returned to kissing her there.

Oh God, and then it was just his mouth, and his fingers, and how it felt as though something was churning low and powerful in her belly, and she never wanted him to stop, and something was building, and she felt it everywhere—in her breasts, all over her skin, there where he was kissing her. And then—

"Don't stop, don't stop, don't—aah," she cried as the feeling hit its peak, and she rode the sensation for what felt like hours before finally returning to some sort of consciousness.

He was still gazing at her intently, a powerful look of satisfaction on his face. "You came, Ivy. How did it feel?"

"You know how it felt," she replied.

"Tell me. I want to hear it from you."

"It felt wonderful. As though I were gliding on a cloud being swept up into the sky." She paused. "Is that how it feels for you?"

"It is. But I think that with you it will feel the best it ever has."

He brought himself back up so he was face-to-face with her. His mouth was moist—from her. His hand rested on her breast, his fingers caressing it lightly.

"And now what?" she asked. She could feel his erection hard and hot against her leg. "And now will you put your cock in my cunt?"

His eyes fluttered closed, and she grinned. To be

able to evoke that much of a response from him, he who had likely done this with many women before. But she knew it was different with her. She knew that, even though she didn't know how she knew that.

"I want to," he answered at last, opening his amber eyes. So beautiful, and so focused on her. "I want to assure you, though, that there will be no . . . consequences."

She frowned in confusion for a moment, then felt herself blush. She hadn't even thought of that when she'd been anticipating the evening. "Oh. Yes. Well. Proceed," she said, lifting her hand in a vague directional manner.

"Proceed?" He sounded amused.

"I don't know what one says in this situation." Her tone was both exasperated and embarrassed.

"Stroke me again, like you were."

She reached down between them to take hold of him, gripping him tightly as it seemed he liked. He throbbed against her fingers.

"Yes, like that," he murmured. The top of him felt wet, the slickness making it easier to slide her hand up and down.

"Are you ready, Ivy?" he asked, placing his hand over hers. The two of them stroked his shaft, him biting his lip as he closed his eyes.

"I am. Now, Sebastian," she ordered, making his lips curl up in a smile of acknowledgment.

"So bossy," he said. He moved to position himself there, and she held her breath as she waited.

She felt something at her entrance, and then he began to push inside. It felt like too much, and she gasped.

"Should I stop?" he asked in a strained voice.

"No." She shifted to widen her legs, reminding herself to breathe. And then he pushed in more, and it felt tight, so tight, and then he groaned and moved so he was entirely inside, his hips pressing against hers.

"Are you all right?" he asked.

"I am fine. And you?" This conversation sounded more like one they would have over tea, not naked on a gaming table. She giggled at the thought.

"You're laughing?" he asked.

"It's—never mind, I'll explain later. Just—just do whatever it is that happens next."

"We might have to work on your words of seduction," he replied dryly. But then he began to move, pulling out, and then pushing back in again. The first few times hurt, but then the hurt began to be accompanied by a pleasantly building pressure, and she moaned, wrapping her arms around him and putting her hands back on his deliciously firm arse.

"Like that," he said. "Move with me."

She did, and her movements seemed to unlock something inside him, and he moved faster and faster, his arms bracing his body above hers, his gaze locked down there where they were joined. She looked, too, and then she couldn't take her eyes away, at the sight of his cock thrusting into her, at his flexing stomach muscles.

He performed a few more urgent thrusts, and then he withdrew entirely, flinging his head back as a warm liquid spilled on her belly. He held himself, giving a few more strokes, and then collapsed on top of her, panting.

"Well," she said at last, when his breathing had returned to normal, "this is certainly going to change our employer/employee relationship."

She felt him start to laugh, and she joined in, both of them giving full expression to their joy.

She would miss this, miss him, when he was gone.

Not that she could think about that now. Now was the time for laughter, for enjoying the passion they'd just shared.

But still. She knew she would never be the same, and it wasn't just because she was no longer a virgin.

"WELL," SEBASTIAN SAID when he could catch his breath. "That was tremendous."

He felt her nod. "It was. And we didn't use the ribbons," she observed.

"Next time," he promised.

He shifted off her, wincing as his knees dragged along the table. If he were going to keep this up, he'd have to invest in some knee-padding.

And then he laughed again.

Had he ever laughed so much with a sexual partner before? He knew the answer to that. He'd seldom engaged in much conversation with any of his partners, to be honest, so he knew he certainly hadn't laughed a lot with them.

"Let me clean you up," he said, leaning off the table to snag his neckcloth from the floor.

"Don't fall!" she said, grabbing his backside.

He turned and grinned at her. "Is that just an excuse to touch me again? Because you don't need one." He wanted to feel her hands all over him. He liked how it made him feel, knowing she admired and desired his body.

"You're quite vain, Your Grace," she said, slapping his arse playfully.

He drew the neckcloth over her belly, tenderly wiping away the evidence of their coupling. "I'm not vain, it is all true. I am the best lover you've ever had—"

"You're the *only* one I've ever had," she interrupted in an amused tone.

"And I am handsome and witty and charming. You cannot deny it. Why else would you be lying naked with me on this somewhat uncomfortable table?"

"And I am famished. Who knew the activity would render one starving?"

"Starving for more of my kisses?" he teased.

She rolled her eyes. "Yes, of course, but you're going to have to hear my stomach rumbling if we go much longer without food."

She wriggled off the table as he kept his gaze on her. Lush, luscious, and utterly naked. He never wanted her to put clothing on again, not now that he knew what she looked like underneath.

He felt his cock stir. Already? He'd just finished, and here he was, wanting to go again, to bury himself in her plush softness. Perhaps bring her to climax when he was inside her this time.

"Let's see what Mac has in the kitchen," she said. She had picked up his shirt, and was pulling it over her head, her delighted face grinning at him as the shirt dropped to midthigh.

He arched a brow at her, then took her shift, which was hanging off the other end of the table, and put it on. The armholes were tight, but otherwise, it fit like one of his nightshirts. It hung to his knees, and he smoothed the fabric down, glancing up to meet her appreciative gaze.

"That is—well, I never realized how sheer that is," she commented, her expression one of frank appraisal.

He looked down, noting the bump in the fabric where his semierect cock was. "Or we could just remove all this and do it again," he said in what he hoped was a persuasive tone.

She shook her head. "Too hungry."

So much for his much-vaunted charm.

"Lead the way," he replied, holding his arm out toward the kitchen at the back. She walked ahead, and he kept his eyes on her round arse as it swayed from side to side under his shirt.

They reached the kitchen, Ivy peering around the room before beckoning him inside. "Nobody's here."

"It's a bit late to worry about that, isn't it, given what we just—?" he asked.

She swatted him on the arm. "Hush." Her cheeks were flushed. From passion or embarrassment?

"Now that you mention it, I am hungry, as well." The sooner they were fed, the sooner they might be able to return to fucking.

And one always needed nourishment for important tasks.

"Mac usually keeps some supplies over here." She examined the cupboards, catching her lip with her teeth as she looked.

She was adorable. And eminently fuckable. Sebastian began to conduct his own examination, trying to figure out the most forgiving surface for his knees.

"Bread!" She held up a loaf in triumph. "And he should have some cheese and butter in the larder." She put the bread down on the large table in the middle of the room, walking over to the small room at the side of the kitchen, reappearing within minutes holding a plate in each hand. One plate held a block of butter, and the other held cheese. She deposited the plates on the table next to the bread.

"We just need a knife," she said, looking thoughtful. "I believe he keeps his—oh, here," she said, opening a drawer and withdrawing a knife. She looked at him with an amused expression. "I don't suppose you would care for some tea?"

He grimaced exaggeratedly. "I am thirsty," he admitted.

"Set the kettle on," she ordered, beginning to slice the bread.

He approached the stove gingerly, spotting the kettle on top of one of the burners. And paused. He had no idea how—

"You don't know how to light the stove, do you, Your Grace?" she asked. She sounded far too amused.

"I am certain it is not that difficult," he replied. "A stove requires fire and . . . something." He glanced around, spotting a jar of matches to the right. "This!" he exclaimed, plucking one out.

"And then what, Your Grace?"

He was going to figure this out if it killed him. "Uh . . ." He bent down and opened the door to the oven, spotting some charred wood. "Wood. I need wood."

"Over there," she replied, pointing to a box filled with logs. He walked over and pulled one from the pile, then thrust it into the stove in triumph.

"And then it's a simple matter of lighting it, you see."

"I do see." She was laughing at him. But he couldn't blame her, given that he was wearing nothing but her shift and attempting to light a fire to make tea, his most loathed beverage.

The wood caught after a few tenuous moments, and he squatted back from the stove feeling inordinately proud of himself.

"Not bad, Your Grace. Here, I've cut some bread and cheese."

She sat on a stool, her knees raised up, her elbows on the table as though she were a mannerless heathen. He grinned and joined her, mirroring her posture. The bread and cheese were cut in neat slices, arranged on a platter between them.

"You serve an excellent postcoital meal, my lady," he said as he picked up a slice of bread and topped it with two slices of the cheese.

"I will take your praise, given that it is the first postcoital meal I've ever served," she replied in a wicked tone of voice.

Would there be others? he wondered. He knew he wanted to do it again, next time preferably in a proper bed. Would she want to do it again? And what would it mean for their working relationship?

"What are you thinking about?" she asked, taking a bite of her own bread and cheese.

He couldn't tell her. Not now, not when it was all so fresh. Not when he knew that if she told him never again that he would immediately try to seduce her, which wouldn't be fair. But it would be him living up to his previous role as an unrepentant rake, something he didn't think he was anymore, even if his cock would disagree.

"About how I might actually enjoy tea in this context."

They both looked at the kettle, which was emitting a slim stream of steam.

"How do you—?" he began.

"When it whistles," she answered, anticipating his question.

"I've learned so many useful things in my position," he mused, putting his food down on the platter. "How to gauge when a customer is in need of another beverage—or not. How to decorate a room quickly and inexpensively. What to say to persuade someone to try their luck again, even if their luck seems to have run out."

"You would never have learned any of that as a duke," she pointed out.

The kettle began to whistle. She stayed him with her hand, getting up and making the tea far more efficiently than he thought he could ever do, regardless of how much practice he'd had.

Which, at this point in his tea-making career, was none.

"There's no whiskey here," she said as she placed the steaming cup in front of him.

He glared down at the clear brown liquid in the cup, then glanced up to meet her laughing eyes.

"This might be the most difficult thing I've had to adjust to," he said.

She frowned. "What?"

He gestured toward the cup. "Not being able to

wave my hand and have whatever I want brought to me. Because I certainly never asked for tea when I was a duke."

"What *did* you ask for?"

SEBASTIAN'S EXPRESSION FROZE at her question, and she wondered what it was that was making him react so strongly. Should she not have posed the question? But no, that was ridiculous; they'd just engaged in a carnal act, or a few of them—she wasn't certain how carnal acts were totaled up—so her asking a question shouldn't be out of line. Because if it was, she was going to have to reevaluate the relative importance of what they'd just done.

"I didn't usually have to ask. Things just . . . arrived."

She arched her brow as she took a sip of her tea. "So at any given moment your door would open to reveal a phalanx of servants bearing whiskey, and deviled eggs, and cakes?"

"Is that your idea of what the nobility longs for? Whiskey and cake?" He tilted his head in thought. "I suppose that is not all that terrible a life."

"I suppose it wasn't." She paused. "You miss being a duke, you said before. Because you're a reasonable person," she added with a snort. "But does it bother you, what you're missing?"

He looked conflicted, and again she resisted the immediate impulse to apologize for her probing questions. Again, naked high jinks, so she was likely fine. She just had to remind herself of that. As though she would forget. She would never forget, for as long as she lived.

"I've tried not to think about it, honestly. Mostly, I miss living with Ana Maria and not having to walk my dogs. Though then I would miss my conversations with your sister."

She smiled.

"And I never realized just how privileged a position I had—it was just who I was, and then when I wasn't, I realized there was so much I had taken for granted. If I were to return to that life, I wouldn't take any of it for granted."

"Though you might have a servant walk your dogs," she replied in a teasing voice.

"Very possibly."

He took a sip of tea, grimacing as he set down the cup. "I will need to think about it eventually." He shrugged as he ran his hands through his hair. Leaving it looking perfectly disheveled, although his appearance was definitely at odds with what he was wearing.

"When it first happened, when I first arrived here, I was determined not to think about it so I wouldn't long for it. It's over and done, and there's no point in bemoaning that. Or moping," he added, his mouth curling up into a wry grin. "But with some distance, it is easier. My cousin and sister very much wish me to consider finding a place in their lives so we can be a family again."

"Are you not a family because you're not a duke? Surely your cousin isn't so haughty." And if he was, then maybe he would stay forever, after all?

She couldn't think like that. She knew the reality of it.

He laughed as he shook his head. "No, Thaddeus is a firm believer in achieving your greatness through merit. He was in the army before having to—to take over."

"So what is the impediment?" She leaned forward, resting her chin on her hands. The sleeves of his shirt fell down her arm, nearly landing in the butter. She jumped and rolled the sleeves up over her elbows.

He grinned at her. "My shirt is most delightful on you." He reached forward, putting his index finger in between the fabric and her skin, drawing the shirt out from her body and looking brazenly at her breasts.

She felt her breath catch at his expression. Of hunger, of desire, of admiration.

She'd never been looked at like that.

Of course, she'd never worn a gentleman's shirt—and only a gentleman's shirt—while cavorting with said gentleman.

"And my shift is—well," she said, scrutinizing him, "it's not the most flattering attire. But you look quite fetching."

He rose, holding his arms out perpendicular to the floor, turning slowly around. The fabric fluttered around his back, around his hard, round arse. His legs were strong, the muscles shifting under his skin as he turned.

She wanted to lick him everywhere.

"What are you thinking about?" he said when he had turned in a complete circle and was facing her. One wicked eyebrow was raised, as though he knew perfectly well what she was thinking about.

"I like your body," she replied.

He licked his lips, his eyelids drooping as he raked his gaze over her. "I can return the compliment."

Her skin began to heat all over.

"You didn't answer the question." This was all too much, too intense. If she wasn't careful, she would end up doing irreparable harm. To herself. She wasn't naive enough to believe he would feel anything more than a passing fancy.

A duke, an unmarried handsome duke, likely knew perfectly well how to navigate a sexual relationship with a person he had no intention of marrying.

She should learn to do the same.

"Question?" he asked.

"Yes, what you were talking about," she explained hastily. "The impediment to returning to your family." The more she understood, the better prepared she'd be.

He sat back down on the stool, but not before giving her a glance full of regret. As though saying, *We could have been doing something much more delightful than talking*, although she could be speaking for herself.

"I didn't want to be like my mother, compromising myself in order to stay in my preferred way of life. And then there is the pride, I suppose." He snorted. "I wanted to prove that I could be on my own without anything, without any help. And to do that, I had to cut myself off from my family, or at least cut myself off from them providing substantive assistance. Ridiculous," he added, after a moment.

"It's not ridiculous," she said softly. "It's admirable." She paused, not wanting to ask the next obvious question, but knowing she'd be a coward if she didn't. "Have you proved it to your own satisfaction?" she asked.

Instead of replying, he stood up and held his hand out to her. She took it, allowing him to assist her off the stool.

"I think we should stop talking," he murmured, pulling her into his arms, then bending down to sweep her up under her knees, raising her against his chest.

She glanced up at him, at the hungry, intense expression in his gaze, at how it felt to be in his arms.

"I suppose," she said in a wry tone, "that this is a reasonable option if you don't intend to answer my question."

He chuckled as he carried her back into the gaming room.

Chapter Twenty

$\mathcal{N}$o, not here," she said in a stern whisper.

It was the day after their tryst, and Sebastian was trying—unsuccessfully—to steal a kiss.

They had spent the whole night together, talking and caressing and kissing. He'd never been naked and supine with a woman for so long before. He certainly had never shared secrets, nor laughed as hard.

They'd implemented his idea for the ribbons, and the image of her wrapped up in all that color was something that would be imprinted on his brain for the rest of his life.

When they'd finally reluctantly parted, he could smell her scent on his shirt.

They'd crept back to their respective rooms in the early dawn, and Sebastian had stolen a few hours of sleep, his shirt tucked against his nose, before Byron and Keats had woken him up insisting their needs be met.

And now it was midday, and Ana Maria's party was this evening. There was a lot of work to do before then, however, which was why they were both in her office reviewing the staff schedule. She wouldn't be on the floor to deal with any potential issues, and she was understandably nervous. So nervous, in fact, that he was trying to distract her—with kissing first, since that was something he would very much like to do, as well.

It wasn't working.

In fact, he needed a distraction from thinking about kissing her.

"Mr. Silver?" The maid, Carter, stood at the door to the office.

"Yes?" He'd given up trying to correct his name.

"There's a gentleman here, he says—"

Nash's broad form appeared behind Carter. "Sebastian."

Ivy glanced between them, a tiny frown between her brows.

"What is it, Nash? I'm working."

"If the duke wishes to speak to you, Mr. de Silva, I am certain I can spare you."

He didn't like it when she used his proper name. Nor did he like it when she spoke so formally.

"Come on, then."

Nash didn't wait, he just turned around and walked back down the hall, likely assuming Sebastian would follow.

"A duke! That is a duke?" Carter said, her eyes wide.

"Go," Ivy commanded, shooing him away. "I don't want a duke to feel ill-treated by Miss Ivy's." Carter nodded her head in agreement.

Sebastian opened his mouth to retort—*I don't want to go with him, I want to stay here and kiss you senseless, perhaps persuade you to join me in an actual bed.* The last caveat because his back and knees were sore from last night's activities.

"Go," she repeated in a sterner voice.

He liked it when she used her bossy tone, but not when she was telling him to leave.

He shrugged, stepping past Carter to Nash, who stood at the end of the hall.

"What do you want?" he said, glaring at his friend. Not that Nash knew he had interrupted what might have ended up being a pleasant afternoon before heading to Ana Maria's party.

But still.

Nash glared back. As Sebastian knew he would.

"Thad asked if we could meet at my house. Now, so we have time to dress for tonight." And then he grimaced, as if he was pained by the thought of tonight's festivities. "So I said I'd come collect you."

Sebastian waited for Nash to say more. Of course he didn't have any more to say, since Nash was nothing if not taciturn. Still, he could have said something.

"Did Thaddeus say what this was about? Why we have to meet now, when we've all got Ana Maria's party to prepare for?"

Nash shrugged. "No."

Sebastian exhaled in exasperation. "Fine. Let's go."

It would take just as long to get Nash to spill everything he might know as it would for Sebastian to travel there, hear what Thaddeus had to say, and return home. He knew that, and yet he had to ask anyway.

"We'll walk," Nash said as they left Miss Ivy's.

Sebastian nodded, increasing his pace to match Nash's long stride. He'd grown accustomed to walking with Octavia or Ivy, he hadn't had to push himself for a few weeks now.

He'd grown accustomed. To living with her and her sister, to actually working for a living, to being valued for his opinion.

And he was walking back to where he used to belong, to go tonight to a party where he'd see everyone who knew he used to belong, and no longer did.

The party. It was so important to Ana Maria. He had to attend.

"So you'll be there tonight?" he asked.

Nash grunted. "She made me promise."

Sebastian snorted in response. "She did the same thing to me."

"Determined," Nash said.

"Yes."

They walked the rest of the way in silence, which was Nash's preferred way to travel. Sebastian would have normally tried to engage him in conversation, just to annoy him, but his mind was too filled with what had happened the night before—and what might happen in the future. Both he and Ivy had skirted around the issue of what their activities might mean. Would they do it again? Sebastian certainly hoped so. Would it affect their working relationship? Would she tell her sister what had happened?

And what did he want it to mean in the future?

What did he want for his future?

He wanted her.

He stopped short in surprise, Nash continuing to stride ahead.

"Watch where yer going, mister," a woman holding a basket of food chided. Nash turned around after a few yards, giving him a quizzical look.

Sebastian gritted his teeth and began to walk again, gesturing to Nash to go ahead.

He wanted her. Forever.

But did she want him? And what would that look like?

If he had still been duke, he would have set her up in a tidy house where he could visit her whenever he had the desire. Which he knew would be frequent.

But even thinking that felt tawdry. He didn't want to *own* her, as a nobleman would a mistress; he wanted to be with her, as if they were partners. Partners in love.

He snorted at how mawkish he sounded. Nash and Thaddeus would howl if they heard his thoughts. The man he was before a few weeks ago would howl and then scoff if he heard his thoughts.

But he was neither howling nor scoffing.

The question was, what would the man he was now do to achieve his goals?

"Oh, Ivy."

Octavia stepped back in appraisal. Ivy smoothed the gown, not because it was wrinkled, but because she was nervous. She, the woman who had fearlessly wagered her and her sister's futures and set up her own gambling house, was nervous.

About wearing a beautiful gown to an evening party.

"It looks good?" Ivy asked, even though Octavia's breathless tone had given her the answer.

"Amazing. Come look."

Octavia shifted the full-length mirror toward Ivy, who took a deep breath before taking a look.

Oh. She did look amazing. She didn't look like Miss Ivy, professional business owner.

She looked like a goddess. A short goddess, but a goddess nonetheless.

The gown's golden threads glittered in the light cast by the late-afternoon sun, the low neckline and simple ornamentation drawing attention to Ivy's pale skin and, as Madame Delyth had already remarked, her lovely bosom.

She had to admit it did look lovely in this context.

Octavia and Carter had dressed her hair in a more elegant style, cajoling a few curls to lay gently against her neck. She wore the gold gloves, and she and Octavia had found some gold earrings in a pawnshop.

"Goodness, miss," Carter said. "You look like a princess."

"Like a queen," Octavia said.

"Thank you both," Ivy replied. She looked at Octavia. "And you look like a fairy."

The gown Madame Delyth had chosen for Octavia was lovely and needed very little alteration. It was pale green with an overskirt of sheer tulle studded with beads. Octavia wore white gloves and had found a small pearl drop necklace.

This was how she would have looked if their father hadn't inflicted such damage to their futures.

But Ivy thought that perhaps the damage had resulted in something better than what would have awaited them otherwise; they made their own decisions, they did what they pleased, and neither of them had to wed anyone whom they disliked.

That Ivy didn't think marriage was in her area of possible futures was something to be thought of at another time.

She felt her lips lift in a faint smile as she recalled the previous evening—she'd done her best to forget about it while she was working, even though it seemed he could not, judging by how he had tried to kiss her.

But now, preparing to return if only for one evening to her previous life, it was difficult not to.

Not that in her previous life she would have engaged in such play. She laughed aloud at the thought of that.

"What is it?" Octavia was in the middle of twirling in front of the mirror, but paused when she heard Ivy.

"Nothing," Ivy murmured, shaking her head. Unable to keep herself from smiling.

"Carter, can you see where I might have put my evening slippers?" Octavia said.

Carter nodded, leaving the room.

Octavia's mouth curled into a mischievous grin, and she raised the skirts of her gown to reveal her evening slippers were on her feet.

"Octavia!" Ivy exclaimed.

"I need to know what happened last night," Octavia replied. "And we don't have much time before the party. Before he sees you in that gown. Have I mentioned you look stunning?"

Ivy felt her cheeks heat. "You did. Thank you." She took a deep breath, which was a bit more difficult than usual because of the closer-fitting gown. "I can't—" she began, only to stop speaking when Octavia shook her head.

"I don't need the details, to be honest. That would be decidedly odd. Sebastian is my friend." She wrinkled her nose at the thought. "I just want to know if you've made good on your promise to think about what you want. What *you* want, Ivy, not what you think other people want."

"I'm not sure I can tell you that," Ivy said slowly.

Octavia frowned, putting her hands on her hips for emphasis. "I am your sister, you can tell me any—"

"Because what if I don't know what I want? And what if I can't have it?" Ivy knew how she sounded—needy, and wanting, and yet still fierce.

Octavia flung her hands up in the air. "That is the whole point of saying it aloud! It's not as though you'd say what you want and that thing would walk through the door and wave hello."

They both reflexively looked at the door.

"But you knew what you wanted to achieve with the club, Ivy. You had a plan, and you laid it out, and then you managed to do it."

"Even though I might just as easily have failed."

Octavia brushed that aside. "Of course, you might have. You might still. But you have to try, Ivy. You can't just do things for everyone else anymore. What about you?"

He had done things for her the night before. Or, more accurately, had done something that had resulted in one tremendous thing. Her knees still felt shaky when she thought about it—that feeling of passion, nearly of rapture, as his mouth and hands had brought her to climax.

"Maybe you really cannot answer now. I understand because I know you." Octavia gestured to

Ivy. "But just know that you should be thinking about it, especially when you're dressed like that."

Ivy raised an eyebrow. "So my looking more attractive means I deserve what I want?"

"That is not what I am saying," Octavia replied in an exasperated tone. "Sometimes I think you say things just to annoy me."

Ivy suppressed a grin. Because Octavia was right.

"I am saying," Octavia continued in a pedantic tone, "that the chances of you getting what you want increase if you are confident. And when you are dressed in something beautiful, and you know you look beautiful, you are confident."

"I appreciate that you are framing this in terms that a gambler can understand—my chances increase with more confidence," Ivy replied, an amused tone in her voice.

So—could she gamble with the most precious thing in the world? Her heart?

And what would happen if she lost?

"Finan!" Nash shouted as he and Sebastian entered Nash's house.

The butler emerged from the hallway, one eyebrow raised. "There's no need to shout the house down, Your Grace. You told me you were coming with this one. That other one is in your library."

"Brandy," Nash said, striding toward the library. He flung the door open, then gestured for Sebastian to enter and followed, shutting the door firmly behind them.

Thaddeus was seated on the sofa, as rigidly at attention as though he was expecting the queen to pay a visit.

"What is it, Thad?" Sebastian asked. "Why did I need to come today?"

Thaddeus looked puzzled, glancing between Nash and Sebastian. "It's not as though I summoned you. Unless . . ." He paused, focusing on Nash. "Did you just order him to come?" He shook his head. "I was hoping we could spend some time together, as we used to, that is all."

"If that's all, I should get back." Back to her. Back to where he'd have to figure out just what he wanted. Back to where he might not get what he wanted.

"Just one drink, Seb," Thaddeus replied.

"Please," Nash added. Nash never asked for anything.

"One drink," Sebastian agreed. He sat on the sofa beside Thaddeus, spreading his arms over the back of the sofa and crossing his legs.

He was not a military man, after all. Nor was he a duke.

Nash sat in the large chair opposite, his broad frame taking up nearly all the available space in the chair.

"Brandy," Finan announced as he wheeled a round table into the room. He brought it to the side of the sofa, then began to pour.

"Here you go, sir," he said, handing a well-filled glass to Sebastian. He distributed the remaining two, then nodded toward Nash and wheeled the table back out again.

"What are we drinking to?" Nash asked.

To her. To all the possibilities. To my future?

Damn it.

"To family. Most especially Ana Maria, whose love none of us deserves." Thaddeus raised his glass as he spoke, and the other two mirrored his movements.

"To Ana Maria," they echoed.

The brandy was excellent, of course. Nash spent little on things that most gentlemen in his position would—women, clothing, horses. But he refused to economize on his liquor, something Sebastian appreciated at this very moment. He hadn't realized he had a headache until now, although of course it stood to reason he would—he'd gotten maybe three hours of sleep and had spent the evening engaged in a delightfully strenuous pursuit.

The brandy helped. Or it was muffling the headache. Either way, it made him feel more like himself.

Although who he was was the question of last night, wasn't it?

"What is going on with you, Seb?" Nash asked. He gestured accusingly toward Sebastian, careful not to spill his brandy. "How is your dalliance with working for a living?" Nash spoke with a mixture of envy and disdain. The former likely because Nash wished he could just live life as a normal person, disdain because he knew he was dependent on his ducal benefits.

"You've proved yourself," Thaddeus added. "We know you can do without us. But I'm not certain we can do without you."

The words made Sebastian speechless. Thaddeus—taciturn, serious, distant Thaddeus—had just expressed an emotion that would have been natural coming from the demonstrative Ana Maria, but from Thaddeus?

Nobody spoke for a long moment.

"He's right," Nash said gruffly as he finished his brandy. He rose from his chair to pour himself another glass. He paused to regard Sebastian, nodded in emphasis, then returned to his seat.

"Thank you," Sebastian replied, his throat thick. He had missed them; he missed the easy comfort of being with someone who'd known you your entire life. Who would remind you, when you were being particularly arrogant, of the time you practiced bowing for four hours straight because you were convinced you would fall over if you got it wrong.

"Drink up," Thaddeus urged. He downed his glass, wincing as he drank. Thaddeus never had been one for drinking. If given the choice, he would always want to be doing something useful rather than indulging himself.

Whereas Sebastian never had had to choose—as he'd told Ivy, things just arrived. Women, power, influence, wealth, and everything else a young, healthy duke might expect.

If he could have returned to his past self, he'd remind that arrogant ass that things could change in an instant. That he should look beyond what was handed to him to see if there was anything else out there that he might prefer.

"So how are things?"

Thaddeus was terrible at making conversation. The way he asked his question made it sound as though he had just recently learned the language.

"Things are . . ." Sebastian began, then paused. Took a sip of brandy. "Things are fine." He exhaled, shaking his head as he leaned over to splash some more liquor in his glass. "Although you two deserve more than that. I wish I could tell you," he said, chuckling. "Some things are wonderful"—*such as Ivy, his friendship with her sister, Mac's food*—"and some things are not." His perpetual concern that he would lose his temper and lose his position. That he wouldn't be up to the responsibility she'd entrusted to him. That she would make enough money so she could close up the club and head off to a remote cottage, as she'd mentioned.

"That's remarkably vague," Nash commented.

"As though *you're* a fount of information," Sebastian retorted. "It's difficult enough to get you to say hello, much less tell us how you're doing. Most of the time I have no idea if you're even happy. Though you should be," he continued in a wry tone, "what with being a duke. Even though you'd say you'd prefer not to be," he added, forestalling Nash's reply.

Nash made a grumbling noise and drank more.

Which, Sebastian mused, could be the title of Nash's biography, given how often he did both things.

"Gentlemen." Thad spoke in his most commanding voice. It worked, too; both Nash and Sebastian straightened in their seats. No wonder Thaddeus had been so successful in the army. "Stop bickering."

"And how are you, Thad? Have you resolved the Great Conflict?" Sebastian asked slyly.

"What great conflict?" Thad asked in a puzzled tone.

"The one between the secretary and the valet."

Nash snorted.

Thad looked nonplussed. "It has been an ongoing battle, to continue your noxious analogy, but I believe we have come to a peaceful resolution."

"In other words, you've flown the white flag," Sebastian replied with a smirk.

Thad gave an exasperated sigh as he waved his hand. "Fine. Mock me."

"Oh, we will." Sebastian grinned as he spoke. He had missed these two, the opportunity to spar with them, knowing nobody would take offense no matter what was said or done.

"As to mocking," Nash said in a leading tone of voice, "you won't escape, even if you have become a common man."

"Oh?" Sebastian said, raising his eyebrow.

Nash leaned back in his chair, folding his arms over his chest. "You might have escaped the torment of being a duke," he said, his expression making it obvious he knew he was being sarcastic, "but you still have to attend functions like tonight. Dance with some ladies who will still accept your request, drink the best wine at one of the most exclusive homes wearing clothing that someone in your new position would never be able to afford."

"And your point is—?" Sebastian said.

Nash unfolded his arms, spreading his hands wide. "My point is that you have to suffer alongside us. Why not suffer but take some of the benefits? I am certain your strategic cousin"—at which point he gestured to Thaddeus—"could figure out some way for you to return. To your home, to your family. We wouldn't have to miss you, you could enjoy the aristocracy's largesse, and you could be satisfied that if things ever went sideways again, you would be fine."

That was the most amount of words Sebastian had ever heard Nash speak in a row. Sometimes, if

Nash was being particularly Nash-like, the most he would have spoken in a week.

Things were definitely not usual if Nash was willingly engaging in conversation.

"I have offered, if you recall," Thaddeus said. "But you declined. Perhaps it's just that I haven't found the right incentive for you to return."

Did Sebastian want to return?

It was tempting, to be certain. Especially since he'd be returning with the knowledge of all that he would never take for granted again.

But he wouldn't have *her*. Nor would he have Octavia, or his friendly badinage with Mac, or even Henry and Samuel's wary suspicion and hopefully growing grudging respect.

He reeled with the knowledge that returning wouldn't be enough. Not without her.

And now what should he do with that knowledge?

"But meanwhile, it's time to get ready," Thaddeus announced. For the first time, Sebastian was grateful for Thad's militaristic approach to time and scheduling. He didn't have to answer Nash. Or himself.

Chapter Twenty-One

*Y*ou came!" Lady Ana Maria rushed up to greet Ivy and Octavia, a delighted smile on her face. She took their hands in hers, glancing from one to the other as she squeezed.

"Yes, and you look lovely."

It was true; Lady Ana Maria wore a striking gown, one more suited for a married lady than a debutante, but it absolutely suited her. It was simply cut, but she'd made up for its simplicity by dressing her dark lustrous hair in a complicated style, winding strands of pearls throughout, a matching strand around her neck. The gown was dusky rose, making her skin look golden in contrast. Her gloves were a dark pink, and she had pearl bracelets on each wrist.

"And you, ladies! Miss Ivy, you look incredible in that color. Perhaps I should have worn gold instead."

"Thank you, but your gown is a perfect color for you."

"And Miss Octavia! I admire your aplomb in choosing such a bold gown." In someone less earnest, the words might have sounded like a cleverly disguised insult, but coming from Lady Ana Maria, it was a sincere compliment. "Come in, come in.

People are dancing already, although I haven't yet ventured out."

Ivy wrinkled her brow. "Not from lack of invitations, I hope?" Because Society was fickle enough to decide to ostracize Mr. de Silva's half sister if they judged her by his antecedents. And if they had, Ivy would have to ostracize them from her club. She'd already spotted a few of her regular customers here.

"No, I'm just—" And she glanced over the ladies' shoulders to the door, a look of hopeful expectation on her face. "Thaddeus is here, of course, but Sebastian isn't yet. I thought he might arrive with you."

"No, he went off with the Duke of Malvern earlier this afternoon." And hadn't returned when they'd left, much to Ivy's consternation. What if he didn't appear? His sister would be so disappointed. Not to mention Ivy.

But Lady Ana Maria was speaking. There was no time for Ivy to get her hopes up about seeing him, perhaps even dancing with him. "I do hope you have fun. And I am so glad you are here. My brother seems so different since coming to live with you—"

"Maybe because he's not a duke any longer?" Octavia interjected in a dry tone of voice.

Ivy nudged her sister in the ribs.

"I suppose, although it's more than that," Lady Ana Maria replied, as though it were a serious question and not Octavia being sly.

"We should let you greet your other guests," Ivy said, glancing back to where a small group of people were clustered at the door. "Thank you again for the invitation."

"Thank you for coming," Lady Ana Maria replied.

Ivy and Octavia wandered around the periphery of the ballroom, coming to stand at the opposite end from the door next to a pillar holding a marble bust of some grim-looking past relative of Sebastian and the duke's.

"This is the best vantage point to see when Sebastian arrives," Octavia said in satisfaction.

"Oh, is it?" Ivy asked.

Octavia rolled her eyes. "As if that's not why you brought us over here. You cannot fool me. You already told me you like him."

Ivy's breath caught. *Like* was such a mild word for what she felt, although her mind shied away from that other word that began with *L*. She couldn't feel that toward him, could she?

"Ivy?"

Ivy shook her thoughts free, looking determinedly toward the dance floor. "I believe that is Mr. Jennings, Lady Massingley's nephew. You remember, the one Sebastian nearly—?"

"Nearly knocked down in the middle of the club? Yes, that's him," Octavia said in a fierce tone. "I wonder how he came to be invited. If he tries anything tonight, if he ruins Lady Ana Maria's night, then—"

"There's no need to be so pugnacious, Octavia. There are plenty of people ahead of you in line to punch the gentleman. I think I might be at least number five down the list, judging from the company."

And then there *he* was, standing at the entrance to the ballroom.

Ivy kept herself from reacting to his presence, at least on the outside, merely acknowledging him with a slight incline of her head. He smiled at her, a "we did things together that were entirely wicked" type of smile, and she felt her knees wobble a little. He crossed the distance between them quickly with his long stride.

"Good evening, ladies," he said.

Octavia narrowed her eyes as she looked between them. "I feel as though I am an unwilling third partner in whatever dance you two have begun. If you will excuse me?"

And she walked away, leaving them alone. Alone except for the hundred or so other guests milling about the enormous room. But alone in that nobody could hear their conversation.

"You look lovely, Ivy," he murmured. His gaze traveled from the top of her head to her shoes and back up again. It felt as though he was stripping her bare. Or perhaps she wished he was stripping her bare.

Was it possible to become addicted to something after just one time?

It was, judging by her experience at the club.

Which meant that it was quite possible she was now addicted to sexual adventures with him.

Drat.

"You look quite fine yourself." She took the opportunity to allow her eyes to soak in his splendor. Like the previous evening, he wore excellently tailored clothing that clung to his muscular frame like a clinging lover.

Perhaps not the best analogy, given her present frame of mind. Or, given that, perhaps the absolute best.

She had never been so contrary before.

His jacket and trousers were black, and his shirt and neckcloth were both white. He wore that same gold waistcoat he'd had on when she had first met him. It was still ostentatious, and he still looked incredibly attractive in it.

Though she might have to admit to finding him more attractive when he was wearing her shift. Or nothing at all.

"I can tell what you're thinking," he said in a low tone. "You'd make a terrible card player," he added with a sly grin.

She resisted the urge to smack him. Or kiss him.

Instead, she just rolled her eyes.

"Would you care to dance?" he asked, gesturing toward the crowd of people in the middle of the room. He held his hand out to her and she grasped it, feeling her heart do something odd in her chest as he squeezed her fingers.

It was just a dance.

But it was also the opportunity for her to pretend, just for as long as it took the musicians to play a song, that she was a normal Society lady. That her partner might be interested in her for something more than a dance, representing marriage and family and security.

"Let us show them how it's done, Ivy," he said in a low tone as he escorted her onto the dance floor.

"How do you know I can dance?" she asked, tilting her head up at him.

His lips curled into a knowing smile, and she

shivered. "Because even if you can't, you know how to move with me. You showed me just that last night."

She released a shuddery breath, allowing him to draw her into his arms.

The music began, and of course it was a waltz. She hadn't danced since her brief foray into Society, and even then, she hadn't been more than adequate.

But in his arms? With him guiding her through the steps, and her listening and reacting to his movements?

It felt as though she'd always known how to dance. As though the movement was as natural as breathing air.

Or more so, given how difficult it currently was to breathe.

"I couldn't picture you in this world before, Ivy. I could only see you as the fearsome owner of the club."

"Fearsome?"

He nodded in mock sincerity. "Oh yes. Fearsome for your ability to garner loyalty from the most irascible group I've ever met."

"That's just Mac," she said, laughing.

"Fearsome for how you manage to contain your ebullient sister."

Ivy released a sigh indicating her long-suffering. Albeit with a smirk on her face.

"Fearsome for how you managed to win first my fealty and then my"—he glanced down, indicating what he meant—"my cribbage board."

She burst out laughing. "Is that what you're calling it?"

"In polite company, of course," he replied in a stuffy tone.

She shook her head, then forgot everything as his arms tightened around her, and he whirled her through the steps of the dance.

This exuberance couldn't last, but she would enjoy it while she could. All too soon she would have to return to her own life.

Though it wasn't as if she was suffering; she owned her own future, she held all the cards in her hand, and she would never have to compromise or bluff her way through any situation.

"Ivy, I—" he began.

"Sebastian!"

The new duke, the military gentleman, had appeared at their side, a nearly delighted expression on his face.

Sebastian's steps faltered, and then he stopped dancing, his body suddenly rigid.

"What is it?" he asked. He glanced at Ivy, his brow furrowed. "I promise you, a happy Thaddeus is not his usual way of being."

"Come this way, if you would. Could you excuse us?" he said to Ivy, not waiting for her reply as he took Sebastian's arm and led him away.

Leaving her on the dance floor alone.

She supposed it was just as well it be now rather than later. It would give her time to grow accustomed to the solitude.

You will be no more alone than you were before he came, she reminded herself. *It will be fine.*

"WHAT?" SEBASTIAN GROWLED as Thaddeus practically dragged him to the edge of the ballroom.

Thad didn't reply, instead glancing from one side of the room to the other before pulling Sebastian behind one of the large pillars lining the room. The pillar held an enormous bouquet of flowers, and Thad jostled it, sending a cascade of petals onto his hair. He glowered, then shook his head like one of Sebastian's dogs after a walk in the rain.

"You recall how we were just speaking about your return. And how I vowed to come to an amenable solution." Now Thaddeus looked smug, making Sebastian uneasy. Thaddeus was seldom pleased with himself unless he'd completed some sort of large-scale military maneuver. "I've just spoken with Mr. Muttlefield, he owns the largest export business in London."

"And?" Sebastian said impatiently. "What does this have to do with me?"

The muscle in Thaddeus's jaw clenched. "If you'll listen. Mr. Muttlefield has just done Her Majesty a great favor. It doesn't matter what it was, but the thing is, he has a daughter of marriageable age. And he will soon be made a baron."

Sebastian didn't say anything, just kept regarding Thaddeus, whose clenched jaw was becoming more pronounced.

"Don't you understand? Mr. Muttlefield wants his daughter to enter our world, *this* world, and the easiest way to do so is for her to marry into it. Now, once other gentlemen hear about the young Miss Muttlefield, you won't have a chance. But the gentleman informed me just now that his daughter has seen you and has taken a liking to your general appearance. She would not be averse to you paying court to her." Thaddeus's expression was triumphant. "It's all arranged, and so quickly, too. You will marry her, and you will have a purpose, helping to manage your wife's fortune. She comes with a healthy dowry, I may have forgotten to mention."

Now Sebastian couldn't say anything even if he wanted to.

"She's over there, speaking with Ana Maria."

Sebastian turned to where Thaddeus was pointing. His sister stood in a cluster of ladies so he couldn't figure out which was Miss Muttlefield.

But he knew it wasn't the lady in the gold gown, who stood in the group. Ivy. His chest squeezed at the thought of her hearing of Thaddeus's plan.

Fuck.

"Well?" Now it was Thaddeus's turn to sound impatient. "Is it too much to hope you'd be grateful?"

"Thaddeus, I really wish you hadn't done any of this. Not without asking me." *I don't want this.*

"Isn't this exactly what you wanted?" Thaddeus sounded bewildered, which Sebastian had never heard from his decisive cousin before. "We spoke about it just this afternoon!" As though bringing it up in conversation was equal to agreeing to whatever machinations Thaddeus might devise.

"It is the last thing I wished for," he gritted out. "It's well-intentioned, but don't you see that this kind of conniving is just as deplorable as what my mother did? Lying to achieve a certain status?"

"A certain status? Or do you mean the only status you've ever known?"

"Stow it, Thad. Even if it was possible to make me a duke again, I wouldn't want it." Saying it aloud made it so much more real. And he knew he believed it. "Not if it means compromising myself and my goals."

"But—"

Sebastian glanced over toward Ivy again, feeling an irrepressible urge to speak with her. Before it was too late. Before she heard.

"If you'll excuse me." He had to go over there and make certain she didn't know about any of this.

Because—damn, because he loved her.

He loved her. And that was worth more than anything.

"Sebastian!"

He ignored Thaddeus calling his name.

"Miss Ivy, you and my brother dance so wonderfully together," Lady Ana Maria said, the warmth of her eyes easing Ivy's discomfort at being abandoned on the dance floor.

"Lady Ana Maria, I didn't know you were Mr. de Silva's sister!" The young lady who spoke was elegantly, perfectly gowned, with a strand of brilliant diamonds around her neck that caught the light.

"I am, Miss Muttlefield." Lady Ana Maria gazed off toward where Sebastian had last been seen. Unlike Ivy, she had not tracked him from the dance floor to behind the pillar.

"He is so handsome," the lady enthused.

"He is." Lady Ana Maria sounded uncomfortable; perhaps she had realized that there was more to their relationship than one of employee/employer? "Miss Holton, may I present Miss Muttlefield?"

The ladies shook hands as Lady Ana Maria kept speaking. "Miss Muttlefield's father is in shipping." Miss Muttlefield looked anxious, as though Ivy was going to stomp off because there was a person from commerce in her general vicinity.

"Miss Holton is a businesswoman herself," Lady Ana Maria continued. "She and my brother . . . work together," she said, fluttering her hands in a vague manner.

"Oh!" Miss Muttlefield said in a relieved tone of voice. "Then you understand how it feels to be here. I am so grateful to the duke for his invitation this evening."

"How did your father make the duke's acquaintance?" Lady Ana Maria asked.

Miss Muttlefield shrugged. "I am not certain. Father doesn't share details of his business with me. He is determined to make a lady of me," she added with a self-deprecating laugh. "I've had lessons in French, Italian, embroidery, dancing, and painting. Watercolors only, of course," she said.

"Of course," Ivy echoed with a smile.

"And he especially wanted me here to see what I thought of all this." Miss Muttlefield's bright expression revealed what her opinion was. "He has given me a great dowry so as to attract the best gentlemen for my hand," she continued artlessly.

"Miss Muttlefield, if I may be so bold, it is not always polite to discuss finances at a party," Ivy said in a quiet tone that she hoped wasn't condemning. More like a wise older sister. "I have discovered that myself," she added in a self-deprecating tone, even though it was a lie. She just didn't want Miss Muttlefield to feel as though she was being reprimanded.

Miss Muttlefield's eyes widened. "Oh, I know that! I just thought that since Lady Ana Maria is his sister that it would not matter as much." She ducked her head. "Father said that Mr. de Silva might be in need of a bride and a fortune. If he is to return to Society."

Ivy's throat closed.

"We have been asking him to come back," Lady Ana Maria said, sounding enthusiastic. "No offense to what he is doing with you, Miss Holton," she added. "This might be the perfect thing for him."

What he is doing with you, Miss Holton.

And what was that, anyway? He had never told her how he felt.

And she hadn't asked.

Nor had she said.

Because it was all temporary, they both knew that.

"Perfect," Ivy said. "If you will excuse me?" She nodded at both the ladies, willing herself not to storm away or fall down in a sobbing heap or anything that would reveal her own feelings.

Which were—well. That would be something she would ask herself another time. Right now, she just needed to leave.

Chapter Twenty-Two

$\mathcal{S}$ebastian saw her walk swiftly toward the entrance, saw Ana Maria and who he presumed was Miss Muttlefield looking after her in surprise. Octavia burst out of nowhere and dashed after her, making everyone look at them.

He was opening his mouth to call her name, never mind that everyone would notice and gossip about it, when he was stopped short by a hard grip on his shoulder.

"Ex-Hasford."

It was Mr. Jennings who'd grabbed him, surrounded by a more sober, more belligerent Lord Linehan and a few other gentlemen whose expressions were equally derisive.

Wonderful. Just what he needed. More entitled disdain when all he wanted was to chase after her.

"Let go of me." Sebastian kept his voice low. He didn't want to ruin Ana Maria's party with a brawl. But he would if necessary. He gave a furtive glance around the room; thankfully, Nash was not in the area, or he knew there would be a brawl.

"I knew you would be here, no matter that you are a bastard," Mr. Jennings practically spat out. As though those two things had anything to do with one another.

He wanted to address the incongruity, but doubted they would follow his line of reasoning.

"Is this what you gentlemen do for pleasure?" Sebastian asked, placing his hand on Mr. Jennings's and yanking it off his shoulder. "Find someone you believe is lesser than you and point that fact out to them?" He shook his head. "Seems like a waste of time to me. Besides which, what happens when someone finds *you* lesser?"

Had admitting he'd fallen in love suddenly increased his ability to philosophize? He was impressed. By himself.

Perhaps he hadn't shucked the duke persona enough.

"You should stick to your own kind. *Bastard*," Mr. Jennings said. "It's a good thing your sister has an excellent dowry," he sneered as he shoved Sebastian back.

He was able to keep from falling down, thank goodness, but he wasn't able to keep his fist from Mr. Jennings's nose.

Oops.

That gentleman was not so lucky, falling down in a heap on the dance floor as the assembled crowd gasped.

"Sebastian!" Thaddeus strode up, pushing through the group that had surrounded Mr. Jennings, who was sitting up and holding his nose while glaring at Sebastian. "Come with me."

"I can't, I—" He craned his neck to see if he could spot her. But she must have already gone.

"We need to speak. Now." Thaddeus gestured to a side door that led, eventually, to Thaddeus's office.

Goddamn it.

Thaddeus pushed him forward. The guests were already backing away from Sebastian, as though worried he would take a swing at them, too.

Only if you malign my sister, he thought.

"Undo it."

Sebastian stood in Thaddeus's office, which was finally beginning to look like Thaddeus's office, and not Sebastian's. There were maps on easels, stacks of papers wrapped in neatly organized bundles, and a large pitcher of water on the small side table next to the most comfortable chair in the room.

Not untidy ledgers, packs of cards for playing patience when he had none, and a decanter of whiskey.

Thaddeus sat behind the desk, both palms flat on its surface, a grim expression on his face.

"I can't undo it. Not without proper procedure."

"Proper procedure?" Sebastian shot back. "What the hell does that even mean?"

"Mr. Muttlefield approached me, knowing of your circumstances." Thaddeus's tone was his most pedantic, and also—not coincidentally—the one that Sebastian hated the most. "He suggested we had a mutual interest in ensuring our family members are able to ascend to a higher place in Society than they are in currently. In his case, he wishes his daughter to achieve greater heights than he could. In your case—well, we spoke about it just this afternoon. I took that as my cue to confirm with Mr. Muttlefield that his plan met with your approval. I didn't want to mention it to you until it was a certainty since I didn't want to get your hopes up. If I was wrong, this afternoon's discussion was the time to inform me you wished to stay ostracized from your family and everyone you love." He sounded thoroughly condescending, and Sebastian wished Nash were here, if only so Sebastian could ask his friend to punch his cousin.

"Goddamn it, Thad." Sebastian paced in front of the desk. "I had already told you I wanted to do things on my own. Make my own way. I certainly didn't intend for you to arrange a marriage for me."

Thaddeus ignored his objections, as Sebastian had known he would. "Ana Maria and I agreed to allow you to indulge your fancy for a time. But we knew you would change your mind."

"So I'm a dilettante now?" The fury roiled inside of Sebastian, nearly making him want to punch Thaddeus in the jaw. Even though that would do no good in the current situation.

"You always have been a dilettante." Thaddeus was firm in his judgment. And he wasn't wrong seven months ago. But then Sebastian's situation had changed. And he had changed. Like he was changing now. "You expect me to believe that you want to take the hard route? When you never have before?"

You don't know me anymore, Thad.

Because you haven't let him.

"Just meet Mr. Muttlefield and his daughter. He appears to be a gentleman, you would never know he is a merchant. And his daughter is quite lovely. A worthy addition to our family."

Sebastian uttered a derisive snort. "You are such a snob, Thad. And here I thought you were all for the common man and earning respect because of deeds, not divination."

"Deeds not divination, hm?" Thaddeus sounded amused.

"It's not amusing." Sebastian paused. "This is my life, my future. My mother and her machinations tried to alter my course, but this is what I have to go from. *This.* Me as a bastard, not as a casual aristocrat who can marry back into everyone's good graces."

"Is it that you're not certain you can? I assure you, Mr. Muttlefield holds considerable sway in our world."

"Our world. *Your* world. Why does it have to be bifurcated?"

"Bifurcated? Your vocabulary has improved, even if your social standing has not."

"Stop treating this like a game, Thad. This isn't a military operation where someone will win and someone will lose. This is my life. I don't want my life to change."

Thaddeus ignored his last words. "I just want you to have the life you were intended to have, despite your mother." Thaddeus's tone was nearly convincing.

But there was Ivy to consider. And there was him, and what he wanted.

"Just think about it, Sebastian. Compare what you would have with what you currently have. Which is nothing."

"I have plenty." Sebastian took a deep breath. "I have work, good, hard work that is rewarding in several ways. I have friends. I have pride. I have the satisfaction of knowing that if someone listens to me it's because of me, not because of what I can do for them. And," he said, exhaling, "I have someone I love."

There. He'd said it. And it felt right.

He exhaled. "I'm sorry, Thaddeus. I know myself now, much better than I did before, and I know I cannot deny how I feel."

"Well, then," Thad said in a gruff voice, "I'll tell Mr. Muttlefield."

And I'll tell her.

"WHAT IS IT?"

Octavia kept asking, and Ivy kept shaking her head.

"You're going to have to tell me," Octavia said in a matter-of-fact voice. "You can't keep anything from me, you promised. Except for *those* details," she added hastily.

Ivy made a strangled noise that was half sob, half laugh.

The two sisters were in a hansom cab Ivy had hailed impulsively as she left the duke's residence. She hadn't waited for her wrap; she presumed Lady Ana Maria would keep it safe for her. She'd just needed to leave.

What if he married? Miss Muttlefield seemed perfectly nice. He could return to his former way of life with a wealthy wife and a stable position in Society.

Would he want that?

And what did she want? She'd been asking herself that for a few weeks now, and she hadn't been able to answer the question. Until now. When it was too late.

"What is it?" Octavia asked for perhaps the hundredth time. Her sister was nothing if not persistent.

The cab slowed, and then stopped.

"There's an overturned cart up ahead," the driver yelled.

Wonderful. More time to sit and think about it all. She might as well tell Octavia; it would pass the time, at least.

"I got introduced to a young lady," Ivy said, forcing herself to speak slowly, "and it was implied that Sebastian might be marrying her."

Octavia leaped back in surprise. "No. No, he can't. He loves you surely."

Ivy shrugged. "I don't know. He hasn't said."

"Have you said?" Octavia asked pointedly.

Ivy rolled her eyes, although her sister couldn't see it, thanks to being in the dark cab. "No, but it's not my place to say."

Now it felt as though she could see Octavia rolling her own eyes. Remarkable talent her sister had.

"For goodness' sake, Ivy, you are a resourceful, powerful woman. You shouldn't resort to submission when there is something you want."

The anger bubbled out of nowhere, startling both of them. "I'm not powerful and resourceful. I am determined. And I am frightened. Do you think it was easy to do all this?" Ivy said, spreading her hands wide. "To gamble with our very lives and to come here with no guarantee that we would succeed? I wish I were powerful." She snorted. "Most of the time I just think about what will happen if I don't continue, and that fear drives me." And just as suddenly, her anger subsided, and she felt flattened. As if her anger had taken all her energy.

Octavia's hands found hers in the dark, holding tight. "I know you feel sometimes as though you aren't brave."

Ivy snorted again.

"But you will do whatever is necessary to protect whomever you love. Why not do the same for yourself?"

Ivy took a deep breath. The carriage rattled over the cobblestones, jostling their shoulders together. Ivy could see the buildings had become less posh, meaning that they were nearing the club. Closer to where she belonged. And, she knew, where she *wanted* to belong.

She didn't want to go back to that life, even if it was offered to her. And she couldn't ask him to make the choice between her and his future, if there was a chance he might return to being who he was.

She lifted her chin, feeling the resolve flowing through her. Better. She felt much more like herself. Not some lovesick schoolgirl who was blind to what life would be like if she compromised, because love was all.

Love was all, but it was love for oneself. One's family. Not discarding everything, one's entire character, because of another person.

"I do love myself," Ivy said at last, smiling in the dark as she heard Octavia's sigh of relief.

"Good. I do not want a sister who doesn't know she's as wonderful as I know she is."

Ivy's eyes teared up, and she squeezed Octavia's hand.

And the carriage rolled up in front of Miss Ivy's, Sebastian standing in front of the club, his expression tense.

She would be fine, no matter what. She knew that. She would just have to make sure he understood that, as well.

SEBASTIAN PEERED INSIDE the cab, but was unable to see who its occupants were. The club was just reaching its peak hours, so there had been plenty of carriages pulling up, only to leave Sebastian disappointed as people who were not Ivy emerged, eager to gamble at the club.

What was taking her so long? He'd expected her to beat him here, but he'd run inside and asked, and nobody had seen her yet.

He hadn't bothered with a carriage back to the club, instead opting to walk, his mind churning with all the possibilities. What if she hadn't heard anything? What if her leaving was entirely unrelated to him?

His previous ducal self would not have allowed that to be a possibility, since everything was about him, but now he knew that there were other factors involved.

And if she had left because of him, what was she thinking now?

Octavia emerged from the cab, and Sebastian's chest tightened as he waited.

She looked at him as she descended, then lowered her gaze as she deliberately shook out her skirts. Her entire demeanor suggested she wanted to avoid him, but that was the last thing he would allow.

Even if that meant he had to return to the habits of his former arrogant self.

"You're back," he said, then winced. Of course she was back. She was here, wasn't she?

"I am," she replied shortly. She walked past him to go in the club. Henry held the door open, glowering at Sebastian as she stepped inside.

That was no different, at least. One of these years Henry would unbend enough maybe to even smile at him, but tonight was not that night.

Octavia made a gesture to indicate he should follow, and he nodded.

"Tell her how you feel," Octavia urged as she went into the club behind him. He glanced back at his friend with an aggravated expression on his face.

"What?" she asked in a pugnacious tone. "Oh, and I'll take Byron and Keats out."

"Thank you," he replied, speeding up his pace. Ivy was already halfway across the club floor, barely acknowledging the staff or customers. Not like her at all.

"Ivy," he called, and her steps slowed, then sped up again.

Damn it.

He began to run so he was abreast with her in just a few moments.

"What do you want?" she asked in a peevish tone.

Good. She had spirit enough to be argumentative, so he hadn't lost her yet.

"I want to speak to you. I want to—" He glanced around, noticing the interested faces all around them. "Damn it, can we be alone, please?"

"That's what got us into all this trouble," she murmured, but she continued to walk, opening the door that led upstairs to the private apartments and holding it open for him to follow.

"The sitting room," she said.

They walked into the room, Sebastian waiting until she had seated herself, shutting the door behind them. He went to the cabinet where she kept the whiskey, bending down to retrieve it from the back of the shelf.

He opened the bottle, pouring two glasses for them. He plucked them both up off the table, holding one out to her. She took it with a raised eyebrow, but didn't say anything.

He sat beside her, resting his forearms on his knees. Now not certain what he should say.

"Well?" she said. "You wanted to speak to me?"

He took a sip of the whiskey, which burned down his throat. Not nearly as painful as how it felt when he saw her leaving the ballroom.

"I don't know what was said—" he began.

"I can tell you," she interrupted. "I am glad you will be able to return to your life. Your real life, not whatever you were doing here." He opened his mouth to object to her derisive tone.

She is hurting, too, he reminded himself. Last night wasn't just something they could dismiss. They had to talk about it. Even if it turned out she didn't want him.

That burned far more than whiskey.

"Did you think what occurred between us was mere indulgence?" he asked.

She shrugged. Her expression was guarded. "I believe you feel—felt something for me. I also believe that you belong there, not here. You have a marvelous opportunity."

His eyes narrowed. "So that is what you want?"

She lifted her chin. "It is not what I want, Mr. de Silva, that is important."

"Sebastian," he said through gritted teeth.

"Sebastian. I am a practical businesswoman. I would not begrudge you something that would allow you to be who you truly are."

"And who am I?" He could feel the bitterness, the anger, churning inside his gut. Did she think so little of him that she thought he could just walk away? Did she think so little of herself?

"You are an aristocrat. You barely know how to shave yourself." The words rankled.

"I've been learning!" he shot back, sounding defensive.

Damn it. This was not how this was supposed to go.

"And we both knew that it was a momentary alteration in your life. I can have your things sent. Unless you wish to just leave them."

He knew she was hurting. She had to be, given that she was saying these things. But—

"That's it? You won't fight for me?"

That chin lifted even more. "I have been fighting ever since that card game, Sebastian." She exhaled. "I am tired. I am tired of fighting." She spoke in a dispirited tone, and just like that, his anger dissipated.

And an idea, a wonderful idea, occurred to him. An idea that could solve everything. He'd need to smooth things over with Thaddeus, but the end result would be what they all wanted. He could give her everything she'd lost.

He put his glass down on the table between them, going to kneel in front of her. He took her glass from her hand, then clasped her hands in his.

"Ivy. What if—what if we could both return?" His enthusiasm increased as he considered it. "What if we were to get married? Thaddeus would gladly give me money, he has offered several times. He would likely allow us to live on one of the many Hasford estates. We could have a home. I refused his offers before out of pride, since I wanted to prove I could make it on my own. But I can, I've shown that. So if we got married, we could go back to our life, and we would have everything we had before. Both of us. Together."

She stared at him blankly. He squeezed her fingers, keeping his gaze on her.

And then she spoke.

"That is your offer?" Her tone was cold, and he stilled. "You think I long to return? That I am so desperate to be a respectable lady once again that I will give this up? My employees will lose their positions. I will have to cede everything I own, everything I am, to you. Because you're my husband. Because you would effectively own me."

Her face crumpled, and he released her hands, leaning back on his heels.

"I thought you had come to know me. Know what I want. I thought you knew sooner than I did." She smothered a sob as her eyes grew bright. "I have finally come to realize that this is who I am, and who I want to be. I want to live my own life, Sebastian."

She rose, shaking with emotion. "I do not want to be obligated to anyone else for my livelihood. That is no way to live. At least not for me." She swallowed, the expression on her face sending daggers to his heart. "You can go back, Sebastian. You *should* go back. That is who you are, no matter what you were playing at these past few weeks. An entitled aristocrat who believes that being kowtowed to is more important than your pride or sense of self."

She walked to the door, flinging it open. "Go now. I can send your things to you, or you can leave them here. I am certain you will soon be able to afford far finer replacements."

"This isn't fair, Ivy," he growled. His anger had blazed back, feeling as though it would engulf him. "You haven't given me a chance."

She uttered a derisive snort. "A chance for what? A chance to try to cajole me to reject all of my hard-won values? A chance to deny who I am, who I have become?" She shook her head. "No. You don't deserve that chance. You don't deserve *me*."

He kept his gaze on her for a few long moments, his heart aching as his fury pounded. Odd how anger and love could coexist inside a person, but there it was.

"Go," she repeated in a softer tone.

He clenched his jaw, the words crashing in a tumult in his brain, but not able to say anything. Certainly not anything that would help.

He strode to the door, yanking it open so hard it crashed against the wall, then slammed it behind him.

"Sebastian?" Octavia stood in the hallway, her eyes wide.

"Not now," he said, walking past her to his room. He whistled for Byron and Keats, then walked across the club floor, ignoring everyone, to leave.

Forever.

Damn her.

"Ivy!"

Octavia burst into the room only seconds after Sebastian left, her gaze taking everything in. She was instantly standing in front of her, the same spot Sebastian had just vacated, wrapping her hands around Ivy's waist and holding her tightly.

The sobs came then, full all-body sobs that poured out from inside her, making her shudder.

"What happened?" Octavia asked.

Ivy's throat was thick. Too thick to talk, certainly. She just shook her head.

"Did he—did he tell you how he felt?" Octavia said.

Ivy was about to nod her head when she realized the truth of it. He hadn't. He hadn't told her he loved her. He'd suggested marriage as the most convenient way for them to be respectable again. A convenient way for them to continue their sexual liaison, she supposed.

If he tired of her—*when* he tired of her—was he thinking he'd just go set himself up with a mistress? Perhaps a woman who was not of his world? Like her?

"Ivy?" Octavia asked. "Can I get you something?" Her sister handed the glass of whiskey to Ivy, who took it automatically.

She drank it, all of it, sputtering as the liquid went down her throat. She felt the heat of it in her belly immediately, the light-headed feeling a welcome one given how distraught she felt.

She could understand why people turned to drink in difficult times.

"I don't want to talk about it, Octavia." Ivy gently disengaged her sister's hands from around her waist. "I want to go into my room, have a cry, and then get back to work. Perhaps I'll have a cup of tea." And then she wanted to cry again because it reminded her of his antipathy toward the beverage.

"You know I am here for you," Octavia said. "Whatever you want to do, I am here for you."

Ivy offered a tremulous smile. "I know. Thank you."

She took a deep breath, then frowned. "I do want to tell you about it, actually. I don't know why I said I didn't."

"Habit?" Octavia offered, a wry smile on her lips. "Because you're accustomed to holding back your emotion for fear it will cause difficulty? Because you're accustomed to doing everything by yourself?" Her sister's expression was fierce. "But I am old enough to shoulder this with you, Ivy. I want to be here with you, as you were there for me when I was too young to understand."

Ivy felt the tears welling up again, but this time they weren't borne of misery.

This was why she had responded so vehemently when he'd made his suggestion. Why she knew that if he was to plead his case she would have the same answer.

It wasn't worth it to give up not only her autonomy, but that of her sister's. She'd already made decisions for Octavia, she didn't want to continue to do so. Octavia should be able to make her own mistakes, not have her sister make them for her.

"Let me tell you what happened," Ivy said, taking Octavia's hand and guiding her to the seat where he'd sat, then placed herself down in her own chair. "You might want some of that, too," she added, gesturing toward Sebastian's half-drunk whiskey.

Chapter Twenty-Three

"What the hell, Seb?"

Nash glared at Sebastian, an irritable look on his face. His butler, Finan, stood behind him, a less irritated but more exasperated expression on his face.

At least he was inciting a reaction from everyone he spoke to?

Small comfort. Or, to be honest, no comfort at all.

Nash swung the door wide. "You'd better come in," he muttered ungraciously. Sebastian walked in, followed by Byron and Keats. As Nash shut the door behind him, the noise echoed in the bare hallway.

His friend wore a black silk dressing gown, making him look even more menacing than usual. It hung open over his naked chest, wrapped at the waist, not quite long enough to hide his bare legs and feet.

"You were asleep?" Sebastian asked unnecessarily. Because Nash's hair was all awry, his eyes were puffy, and his cheeks were heavily stubbled.

"Yes, you idiot, because it is five o'clock in the morning."

"It is?" Sebastian said in surprise. He hadn't taken note of the time when he'd left Miss Ivy's, but it couldn't have been much past one o'clock. Had he truly been wandering for over four hours?

"Come into the study." Nash whirled in a flurry of black silk, stalking down the hall to open the door, holding it wide for Sebastian. "Bran—" he began, only to be cut off by Finan.

"I know, Your Grace, brandy and brandy and more brandy," the butler said in an aggrieved tone. "People coming at all hours of the day and night causing havoc," he muttered as he retreated down the hall. "And with their dogs, too," he added.

"Insolent beast," Nash commented as he shut the door. His tone held no rancor, however, and Sebastian had to chuckle.

Nash sat down, tucking the fabric of his dressing gown around him so as to preserve his modesty. Sebastian appreciated that his friend was alert enough to spare Sebastian's eyes from the sight.

"What is it?" Nash said, sounding almost sympathetic.

"I look that bad, hm?" Sebastian replied. Byron and Keats settled at Sebastian's feet.

Nash shrugged. "No, honestly. You look as you usually do. It's just not like you to show up, banging on my door at such an hour. Not to mention I saw the lady scurry out from the ballroom and you follow after with a determined expression. Tell me what happened."

Sebastian began to speak.

Finan kept their glasses filled through the entire story, from the cribbage board incident to Ivy's refusal.

"You wanted her to be—what? A bastard's bride dependent on her husband's family?"

Uh. "Well, put that way—"

"What other way would you put it, Seb?" Nash asked, swallowing the rest of his brandy and holding it out for Finan without taking his eyes off Sebastian.

"I wanted her to return to who she was." He sounded defensive even to himself.

"Who she *was*?" Nash replied, emphasizing the last word.

Sebastian frowned. "What do you mean?"

"I mean, you idiot, that she has clearly become more than what she was. Tell me," he continued, pointing an accusing finger toward Sebastian, "would you have paid attention to her at all if she had been Miss Ivy—I don't know her last name . . ."

"Holton," Sebastian supplied.

"Holton. If she had been Miss Ivy Holton, and had been presented to you in a ballroom wearing white and a demure smile?"

When had Nash ever been this loquacious? Or had he always been able to converse, but nobody had ever asked it of him? Required it of him?

Perhaps they all had hidden depths that were only discovered when difficulties arose.

He opened his mouth to reply, then snapped it shut again. "No," he said at last. "I wouldn't have."

"Exactly." Nash paused. "So why do you want her to be someone you wouldn't have paid attention to? Why don't you want her to be *her*?" A pause. "And why don't you want you to be you? The person you are now?" A philosophical Nash was almost too much to bear.

Fuck. Nash was right. They both knew it. Finan knew it. Likely Byron and Keats knew it, too.

"I've ruined it," he said. "If I go back to her and try to persuade her that I don't want her to change—how could she possibly believe me? I still don't have the means to support her—"

"Does she need supporting?" Nash interrupted.

Sebastian began to sputter, only to give in to Nash's irrefutable logic. It was only custom that he feel obliged to provide for his wife; there were certainly ladies whose fortunes or skills allowed them to be the primary breadwinner. He just didn't know any of those people himself.

Because you've only ever known aristocrats, a voice whispered pointedly in his head.

"Does she need supporting?" Nash asked again, this time in a more acerbic tone.

"No. But—"

"But nothing." Nash downed his glass of brandy, waving Finan away when he would have refilled it. "You need to decide what you want to do, Sebastian. You idiot. Do you want to suffer the rest of your life without love because of your pride, or do you want to go to her, grovel in a thoroughly satisfying manner, and then kiss her senseless?"

Put that way— "Yes."

Nash frowned. "Yes, what? Suffering or groveling?"

"The latter, I believe, Your Grace," Finan interjected.

"Precisely," Sebastian replied.

Nash made a shooing gesture. "So go, you idiot. Grovel well. Your future depends on it."

Sebastian rose, glancing down at his dogs. "Could you—?"

"Yes, leave them here. They can have some brandy, too," Nash said in an impatient tone of voice.

"No brandy for dogs, Your Grace," Finan chided.

"Beef, then. Whatever they want. Just go."

Sebastian nodded toward Nash and Finan, then spun on his heel and nearly ran out of the house. It wasn't too late. Was it? It wouldn't be too late. He had to tell her how he felt. And if she didn't want him after that?

Well, then, he'd try again.

And again.

And if she never said yes?

He would work to be the man she deserved, even if she never accepted him. He would not compromise. Not with his goals, his marriage, his future.

She'd shown him the importance of that.

Now he just had to figure out a plan.

"You want to—what?" Thaddeus narrowed his gaze at Sebastian. They were back in Thaddeus's office. The town house was still being cleaned after the party, and Thad had told Sebastian that Ana Maria was still asleep.

The party had been a grand success for her, and for Thaddeus's first official appearance as the Duke of Hasford, Thad reported.

Sebastian sat in front of Thaddeus's desk, no longer noting the changes in the office with regret. That time of his life was well and truly over. And he did not wish to return.

"I want to take up your offer. Not the one involving me marrying Miss Whatshername," he added hastily.

"Muttlefield," Thad supplied.

"But the one where I go to a Hasford country estate and try my hand at management. I've learned a lot at Miss Ivy's"—*including how to fall in love*—"but I want to make my own way. That's why I want to be anonymous."

"They won't recognize you?" Thaddeus asked.

"The one we grew up in, yes, of course they would. But there are others, ones that my mother deemed not ostentatious enough to patronize." He couldn't keep the bitterness from his tone. One day, perhaps, he'd forgive his mother. As Ana Maria wished.

But that day was not now.

At least her overt snobbery meant that there were places he could go without being recognized. An upside to her complete and entirely offensive persona.

"Why do you want this?"

It was an honest question, and one Sebastian hoped he could answer honestly.

"I've changed, Thad." Sebastian glanced away from Thaddeus's direct gaze, trying to find the words to explain. "You presented me with an option that might have suited me if it had come up right after hearing about the title. I don't know. Maybe. It's a reasonable option, one that any somewhat disgraced gentleman would leap at if it meant he could return to the world he knew."

"You weren't disgraced," Thad said gruffly. "You were always you, it is just that—"

"That I was no longer the duke. I know. And you were right when you said I usually took the easy way. I never thought before about the easy way or the hard way. I just assumed that things occurred because of me. Not what my lineage provided."

He looked back at Thaddeus, whose expression was intent. Listening to Sebastian as he'd never listened before.

First Nash, now Thad. Was everyone different?

"At first, after losing everything, all I knew was what I didn't want. I didn't want to be a charity case, I didn't want to do the same things my mother had."

He took a deep breath. "And when I did think I knew what I wanted, I set my sights too high." Yes, he could eventually get enough money to become an investor. But that would take years, and meanwhile, he had a life to live, and a woman, hopefully, to love.

"But that's not enough now. I think I know what I am capable of. I just want a chance to prove it. And since I have no recommendations, I have to ask you for this favor. But if you agree, you cannot tell anyone—not Ana Maria, not anyone—where I am. I need to do this on my own."

Thaddeus gave him a long searching look, then grunted in assent.

Sebastian exhaled in relief. "Excellent. Thank you. And I promise, I will return."

"Just—just take care of yourself," Thaddeus said.

Sebastian stood up and stuck his hand out, and Thaddeus rose, as well.

"I promise I will," he said as they shook hands.

"Do you regret telling him to leave?" Octavia held Ivy's arm as they walked down the street. Once again, like that previous time, in search of apples, bread, and cheese. Octavia had also vowed to make Ivy choose a new hat, saying, *You might be miserable, but at least you'll look pretty.* Ivy didn't want to argue with Octavia, since her sister was being remarkably supportive.

And Octavia had taken over some of Seb's duties at the club, now coming up with creative ways to please their customers, so she didn't want to annoy her either.

Ivy sighed. "I don't regret it. It wouldn't have worked, what he planned."

"Of course not!" Octavia rejoined. "I am so glad you know what you want now."

I want him.

"And that the club is continuing to do so well."

One of the first things Octavia had done after that fateful evening was to choose a night to try Sebastian's plan of clever wagers. It had been successful, more than what Ivy had hoped, and they had nearly enough money to go buy that cottage by the sea, if that was what they wanted.

But Ivy didn't want that anymore.

She squeezed Octavia's arm as she spoke. "I have to thank you for keeping me from falling into melancholy." Octavia had gone so far as to surprise Ivy at odd moments by dashing into whatever room Ivy was in and dancing a spontaneous jig.

"It's because I care about you, silly," Octavia replied, sounding embarrassed. "You would do the same for me. Although it's not the same as staking my future on the turn of a card, or anything—"

"Hush!" Ivy exclaimed. "I didn't tell you that so you could tease me about it at any possible moment."

"No, but you do have to admit it's like me to do so," Octavia countered.

"Do you know where he went?" Octavia asked after a few moments.

A lump formed in Ivy's throat. "No. And it's not really anything I can ask."

"I could ask, if you want. Lady Ana Maria is so friendly anytime I stop to visit Byron and Keats."

Ivy knew Octavia was visiting Sebastian's half sister, but she hadn't wanted to ask anything about that either. Not because it would be odd or inappropriate, but because she didn't want Octavia to have to deal with the sight of her sister crying.

Besides, there was enough crying in the middle of the night when everyone had gone to bed.

"If he wants to see me, he can come find me."

They had reached the baker's stall by now. Piles of freshly baked bread were stacked on a cart, while the merchant stood behind the stall, patches of flour on her gown and a wide smile on her face. "What can I get for you, ladies?" she asked.

"Mac said he needs five loaves," Octavia said. "He's making sandwiches for the whist players. They spend a lot, we don't want them to leave because they're hungry."

"Five loaves, please," Ivy said.

The woman gathered the loaves and put them into two bags as Ivy handed over the money for them.

"Apples next?"

Ivy nodded. "Yes, but those are just for us."

"And the cheese?" Octavia asked in a hopeful voice.

Cheese. That night. She would not let her memories ruin the taste of one of the most delicious things ever invented. "Let's get lots of cheese for us," Ivy replied.

"If he did come find you, what would you say?" Octavia had torn off the end of one of the loaves, and had some of it stuffed in her mouth, making it difficult to hear.

"Don't talk with your mouth full," Ivy said automatically.

"Humph. You understood me, didn't you?"

Ivy rolled her eyes, but Octavia wasn't looking at her.

"I don't know what I'd say," she said after a moment.

"But you love him, don't you?"

Had she been grateful for her sister's solicitousness? She might have to revisit that opinion.

"I do," she admitted.

"I feel terrible he is such an idiot," Octavia continued. "He could have had you, and he tried to offer some sort of weak compromise without ever asking you what you wanted."

"Is this supposed to be making me feel better?" Ivy asked wryly.

"Well, no. But if we talk it out, eventually it won't be a big gaping wound in your heart." Octavia spoke in a matter-of-fact voice, making it that much more painful.

"Just a small gaping wound."

"At least you haven't lost your sense of humor." A pause. "No, wait, perhaps you've gained one, since you honestly were never that funny before."

"Thank you?" They had reached the cheesemonger's stall, thankfully, so Ivy was able to distract herself with choosing what types of cheese she wanted to drown her sorrows in.

They were heading toward the applecart when they heard their names being called.

"Miss Holton! Miss Octavia!" It was Lady Ana Maria dashing on the cobbled streets, a beleaguered-looking footman running after her.

"Good afternoon, Lady Ana Maria," Ivy said. Lady Ana Maria looked entirely out of place in the common marketplace; she wore an exuberantly colored gown of deep pink, with a darker pink spencer on top. Her hat was festooned with a variety of feathers and blobs of plastic fruit that dangled precariously off the side.

"Have you heard from my brother?" she asked. "I meant to ask when you were visiting his dogs the other day, but I forgot." She addressed Ivy. "Your sister is delightfully witty, she had me laughing so hard."

Octavia glanced at Ivy, then answered, "No, we haven't heard from him. Do you know where he went?"

Lady Ana Maria shook her head. "No. Thaddeus knows, but he won't tell me. He says Seb is safe and doing well, and that he will come back when he is ready. I miss him dearly."

She looked so mournful Ivy wanted to hug her, even though that would be entirely inappropriate, and likely rather odd.

But she could do something. "Lady Ana Maria, would you like to come to the club some evening? We have whist on Mondays—tonight, actually— and it can be fun."

"You are so lovely to try to take my mind off things," Lady Ana Maria said. "I will come. Nash— that is, the Duke of Malvern—has been there. I would very much like to."

"Excellent."

The ladies said their goodbyes, Ivy and Octavia heading to the applecart, Ivy able to sufficiently distract Octavia with a discussion of the juiciest type so that her sister wouldn't continue to press the point.

She loved him, he'd left, and she would have to adjust to that. She didn't regret her decision, but she did sorely regret his.

Chapter Twenty-Four

$\mathcal{T}$hey should be ready to harvest in another month."

Sebastian followed Clowster's gaze, looking with satisfaction at the emerging turnip greens.

"I don't know if I've ever eaten turnips," he remarked.

Clowster snorted. "Of course you haven't, Your Grace."

Sebastian gave Clowster a good-natured shove, and he responded by grinning and waggling his eyebrows.

The day was warm, and Sebastian could feel sweat trickling down his back. He wore his usual work garb of worn trousers and an equally worn shirt, both the hand-me-downs from an earlier worker, a gentleman who had a similar frame to his, but was at least half a foot shorter, meaning that his trousers ended at his lower shins.

Sebastian had chosen to come to the Hasford estate the farthest from London, not just to escape, but also so nobody would know who he was. He hadn't visited this estate since he was a boy.

It had taken all of about half an hour before he was recognized, however. A combination, perhaps, of Sebastian's inability to disguise his patrician accent and his looking remarkably like one of his ancestors, whose painting hung on the wall. Once the staff had stopped treating him as some unidentifiable anomaly, they'd taken to using Ivy's nickname for him, unaware she'd coined it first.

It had smarted, hearing it from someone else's lips, but he had grown accustomed to it. He'd grown accustomed to many things: waking up at dawn, working all day, being told what to do by someone he wouldn't have noticed before.

And he'd grown accustomed to the pain of missing her. He didn't think he would ever not feel it, but at least he could endure it. It helped that he was constantly busy.

Mr. Clowster made certain of that. He was the estate's current steward, the third such Clowster to hold the position.

"De Silva." Mr. Clowster's voice penetrated his thoughts, and he turned to regard the steward. His current boss.

Not as lovely as his previous one, but Mr. Clowster didn't have to worry that his worker would threaten his livelihood with his arrogant anger.

Mostly because the livelihood comprised a variety of vegetables, and Sebastian couldn't manage to be offended by any of those, no matter how stubbornly they refused to grow.

"What is it?"

It was close to dusk, and the sun was beginning to shift in the sky, indicating it wouldn't be long before the shadows lengthened and they had to go inside. The housekeeper, Mrs. Werriter, would be anticipating their arrival. Sebastian had noted with some humor that she was sweet on Mr. Clowster, who hadn't noticed a thing.

"It'll be time for you to go soon."

"What?" Sebastian asked in surprise. "Go where?" If it was to the market, they'd gone just the other week.

"You have to deal with it, lad. Whatever it is that you were running away from." Mr. Clowster jerked his head toward the rows of turnips. "These'll be coming up with or without you soon enough. You've spent time learning how to listen, and what to do, and I s'pose that is what you needed. Am I right?"

Sebastian folded his arms over his chest and glared at Mr. Clowster. "Did the duke tell you? Or the other duke?" Because he wouldn't put it past either Thaddeus or Nash to have alerted the staff about his heartache, damn them.

Mr. Clowster snorted. "I'm not in the habit of corresponding with dukes, Your Grace," he said in a pointed tone. "Even the one who owns this estate. It's obvious. We all knew there was a reason you came here, but we thought we'd just help you along with it." He nodded, making a shooing gesture. "And now you have. Too bad you won't get a chance to taste your turnips."

Now it was Sebastian's turn to laugh. "I'm that obvious, hm?"

"You're in love. You should talk to her." Just what Nash had said, only Sebastian hadn't been who he needed to be then.

Was he now?

And if he was, what would she say?

"Oh."

Ivy covered her mouth with her hand. He was here. He was here, after not being here for two months.

Or fifty-seven days, six hours, and forty-seven minutes, if one had been counting. Which one had not been.

She had expected the knock at the door to be one of the constables who checked in with her every day. To ensure the club was safe, but also to receive whatever was left over from Mac's cooking the night before.

The words burst out of her before she could even think. "Where have you been?"

"It's good to see you, Ivy." His gaze was intense, as though he was trying to see all of her all at once. It felt too much. It wasn't enough. "Can I come in?"

"Yes." She opened the door wider, and he stepped inside. He wore a plain suit with a white shirt, the clothing looking as though it had been chosen for its usefulness rather than its ability to make its wearer look handsome.

Not that he needed any help there.

If anything, he looked handsomer. He'd allowed his facial hair to grow in, so he had the start of a beard on his lean cheeks. It was golden brown and drew attention to his mouth. His gorgeously shaped mouth. His hair was longer, too, giving him an even more rakish look.

"Do you—would you like anything to drink?"

"Tea, perhaps?" he said with a hint of a grin.

She chuckled in surprise. "I can make—"

"I don't need anything, Ivy," he said. He paused, and his gaze seemed even more searching. "Except you."

SEBASTIAN HAD NO idea what he was going to say to her. Just that he was going to say *something*.

His brain felt fuzzy, the only persistent thought that he needed to see her. To talk to her. To tell her—something.

He hadn't expected that something to be a joke about his dislike of tea within a few moments of greeting her, but then again, everything about her was unexpected.

How he felt seeing her was not unexpected, however. It felt as though he'd been whacked in the chest by a powerful object, but the powerful object was a fierce emotion that was wonderful and tormenting all at the same time.

Was that love? It must be love. Now the Romantic poets he'd read back in the day made a lot more sense, what with always walking around with a mixture of agony and desire and yearning.

Well, if she turned him away, perhaps he could find a third career as a poet. Because that was doubtlessly lucrative. He'd snort at himself if he wasn't so on the edge.

"Well," she said, clearly composing herself, "would you like to sit down?" She gestured to one of the tables in the gaming room. It wasn't their table, much to his regret.

"I would." He waited for her to walk to the table, then followed, his mind buzzing with the overwhelmingness of everything.

Just say it all, his brain reminded him. *All the things you went over while you were at the Hasford country estate.* In between settling disputes between the housekeeper and the stable master, hiring temporary help for the harvest, and gently rebuffing the advances of the squire's widow.

She sat, folding her hands in her lap. She looked calm, but he could see her fingers moving as she clenched and unclenched her hands.

He drew a chair to sit opposite her. If he leaned forward, he would likely kiss her.

He wanted to kiss her so badly. It took an effort to keep his back rigid against the chair so as not to close the distance between them. But he would not intrude on her that way, not without saying everything he had to say—whatever that was—first.

"Well?"

"Well."

He couldn't sit in the chair. It didn't feel like enough. He rose and went to kneel on the floor in front of her. The hardwood hurt his knees, and yet the pain was welcome—feeling it meant it was real, that he was here with her now.

"Ivy, I—" And then he paused, the enormity of his emotions making his chest swell. "I was wrong. I want to tell you everything, tell you how I feel. And if at the end of it you don't want to see me again, I will accept it. But I am hoping you will hear me out."

"You're asking me," she said. "Not telling me." She sounded faintly surprised, and he felt a wry smile tug at his lips.

"I am asking. I'm asking for so many things." *Please give them to me. Because if you don't, I will have to resort to writing what will undoubtedly be bad poetry.*

"What are you asking for?"

He took a deep breath. "Ivy, before, when I asked you before, I made it seem as though I would be doing you a favor. I barely even asked you, I just sailed over it. I could say that wasn't what I meant at all, but I'd be lying. Even then, even after spending time with you and talking with you and eating cheese and drinking tea, I thought that you wanted to go back to that life we both used to have. It was arrogant of me"—at which she nodded—"and I have regretted it every moment since."

"You didn't drink tea," she pointed out, a trace of humor in her voice. Thank goodness.

"And what I didn't know then, but I know now, is that there is nothing about you that I would change. I don't want you to be a Society lady, worrying about your latest gown or who has accepted an invitation to dine."

She kept her gaze steady on him.

"But just as important as that is that I don't want to change. I don't want to change who I am now—a man, a man with faults and stubbornness and occasional arrogance"—at which her lips quirked up in a smile—"who loves his sister and his dogs and—and you. I love you, Ivy. And because I love you, I know that you would not be who you are, the strong woman I love, if you hadn't made your choices. Gambled on your own future. And I wouldn't be worthy of you if I let someone else dictate what was going to happen to me. That's why I left."

"Where did you go?" she asked. "You've been away so long." She sounded mournful, and he dared to hope.

He gazed over her shoulder in thought. Because if he kept looking at her lovely face he'd forget his words, and she should hear them so she could understand. Because he finally understood, thanks to his sojourn away from it all, and the work, and possibly even the turnips.

"I needed to discover what it was that had changed in my life. It was you, and Octavia, and the club, but it was also me: my resolve, my confidence, my goals. I don't want to be someone who just gets things handed to them. And I don't want to take them either. I want to ask for them." He reached around to his back, withdrawing the thing he'd kept as a reminder of what he was working toward.

"A—cribbage board?" she asked, sounding startled.

"*The* cribbage board," he replied. He flipped it upside down, sliding the bottom panel out to reveal the storage space. He withdrew the ring, clasping it tightly in his fist.

"Ivy," he began. "I won't say I don't care where we live. I *do* care. I don't want to live in a spacious town house. I don't want to sleep on satin sheets and have more servants than I can count. I want to live with you, in a home of our own making, wherever that might be. I want us both to risk it all, gamble on our future together."

"You'd make a terrible card player," she said, her eyes bright.

"I would. I do. I am showing all my cards, Ivy. I don't have any other tricks up my sleeve. I am Sebastian de Silva and I love you. So now I am going to ask." He swallowed, holding the ring out to her. "Ivy, will you marry me?"

"Yes."

IVY GRINNED AS he leaped to his feet, grabbing her up and out of the chair to whirl her in his arms.

They both looked down as they heard a noise on the floor.

"The ring!" he exclaimed, dropping down to retrieve it from where he'd dropped it. He shuffled over on his knees, a wide smile on his handsome face. "I want to hear it again. Ivy, will you marry me?"

"Yes," she repeated, and he slid the ring on her finger, then kept hold of her hands as he stood up. He placed one palm on the side of her face, his fingers caressing her tenderly.

"And now, Ivy, may I kiss you?"

"All this asking, Mr. de Silva." She licked her lips, which had gotten suddenly dry. "How about you tell me what you want."

His eyes lit up at her words, and his mouth curled into a wicked smile. "First, Miss Holton, I want to kiss you."

And he did. He slid his tongue in as she opened her mouth, and then his hand moved to the back of her neck, holding her in position. His other hand went to her waist, then slid up her rib cage to her breast, and he rested his palm there. Her whole body ached for him to touch her. He broke the kiss, his breathing already ragged. "And then I want to stroke your breast"—at which point he did just that and she gasped—"and if you'll let me, I'll undo your exceedingly practical gown so I can see your gorgeous body."

"Mm," she replied, turning around to present her back.

She felt his fingers at her buttons, and within a few moments, he'd slid her gown off her shoulders, holding it wide so she could step out of it.

She turned back to face him in her shift. "And this?" she asked, gesturing to it.

"Please."

Meanwhile, his hands were at his neckcloth, unwrapping it with one quick movement, then he removed his jacket and began to undo the buttons at his shirt.

She stood in just her stockings and shoes, her hair a tumbled mess around her shoulders.

His eyes drank her in, and she felt as though she were dressed entirely in his love.

And then he undid the placket of his trousers, toeing off his shoes as he shucked the fabric down. His erection stood proudly out from his small-clothes, and she couldn't help but lick her lips as she regarded it.

"Christ, Ivy, you'll be the death of me before we even marry," he growled, sweeping her into his arms, picking her up to deposit her on the table. Another table, not their table.

"Is it your intention to christen each one of these?" she asked, glancing around the room.

"If it means I can fuck you on every one of them, then yes," he said. His clever fingers finding her nipple, beginning to stroke it to a hard point.

She felt herself getting wet down there, and her hand moved of its own volition to caress the part of her that ached.

He still stood on the floor, his erection right at her eye level.

"Mm, yes, Ivy. Show me what you like." His gaze was rapacious on where her hand was stroking herself, and his hand went to his cock, gripping it tight as he began to slide his fist up and down.

"Ivy, I need to be inside you."

"Another order?" she said with a grin. She shifted over to make room, but he shook his head.

"No, not that way. Over here." He grabbed hold of her legs, spreading them wide so she was bared to him, then urged her forward to the edge of the table so her legs dangled off. He stepped forward so his cock was right there at her entrance. His stomach muscles were flexed, the hard ridges defining them a delicious sight. He took his shaft in his hand and pressed himself inside as she caught her breath. He slid inside as he took her leg and wrapped it around his waist. She did the same with the other leg and then he grabbed hold of her waist, holding her off the table entirely. He was certainly strong. It felt so good for him to be inside, and she bit her lip as she shifted against him. "That's it, Ivy. Goddamn, woman, yes. Fuck me." And then he managed to deposit them back on the table, still connected, only now she was on top astride him. She blinked in surprise as he urged her up, then down, until she got the rhythm of it. And then it was delicious, the pressure increasing inside her as she rode him, his gaze hungry on her, his hands roaming all over her body.

His fingers found that spot that was begging to be touched, and he stroked her as she kept moving, the momentum building until she hit that peak, flinging her head back to cry out as the enormity of it engulfed her.

"You are beautiful when you come," he said. His hair was damp from their exertions, and she could feel him inside her, hard and demanding. She kept moving up and down, faster and faster, until his eyes closed and the tendons in his neck stood out.

And then he arched his back and groaned, and she could feel the hot liquid spill inside her. Her hands went to rest on his chest, and they were both panting and she had never been happier in her life.

At last, after a few long moments, he opened his eyes and his lips curled into a wry smile. "Do you suppose after we are married we could try this in an actual bed?" He arched a brow. "And possibly try some turnips? I hear they are delicious."

"Yes," she said. "Yes, yes, yes."

Epilogue

"The ceremony was lovely," Ivy said as she and Sebastian entered their bedroom.

Thaddeus had lent them enough money to purchase a small home close to the club with the understanding—from Sebastian at least, Thaddeus didn't care—that they would pay the debt over time.

Octavia was fully in charge of Miss Ivy's and had forbidden them to return until a week following their wedding.

Ivy was chafing at the restriction already, but she was looking forward to spending time with Sebastian without worrying about anyone coming in. Not to mention the thought of spending time with Sebastian in a bed.

Byron and Keats were with Ana Maria, though they were coming to Ivy and Sebastian's home after their week alone.

"Can I help you with that, my lady bride?" Sebastian asked as Ivy began to tug on her headpiece.

"Please."

Ivy stood still as he gradually undid all of her clothing, from the top of her head to the soles of her feet. His smile grew increasingly wicked the more naked she got, and she was laughing by the time he reached her stockings.

"Come, wife," he said, drawing her toward the bed.

She froze, her eyes wide. "A bed? An actual bed? Whatever are we going to do in there?" she said in mock dismay.

He hoisted her over his shoulder and plopped her onto the mattress, making her bounce as she laughed.

And then he crawled toward her as he shed his clothing, his neckcloth sailing over his shoulder, his vest flung on top of the dresser nearby, his boots thumping on the floor.

"We are going to do everything, wife."

Her brows rose. "Everything?"

"Everything," he confirmed.

"Oh, good," she sighed, pulling him down for a kiss.

"I love you," he murmured before his mouth pressed to hers.

"I love you, too," she replied, her words muffled.

Keep reading for a sneak peek at the next book
in Megan Frampton's Hazards of Dukes series

Tall, Duke, and Dangerous

Coming soon from Avon Books!

Chapter One

If Nash, Duke of Malvern, had envisioned at all the scenario in which his life was to be irrevocably changed—which he had not, by the way—he would most certainly have thought he would have been wearing trousers.

He was not.

He was not, in fact, wearing anything at all. Excellent attire if one were planning on posing for a statue of some ancient Greek god, or taking a refreshing dip on a hot summer day in the privacy of one's personal estate. But not for life-changing events.

Unconventional though he was, Nash would have imagined trousers in that scenario.

And yet here he was.

"Get up."

Nash reluctantly opened one eye, wondering if he'd have to clock the person who was speaking for disturbing him so early in the morning. He definitely did not recognize the voice, and it was definitely not friendly.

But waking him was not a clockable offense. He chose his battles carefully, only getting into fights with someone who deserved it.

"Get. Up." This time, the irascible words were accompanied with a poke to his lower limbs, making him snarl. Perhaps he'd have to lower his "who to clock" standards.

"Your Grace, this is the Dowager Duchess of Malvern." That voice he recognized as belonging to Finan, but he'd never heard his valet sound so apprehensive.

Nash rolled over onto his back, opening the other eye. He stared up at the ceiling, blinking in an attempt to clear his head.

"Disgraceful." The dowager duchess's words were no less harsh than words Nash had spoken to himself, but he did not appreciate someone else pointing out his faults. Besides Finan, that is.

He sat up abruptly, the covers falling to his waist as he saw the lady, who immediately made some sort of yelping sound and turned to scurry out of his bedroom, her cane thumping on the floor.

"Told you you should wear a nightshirt," Finan grumbled.

"If going to bed naked means I frighten elderly aristocrats from my bedroom then why would I ever bother with a nightshirt?"

Finan just shook his head. Nash shrugged. It was a reasonable question.

"I will wait for you in the blue salon," the dowager duchess's voice came from down the hallway. "Come as soon as you are properly dressed."

Finan marched to the wardrobe and flung it open, yanking clothing out and dumping it at the end of Nash's bed.

"You heard her. Get up."

Nash glared at Finan, who glared back. One of the reasons he was able to tolerate the man's company as well as he did—Finan never kowtowed to him, nor did he let Nash get away with anything both of them knew was privileged nonsense.

"Just how terrifying is she?"

Finan folded his arms over his chest. "Somewhere between a loaded cannon and jellied eels."

Nash winced. "That bad." He threw the covers aside and walked to the washbasin, dipping his hands into the water and flinging it onto his face. The water was cold, and he shuddered at the shock of it on his skin. But he'd need to be as alert as possible to confront his grandmother—a woman he barely remembered.

"What do you think she wants?"

Finan snorted. "I have no idea. I wouldn't dare to ask her, either."

Nash felt an unsettling feeling of dread in his stomach. Not something he was accustomed to feeling; he was Nash, Duke of Malvern, naked sleeper determined to do what he wanted when he wanted. Always.

That he was also determined to do right by his responsibilities was likely why he had that dread. It was clear the dowager duchess was here on a matter of some importance, since he hadn't seen her in at least ten years. His father had cut off visits from all respectable members of his family, effectively isolating Nash from anyone who might help him.

Had she heard about his work assisting his father's bastards? It was the least he could do, given how many lives his father had ruined. Hopefully she didn't know his butler was also his half-brother.

Actually, he didn't care if she knew. It was the right thing to do, along with only inflicting his temper on people who deserved it.

Why else would she be here, though? He couldn't imagine anything that would bring any of his family members into willing contact with him—his father had burned all the family bridges, and Nash saw no need to rebuild them. If they wanted to know him, they would have to take him as he was.

Well, he wouldn't find out the answers to any of his questions by staying here.

Fifteen minutes later, Nash was dressed nearly appropriately, though he'd refused to put on a cravat, despite Finan's pleading looks.

"Your Grace," he said as he walked into the blue salon. He rarely used this room, much preferring his library, which had a sofa made especially for his long frame. The sofa here was more of a loveseat, which would be fine for two normal height people to sit on, but not for someone of Nash's size.

The dowager duchess was seated primly on a chair that matched the loveseat, her equally prim maid standing behind her. The poking cane leaned against the chair, inches away from the dowager duchess's hand.

Both ladies managed to look down their noses at him, despite their height differential.

Remarkable feat.

He hadn't gotten a good look at her when she'd been in his bedroom, what with her running away at the sight of his naked chest. But now he could see the resemblance to his father, both of them with strong cheekbones, dark brown eyes, and a general look of hauteur.

A resemblance he knew he shared, unfortunately.

Unlike his father, however, his grandmother was slight, with gray hair pulled away from her face and fastened on the top of her head with an enormous bow. Her eyes looked keenly intelligent, and held a cordial warmth he had certainly never seen from his father.

He found himself regretting, for just a moment, not wrapping a hellcloth around his neck.

"Your Grace," the dowager duchess said, inclining her head a fraction. "I have been remiss in not coming to see you—"

"Perhaps because I haven't extended an invitation?" Nash cut in.

It was best to let her know who he was as soon as possible. That way she wouldn't be disappointed later on.

She sniffed. Apparently made of strong stuff, his grandmother. A tiny part of him had to respect that.

"But I am here now, and I have some urgent business to discuss."

Well, he knew that already. Else why would she have come? He crossed his arms over his chest and waited. Bracing himself for her disapproval.

"Sit down." She spoke as though there was no possibility of his not doing as she commanded.

So he sat, holding his breath as he lowered himself onto the matching chair. It only creaked a little, and he gripped the armrests in a futile attempt at controlling whether or not it collapsed.

Perhaps he should redecorate. He had taken possession of the town house after his father died three years ago, but hadn't bothered to change anything, even though he disliked most of it. Or do much that a duke was supposed to do, to be honest.

Of course he discharged his responsibilities—he wasn't like his father, ignoring everything except that which brought him pleasure—but he didn't do the superficial things, like attend parties or be seen in the most fashionable parts of town engaging in frivolous activities.

Could that be why she was here?

And if that was so, why hadn't she come when her son had died? Why was he just seeing her now?

His last memory of her must've been from when he was about ten years old, not long after his mother left. He'd been too confused, too distraught, and too terrified of his father to pay attention to visitors.

"Well?" he said impatiently.

She looked unsettled, and he wondered just what the hell kind of business she had to discuss.

"Is this about an allowance? I don't know any-thing about those things, I let my man of affairs handle that." His man of affairs who was also his half-brother.

"No. My allowance is adequate, thank you."

"Good."

The silence stretched, and Nash began to shift in his chair, the creaking noise audible in the room. His grandmother arched a patrician eyebrow.

"I did not like your father. My son," she said.

That would explain why he hadn't seen her in all these years.

"We have that in common then."

"I regret his behavior toward your mother. When I realized what was happening, I did as much as

I could, which wasn't very much, unfortunately."
She spoke in a tight tone.

The familiar tension—the anger that simmered
within at all times—rose up in his chest, and he
clamped down so he wouldn't reveal his emotions.
As he always did.

"I gave her money to escape. Your father found
out, and forbade me to come in contact with you. I
should have come earlier. That is my fault."

He couldn't speak. "Escape. Do you know where
she is?"

She shook her head. "I do not. I just hope she is
safe."

Letters had come sporadically, smuggled to him
from sympathetic servants, so he knew she was
alive, and that she cared deeply about him and
worried about him. It had been a relief to know
she was doing well, even if she was helpless to
save him.

His father's death was the only thing that could
rescue him.

"So you're not here about my mother, then."

His grandmother's expression grew somber.
"No. But I need to interfere where I wasn't able to
before." She took a deep breath. "It seems that your
heir, Mr. John Montrose, has some of your father's
more . . . unpleasant habits." She paused. "You
hadn't heard?"

Nash shook his head no as he bit back a snarl,
his grip on the armrests tightening. "I don't speak
to many members of the family." At least not the
legitimate ones.

"I have it on good authority that you are not at
all like my son." He could hear the pain and regret

in her voice. She took a deep breath and gave him an intent, purposeful look. "The dukes of Malvern stretch back to Henry VIII's reign, and it is an honorable title."

"Honorable until my father." Memories flooded his brain, memories he usually expunged by getting into a brawl, or drowning with brandy. His mother, pleading with his father not to hit her. A young Nash grabbing his father's arm so he wouldn't strike again.

A young Nash splayed out on the floor, his nose broken.

She spoke again. "I have heard rumors that you intend never to marry."

Because he would not subject any woman to the possibility of his father's behavior. She continued in an urgent tone of voice. "But you must. The sooner your cousin has no possibility of inheriting, the better. He has heard the same rumors about you, and is borrowing heavily against his future, and his behavior is growing bolder. It is therefore imperative that you marry and produce an heir. Immediately."

Nash's throat closed over.

"I will stay here to assist you in your search for a bride," she announced. "It must be a lady of the highest birth, one who will do her duty as your duchess and provide children."

"What? No!" Nash said. He didn't know if he was saying no to her staying with him or a bride.

He just knew he didn't want any of it.

"Stand up."

He rose before he'd realized he'd obeyed her orders.

"You are quite handsome." It didn't necessarily sound like a compliment. "Excellent height, and your shoulders are quite broad. More suitable for a blacksmith than a duke, wouldn't you say?" she said, turning to look at her lady's maid. She turned back around without waiting for a reply. "We'll have to ensure you are dressed properly, and that your hair is neat, although I understand some ladies like that disheveled look." Her tone was disapproving.

"I've never had complaints before," Nash said, folding his arms over his chest.

His grandmother made another one of those disdainful sniffs. He did like her, in spite of what she was asking him to do.

What she was asking him to do—he'd almost forgotten. He sat down abruptly, the chair moaning its displeasure. "I have no desire to get married."

She narrowed her gaze at him. "Do you want another duke like your father? Do you want to allow someone like that to oversee the tenants and the household staff?" She raised her chin. "I have heard of your kindness toward Richard's . . . mistakes," she said, as though a child was a mistake. "Do you want your cousin to have power over them?"

"Fuck."

Her horrified expression told him he'd said the word aloud.

"My carriage is arriving soon with my luggage. If you will ring for your butler I will retire to my chambers." She rose as she spoke, and Nash saw her wobble for a moment before her maid clasped her arm to steady her.

Nash gritted his teeth. "Yes, Your Grace."

Because what else was he to say? The lady was determined to stay, and he couldn't very well throw her out, even if she had woken him up and demanded he marry, two things he did not want to do. Ever.

Not to mention she poked him with a cane.

But she was his family, and she had already admitted she loathed his father. And he did already like her, despite himself. And that blasted cane.

"Meanwhile," she said as she made her way slowly to the door, "please review your invitations so we can discuss what social events you should be attending. I will see you at dinner. Five o'clock, I presume."

Nash's mouth opened in protest, but no words emerged.

As soon as the door shut behind her, he did the only thing that he could—he picked up the chair she'd been sitting on and smashed it against the bookshelf, the pieces scattering over the plush carpet. But because of the damned carpet, the pieces didn't make a satisfying cacophony, but instead thumped softly on the ground.

He stared down at the now broken chair, that previous dread turning to panic as he realized what he'd just done—reacted in a violent way to unpleasant news.

Like his father.

He had to take control. He couldn't allow himself to lash out without cause. He'd never used violence without cause—that was how he justified using his fists to exorcise his demons. There were plenty of reprehensible people he could pick fights with to assuage his constant anger, if only for a short time.

But the broken chair had done nothing to him. A ridiculous thought, of course, but what if he erupted around a person who had done nothing to him?

Could he trust himself?

"Achoo!"

Ana Maria blinked to clear her damp eyes.

"My lady?" Jane, her lady's maid, held out a handkerchief.

"Stop calling me that," Ana Maria said in a grouchy tone, taking the handkerchief and wiping her nose.

They were seated in Ana Maria's salon, newly redecorated in colors that made Ana Maria's spirits soar, nothing like the room's previously staid blues and browns. Bright reds and purples and pinks created a fantastical setting that made Ana Maria grin every time she walked in, only now the room was also filled with flowers that were just as bright, but they made Ana Maria sneeze as well as smile.

She had to figure out which one was the culprit and forbid them entrance to the house. She hoped it wasn't the tulips. She loved tulips. Though she loved all flowers, so a tiny part of her hoped it was just dust. She did not like dust.

"You've been my lady for as long as I've known you," Jane replied tartly. "It's just the dragon wouldn't let us call you that."

"The late duchess," Ana Maria corrected.

"The dragon duchess," Jane said, accompanying her words with an eye roll.

"But can't we just be Ana Maria and Jane here, as we used to?" Ana Maria couldn't help her plaintive tone.

The words weren't even out of her mouth before Jane had folded her arms over her chest and was shaking her head. "You have to accept it, my lady. You're a lady, daughter of a duke, cousin to another duke. Like it or not, you are entitled to being treated as though you are a special person." Her voice softened. "And you *are* special, it is just that the dragon—that is, the late duchess," she said, at Ana Maria's stern look, "was determined to keep you in a particular place. And now that she's gone, you should take your rightful place among all those other ladies."

My rightful place. What place was that, Ana Maria wondered? For more than twenty years, she'd been the late duchess's unpaid and unappreciated dogsbody, doing anything that required doing, if the duchess ordered her to.

And now? Now she was supposed to become a lady overnight, a person who didn't know how to polish silver, who would order a bath without considering just how long it would take to boil water, and who treated the help as though they were just that—help, not people or even friends. Who did not have an opinion about dust, because she wasn't aware it existed.

But even if her status was suddenly elevated, she was not.

If only her half-brother, Sebastian, had remained as the duke she would have been far more comfortable. But Sebastian was not the rightful duke, not since it was discovered that the late duchess—in this particular case, the dastardly duchess—had lied about her relationship to Ana Maria's mother. When it was revealed that the two duchesses were sisters, not cousins, it had invalidated the second marriage, making Sebastian a bastard so the title went instead to their cousin Thaddeus.

Thaddeus was kind, in his way, but he wasn't Sebastian. Ana Maria had only wanted to become a lady because Sebastian had seemed to want it for her so desperately. And now that he was established in his new life with his new lovely wife, it all seemed so pointless.

But it wasn't as though she could toss off her elegant clothing and grab an apron and pretend things hadn't changed.

They had. This room, redecorated to her taste and overflowing in flowers from potential suitors, proved it.

She liked the flowers—even if some of them made her sneeze—but she did not appreciate the attention. The gentlemen who sent them would never have noticed her when she'd been wearing her apron, and she knew full well why they were noticing her now. Thaddeus, continuing what Sebastian had promised, had bestowed a generous dowry on her, one that was drawing all of Society's eligible bachelors like—like ants to sugar.

"What are you thinking about then, my lady?" Jane's voice said, interrupting her thoughts.

"Flowers, ants, and sugar," Ana Maria replied, snorting at her own words.

"It'd be better if you were thinking about your suitors and which one of them you'll decide on. I like the looks of that earl's son, Lord Brunley. He's quite handsome, and has nearly all of his teeth."

"High recommendation," Ana Maria replied dryly. "So I can look at him while he chews." Is that what marriage was? 'Dearest, let me pop that toast in your mouth as I gaze upon you.'

"What else is there to require in a husband?"

It was unfortunate Jane asked so many questions. So many questions Ana Maria could answer, but not to anyone's satisfaction but her own.

What else is there to require? A kind soul, someone who would listen and care for her? Someone who would want *her*, not the daughter and cousin to a duke with a fortune?

How would she be able to tell if a suitor truly cared for her? Someone who would ask her why she was thinking about flowers, ants, and sugar instead of regarding her with a horrified look because she wasn't thinking about proper ladylike things?

Someone tall, and protective, and solid.

Someone very like—no. She could not finish that sentence, not even in her own mind.

She'd rather die by sneezing than admit to her own interest. If Sebastian, or Thaddeus, or worst of all *him* at all suspected she harbored a secret fascination for a certain tall, grunting gentleman with a penchant for frequent pacing she would be completely mortified, and it wouldn't do any good anyway.

He treated her as a sister, and not even as a much beloved sister. More like a forgotten sister who was only noticed when she was a nuisance. And since Ana Maria was so well-behaved, she was never noticed. Not by him, anyway.

No. Better to consider the gentlemen who were now noticing her. Or even better, figure out something that didn't involve gentlemen or marriage so she could at least be satisfied in her own life, even if she ended up alone.

"My lady?"

"What is it, Fletchfield?" Jane answered.

The butler gave a slight frown, indicating what he thought of Jane's presumption.

"Miss Octavia Holton is here to see Lady Ana Maria."

Ana Maria smiled. "Please see her in, Fletchfield. We will take tea as well." Miss Octavia was Sebastian's young sister-in-law, and a welcome addition to Ana Maria's acquaintance, though their ten-year age difference made it seem as though Ana Maria was Octavia's older sister. Until Octavia, Ana Maria hadn't had any friends in her new world, and the friends from when she was a drudge all treated her differently now.

Even Jane.

Fletchfield bowed, and Ana Maria turned to Jane. "I'll be up later this afternoon to discuss what gown to wear this evening."

"I thought the blue—" Jane began.

"Later this afternoon," Ana Maria interrupted. One of the few good things about being a lady— besides not having to scour kitchen grates and sweep dirt—was getting to choose which of her new gorgeous gowns she'd wear. And Jane had an opinion, as she always did, but Ana Maria was beginning to trust her own taste better than her lady's maid's.

That felt wonderful, at least. To know she was looking her absolute best thanks to her own decision.

She'd never had that kind of confidence. Not least because she always wore whatever castoff her step-mother allowed her to. But also because nobody had entrusted her with making any kind of decision her entire life—and even now that she was supposedly a lady in the highest echelon of society she was denied the same choice.

Well, she'd have to say no, thank you, to that. She was going to make her own choices and live her own life, which meant not marrying someone merely because he sent her some posies and could chew on his own.

It wasn't much as standards went, but it would do for now.

Fletchfield held the door open for Miss Octavia, who stepped inside, her customary lively expression on her face. "Good afternoon, my lady." Her eyes widened as she scanned the room. "Look at all those glorious colors!"

Ana Maria felt the unfamiliar warmth of a welcome compliment. "Thank you." She patted the cushion of the seat next to her. "Do sit down. Tea is on its way."

"Please tell me you decided on everything entirely on your own."

That warmth furled throughout Ana Maria's whole body. "I did." She tilted her head to regard the bright silk of the curtains. "I've never done anything like this, I wasn't certain I'd like it."

"You have to tell me where you got all this. Or better yet, take me yourself." Miss Octavia squinted in concentration. "You have a real talent."

"Thank y—achoo!"

"You're achoo-welcome," Miss Octavia replied with a cheeky grin.

Her friend's exuberant delight infected Ana Maria, making her want to cast off all the doubts and hesitations that had claimed her imagination since she'd first been elevated to her current social status.

And why shouldn't she cast them off? Wasn't the whole point of being independent to be . . . *independent*? To stride forward in life without worry?

"What in heaven's name are you thinking about? You have the most intense expression on your face." Miss Octavia wrinkled her nose. "You look like my sister, Ivy, when she's puzzling out a particularly difficult bookkeeping problem."

Ana Maria shook her head. "Nothing nearly that complicated." *Only the rest of my life.* She smothered a secret smile as Fletchfield arrived bearing the tea things, including some of Cook's most excellent lemon scones.

She would decide on her future after she had some tea and possibly a few scones. A person had to have their priorities straight, after all.

Next month, don't miss these exciting new love stories only from Avon Books

The Pursuit by Johanna Lindsey

What was to be a grand adventure for Melissa MacGregor seems to pale before the promise in the passionate gaze of Lincoln Ross Burnett. Though they exchange only a few words before parting, Melissa instantly knows this bold stranger is her destiny, while Lincoln realizes his heart has been claimed forever, and he will never be complete until Melissa MacGregor is his bride.

His Secret Mistress by Cathy Maxwell

Brandon Balfour made the mistake of trusting his heart to the exquisite, strong-willed actress, Kate Addison, with whom he shared one intimate night before fate intervened. Now a decade later, Brandon is a leading member of the Logical Men's Society—for no woman since Kate has managed to captivate him. Loving her exiled him. Trusting him ruined her. And now, a clash of passions threatens *everything* each of them ever desired.

Engaged to the Earl by Lisa Berne

Christopher Beck strides into a glamorous London drawing-room and can't believe his eyes. The last time he'd seen Gwendolyn Penhallow, she was a dreamy, strong-willed girl with a wild imagination, and now she's a beautiful and beguiling young lady . . . who's engaged to the Earl of Westenbury. Christopher had fled England to seek adventure elsewhere. Has he found it here too — the most delightful adventure of his life?

Discover great authors, exclusive offers, and more at hc.com.

REL 0220